THE BIRTH

of

BLUE SATAN

by

PATRICIA WYNN

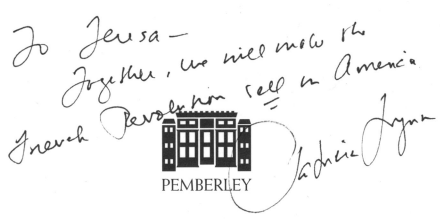

To Jensa —
Together, we will make the
French Revolution sell in America

PEMBERLEY

Published by

PEMBERLEY PRESS
PO Box 5840
Austin, TX 78763-5840
www.pemberleypress.com

A member of The Authors Studio
www.theauthorsstudio.org

Printed in the United States of America
October 2001
Cover design: kat & dog studios
Painting: Peter Angellus, Conversation Piece, Tate Gallery, London,
Art Resources, N.Y.
Chapter verses: *The Rape of the Lock*, by Alexander Pope

Publisher's Cataloging-in-Publication

Wynn, Patricia.
    The Birth of Blue Satan / by Patricia Wynn.
    p. cm.
    LCCN 00-092540
    ISBN 0-9702727-3-1

    1. Great Britain--History--18th century--Fiction.
    I. Title

PR6073.Y55B57 2001   823'.914
                      QBI00-901411

ɸ

This book is dedicated to
my mother,
Marguerite Johnston Barnes,
for her loving help
and her writer's genes
and to
my father,
Charles Wynn Barnes,
for
his constant encouragement
and for having enough faith in me to offer
to back this project.

Also by Patricia Wynn

The Parson's Pleasure

Sophie's Halloo

Lord Tom

Jack on the Box

Mistletoe and Mischief

The Bumblebroth

A Country Affair

The Christmas Spirit

A Pair of Rogues

Capturing Annie

Acknowledgements

I must express my appreciation to Alexander Pope for the wonderful verses used in this book. They come, of course, from *The Rape of the Lock*, his satirical masterpiece. Those who know the work will find it strangely used here, but out of context, it proved to be too perfect to resist.

I would like to thank my beloved family for all their many considerations: my husband, Tom, for supporting me through this and all my many ventures; my daughter, Virginia, for her valuable assistance and opinions; and my son, Ian, for his forbearance whenever it was needed.

There are not sufficient words to express my gratitude to Penny and Rod Chalmers and Mr. and Mrs. Duncan Bluck who so generously invited me into their lovely homes in Kent. Their hospitality, while I researched the villages and countryside in which this novel is set, will always remain a special memory.

My heartfelt thanks, also, go to the members of The Authors Studio, without whose advice, friendship, and expertise this book would never have been published, and to Alicia Rasley and Polly Coleman for their sensitive and thorough editing.

The British Succession

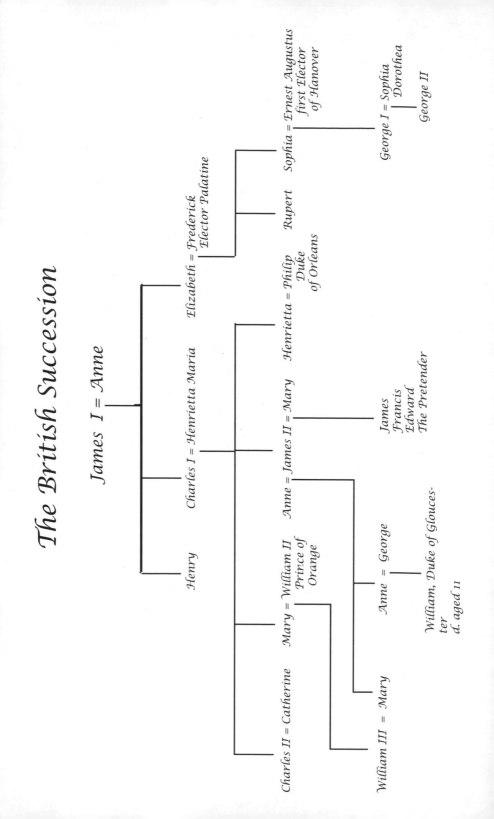

James I = Anne

Charles I = Henrietta Maria   Elizabeth = Frederick
                                            Elector Palatine

Henry

Rupert   Sophia = Ernest Augustus
                    first Elector
                    of Hanover

                    George I = Sophia
                               Dorothea

                        George II

Charles II = Catherine   Mary = William II   Anne = James II = Mary   Henrietta = Philip
                                 Prince of   Duke
                                 Orange   of Orleans

William III = Mary   Anne = George   James
                                       Francis
                                       Edward
                                       The Pretender

William, Duke of Glouces-
ter
d. aged 11

Historical Background

The trouble might be said to have started when James II took a second wife.

His first wife was a Protestant, who bore him two daughters, Mary and Anne. His second wife was a Catholic, and she provided him with a Catholic heir, James Francis Edward Stuart. Unwisely in those days, the birth took place with no official witnesses, so a rumour immediately began to circulate that the boy had been born of a commoner and smuggled into the palace in a warming pan. Thereafter, a warming pan became the emblem for those who opposed the Stuart cause.

James II was an authoritarian who threatened the powers of the oligarchy. As a Roman Catholic, himself, he also presented a threat to the newly restored Church of England. Religious wars had ravaged England for the better part of a century, and few wished to return to those days of strife. So, in 1688, immediately after the birth of the suspect baby, the newly created political parties, the Tories and the Whigs, united briefly to overthrow James II in what became known as the Glorious Revolution— "glorious" because it preserved the Protestant faith. James was toppled by armies led by William of Orange, his son-in-law, who became William III and reigned jointly with his wife Mary. Since neither they nor Anne produced a surviving heir, Parliament passed an Act of Succession, which stipulated a new order of succession to exclude Roman Catholic heirs, namely James Francis Edward Stuart.

From the beginning, there were those who opposed the revolution, including many priests in the Church of England. Their position was based on the principle of the divine right of kings and a recognition of the absolute authority of the Church, which had consecrated James as king. These priests refused to take the oath of loyalty to William and Mary, and so were called nonjuring priests. They refused to swear loyalty to all subsequent monarchs under the Act of Succession, and as a result, lost the right to hold positions in the state Church, schools, and universities. They found refuge under the patronage of wealthy High-Church Tories who agreed with them.

Mary's sister Anne succeeded the joint monarchs. When Anne's only surviving child from eighteen pregnancies died, Sophia of Hanover, a Protestant granddaughter of James I, became next in the line of succession.

In 1714, Sophia predeceased Queen Anne by two months. So, on Anne's death, the Crown passed to Sophia's son, George, who became George I, King of Great Britain and Ireland. The current British monarchs, the Windsors, are descended from George.

The Hanoverian Succession, as it was called, was not only unpopular with the nonjuring priests and High Churchmen, but with Catholics, conservative country squires, and the Highland Scots, who regarded the Stuarts as their hereditary kings. Most of the aristocracy initially accepted George's accession; however, before he succeeded to the throne, he was so successfully courted by the Whigs that he mistrusted all Tories, whom he suspected of being Jacobites, the term given to adherents of the deposed James II and his Catholic heirs (from *Jacobus*, the Latin for James).

Queen Anne's last ministry had been a Tory ministry. When she died in August of 1714, the Regents appointed by George to hold the throne until he could arrive from Hanover, were nearly all Whigs. Before the parliamentary election the next Spring, George called upon his citizens to return men who would be true to the Protestant cause. He turned his back on the idea of a shared ministry, snubbed many Tories, and forbade many of them his Court.

Although no attempt was made to place the Pretender on the throne immediately after Queen Anne's death, George's subsequent actions drove many Tories to the Pretender's cause. It is during this unsettled time that this novel takes place.

What dire offence from amorous causes springs,
What mighty contests arise from trivial things . . .

With beating hearts the dire event they wait,
Anxious, and trembling for the birth of Fate.

Say, what strange motive, Goddess! could compel
A well-bred Lord t'assault a gentle Belle?

And now (as oft in some distempered State)
On one nice Trick depends the general fate.

CHAPTER I

THE tall, young gentleman with long, fair hair and aquiline features lounged impatiently before the looking-glass. He drummed his long, slender fingers on the dressing-table to quell his annoyance.

The longcase clock in the chamber next door had just rung eleven, yet his shoulder-length peruke was still resting in the same place it had an hour ago—on its stand instead of his head. His valet, the little Frenchman who was busying himself in a corner, would never allow himself to be rushed.

Philippe withdrew from the Boulle armoire and returned with a familiar object draped over one arm. His eyebrows raised with a soupçon of hope, he dropped to one knee to display it.

"Would *Monseigneur* condescend to wear his new satin cloak this evening?"

Gideon gave it a look that conveyed his disgust. The offending garment, a voluminous cloak with three large shoulder capes, all in deep sapphire Duchesse, was precisely the sort of showy tog he abhorred.

"No, Philippe. I will not condescend to wear it this evening . . . nor any *other* evening, so you will please refrain from holding it out for my inspection."

As Philippe's face sagged, Gideon Viscount St. Mars gave an involuntary laugh. "No one but a damned popinjay would be caught in the street in a rig like that! I cannot conceive why you persist in wasting my allowance on things I would much rather eat than wear."

"But, *monsieur!* I have already explained myself with such perfection, if *monsieur* would but listen. It is precisely the shade of blue—though *monsieur* refuses to wear it—which will bring out the colour of *monsieur's* so-beautiful blue eyes."

"Blue eyes be damned!" Gideon muttered, feeling a rush of heat to his cheeks. He tossed a hasty glance in the mirror and was reassured by his glowering expression and the harsh contours of his face. "I have told you I will not be dressed like a *petit maître* at Versailles. I am an English gentleman, not a French courtesan."

"So much is evident, *Monseigneur.*"

"Well, you don't have to agree with me in that dismal tone of voice. I am not completely loathsome, I hope?"

"*Mais non, non, non! Monsieur* is blessed with a noble countenance and a pair of shoulders one can only call *magnifique*. It is *tout simplement* that *monsieur* fails to take advantage of his splendid physique."

"I took advantage of my splendid physique when I rode *ventre à terre* to arrive in time to dress for the ball. You should be pleased with me."

"*O là!* As if *monsieur* has given me half the time I require to make him *présentable!*"

"If you would stop lamenting that damned blue cloak, which I have instructed you to burn, I should be dressed and at Lord Eppington's house already."

"Very well, *Monseigneur.*"

Philippe's shoulders drooped, but Gideon noted that he folded the cape and carefully placed it in the armoire to bring out at a later date, when he might find his master more tractable.

Gideon grinned at his impudence. The heir to an earldom must have a valet, though he would happily have managed without if Philippe did not entertain him so.

Right now, Philippe had forgotten about the cape in his absorption over Gideon's *maquillage*. A nearly imperceptible layer of white paint, a faint colouring of rouge, and a dusting of fine powder were all the cosmetics Gideon would allow, although his resulting pallor when combined with a grey-powdered wig made a touch of red all but essential to his lips.

"And the patches, *Monseigneur?*" With a long-suffering sigh, Philippe held up his porcelain box with its assortment of shapes and sizes.

"Two," Gideon said.

"But two!" The little valet's resignation crumpled. "But, *monsieur!* My reputation will be ruined if you do not wear eight at the very least!"

"Two," Gideon repeated firmly. "And none of your hearts or crosses, mind."

Philippe drew himself up like a martyr, the box clasped like a stake to his heart. "Very well, *monsieur le vicomte.*" He was truly offended now, as his flared nostrils revealed. "It shall be precisely as you wish, but I hope you do not live to regret the advice Philippe has given you when Mademoiselle Mayfield marries the *Duc de Bournemouth* instead."

Gideon turned in his chair so rapidly that Philippe took a hasty step backwards. "You little imp! What the devil do you know about me and Isabella Mayfield?"

"I know nothing, *monsieur*. And I fear I shall know nothing at all if *monsieur* refuses to listen to Philippe."

Gideon fixed him with a glare fierce enough to make a stronger man quail, but Philippe knew his master too well to be afraid. In order to keep his position, however, he endeavoured ι look contrite.

Reluctantly, Gideon restrained his temper. "Cut loose, you noisome piece of bait! What do you know about Isabella Mayfield and the Duke of Bournemouth? And how do you come to know it?"

"*Quand même —*" with an exaggerated shrug, Philippe grew very French— "one may be a mere servant, *monsieur*, and not be completely *hors du courant*."

"By that, I suppose you to mean you have been talking to someone else's servant. Is that it?"

"My lips are sealed."

Gideon would have laughed at the improbability, but he could not allow his valet, or any other servant for that matter, to gossip about the lady he intended to wed. He could do nothing to prevent rumours from spreading outside his own household, but he exercised a considerable authority over his own staff. And, in this case, he would use it.

"You had better seal those lips, or you will have to find another pair with which to eat your dinner. Do you perfectly understand me, Philippe?"

"*Oui, Monseigneur.*" The Frenchman lowered his voice to a confidential whisper. "But, since we find ourselves alone, would monsieur not wish to hear what Philippe has heard?"

Gideon's usual dislike of gossip warred with a distressing curiosity. He could not deny that the pairing of Isabella's name with the Duke of Bournemouth's had caused a nasty turn in his stomach. "Very well." He feigned an indifference he could not feel, which would not fool Philippe for a moment. "Get *on* with it, curse you, so I can get to the ball."

Philippe took up his hare's foot to brush a tiny speck of powder off Gideon's cheek. The eagerness in his tone did nothing to calm his master's anxious pulse. "*Bon!* It is said that his Grace is expected to offer for Mademoiselle Mayfield very soon, and that the lady is not at all averse."

"Nonsense! You may tell your sources that the lady would never dream of marrying that dried-up *roué*. And, besides, that she will soon be affianced to me."

"*Exactement!* That is precisely what I said, *monsieur le vicomte*. I could not allow *Monseigneur* to be so insulted."

Gideon gave a short laugh. "Defended me, did you? Damn, if I won't raise your wages for that!"

"*Monsieur* is too kind." With a scattering of grey powder, Philippe retreated a step, clasping the hare's foot to his chest.

Then, turning deadly serious, he stooped to bring his lips close to Gideon's ear.

With black eyes meeting blue ones in the mirror, Philippe spoke in a portentous voice. "If *monsieur* will please but consider, the *Duc de Bournemouth* is not so old that he cannot attract a younger lady with his wealth—*monsieur* must trust Philippe on this. And *monsieur le duc* is a *grand seigneur* who knows how much the elegant wig and the skillful placement of a patch can please a beautiful lady."

Gideon knew what his servant was about. He wanted to use his master's jealousy to get his way. At the same time, Gideon had heard those rumours himself, and he knew how much Isabella valued a fine appearance. If she did not care so much for fashion, he would never let himself be painted at all.

"Oh, very well," he said. "Three patches, or I don't suppose I shall ever get out of this house. And you may choose the shapes you wish and put them wherever you like. Just hurry, blast you! I would like to appear at Lord Eppington's house before midnight."

Philippe was hardly appeased by the thought of a mere three patches, but he went speedily to work. "*Monsieur* would have been at the ball already if he had not arrived so late and in such a state as I hope never to see him again."

"I had business with my father." Gideon's curt reply was intended for a warning that this was one subject Philippe had better not broach.

The object of Gideon's visit to Lord Hawkhurst had been the very lady they had just discussed. And the recollection of the argument he had had with his father over Isabella brought a tightness to Gideon's throat.

He had been summoned home three days ago—he had thought—to acquaint his father with the latest attacks on the former ministers. The news Lord Hawkhurst sought was not to be found in the prints, for King George had ordered all justices of the peace to execute the laws against printers and publishers. Knowing how desperately his father wished to keep up with his country's affairs, Gideon had put aside his own engagements to visit White's Coffee House, a Tory stronghold, to hear the version of events his father would prefer.

The news was not good. The Whig Parliament had threatened the former Tory ministers with impeachment, and nothing Bolingbroke, their leader, could say to justify his actions as secretary of state had managed to turn the Whigs' temper. Even Atterbury, Bishop of Rochester and a confidant of Lord Hawkhurst's, had reason to be afraid. He was believed to be the leader of a group that had planned to proclaim the Pretender as James III at the moment of the late queen's death.

Gideon could not send anything controversial through the post. It was said that all letters were being opened. So he rode down, travelling the more than seventy miles from London to Hawkhurst rapidly by stages. After a wearying day in the saddle, he arrived at Rotherham Abbey, where his father resided in exile from Court, to discover that the earl had already retired for the evening, exhausted by the gout.

If he had known that gossip had carried his intentions to wed into Kent, he would have been more prepared for the vituperative anger he'd faced. As it was, he was blind-sided by his father's wrath.

Gideon presented himself in his father's library early the next morning when, according to their ancient ritual, he went down on bended knee to receive his father's blessing. It was at that very moment when he, with bowed head, was humbling himself, that Lord Hawkhurst charged him with the rumours he'd heard—that his son and heir had formed the ludicrous intention of offering for a girl who was "nothing better than the latest toast of the Kit-Kat Club."

When Gideon, feeling the heat beneath his neckcloth, confessed to his feelings for Isabella, he was treated to a display of anger such as he had never witnessed, a tirade in which Isabella, her family, and her morals were reviled in every possible way.

His temper flared, and he gave in to the need to defend the girl, his passion for her lending a loudness to his voice. "If you do not refrain from speaking of her in this manner, my lord, you will live to regret it!"

"Do not threaten me, sir!" Lord Hawkhurst bellowed, loudly

enough to rattle the panes in their glazings.

"I have done nothing more than express my outrage for your unwarranted insults to Mrs. Isabella in the manner they deserve."

"Unwarranted?" Lord Hawkhurst leapt too eagerly on the word. "Do you tell me these tales are unfounded, my boy?" The gleam that sprang into his eyes made Gideon feel more furious for the guilt it provoked.

Gideon loved his father, and he did not usually allow Lord Hawkhurst's rages to rouse him to such an alarming extent. But whenever he even thought of Isabella, his pulse drummed so furiously that he could scarcely think at all. All he could do was struggle to conceal the intensity of his desire, so as not to make himself the laughing-stock of London.

Weeks of such frustration had fed his impatience. His father's taunts had heated his blood, so that now he was stretched so taut as to be beyond all reason.

"I say *unwarranted*," he bit back, "for you have judged Mrs. Isabella sight unseen. You cannot imagine the goodness of the angel you have maligned."

"Bah!" His father's craggy brows snapped together again. "Don't talk to me of angels, boy, when you have been trapped by a pretty face and a handsome pair of breasts, whose owner knows well how to use them to distract you from her faults."

"I warn you, Papa—"

"You *dare* to warn me? I have my spies, sir. I have heard of this girl. They say she is a flirty piece. The rage of the town . . . *Ha!* As if that were enough to make her a fitting countess for my son!"

"Isabella is more than fitting. She will grace our house."

"She may—" his father's words were only briefly deceiving— "until her bloom wears off, and then what? What can she bring to this family besides her fleeting beauty? Her mother is no better than a harlot herself—a gamester who came near to ruining that fool Mayfield, who was a fop and a Whig besides! The girl has no dowry to speak of from what I hear."

"Her dowry is adequate. You above others know that I have no need to wed for funds."

"Adequate? Need? When have I ever given you the notion that a portion of three thousand pounds is enough to gain admission to this family? For such a paltry sum, I wouldn't accept her if she was the Virgin Mary herself! And if she's inherited her mother's tendencies, I can assure you she is far from that. I will not allow you to be caught by a buxom figure. You can find your fill of those in Drury Lane. And above all—"

As his father paused to gather his breath, Gideon braced himself for the words he knew would come.

"— I will never permit a son of mine to marry the daughter of an accursed Whig!"

Gideon winced as his father launched into another tirade, not about Gideon's betrayal, but about his duty to their party. It was a theme he had been lectured upon all his life.

But for once he had heard enough of his father's diatribes. He refused to allow Lord Hawkhurst's bitterness to rule his heart.

So, in a terrible calm, he asked, "How do you mean to stop me, my lord? I will not have my love for Isabella sacrificed on this altar of yours. I intend to wed her, and so I ask you—how do you plan to stop me?"

At his quiet words, Lord Hawkhurst grew so enraged, Gideon thought he would surely burst a vessel. The flesh on his face turned a purplish hue.

"I shall withhold your allowance," Lord Hawkhurst blurted finally. "That should bring you to heel."

Despite the tension between them, Gideon nearly smiled. Every time his father was the least bit annoyed, he threatened to withhold Gideon's allowance. The problem was that Gideon possessed a sizeable fortune of his own, derived from an estate in France, which had been bequeathed to him by his maternal grandfather. It would suffice to maintain him and a wife in a comfortable style. Given this, as well as his disinclination to waste money on vices, and Lord Hawkhurst's threat lacked punch.

"I hate to inform you, but you have done such an admirable job in raising me that I save much more money than I spend. It will be a very long time, I fear, before this deprivation can cause me any hardship."

Lord Hawkhurst's expression had begun to relax, and his tantrum might have ended there if Gideon had not perversely added, "So, I shall have to marry Mrs. Isabella without your blessing."

This last statement was a leap of faith, since Gideon had not yet proposed and Isabella had not yet accepted. But Lord Hawkhurst did not know this, and his age-lined face hardened again.

"Then . . . it is over, sir. But I warn you, St. Mars, that that Whig's daughter shall never enter this house."

They parted on that hostile note. As Gideon angrily left by way of the antechamber, James Henry, his father's receiver-general, glanced up from his work to give him a condemning look. Enraged by this impertinence from his father's favoured servant, Gideon strode quickly past the white-faced stares of the liveried footmen, who waited in the hall for their master's orders, and stormed out of the Abbey.

His anger, normally quick to fade, remained with him throughout the long, cold journey back. Changing horses at the posting houses he had used on the way down, he pushed them each so hard over the deep Wealden roads as to cover them with mud and sweat. The last horse was his, a handsome bay with a great deal of strength. But, when he saw how badly he had tired it, he walked it over London Bridge instead of taking the horse ferry at Lambeth.

It was after dark by the time he guided his exhausted mount through the shops and the traffic on the bridge, only to find that the City streets were more than usually teeming. In spite of the bitter March air, men spilled out of the coffee houses and taverns, discussing—some in shouts and some in whispers—the day's disturbing news. Bolingbroke, Viscount St. John, had tried unsuccessfully to justify his actions before Parliament in negotiating the Treaty of Utrecht. Mr. Walpole, the paymaster general of the armed forces—and an up-and-coming force—would chair a Committee of Secrecy to investigate the former ministry and its dealings with France.

Such an investigation, Gideon knew, was likely to turn up Bolingbroke's communications with the Pretender, for like many careful men he had hedged his bets, publicly welcoming King George while secretly encouraging James Stuart.

Gideon had learned this from remarks his father had let drop while bemoaning the lack of leadership in the Stuart cause. But the Jacobites must be aware of it as well, for those in London had clearly been roused.

He passed an alehouse known to be a Jacobite haunt and heard an itinerant singer chanting the words of an old and treasonable ditty.

> The Baptist and the Saint
> The Schismatick and the Swearer
> Have ta'n the Covenant
> That Jemmy comes not here, sir
> Whilst all this Pious Crew do plot
> To pull Old Jemmy down . . .

Although it was not the deposed James II, but the new Jemmy, his son—the Pretender, James Francis Stuart—who inspired them now. The working people would never tire of the rowdy verses that poked fun at the Whigs and Dissenters, the German, and the Dutch, which dated from the time when James II had been overthrown by the Dutch William of Orange. Even with George of Hanover securely on the throne, the treacherous songs were still sung.

Their harmless words could only rankle Gideon's feelings now. Bitterness gnawed at his tongue when he thought of how his father's political sentiments had driven them apart that morning. Their confrontation had confirmed his fears, that the politics practiced by Isabella's father would count much more heavily against her than a lack of dowry or her mother's morals. Gideon had known all this, and the state of his father's mind was the reason he had not informed him of his wish to marry Isabella.

Lord Hawkhurst lived at his country estate rather than play the hypocrite to Hanover George. Even if he had not chosen to absent himself from St. James's, his Majesty had made it abundantly clear that Lord Hawkhurst and other High Church Tories would not be welcome at his court.

Lord Hawkhurst was a Cavalier of the old school, who would rather draw his sword on a Whig than speak civilly to him. If he would seldom remain in a room that a Whig had entered, he was unlikely to permit his son to marry one. Gideon did not agree that his father's politics should decide whom he could wed, especially when Isabella had no professed opinions of her own. She was young and had no interest in the country's affairs. Even if she had, Gideon had grown so weary of the political strife tearing his country apart that he had made up his mind that party politics would not rule his life as it had his father's.

Now that his temper had had time to run its course, however, he regretted upsetting his father at a time when he had suffered so much disappointment. Lord Hawkhurst had been among the men who had gathered in Kensington at the time of Queen Anne's death to wait for their Tory friends in government to proclaim James III as king. But the party leadership had failed them. The Whigs had moved faster, taking their places as regents to hold the throne for George's arrival nearly two months later. Gideon did not know how his father had survived the blow of seeing the Pretender's best chance wasted through hesitation. He could only be grateful that Lord Hawkhurst's fiery opinions had never led him to take a rash part in one of the rebellions that had occurred in previous years.

He hoped for a chance to repair the breach between them. And he consoled himself with the knowledge that Lord Hawkhurst's tantrums never lasted long. If past experience could be his guide, he would receive a new summons in a pair of days, bidding him come for a reconciliation. Still, he could not convince himself that Lord Hawkhurst's opinion of Isabella would undergo as rapid a change.

While Gideon would permit no faults to be ascribed to her, he had to admit that her mother, Mrs. Mayfield, might have merited his father's opinion. A shrill voice and the occasional hint of hardness in her eyes had blighted a once-famous beauty. The Honourable Geffrye Mayfield, a man of impeccable lineage, was said to have eloped with her within a month of their first meeting, an unseemly haste which had given rise to speculation. But whatever the reason for it, Lord Stokely, Mr. Mayfield's father, had cut his son off with barely a groat. If Mr. Mayfield had not secured a position at Court with the help of a maternal relative, his family would have suffered much.

But Isabella was so far superior to her mother in every way that Gideon believed it grossly unfair to hold Mrs. Mayfield's sins against her. He had no fears on the subject of Isabella's fitness to be his wife. Last autumn, he had returned from three years' study abroad to find her joy and innocence a welcome contrast to the cynicism and experience of the ladies at the European courts. But in spite of her artless youth—or perhaps because of it—she had raised a desire in him such as he had never known, not even in his earliest encounters with women. He knew he must not marry just to satisfy his carnal desires—the Church was very clear on the subject—but he could not help yearning for the moment he could make her his.

Consumed by these thoughts, Gideon had ridden back to Hawkhurst House, across from Green Park in Piccadilly, still in such a foul humour as to speak curtly to the new boy in his stables who was slow to take his reins. Normally quick with a smile for his servants, he soon regretted his angry tone and resolved to go out of his way to speak kindly to the boy on a future occasion. But he was so anxious to see Isabella, to have her smile reward him for his loyalty, that he could not be bothered with such a trifling matter then.

Now Philippe's insinuations about the Duke of Bournemouth increased his impatience. His longing to speak with Isabella deepened with every passing moment, so he resisted his valet's more elaborate attempts to arrange his long, powdered wig.

Eventually, clad in a knee-length coat with deep cuffs, a matching waistcoat in peach-coloured silk with elaborate brocade, a pair of silk inexpressibles, a fall of long, blond lace at his throat, clocked silk stockings and high-heeled shoes, a gold-hilted sword riding at his hip, and a three-cornered hat, Gideon was at last able to leave the house. He had already sent word to have a fresh horse saddled, aware that riding to the ball would get him there sooner than taking a chair. In truth, he still had an edge to his passion to work off before seeing Isabella.

Stepping out into the wide courtyard of the house, he spied the stocky figure of Thomas Barnes, his groom, walking his mare. Noting the scowl on the face of the man who had guided him and watched over him since his fourth birthday, Gideon smothered an impatient sigh. He was sure to get a sharp scolding, both for his abuse of the horse today and for his intention to ride out unaccompanied so close on midnight.

No moon was in evidence, and the small bit of light that might have been expected from the stars had been smothered by a layer of cloud. On a night like this, the streets would be thick with thieves, eager to strip an unwary man. Tom would be sorely displeased. But Gideon was not in the mood to take a scolding, not after the one he had received from his father.

"Good evening, Tom." Affecting not to notice his servant's scowl, Gideon reached to take the reins.

"'Tis more like good morning, my lord."

"Do you think? I have not heard the clock strike, but perhaps the chimes are not working. You must remind me to have them checked."

Gideon's irony was seldom lost on Thomas Barnes, who snorted. "Your lordship knows full well what time o' the clock it is, *and* what your lordship's asking for t' be riding out at such an hour."

"Now, Tom, you must be aware by now that I am a man fully grown, and as such I may keep the hours I like."

"If you are so fully growed, how come your lordship don't know there's footpads wandering these streets just a'waiting for a pigeon like your lordship to pluck?"

"A pigeon? Tom, I fear you do not flatter me."

"No. Nor I won't be flattering your lordship neither till you shows a bit of the sense your father give you."

Reins in hand, and reaching for the saddle, Gideon froze. His words, when they came, were very low. "Thomas, this scolding will have to cease or I shall be forced to find a groom who does not seek to remind me that he instructed me to hold the reins. It is quite beyond my limits to have you pull a prosy face in front of my friends."

"I don't see no friends about," Tom mumbled, as he bent to give his master a leg up, but he threw Gideon up into his saddle without further comment and made the final adjustments to his straps. There would be no point in remonstrating further when my Lord St. Mars took on that tone.

Not that Gideon's voice had betrayed anything more than a wry amusement, but Tom had sensed the steel underneath. And his experience told him that nothing would shake St. Mars from his reckless course when he took the bit between his teeth.

Tom could not be certain why his lordship was in such a pent-up mood of late, but he had a fairly good notion. He had ears just as keen as that fancy French valet's. And, knowing both my Lord Hawkhurst and his tantrums better than the Frenchy did, Tom could well imagine the scene that had just transpired at Rotherham Abbey. His sympathies were divided fairly equally on this occasion, but no words of his would improve Master Gideon's disposition. And it was not for a servant like him to tell my Lord St. Mars whom to wed.

"Foolish is as foolish does," he muttered to himself as he helped his master's diamond-buckled shoe into its stirrup. "And I wonder how he thinks he's going to look, struttin' about her ladyship's ballroom after a ride in them fancy clothes?"

Tom followed Gideon's horse to the immense wrought-iron and gilt gate that shielded Hawkhurst House, with its thirty rooms, its stables and its outbuildings, from the roughness of the city streets. He moved past him to swing the heavy gate open, and Gideon walked his horse through it. There was no more need for talk. Gideon knew the risks he took and had no patience with his servant's worries. For his part, Tom knew that he would not sleep until his master was safely home that night.

The night was as black as the depths of a well, the park uncannily empty, the street immensely quiet, as Tom swung the gate closed. Gideon turned in the street. "On my return, I do not wish to find you manning this gate. The porter wil let me in. It is, after all, his job.

Tom was on the point of responding when he heard a horse

coming slowly, then faster down the darkened street, its iron-shod hooves ringing sharply on the cobblestones.

With a sudden worry, he swung the gate open again, starting forward just as the shadowy form of a rider came within view.

Gideon swiveled in his saddle to peer at the approaching figure. "What the—"

The stranger was hurtling towards him like a kite diving for its prey. Tom strained to make out the man's face, but nothing could be seen on this moonless night except a black, fluttering mass riding swiftly towards them, its features shrouded or obscured. He had an uneasy impulse to reach for his master's reins, but Gideon stopped him, spinning his mare, one hand reaching for his sword.

"A word with you, St. Mars!" the rider called out, easing up on his horse.

Gideon released his hilt.

It's a messenger, Tom thought with relief—relief still tinged with a nagging anxiety. *A messenger belike from the Abbey and Gideon's father.*

But, then, as the stranger's horse moved within the circle of light thrown by the gate's one lamp, the figure, which was swathed in a long black cloak, began to ride at Gideon at full tilt.

He wore a Venetian mask. His hair was covered by a long, black hood. A glint of steel flashed in his hand.

"Master Gideon, your back!"

Gideon's horse spun on its two hind hooves, knocking Tom aside. As the rider flew past, he raised his weapon and slashed. Reaching for his own sword too late, Gideon jerked with a cry. His horse reared and twisted, flinging him hard to the ground.

Fair Nymphs, and well-dressed Youths around her shone,
But every eye was fixed on her alone.
On her white breast a sparkling Cross she wore,
Which Jews might kiss, and Infidels adore.
Her lively looks a sprightly mind disclose,
Quick as her eyes, and as unfixed as those:
Favours to none, to all she smile extends;
Oft she rejects, but never once offends.
Bright as the sun, her eyes the gazers strike,
And, like the sun, they shine on all alike.
Yet graceful ease, and sweetness void of pride,
Might hide her faults, if Belles had faults to hide:
If to her share some female errors fall,
Look on her face, and you'll forget 'em all.

CHAPTER II

MASTER Gideon!"
As the stranger galloped away, his long, black cape streaming after him like the wings of death, Tom rushed to kneel at his master's side.

"Go after him, Tom." Gideon struggled to sit, clasping a pale hand to his left shoulder. "Take my horse and ride after the devil. Take my sword."

"No, sir! You're hurt!" Tom reached shaking fingers to feel a spot that was widening on Gideon's sleeve.

"Go after him, I said! The damned coward's getting away!"

"Aye, but there's nothing can be done about that now. His lordship would eat me for dinner if I let you bleed in the street."

Ignoring Gideon's swearing, Tom scooped him up and staggered towards the door. A warm, sticky liquid pooled in the palm of his hand, giving him strength. In a matter of seconds, he had crossed the courtyard and climbed the steps to the house.

"Open up!" he shouted, kicking furiously at the door.

"Curse you, put me down!"

"Not on your life, my lord." In the shock of the moment, Tom had forgotten to use his master's proper address, but he was reminded of it now.

"Loose me, or I'll be the one to have your head on a platter!"

The fact that Gideon had barely struggled in his arms told Tom that he was weaker than he would admit. But at least he could speak. He had not lost consciousness. Perhaps the wound was not as severe as Tom had feared.

"Very well, my lord, but if you get dizzy, you must lean on me."

The door opened slowly at first, but once the liveried footman saw who was waiting outside, he threw it wide.

"My Lord St. Mars!"

"I am quite all right, Will," Gideon said as Tom gently lowered him to his feet. "'Tis nothing but a scratch."

A scratch that was making an ever-widening stain on his lordship's upper sleeve, as both servants could see in the candlelight that spilled from the hall. Still, when Tom saw that his master's torso had been spared, his chest filled with blessed relief.

The housekeeper hurried forward from the servants' hall. When she saw the blood on Gideon's coat, she shrieked. "Oh, my lord!"

"Have Philippe called to my chamber, if you please, Mrs. Dixon. I shall be requiring a change of clothes."

"And a surgeon, too." Tom was ready to run into the street. "Shall I fetch the Watch, my lord?"

"Yes." As Gideon mounted the stairs, he turned. "No— wait. I do not wish to be bothered with either this evening. You may fetch them in the morning."

"But, my lord—"

"No, Tom. I shall be fine, truly I shall. I do not wish to be questioned now. It would be a complete waste of time in any case, since they will never catch the scoundrel. And I must not miss Lord Eppington's ball."

With that, he turned his back and continued to climb, leaving his three servants below, and speechless.

"But—my lord!" Tom was the first to find his voice.

He was given no further chance to use it, for Gideon ignored him as he disappeared at the bend in the stairs.

"Now, there's a queer start," Will said, looking to Tom for

enlightenment.

Tom was so angry with his headstrong master, he could not stomach any remarks about him right now. "Mind your tongue!" he said sharply. "And don't be speaking about the master in that impudent way. Get along with you, now!"

The footman knew the privileged position Thomas Barnes held in my Lord St. Mars's household. Thus, he held back the retort he could have made and, with a haughty sniff, retired to the back of the house to tell his fellow servants what he'd witnessed up front.

Gideon slowly made his way up the last two steps, aware that to hurry would cause him to lose more blood. He could not afford to take that risk since his head had already begun to swim.

In the hall, he was met by his anxious valet. "*Tiens!*" Philippe exclaimed. "But *Monseigneur* is hurt! *C'est grave?*"

"I think not," Gideon said, leading Philippe back through his chamber, lit only by the embers of a dying fire, then into his wardrobe. He lowered himself gingerly onto the dressing-table chair. "But you shall have to bind me up and bring me a fresh suit to wear."

"*Mais, non, non, non! Monsieur* cannot possibly think he is going out." The Frenchman scurried about the room, lighting the candles again.

"Philippe—" Gideon closed his eyes and spoke through gritted teeth— "I have had enough words on this subject from Thomas Barnes. You will do as I have asked."

Philippe swallowed his next remark. With a muffled "tsk" he went to work, removing Gideon's ruined coat and vest, and his lace-trimmed shirt. This last was most difficult, for its upper left sleeve was drenched in blood, which had begun to clot.

The removal of his shirt revealed a long, deep slash, running across the top of Gideon's left arm.

"*Mon Dieu!* Who is it who has dared to harm *monsieur* in this manner?"

"I wish I knew," Gideon said, trying not to wince as Philippe wiped the blood from about his wound. "But Tom—damn him!—

refused to ride the blackguard down. He might have caught him, too, if he hadn't insisted on playing nursemaid to me."

"For once, *monsieur le vicomte*, I find myself completely in agreement with this Thomas."

Fortunately for Gideon's temper, Philippe quickly became engrossed in dressing his wound, so Gideon was spared further comment. The attack had left him more shaken than he cared to admit. Not so much from the wound, though the loss of blood was making him light-headed, but from the purposeful way in which it had been dealt.

Who could have wished to do him harm? Someone he knew for certain, for the man had called out his name to put him off guard. Even stranger had been the fact that his assailant had not lingered to finish the job, though perhaps Tom's presence could account for his good fortune. If the man had truly wished to finish him, he might have expected to easily with no one but an unarmed servant to stand between them. Only an intimate could have known how fiercely Tom would have fought in his behalf.

Had his attacker known?

Gideon had no time to ponder this or any other question, or he would never make it to the ball. And he must go. Isabella would certainly take pique if he failed to appear, and if she was seriously considering the Duke's suit, Gideon's absence might be just enough to tip the scales in his Grace's favour.

He had also begun to think that tonight would be his best chance to press Isabella for an answer. He could speak to her when they were dancing, more intimately than he could at her house. Private balls were rare, and a Court ball would not be as easy a place to get her alone.

His bandaging complete, Philippe helped him to ease into another shirt with a ribbon tie, a long-sleeved vest heavily embroidered in the light cream he most often wore, another lace neckcloth, and a fine coat of palest brown embroidered with hummingbirds aflight. His neckcloth was loosely tied, which Philippe would not have permitted if Gideon had not been injured. The sleeves of his vest and coat, which were fashionably wide, permitted movement without additional pain.

His plan to ride was now put aside. Gideon called for his father's carriage and cautiously stood. Finding that his head only spun a bit, he straightened himself and proceeded to the ball.

ɕ

The *piano nobile* of Lord Eppington's house in Golden Square was glittering with light from a dozen cut-glass chandeliers, its furniture draped in crimson satin and shod in gilt. The large reception rooms were filled to overflowing, the gentlemen resplendent in brocade and Mechlin lace, their faces painted and patched, their shoes sparkling with diamond buckles and high, ruby-coloured heels.

In comparison, the ladies seemed almost subdued, their silks in paler hues and their curls trained simply down their backs, at once more natural and more artful than the gentlemen's elaborately brushed and curled wigs. Still, with their waists nipped in as tightly as figures would allow and plump breasts brimming over low necklines, they had a lesser need for paint.

Young black pages threaded their ways through the clusters of guests to procure orgeat for their mistresses. Lady Eppington's pet monkey chattered away in her lap, winning laughter with its antics.

The pall of stale perfume permeated the air, the different essences long since blended into one familiar, rancid smell. The violins and harpsichord hired for the evening played a continuous round of country tunes and minuets. The youngest of her ladyship's guests had been dancing for three hours at least, their less-adventurous elders absorbed in gossip or in cards.

Isabella Mayfield, the season's toast, had not been obliged to sit out even one common dance, but her cousin, Hester Kean, had more often than not found herself overlooked. Hester was standing in a corner beside her aunt, hoping for a gentleman to lead her out. Since this was Hester's first London ball, she had dared to hope that she might have her hand solicited for most of the livelier country dances, but in this she had been sorely disappointed. She endeavoured to conceal these feelings, however, aware that a sad expression would do nothing to improve her chances of securing a partner. Still, she could not suppress a sigh at the sight of Isabella with her pretty cheeks flushed and her happy eyes sparkling as she was escorted through the steps of a complex minuet.

Hester's aunt, Mrs. Mayfield, must have heard her sigh over the sweet notes of the violins and the tinny plunking of the harpsichord, for she made a sudden pronouncement which, from Mrs. Mayfield, might be taken as an attempt at counsel.

"You may wish to dance, Hester, but you cannot expect to be favoured by gentlemen when you have no beauty or fortune to recommend you."

"I am sure you are correct, Aunt," Hester replied. Mrs. Mayfield's words could hardly offend her, for they were true. They did nothing to contradict her own dismal assessment of her prospects. If she could not find a suitable husband soon, she knew what destiny would await her.

Orphaned but a year ago by the death of Mrs. Mayfield's brother, the Reverend Mr. Henry Kean, Hester had been offered a home in the clear expectation that she would act as her aunt's waiting woman. If Hester had not been aware of the precise terms of her deliverance from impending destitution, she had learned them quickly enough upon her arrival at Mayfield Park.

If Mrs. Mayfield forgot her shawl in her bedchamber, she was sure to call upon Hester to fetch it, when any one of a number of servants might have performed the task. Hester, also, was the person Mrs. Mayfield relied upon to act as her secretary, writing her dictated replies to the scores of invitations she and Isabella received, keeping her accounts, dealing with the household servants, and staving off Mrs. Mayfield's most importunate creditors. Hester brought certain talents to these tasks, since the Reverend Mr. Kean had employed her in much the same capacity. Even at nineteen Hester possessed just the sort of ingenuity and tact her relatives lacked. Taking into account Mrs. Mayfield's shrewdness and her perfect awareness of the situation that had reigned in her brother's household, it was hardly astonishing that she had had the foresight to offer Hester a place in hers.

Hester did not nourish any exaggerated notions of her own attractions. Thin and a bit on the drab side by her own admission, with light brown hair and a plain, even face unrelieved by any particular distinction save for a pair of intelligent grey eyes and a set of even teeth, she had no beauty to compensate for her lack of dowry. The best she could hope for would be to wed a clergyman whose lot might be improved by the assistance of a thrifty wife. As there was little likelihood of encountering such an uninspiring gentleman in Lord Eppington's opulent ballroom, Hester had for once indulged herself in daydreams of a more fanciful sort.

Well, she sighed, as the minuet drew to a close. *There's no harm in dreams, as long as I don't allow myself to believe in them.*

Isabella's escort, Sir Harrowby Fitzsimmons, his long, black wig trailing below the shoulders of his embroidered puce coat, was mincing his way to Mrs. Mayfield's side, his partner's tiny hand rested lightly in his. His fatuous gaze shifted often from Isabella's face to those of the gentlemen they passed. Clearly the other men's envy added to the lightness in his step.

All eyes had turned to watch Isabella's progress through the room, naturally drawn to the sight of golden curls, radiant cheeks, and a generous bosom spilling over the bodice of a damask gown. Mrs. Mayfield had spared no expense on Isabella's ball dress, her cunning eye knowing just the hues to enhance the effect of Isabella's natural charms. Tonight's pale pink, with her smooth, white skin and her lovely blue eyes, made her appear a delectable confection of softly spun sugar, sure to be sweet to the tongue.

Returning Isabella to her mother's side, Sir Harrowby paused to make her a perfect bow while raising her fingers to his lips.

"Mrs. Mayfield," he said, in his arch voice. "I protest, I vow! My enchanting partner informs me that I must surrender her to you, for she insists that his Grace of Bournemouth has claimed her for the next dance. I implore you to use your kindness in my behalf and persuade her to forsake his Grace, or she will surely break my heart."

Isabella giggled, her ringlets bounced, and she tapped Sir Harrowby with her fan. "Why, sir, your pretty speech has given me such a blush, his Grace will think I've been out in the sun."

"Fie, Sir Harrowby!" Mrs. Mayfield exclaimed. "You have a silver tongue, sir, and you mean to sway my little girl yet. But you must not, you know, for you would do her great harm if you was to make her offend his Grace."

Beneath her aunt's bantering was a harsher note. Hester knew it for a warning. Mrs. Mayfield would never consent to Isabella's marrying a mere baronet if she had any chance of catching a peer, and Isabella's odds in that direction looked remarkably high.

Since her first appearance at Court, Isabella had turned the head of more than one young gentleman, including Sir Harrowby's cousin, the Viscount St. Mars, who for the past two months had appeared the clear favourite for her hand. Handsome and wealthy, and in line for an earldom, Gideon Fitzsimmons had fulfilled all of Mrs. Mayfield's dreams—until the Duke of Bournemouth, a man of fifty, with his headier title already secured, displayed an interest in the race.

Isabella seemed delighted with her current partner, although she was not above throwing his rivals in his face. Sir Harrowby had the perfect combination of manners and address, minute attention to his garb, and (to Hester's way of thinking) complete lack of mental spark to appeal to Isabella's tastes. If she longed to hear insipid verses and naughty jokes, Sir Harrowby would be more than willing and able to oblige. But to win her, he would have to do better than claim, as he had throughout the evening, that King George was thinking of conferring a Household office upon him.

Hester had not yet gone to Court. Mrs. Mayfield said she did not own a gown that was fine enough to pass the Beefeaters' scrutiny. Still, she had heard the gossip that said his Majesty had been shockingly slow in making his appointments. Since his grand procession from Greenwich to Westminster last September, he had kept much to himself, refusing to fill the most important posts with Englishmen. Instead, he had surrounded himself with the dozens of Germans he had brought from Hanover, his two German mistresses, two Turks whom he had made grooms of the bedchamber, and a dwarf who seemed to fill no purpose at all.

Unable to speak English, he held no levees or drawing rooms. He did not yet keep a public table or admit gentlemen to his bedchamber. If it were not for the drawing rooms held by the Prince and Princess of Wales, which he occasionally graced, few people would have seen him.

But Sir Harrowby, through connections on his mother's side, had been allowed to approach King George on more than one evening, when his Majesty received visitors in his private closet. Such admittance could only be gained through introduction by a gentleman of the bedchamber or a secretary of state, so undoubtedly Sir Harrowby had reason to hope.

Unfortunately, no Royal Household office could ever compete with a peerage, especially a grand title with its accompanying estates and income for furniture, jewels, and gowns. Sir Harrowby stood little chance in the race for Isabella's hand.

Right now he seemed content to stand at Mrs. Mayfield's side and entertain her while the Duke of Bournemouth approached Isabella to claim her hand for his promised dance.

The throng parted to allow his Grace to make his way across the floor. With all eyes drawn to Isabella, the recipient of his favour, Hester could almost taste her aunt's elation.

The Duke's black *habille à la française*, with its elaborate silver embroidery, cast even the elegant Sir Harrowby's coat into the shade. Diamonds twinkled from the folds of lace at his Grace's throat and from the chain across his chest. A large ruby flashed from a ring, and silver ribbons fluttered brightly at his knees. When Mrs. Mayfield made him her deepest, most reverent curtsey, his nod in her direction was perfunctory at best. His acknowledgement of Sir Harrowby, a noted leader of fashion, was only slightly more polite. To Mrs. Hester Kean, a spinster of no repute or fortune, he paid no notice at all.

Privately, Hester doubted that his Grace's intentions were of the sort that led to marriage, but she kept her cynical reflections to herself. They were certain to be unwelcomed by her aunt, whose ambition knew no bounds and whose heart was firmly set on being mama to a duchess. If Hester had thought Isabella's heart engaged, she might have issued her a warning. But as matters stood, she did not believe Isabella would suffer overmuch if and when the Duke passed her over for a more suitable bride. Hester's only concern was for Lord St. Mars, whom she deemed more worthy of Isabella's affections than any other of her suitors, and whom she would hate to see cast down if cast aside.

"'Pon rep!" Sir Harrowby's indignant tone caught her attention. He had turned his gaze from the retreating couple to raise his prospect glass to his eye and was examining a tall gentleman just entering the room. "'Tis that fellow, Letchworth, by gad! What can have possessed Eppington to invite him?"

"Lud, Sir Harrowby! Do you not know he is received by everybody, even his Grace? They say he is possessed of the greatest fortune in London and that even his Majesty approves him. He keeps a fine stable and gambles his money like any gentleman. I know I should not be too proud to bestow my Isabella upon Mr. Letchworth if she could not do better for herself. Mr. Letchworth will do exceedingly well for one of the other young ladies present, I'm sure, and so her ladyship knows. Think of the jewels his wife will have!"

The object of their speech made his way through the room, stopping only to give a short bark of greeting to one acquaintance, before directing his footsteps in their direction. Mr. Letchworth was an ill-favoured man, long-boned and large-featured, with an unbecoming tendency to wear thick paint on his face. His clothes were costly, but tonight his coat of olive velvet did not sit well with his pasty complexion. He always seemed to have dressed hastily, though it was said he had the services of an expensive *valet de chambre*. It was as if the gold thread that adorned his stockings and the jewels that twinkled from his fingers should be enough to claim his position in the world.

Fortune would secure his welcome in this gathering. But Hester wondered how annoyed he would be to find that his late arrival had given Isabella the excuse she needed to avoid dancing with him.

Reaching Mrs. Mayfield's side, Mr. Letchworth sketched her a bow just as Sir Harrowby turned to hail a friend.

Moving aside to let him pass, Hester returned to her place in time to hear Mr. Letchworth compliment her aunt on Isabella's appearance this evening. He suggested that rubies would become her daughter very well. Mrs. Mayfield accepted these comments with all her usual pride but she could not hide her relish in informing him that Isabella's dances had been claimed for the rest of the night. Seeing that neither he nor her aunt intended to include her in their conversation, Hester turned her attention to the dancers and missed witnessing his disappointment. A few moments later, she saw him retreating in the direction from which he had come.

At that moment, Sir Harrowby bid his friend goodbye. Turning back, he noticed Hester and gave a start. "Ah, there you are, Miss Kean. I vow, you are so silent, ma'am, I had no idea you was here. What say you about that fellow who was just speaking to your aunt? Would you care to set your cap his way?" He giggled at his joke.

Hester smothered her annoyance at hearing herself addressed as "miss" when politeness dictated that ladies both married and unmarried were to be called "Mrs." Instead, she bestowed a tolerant smile on Sir Harrowby, whose intention was to include her in their speech as one of Isabella's family, even if she was only a servant.

"I think not, sir," she said. "I am afraid Mr. Letchworth is too stern a gentleman for me."

Her aunt stepped between them, issuing a sharp snort of laughter. "Fie on you again, sir! Next, you will be turning my niece's head with thoughts of my Lord St. Mars, as if his lordship and Mr. Letchworth was not both head over heels in love with my Isabella. I vow, the letters that gentleman writes are so hot with passion as to put her mama to the blush! Lucky for you, Miss Kean has no illusions about the nature of her own attractions, else your sport would be cruel indeed."

At her spiteful tone, Sir Harrowby gave a blink, before something she had said seemed to catch at his mind. "Do you mean to tell me, ma'am, that Mr. Letchworth has been courting Mrs. Isabella?"

Hester's aunt turned more playful. "Can you doubt it, Sir Harrowby? My Isabella has all the gentlemen wooing her."

"Zounds, madam! But that is infamous! What infernal impudence!"

"I think I know what you are about, naughty sir! You would have all my daughter's suitors passed on to someone else so that you could have a clear field for yourself."

She tapped him playfully on the arm. "Confess now, sir! That was what you was about. Lud, but you gentlemen are all alike where my daughter is concerned—playing off your tricks and making threats to cut each other out—but you cannot win her from me that way, and so I shall warn Isabella." With a smirk, she spread a chicken-skin fan and fluttered it before her painted face.

"I trust you have informed Mr. Letchworth of the futility of his hopes," Sir Harrowby said, raising his brows with a hint of offence.

Since Mrs. Mayfield had done her best to do just that with respect to himself, he was not best pleased when she said, "Why, no, sir. It is not for me to be scaring off my daughter's suitors, though I hardly need tell you that that particular gentleman is not on the list of my daughter's favourites. Family as you are to my Lord St. Mars—"

A movement near the door caught her eye. "Why, here he is at last! I wondered what was keeping his lordship, since he particularly asked my Isabella to save him a dance."

Hester turned reflexively, in time to see St. Mars give one quick glance about the room, before spying Mrs. Mayfield and heading purposefully towards her. He ignored the few hostile looks, as he made his way through the largely Whig crowd. By inviting St. Mars, Lord Eppington had proved himself an advocate of the new politeness, which maintained that party differences should be set aside for the enjoyment of society. Hester was glad for the openness that had brought St. Mars within their circle, even if she had no illusions about his interest in her. It was enough simply to have known such a perfect gentleman.

He seemed to sense her scrutiny, so she averted her gaze until his arrival could render her attention more appropriate. But those few moments' lack of guard had been enough to set her pulse to thumping. No matter how hard she tried to restrain it, her heart would always flutter when my Lord St. Mars was near.

St. Mars never gave the impression of a gentleman who belonged in a ballroom, although none could fault either his manners or his dress. The trouble was the feeling that issued from him, of an immense energy threatening to burst its restraints—a need for greater space than a ballroom allowed, which always left Hester with the sense that he would rather be flying over hedges on a horse than sitting inside. She had formed this opinion of him when he had made his initial call upon Isabella only two months ago. Although his deportment had been without exception correct, Mrs. Mayfield's drawing room had scarcely seemed large enough to hold him.

As he reached them and greetings began, Hester was at last free to take in his handsome features, the grace in his movements, and the sinewy strength of his hands.

St. Mars made them each a courtly bow, Hester included. Not for Lord St. Mars the sneering nod or the indifferent stare. His lordship's manners were so engaging, he made each recipient of his attention believe he had no one else in mind. The smile he gave Hester was both inclusive and warm. It sent a tingle down her spine, even as she noted how soon his gaze left hers to search the crowd for Isabella.

"Your servant, Mrs. Mayfield, Mrs. Kean, Harrowby. I do not see Mrs. Isabella Mayfield this evening. I hope she is well?"

This was another thing that Hester appreciated about St Mars. He never neglected to address her as a woman of distinction. Her aunt had often slighted her when presenting her to Isabella's suitors, who usually followed her lead. Lord St. Mars had just as politely ignored it.

Mrs. Mayfield was answering his question. "My Isabella is as well as can be expected, my lord, for a girl as has had to dance these past three hours and more without a moment's break." Her look was arch as she pointed her fan towards Isabella, who was curtsying to the Duke. "I vow, I shall have to put my foot down and insist that she rest a bit before supper, else she'll never choke down a bite, she'll be so worn out."

St. Mars's blue eyes dimmed as he noticed the identity of Isabella's partner, and Hester's heart went out to him. Something about him this evening did not appear quite right. He seemed unnaturally subdued, and his face was colourless above the white lace at his throat.

"I hope you will not be adamant on that subject, ma'am, before I have had a chance to dance with her myself."

"Why, as to that," Mrs. Mayfield began coyly—she would not wish to offend St. Mars, not until the Duke was firmly caught— "I think I could bring her to take one more for your lordship's sake. But it would seem, my lord, that if you was wishing to have my daughter's hand in a dance, you would have come earlier this evening. You know how sought after my Isabella is."

"I wished to do so, but was detained. Nothing but an urgent call from Rotherham Abbey could have made me appear this late."

"From your papa?" Mrs. Mayfield asked, a bit too eagerly. "Now, what can Lord Hawkhurst have wanted, I wonder?"

The freezing look Lord St. Mars gave her was so unlike him that Hester winced at her aunt's impertinence. There was something in his glance that made her fear Lord Hawkhurst had had nothing good to say about his son's feelings for Isabella.

"It was nothing that should interest you, ma'am." He turned his back on Mrs. Mayfield's impudent stare. Keeping his eyes off Isabella and her partner with a remarkable show of will, he turned to Hester instead. "You are not dancing, Mrs. Kean. May I beg your hand to finish this set?"

Hester started to smile, a quiver mounting from her stomach into her throat, though a drawn look about his eyes made her hesitate just an instant too long.

"Now, my lord—" with a quelling look at Hester and a frown that threw daggers, Mrs. Mayfield intervened— "you would disturb the lines if you was to enter the dance this late. The set is just about over, I believe."

St. Mars was turning towards her in astonishment, when he caught Hester's rueful expression, and an unmistakable flicker of amusement lit his eyes. A look of understanding passed between them. Faced with his awareness of her aunt's machinations, Hester could not restrain a smile, and she had to bow her head to hide it.

"We shall wait, then," his lordship said, with a profound bow—

more to disguise his own grin, she guessed, than to punctuate his statement— "until the start of another dance."

Hester did her best to squelch the feeling of hope these words gave her. Chances were, she and Lord St. Mars would never have that dance. But the look he had given her, a recognition that she was possessed of a wit he could enjoy, had done more to speed her heartbeat this evening than any other gentleman's more formal attentions.

The Duke of Bournemouth escorted Isabella back. Greetings followed in which Hester played no part. Being ignored allowed her to observe the gentlemen's faces to see if she could determine the depth of their feelings for her cousin or indeed Isabella's for them.

As she'd expected, his Grace showed none of the need to feast his eyes on her cousin that the younger men did, though St. Mars did his best to conceal his desire. Much to Hester's annoyance, the Duke seemed amused. An air of superiority attended all of his remarks, since he knew fully well his claim would be favoured over any other's, should he choose to make it.

But there was something in his attitude tonight that made her believe he had wearied of Isabella's charms. Mrs. Mayfield would have noticed that his Grace had solicited her daughter's hand for only one dance, when more would have been allowed. And, contrary to his behavior at their last two meetings, he had made no attempt to get Isabella alone.

Now Hester saw a distance in his expression, and she experienced a pang, the cause of which she instantly recognized. She could not be entirely thrilled that St. Mars would have an unobstructed path to her cousin, even though his plans to wed could have nothing at all to do with her. She simply believed that he could do much better for himself—that he would find greater happiness if married to someone other than Isabella. Someone with a livelier intelligence than her cousin possessed.

Isabella had spoken to him with all the unaffected pleasure with which she greeted her swains. But she had quickly turned away and now was tapping her foot and looking about the ballroom at the ladies' finery, to all appearances unaware of St. Mars's burning gaze.

If he would only look at *her* with that heat in his eyes, Hester thought, she would swoon on the spot. But, she reflected, neither St. Mars's desire nor his looks should be of interest to her.

When the Duke of Bournemouth took his leave, Mrs. Mayfield endeavoured to keep Sir Harrowby engaged in conversation so as to allow Isabella and St. Mars to talk aside. Anxious not to appear to be overhearing them, but trapped beside them in the crush of people, Hester turned her back so they would think she was enjoying the sight of the dancers she had been forced to watch all night.

St. Mars's voice, with its deep, masculine tones, still reached her.

"Forgive me for arriving so late this evening, Mrs. Isabella. Dare I hope you've saved at least one dance for me?"

"Faith, sir, you will have to ask my mama, for I've made so many promises, I've well nigh forgot to who. Apply to her now, if you will, for I see Lord Kirkland bearing this way, and the next is his."

"Isabella—"

Hester winced at the urgency in St. Mars's voice before he was cut off by a gentleman demanding Isabella's attention. After a few polite exchanges, Lord Kirkland swept by Hester, leading Isabella out onto the floor.

Hester would not let herself turn around. She would not turn around to see the light going out of St. Mars's eyes.

After a few moments, he stepped up beside her. His lips were compressed into a thin, bloodless line. When he felt her sympathetic gaze, he responded with a self-disparaging grin, which lightened his features but did not remove the worry from his eyes.

"Mrs. Kean—" he bowed with a flourish— "would you take pity upon me and favour me with this dance?"

Hester made a quick search over her shoulder, but Mrs. Mayfield was more than ten feet away, engaged in conversation with a countess, and so could neither frown at Hester nor interfere.

"I should be delighted, my lord." Hester started to smile, before St. Mars, stepping forward to take her hand, suddenly turned a ghastly pale and wavered on his feet. She reached one hand to grasp his elbow. "My lord?"

"It is nothing." The colour of his cheeks and a hint of sweat upon his brow belied his words. "However, it might be best if we sat this dance out, if you will forgive me."

Suppressing her keen disappointment, Hester looked quickly about and spied two chairs just being vacated in an alcove to the right. "Certainly, my lord. Will you come this way?"

Gideon offered her his arm and did his best to lead her in the direction she'd indicated, without passing out from the sudden dizziness that had seized him. His infernal wound had begun to throb, to which must be added the effect of the frustration he always felt in Isabella's presence. He tried not to lean on Mrs. Kean, but he found he needed her support. Fortunately, she gave it without appearing to mind, as she remarked on the beauty of Lady Eppington's decorations.

A likeable girl, Mrs. Kean. Now that he thought of it, he had always enjoyed her company, ever since that first day they had met in Isabella's drawing room. There was something in those cool, grey eyes of hers that was reassuring. A man always knew where he stood with Mrs. Kean—she was honest, and she seemed to have a sense of humour, too. She had not called anyone's attention to his dizziness either, for which he was sincerely grateful.

They reached the alcove, and Gideon insisted on seating her before he lowered himself into his own chair. "I'm sorry," he said. "I cannot think what came over me. But I would not wish to embarrass you on the ballroom floor."

"Are you sure you are all right? I could fetch a doctor."

He gave a laugh. "Now you sound like my groom."

At her quizzical look, he explained, "I meant that quite kindly, I assure you. My groom, Thomas Barnes, has taken good care of me since I was a babe in leading strings, which makes him inclined to assert the privilege of a nurse. I have just had to discourage him from hovering over me in the most discountenancing way."

"I see." In spite of these words, she studied him cautiously as if worrying out a puzzle. "Was there some reason, my lord, why your groom believed you should have a doctor called?"

"No, nothing—" But Gideon found he could not lie to Mrs. Kean, not with those intelligent eyes of hers fixed upon his face. "That is to say, I did have an altercation earlier this evening, which is one of the reasons I was late. A fellow assaulted me in the street, but I only took a scratch."

Her eyes flickered. "An assault, my lord?"

He chuckled and tried to shrug, but his arm had begun to ache miserably, and the room seemed to turn before his eyes. He could hardly conceal his pain. "Yes, but it is no matter now. Tell me something about yourself, Mrs. Kean. We have talked about me long enough."

"I shall tell you about myself if you like," she said slowly, "but only if you promise that you will alert me the instant you wish me to stop. The look of your brow makes me think you are taking a fever."

"Does it?" Gideon reached up and felt the dampness on his forehead. When he moved the arm from his side, he felt a sudden chill. "Very well, I promise to let you know. But you made a promise to divert me, and I am determined to hold you to it."

"If you insist, but I must warn you. My life is so far from fascinating, you would do better to let me tell you a fairy tale."

"That would be cheating."

"Would it? Oh, dear. As you like, then . . . ."

She seemed at a loss where to begin. In spite of the stabbing pain in his arm and an uncontrollable shiver, Gideon felt a smile tickling the corners of his mouth. It was refreshing to find a woman who was not too eager to talk to no purpose. Mrs. Kean had a restful way about her. If he had wanted a respite while waiting for Isabella's return, he could have found no better companion.

He knew something of her story. Mrs. Mayfield had taken her in after the death of her father, a country parson with no fortune to dower her with. Her only brother, a wastrel, had been too poor to offer her a home. On learning this from Mrs. Mayfield herself, Gideon had been relieved to discover this much kindness in his future mother-in-law, especially in light of her other children, living with their brother in the country and yet to be established. But he had squirmed at the tactless way in which she had imparted the news. He had applauded her generous intention to take Mrs. Kean to Court, but lately he had found her treatment of her niece to be less than kind.

The young lady's dress was not remotely as lovely as Isabella's, being unrelievedly dull and of a sober cut not likely to attract a suitor. Gideon supposed Mrs. Kean might have inherited a serious turn of mind from her father, a juring clergyman, which made her choose such a gown when she might have worn something more complimentary to her colouring. As it was, that brownish-yellow was unbecoming, although the dress fitted her slim figure well. It would be a shame if Mrs. Kean, who was a good, deserving girl, had not a taste in clothes to help her attract admirers.

But none of these thoughts did he allow to show, and soon he forgot them himself in their conversation.

"You come from the north, as I recall. Do you never miss it?" he asked.

"The wuthering of the wind, the treeless moors, and the blinding snow, my lord? You must think me mad." She gave a shudder. "I have far too much love of a warm fire."

"You prefer a milder climate, then? If so, you must come into Kent. You can always count on the warmest winds at Rotherham Abbey. What think you, Mrs. Kean? Will I be successful if I try to prevail upon Mrs. Isabella and her mother to bring you into Kent?"

As he spoke Isabella's name, Gideon let his gaze seek her on the ballroom floor. She was dancing still with Kirkland, her infectious laughter lighting up the room. Gideon felt an instinctive pang when he noted how much her current smile resembled the one with which she always greeted him, as if it had no particular significance.

Of course, he reminded himself, that was one of the things he loved about her, her constant glow. From where else could such a smile come, if not from some deep fountain of goodness?

"I should be delighted to accompany Isabella to your house, my lord," Mrs. Kean said so quietly he almost did not hear her.

Gideon turned to find that she was observing him closely. The pity he saw in her eyes gave him a jolt.

"Mrs. Kean," he said, "you will not be offended, I hope, if I confess to you my aspirations."

"My lord." Her smile gently teased him. "You will not be offended, I hope, if I tell you I have guessed them long ago."

Gideon found himself relaxing again at the evidence of her humour. "Have I been so awkward as that?"

"Not awkward—no." Her haste to reassure him on this point made him worry all the more.

Gideon studied her face and noted her unease with a sinking heart. "Have I a serious rival, then, or would you rather not say?"

"I should rather not say, but since you desire it, I will do my best to put the case in the fairest way I can. My lord—" she regarded him solemnly before taking a deep breath— "I can only say that both my aunt and cousin look upon your suit with great favour. But you must realize that Isabella has more attention than any dozen girls could ever hope to have. And, because of that attention, I do not think she is always in a position to know her own heart."

Gideon felt a frown crease his brow. He did his best to erase it, but he was feeling sick. The wound on his arm was aching more and more with every minute. Fever had begun to blur his eyes, and Mrs. Kean's words had struck at his worst fears.

He would have thanked her all the same. He took her remarks for a careful warning that he must do his best to secure Isabella's hand with all haste. But, just then, a shrill cry interrupted them.

"Hester!"

Mrs. Mayfield's vicious note shocked him.

"I have been looking for you this past quarter hour and more! And where you had gone to, nobody could tell me. I need you this instant to fetch my pink shawl from the carriage. The air has grown quite chilly in here, and I swear I shall catch my death of cold before supper."

Gideon stood abruptly. A wave of dizziness seized him, but he tried to ignore the stabbing pains in his arm that had caused it. Catching his balance, he gave Mrs. Mayfield a stiff bow. If he needed any proof that Mrs. Mayfield regarded him as her daughter's property, her offence at his attention to Mrs. Kean had given it. He supposed he should feel delighted, but he could never wish to see a girl as decent as Mrs. Kean treated so unfairly.

"Pray allow me, madam, to find a page to fetch your shawl. Mrs. Kean has been kind enough to sit with me." He might have added that she had done so while he waited to dance with her cousin, but such a comment would only serve to diminish Mrs. Kean and his pleasure in her company.

Gideon saw that his politeness had done nothing to take the edge off Mrs. Mayfield's offence. The smile she gave him did not reach her eyes—nor did it include her niece.

"La, my lord! How can you think I would ever ask your lordship to bother yourself over a trifle like this?" Turning to her niece, she said, with a false cheer that failed to conceal her displeasure, "Be a good girl, Hester, and run along to the carriage."

Gideon watched Hester's face as she curtsied to him, accepting her aunt's command with no sign of resentment. None of the annoyance he had felt seemed to have bothered her, which was good, he told himself, since she undoubtedly would have to put up with Mrs. Mayfield's whimsical humours until she married. For her sake, Gideon hoped it would not be long.

Here stood Ill Nature like an ancient maid,
Her wrinkled form in black and white arrayed;
With store of prayers, for mornings, nights, and noons,
Her hand is filled; her bosom with lampoons.
There Affectation, with a sickly mien,
Shows in her cheek the roses of eighteen,
Practised to lisp, and hang the head aside,
Faints into airs, and languishes with pride

This day, black Omens threat the brightest Fair
That e'er deserved a watchful spirit's care;
Some dire disaster, or by force, or slight;
But what, or where, the fates have wrapped in night.

Methinks already I your tears survey,
Already hear the horrid things they say,
Already see you a degraded toast,
And all your honour in a whisper lost!
How shall I, then, your helpless fame defend?
'Twill then be infamy to seem your friend!

CHAPTER III

HESTER did her best to keep her composure until she passed from the crowded room. She would not wish St. Mars to see how embarrassed she had been by her aunt's churlish humor. *As if Isabella suffered any competition from a parson's drab daughter!* she thought, hiding her flaming cheeks from the people she passed, and hoping the cool of the night would tame the flush that heated them.

At the door downstairs, she was checked by a footman who inquired whether he might perform her a service. Hester had enough sense not to insist upon searching for Mrs. Mayfield's carriage herself. With the crush of vehicles awaiting their owners outside, she might spend an hour dragging her skirts through the mud and the cold air while she tried to discover the right one. Not that she supposed Mrs. Mayfield had any need for the garment, but neither could her aunt now pretend she did not, having expressed herself so strongly in front of St. Mars. There was humour in that thought, at least, which made Hester feel a bit better while she waited for the footman's return.

She stood to one side of the hall, her back against the wall, where she could observe the arrivals and departures of Lord Eppington's guests. The number of goings and comings had greatly fallen off this close to the supper hour, so that the noisy arrival of a gentleman, dressed in a riding costume rather than the finery required for a ball, his tall boots splattered with mud, could hardly escape her notice. The man's Puritan-style clothing and grim expression gave her the unhappy feeling that he had come to deliver bad news.

Just then, the footman returned with Mrs. Mayfield's shawl. Hester was obliged to take her eyes off the newcomer in order to thank the servant for his help. By the time she turned again, the gentleman had moved up the stairs in the direction of the ballroom, leaving a stream of murmurs in his wake. His sober clothes alone would have caused remark, to which his solemn expression could only add.

With a sense of impending calamity, Hester followed him back upstairs, through the hallway and into the ballroom.

She trailed him to within feet of her aunt. He stopped and bowed before my Lord St. Mars.

St. Mars, his colour heightened since Hester had left—perhaps by the fact that he was enjoying Isabella's company at last—noticed the gentleman and his eyebrows shot up in surprise. He seemed to recognize him at once, although Hester could not hear what passed between them until she stepped closer. When she did, she felt her breath die in her throat.

"My lord," the gentleman said, "I regret to inform you that your father, Lord Hawkhurst, has been murdered."

"Murdered?" Gideon raised a hand to his forehead, gone suddenly chill as the blood drained from his face. A sense of unreality had been slowly spreading through him as the dancers pranced and Isabella toyed with her fan, refusing to hear his entreaties. But now the room transformed itself into a whirligig of faces. Lord Eppington's guests disappeared in a revolving cloud of noses, wigs, and eyes.

Someone grasped him by the arm, and an intense pain shot through him. He tried to muffle his cry, but the unexpectedness of the pang made him jerk to protect his throbbing shoulder.

"My lord!" Sir Joshua Tate, the justice of the peace who had brought him the news, stared down at a smear of blood on his hand.

A gasp tore through the room. Isabella shrieked. His arm—his wound had bled. It must have been oozing through his bandages and had alarmed her.

"It's nothing," he said. But his tongue would not obey his commands, and his speech sounded slurred even to his own ears. He tried to speak more clearly. "Mustn't be frightened, Isabella."

"My lord, you should sit down." Mrs. Kean's calm voice came as if from far away. "You have suffered a grave shock."

A shock? Oh, yes, Tate had come to tell him—something that had upset him. His father—his father couldn't be dead.

Gideon wished the humming that filled his head would cease, so he could make sense of it all, but the noise only increased.

"You said my father has been murdered?"

"Yes, my lord." There was an odd note in Sir Joshua's voice. "He was killed by a man who was himself injured in the attack."

It made no sense to Gideon that Sir Joshua should be the one to inform him of his father's death. Lord Hawkhurst had detested this man and his Puritanical ways.

"What brings you here? What attack?"

"My lord—" that quieter, gentler voice urged him to calm— "my Lord St. Mars, you must be seated. You are weak."

From another direction Mrs. Mayfield's harsher tones sliced through it. "Come away from there, Hester. Isabella can tend to my Lord St. Mars—Lord Hawkhurst, I should say."

Gideon ignored the murmuring voices about him, the worried glances and the shuffling feet. This was all too confusing, though he thought he heard a whispered protest from Isabella among her mother's forceful remarks. Of Mrs. Kean's calm tones, he heard nothing more.

The room was spinning. Hands reached out to grasp him. He was pushed into a chair.

"I am sorry." He tried to form words, but his tongue was heavy, as if he had bitten it. The sounds that came out of his mouth, he hardly recognized as his. "Tate, please tell me again what you said."

Sir Joshua repeated the horrible news. Still unchanged; still unbelievable. Gideon pictured his father so full of life, purple with rage the last time they had met.

When had that been?

He tried to think, but he could hardly form a cohesive thought. "I was with him—this morning I think. We had a quarrel."

"So I was given to understand, my lord."

Some of the hum that confused him came to a sudden halt. Even over the ringing in his ears, Gideon heard the silence that had come over the room.

Why had everyone stopped whispering? His brain was refusing to think, or to tell him what to do. Was it shock? He had thought himself almost recovered from his injury until Tate had come, though Mrs. Kean, observant girl, had noticed his growing fever.

"Lord St. Mars—" Sir Joshua spoke again— "I suggest that you come with me. I will take your statement at Hawkhurst House."

His statement? Gideon's eyes flew open and he sought the justice's face. What the devil did he mean?

He peered out at the hazy room and saw the crowd of guests, frozen in place, their horrified stares surrounding him. Lady Eppington was leaning on a gentleman's arm, being fanned by her black page.

"Yes, we must go." Gideon tried to pull himself together for the sake of his hostess. He should try not to spoil her ball. He only wished he could hold on to Isabella but she was nowhere near.

From a distance, feeling as powerless as a mother whose son was going off to war, Hester watched St. Mars depart with Sir Joshua Tate and Sir Harrowby Fitzsimmons. A few gentlemen moved together to speak, closing the gap behind them before they, too, left the ballroom. Those who remained seemed strangely tight-lipped, their faces worried and drawn. And no wonder. St. Mars had stated that he had quarreled with his father before Lord Hawkhurst had been found murdered. They had seen his blood and heard the justice of the peace state that the earl's attacker had been wounded.

The shock on their faces told Hester exactly what they thought, though knowing St. Mars only this short while, she could not credit their suspicions. No means on earth would convince her that St.

Mars had done his father harm.

He had no sooner left the room than it became a buzz of speculation. No one dared to voice the most startling thought— not when Gideon Fitzsimmons was now an earl. But Hester could see the condemnation in their arching brows. In this Whig assembly, with many of the gentlemen either peers or members of Parliament, St. Mars had no more friends than his father would have had.

"Now, here's a coil." Mrs. Mayfield snatched the forgotten shawl from Hester's hands. "'Tis time we left."

"But, Mama—"

Hester was relieved to hear her cousin's protest, until Isabella finished, "I have promised five other dances, and Lord Kirkland to take supper with him."

For once, Hester was in complete sympathy with her aunt when she rounded on her daughter, hissing, "Foolish girl! Have you no notion of what has just occurred? We must hurry home to think this business through." Grasping Isabella by the wrist, she bustled her party out, hardly stopping to thank their prostrate hostess.

Inside the carriage, Isabella complained of the unfair treatment, but Mrs. Mayfield seemed deaf. Sitting in the dark, Hester could almost hear the mill-wheels churning in her aunt's head. Mrs. Mayfield waited, however, until they arrived at their rented house in Clarges Street before she referred to the evening's episode.

When she did, the direction of her speech took Hester completely by surprise.

"How fine dear Sir Harrowby Fitzsimmons looked this evening," she began, as Isabella and Hester followed her into the house. "We must be sure to invite him to dinner."

They crossed the vestibule quickly and mounted the stairs to the withdrawing room. In only a fraction of the time this took, Hester had understood the turn in her aunt's thoughts. With anger poised on the edge of her tongue, she waited to see if Isabella would come to a similar conclusion.

"But, Mama—" Isabella yawned as she pulled at the ribbon tied about her neck— "I thought you didn't want me to encourage Sir Harrowby by showing him any particular regard."

"Nonsense, child," Mrs. Mayfield clucked as she helped her daughter off with her cloak. "Sir Harrowby Fitzsimmons is as elegant a gentleman as the world has ever known. And if not for the fact that his prospects have not always been the best, why, he would be the very man I would pick for you myself. And so, I hope, he knows.

"You mustn't think," she added, as she fussed about her daughter, tucking a curl behind her ear, "that Sir Harrowby's hopes will be unduly raised by a simple request to dine. Why, all the world will be wanting him! For who else could explain this curious business between Lord Hawkhurst and his son?"

Hester stared at her angrily, but Mrs. Mayfield's gaze had fixed upon an invisible speck of mud on Isabella's cloak. When Isabella, who seemed to have slipped into a state bordering on sleep, failed to react to her mother's words, Hester decided she had no choice. She tried to speak as calmly as she could.

"I should think you would wish to hear Lord St. Mars's own account of any event that so regards him, ma'am."

"And so we shall, Miss Prig, if his lordship is free to make it."

Mrs. Mayfield's affronted glance challenged her niece to put herself forward again, but the next question came from Isabella herself. "Why should St. Mars not be free to do anything he pleases, Mama? Isn't he an earl now?"

"Why not, indeed?" Of a sudden her mother bustled her towards the door. "We must all be tired if we're thinking up such foolish questions. All the same, my dear, it might be wise if you was not to be seen with my Lord St. Mars for the time being."

Hester spoke wryly. "And what will his lordship think, if Isabella refuses him the attentions she has granted him so willingly in the past?"

This question brought her aunt up short. Mrs. Mayfield paused with one hand still clutching her daughter's arm to study the expression on Hester's face, and a realization made her frown.

"What will he think, you say?"

She struggled with the answer as she stood rooted to the floor. Isabella glanced back over her shoulder, but she was much too sleepy, and too used to that calculating expression on her mother's face, to protest, even though Mrs. Mayfield's fingers dug deeply into her arm.

"He will think, ma'am, that Isabella is not loyal," Hester said.

"Hmmm." Mrs. Mayfield drew her daughter back into the withdrawing room and closed the door. "You are quite right, Hester. I knew you was a smart girl."

This was not the precise result Hester had wished for. Still, she knew Mrs. Mayfield would take everything her own way.

"Let me think on this."

"Mama—"

Isabella's sleepy plea was abruptly cut off. "Hush, child! This is much too important."

Since Mrs. Mayfield, for all her harshness, rarely spoke to her beloved daughter in any way other than a croon, Isabella's eyes grew round.

"What it is, Mama? Why are you so upset?"

Her mother ignored her. Hester took her cousin by the arm and led her to a damask-covered loveseat. "Why don't you sit with me, dear, until your mother's had time to give the problem a little thought. Perhaps you will tell me about your partners this evening."

As sleepy as she was, Isabella summoned a delighted laugh as she collapsed on the cushions. "They were all vastly pleasing. Did you ever see the like of his Grace's coat? I vow that silver stitching must have cost him a fortune!"

Thinking she heard a distinctive note of pleasure in her cousin's voice, Hester's heart sank. "Are you in love with his Grace, then, Belle?"

"Oh, no!" Isabella seemed shocked. "I would never dream of such a thing. It is vulgar to talk about love, Mama says."

Hester took a deep, bracing breath to tame her impatience. "It is quite all right to love one's husband in my opinion. Nevertheless, if the term offends you, we can employ another. Do you favour the Duke of Bournemouth's suit over the other gentlemen's?"

"Well, I must, mustn't I? He's a duke, and Sir Harrowby is nothing but a baronet."

"But my Lord St. Mars? Have you no feelings for him?"

"He is very handsome. All the gossips say so."

"But what do *you* think, Belle? Whom do *you* wish to marry?"

"Hester, that is enough!" Mrs. Mayfield emerged from her musings to scold her niece. "I will not have you encouraging Isabella with your ill-bred notions. As if a girl of her class should choose her own husband!"

"I might like to pick my husband, Mama. If Sir Harrowby Fitzsimmons were a duke, I think I should like to marry him. He is always so diverting, and he dresses better than many richer men."

Stunned by her cousin's preference, Hester could only await the sound of her aunt's displeasure.

Surprisingly, Mrs. Mayfield made little protest. "He cannot be a duke, my dear . . . but he might become an earl. And if he does, I should do nothing to stop you from having him. Not unless his Grace comes up to scratch." This was said with a sigh that suggested forlorn hopes.

"How can Sir Harrowby be an earl, Mama, when Lord St. Mars stands before him?"

"Never you mind." Mrs. Mayfield stood. "It is getting very late. It must be on three o'clock and seeing we've left the ball early, we might as well seek our beds."

With a smothered yawn, Isabella rose from the loveseat. "Are you coming, Hester? I need someone to brush my hair, and I like the way you do it better than my maid."

Despite the thoughtlessness of her cousin's request, Hester seized on the chance to speak to Isabella privately. "Of course, I'll come," she said. She would not be able to sleep soon in any case. Agitation would keep her awake.

Together they walked from the withdrawing room and up the stairs. Isabella's bedchamber occupied the second floor, alongside her mother's. Hester's was another flight up, near the servants'.

The differences between their rooms did not stop with their floor. Mrs. Mayfield had decorated Isabella's boudoir as if she expected gentlemen to attend her daughter's levee. An elaborately japanned screen separated a pair of seldom-used, French chaises from the part of the chamber devoted to Isabella's more intimate functions.

Mrs. Mayfield knew that fashionable ladies received their callers while they dressed. Hester found the whole arrangement ridiculous. England, after all, was not France.

There was no point in questioning Isabella until her maid had helped her off with her clothes and into a lawn nightgown, before going gratefully to her own bed. But later, as Hester stood behind her cousin, seated in front of the reflecting glass, brushing her thick, golden curls, she found her moment.

"Bella," she said, once her drowsy cousin had fallen silent, "did you truly mean you do not love St. Mars?"

"I think he is handsome, but he does not dress as well as Sir Harrowby."

"Perhaps not, dear, but do you see nothing else in him to admire?"

"Mama says his fortune will be immense when his father dies. Oh!" she exclaimed. "I forgot. His father is dead now, so he must be quite rich."

"I meant rather some quality of his, beyond his wealth. His strength, perhaps? Or his extraordinary gentility?"

"Gentle? St. Mars? I do not think him gentle at all. He is so . . . so very vigorous! And he is grown so serious, when he used to be vastly more amusing. You have not seen him, Hester, when he looks at me so fiercely."

Hester gave a start. "I am sure St. Mars would do nothing to harm you, Belle. He loves you far too much."

Isabella giggled as if Hester and she had entered into a secret. "That's what Mama said," she confided, "when I told her that St. Mars stares at me in a way I do not like. Not at all like Sir Harrowby, who's the perfect gentleman. He knows how to make pretty speeches without making me feel anything at all. Mama says that gentlemen like St. Mars are so passionate, they cannot always think before they act. She said that could turn to my advantage if I wanted."

Hester felt a cold, sick fury in the pit of her stomach. So St. Mars's love was to be used, wasted, and despised? In spite of her own attraction, she found herself aching at his failure to attach Isabella. Bella was the girl he wanted, and was, therefore, the wife he should have. The only hope for his lordship that Hester could see was that her cousin might learn to reciprocate his passion in time.

"Bella, what do you know of the intimacies of marriage? Would you not rather kiss St. Mars than any other of your swains?"

"No." Bella seemed firm on this point. "I think I would prefer Sir Harrowby. He makes me laugh."

"I am sure he does," Hester said wryly. She couldn't understand her cousin at all, but clearly Isabella's passion had not yet been tapped. Not that Hester's had been given a chance to flower either, but she had always been blessed with a fertile imagination.

Sighing with genuine fatigue, she reached for Isabella's cap. "Go to bed, dear," she said, tying the ribands under her cousin's chin. "We've talked enough for tonight."

Isabella thanked her prettily for brushing her hair and, yawning mightily again, stumbled off to bed as Hester took a tallow candle up to her room. One of Mrs. Mayfield's economies forbade the use of wax in the bedchambers.

Upstairs, there was no maid and no dressing table. Her furniture consisted of an old-fashioned bed in sturdy English oak and an ancient cupboard that was quite sufficient for her modest wardrobe.

Hester set the sputtering candle on a small table and prepared for sleep. The startling events at Lord Eppington's ball, the sight of St. Mars so ill and feverish, the guests' suspicions, and now Isabella's complete indifference to St. Mars's plight distressed her so much she doubted she would sleep. She wondered what the justice of the peace intended to ask St. Mars. His implication had been that his lordship would have to explain the quarrel he had had with his father.

Hester worried that no one would take care of his wound, which might go septic. Fevered and upset, would St. Mars be able to defend himself?

She told herself she had no right to feel this sharp an anxiety. Lord St. Mars—Lord Hawkhurst now—was a man with more power and influence than she could ever have. It would be presumptuous of her to think he could need her help.

Yet, these were treacherous times. The Jacobites had not stopped complaining about King George's accession, and rumours that the Pretender had landed on British soil continued to stir fears among the loyal populace. His Majesty had shown such a preference for the Whigs that he had created hostility even among those Tories who had pledged him their loyalty, and both parties were so acrimonious that no one could feel secure in this climate of smears and lies.

Lord Hawkhurst had been a Tory, and Sir Joshua Tate, clothed as he was, could be nothing short of a Roundhead. He had shown no sympathy for St. Mars. On the contrary, he had seemed to regard him from the first with suspicion.

He might think a greater motive for murder existed than a simple family quarrel. The Hawkhurst estate was one of the oldest and greatest in England; the Fitzsimmons family could trace its line back to the Norman Conquest, if not to William himself.

Why would a son who was certain of inheriting that fortune be so foolish as to kill his own father? The question in itself was ridiculous. Still, Hester could not help wondering why the two men had fought.

There was an old chipped mirror on the wall of her chamber, which told her little about her looks. Nevertheless, tonight Hester carried the candle over to it and spent some time examining her features in the glass. She could find very little to recommend her, but a good, straight set of teeth. If Isabella had a flaw, it was a smile that seemed to beg for a set of false ones, but she was so like most other ladies in that regard, no one would notice the fault at all.

"Poor St. Mars," Hester sighed aloud. "I would return your affection if you loved me as you love Isabella, but I will not be so foolish as to hope for that."

She would ache for him on the day when he should learn how shallow Isabella's feelings were. Most gentlemen, she knew, would be content just to have such a divine creature in their bed. But if Isabella could not return St. Mars's love. . . .

The heat Hester had seen in his eyes when he'd looked at her cousin had been enough to make her knees go weak. Even now, as she pondered the strength of his desire, she grew quite restless. Thoughts of my Lord St. Mars and his wants were enough to send her hastily away from the mirror and its truths.

Climbing under her moth-eaten covers, she made a firm vow. If it would make St. Mars happy to have her cousin Isabella, then she, Hester, would do everything in her power to see that he was not disappointed.

Ye Sylphs and Sylphids, to your chief give ear!
Fays, Fairies, Genii, Elves, and Daemons, hear!
Ye know the spheres and various tasks assigned
By laws eternal to th'aerial kind.

In various talk th'instructive hours they past,
Who gave the ball, or paid the visit last;
One speaks the glory of the British Queen,
And one describes a charming Indian screen;
A third interprets motions, looks, and eyes;
At every word a reputation dies.
Snuff, or the fan, supply each pause of chat,
With singing, laughing, ogling, and all that.

CHAPTER IV

DISTRESSED by the attack on St. Mars, Thomas Barnes had disobeyed him to stay awake until he was safely home. Then, the justice of the peace from Kent had arrived and, within minutes, Lord Hawkhurst's household had learned that the harsh, proud, but just man they all called master had been brutally killed. Sir Joshua Tate, informed of St. Mars's whereabouts, had gone to Eppington House to deliver the news.

Anxious and grieving, Tom awaited the return of the new Lord Hawkhurst. He knew that sorrow would prevent his young master from welcoming his honours. Still, Tom wanted to be the first to bend his knee to him as a peer.

The sound of wheels turning into the courtyard brought him eagerly to his feet. But the sight of his lordship's strange retinue, consisting of two carriages, Gideon's cousin, Sir Harrowby Fitzsimmons, the justice of the peace, and two sober-faced constables, alerted Tom to the fact that something even worse was amiss.

The footmen who had run alongside Gideon's carriage hurried to open the coach door on which the Hawkhurst arms were emblazoned. As Tom moved nearer, flanked by two stable boys and the retreating footmen, he saw Gideon emerge.

His normally sanguine mien was defaced by lines of pain. A cloud seemed to have affected his eyes, and perspiration beaded his face.

The footmen recoiled in shock.

Tom rushed forward.

Gideon took a few steps his way, then reached out for his arm. Tom could feel him trembling with an uncontrollable chill.

"Tom—" Gideon spoke through chattering teeth—"help me upstairs and call for Philippe."

"Just a moment, my lord." Sir Joshua came after him, protesting loudly. "There are questions to be asked."

In fear, Tom caught his master about the waist just as Gideon's legs collapsed. "Can ye not see his lordship's hurt?"

His anger must have pierced Gideon's oblivion, for he gave the ghost of a smile. "Tell them I shall speak to them in the morning," he murmured, before he was overcome by the next wave of shudders.

"Don't you be fretting about them gen'lemen, Master Gideon. They can wait." As Tom felt his master's weight slump against him, alarm shot through him like birds flapping frantically in a cage.

St. Mars was burning.

"Open the door for my Lord St. Mars!" he cried for the second time that evening. Nearly dragging Gideon into the house, Tom prayed he would not lose both his masters on this one horrible night.

Mrs. Dixon had stayed awake since receiving word of Lord Hawkhurst's death, and entering the vestibule now, she gave one glance at Tom's frightened face and ran for the kitchen. A harried footman took Gideon's legs, and with Tom cradling his shoulders, together they carried him up the marble stairs.

"Send for the Frenchy!" Tom called down. Much as Philippe annoyed him, Tom knew the little fop would be his master's ablest nurse. He only hoped Philippe had the fortitude to treat a festering cut.

The Frenchman, he found, had also awaited his master's arrival. As the two breathless men carried Gideon into his chamber, they found Philippe at work over his master's suit of bloodstained clothes. With a gasp, Philippe saw the red on Gideon's fresh coat, and instantly became a whirlwind of efficiency.

"*Mettez-le là!*" Forgetting his English, he gestured towards the large curtained bed. "There! *Là!* Just so."

He felt Gideon's forehead, and a frown disturbed his carefully painted face. He whispered, "*Sacré Dieu!*"

Tremors were now racking Gideon's whole body. His face was flushed, and he moaned. Tom cushioned his head.

"Help me to remove milord's coat," Philippe said. To the footman he added quickly, "Fetch the water and fresh linen and a leaden plaster. *Vite! Vite!*"

As the footman hastily quitted the room, Philippe and Tom got Gideon out of his clothes. His shirt had stuck to his wound which had turned an unhealthy colour.

"Mayhap you should soak it," Tom suggested, wincing as the Frenchman moved to pull at the garment. "You'll make him bleed again."

"The bleeding will not hurt him. With this fever, he would need to be bled *de toutes façons.*"

"Should I fetch a surgeon?"

"*Non!* Your surgeons are all butchers, whereas, *me*, I trained as a barber before becoming a gentleman's servant. I know what to do for *Monseigneur.*" Philippe raised his face to stare Tom in the eye. "You will assist me, *non?*"

With a stiff nod and an even stiffer back, Tom mumbled, "Just tell me what to do."

Philippe inclined his head before returning to his patient. In this emergency, he seemed willing to overlook the serious offence of a stable servant's coming into the master's bedchamber.

The footman returned with the plaster and water, accompanied by Mrs. Dixon, who said that Sir Harrowby had called for his physician. Then she asked anxiously if Gideon would be able to receive visitors soon.

"*Mais non!* Can you not see that *Monseigneur* is out of his head with fever! Regard you the blood he has lost!"

She reacted queerly to the Frenchman's angry tone. Clearly she had suffered a shock which could not be attributed entirely to the sudden death of the earl no matter how much that had affected them all. She seemed on the point of tears when she said, "Sir Joshua insists upon posing Lord St. Mars some questions."

Philippe and Tom exchanged involuntary glances. As Tom felt a new, ill-defined worry stealing over him, Philippe dismissed the housekeeper. "You may tell the gentlemen that milord is very sick— much too sick to be molested with their nonsense. I, Philippe— with the help of this Thomas—will know how best to take care of milord. He is not to be disturbed until I say."

"But Sir Joshua said he will not leave the house until he has spoken with my Lord St. Mars!"

Again, the two servants exchanged uneasy looks. Tom felt a prickling at the base of his neck.

He growled, "Well, tell 'im he can wait. But he may have a good long time of it."

Mrs. Dixon nodded and retreated without another word. During all this, Philippe had been cleaning St. Mars's angry wound, scrubbing it with water-soaked linen to remove the unhealthy tissue that had formed around it. Now, from his valet's closet, he fetched a gallipot with a green salve. Taking a small bit in a spoon, he held it over a candle until it melted. He dipped a tent of linen into this and packed it into the open gash.

He asked Tom to raise his lordship, so that he might wrap linen strips about his torso to secure the dressing.

As Tom moved Gideon, he felt the young man's heat so strongly that he, too, began to sweat. He held the slim, young body against his broad chest, exactly as he had when a younger Gideon had broken his leg, falling off of one of his father's wilder horses. Tonight, when St. Mars had reached out for him, for one brief second, he had seen that boy again—a boy who needed him. There had been a plea for sympathy in Gideon's eyes, more for the loss of his father, Tom believed, than for the fever that racked him so mercilessly.

What would Lord Hawkhurst have said if he had known how miserably he had failed to protect his son? Tom rebuked himself repeatedly to cloak his more unsettling emotions.

Soon, Mrs. Dixon's remarks made their way past his anger to

fester in his brain. If a justice of the peace insisted on speaking to Lord St. Mars, and refused to leave, he must suspect his lordship of something.

"I wonder what those gen'lemen wants."

Philippe looked up. His sudden motion made Tom realize that he had spoken aloud. "This man who attacked *Monseigneur,*" he said, "you saw him, *n'est-ce pas?*"

Tom frowned. "O' course I saw him. What's that got to do with them fellows downstairs?"

Philippe's face, normally expressive, appeared unnaturally blank. "When this gentleman you call the justice of the peace came to tell us of milord's death, he said that milord had wounded the villain who killed him."

It took less than a second for Tom to spring to his meaning. He snarled, "His lordship was hurt here in the street! I saw it myself!"

The valet drew himself up. "Do you think Philippe does not know this? I—*moi*—who dressed his lordship twice for the ball? Who would know he was not wounded until this evening, if not myself?"

Tom grunted. "Then what are ye blatherin' about?"

"Because, *imbécile*—" Philippe gave him an impatient sniff— "it is these gentlemen who must believe, not you—and not me!"

"Well, I'll tell 'em. Just as soon as you get his lordship tooken care of."

The dubious look on Philippe's face caused Tom's stomach to flip.

"I hope, *mon cher* Thomas, that your word will be enough." The Frenchman shook his head. "I hope your English law will believe two servants of *monsieur le vicomte*. In my country, they would not."

"Then it's a damn good thing this is England," Tom growled, but the Frenchy's comment had unnerved him. What if he was not believed? No English jury would believe a Frenchman—the French were known to be liars. And no one else could swear to the fact that Lord St. Mars had been wounded in the street except his groom, who was known to love him.

A slower man than Tom might have worried that the words of a servant willing to die for his master would carry little weight. What if the justice of the peace already believed Lord St. Mars had killed his father?

But no—they couldn't hang a peer on only one man's supposition. It was a worry, though, to think that St. Mars would be bothered with such foolishness when he was ill and grieving.

If only he had done as Master Gideon had ordered and pursued the attacker, he would have had his proof. But he had not. And his master was too delirious now to tell him what he should do.

✄

By the second day after the ball, all of London had been stunned by the news of Lord Hawkhurst's murder. Knowing of the rumours about Isabella and Lord St. Mars, ladies who had seldom visited Mrs. Mayfield paid evening calls on her in the hopes of gleaning gossip for their friends. Not even the news that Niccolini had returned to the opera, the rumblings from Parliament, or fears of the Pretender could eclipse such a shocking event in their midst.

More than once that next week, Mrs. Mayfield had the tea table set out in the withdrawing room. She had bought it in a moment of riotous indulgence after her last successful round at the bassett tables. The tiny tea dishes had come all the way from China, as had the tea, which cost more than the household budget could spare. But for once Hester had more on her mind than their precarious finances.

From each visitor they learned a bit more. That St. Mars had been carried into his house in a raging fever. That Sir Harrowby's personal physician had been called to attend him. That his lordship's condition was very grave.

The round tea table only seated five with comfort, so during these visits Hester occupied a chair against the wall, using the time to ply her needle. Her aunt hardly wanted her to indulge in the expensive tea, so her work became her aunt's excuse for excluding her from the treat. As annoying as this was, it did give Hester a chance to observe the ladies' faces without being observed herself.

It never took long for visitors to begin speculating about St.

Mars. Today, Lady Dimsborough stunned them with news she had learned from her husband.

"They say that the magistrate from Kent has grown tired with waiting for Lord St. Mars to recover, and that he has set two constables to guard Hawkhurst House."

Hester's hand froze. For a moment none of ladies responded. She could see the tension in her aunt's back.

"What does he want to speak to St. Mars about?" Mrs. Mayfield asked.

"According to my husband, Sir Joshua has some questions concerning the argument he had with his father the morning Lord Hawkhurst was killed."

"Does anyone know the subject of their quarrel?"

Two of the ladies exchanged embarrassed glances.

"There have been rumours," Lady Dimsborough replied with a glance at Isabella, "but I hate to repeat them. They may be false. All I can say is that Dimsborough always did say that the Fitzsimmons family has a violent temper. And he said it would get them into trouble one day."

No one could have missed the implication. St. Mars had argued with his father about his plans to marry Isabella, and in a fit of temper he had killed his father. Hester would not be surprised if the reason for their quarrel was just that. Isabella would not be the choice a man as powerful as Lord Hawkhurst would make for his son. Her portion was much too small.

But her aunt would never admit that any such considerations should be made when it came to her daughter.

Apparently St. Mars had ignored his father's objections, for he had clearly been intent on pursuing her the night of the ball. He must love Isabella very much. But would he have continued to love her in the face of his father's disapproval? They would never know.

"Well," Mrs. Mayfield said, and something in her shrug caused Hester a twinge of anxiety, "I'm sure I do not know what to make of it all. All I do know is that St. Mars was in a very queer frame when he arrived at Lord Eppington's ball. He nearly bit my head off when I made a polite inquiry after his papa. It struck me as queer at the time for wherever I go, I am usually treated with the greatest respect. I remember wondering how he could be so intemperate with Isabella's mama. He has been quite wild for her, you know."

Hester had to bite her tongue. She looked up from her stitch and poked the needle into her thumb.

One of their other visitors asked Isabella, "Did *you* notice anything odd about him, my dear?"

"No." Nibbling on a piece of cake, Isabella shook her head— truthful, at least, if unconcerned. "Not until that man took him by the arm and I saw his blood. That made me scream."

"She didn't notice, naughty puss," her mother inserted quickly, "because she was busy dancing with so many fine gentlemen. But I am certain she would have noticed that there was something wrong had she not been so distracted."

Hester thought it very unlikely. Isabella seldom noticed anything but her own pleasure. Certainly no one but herself had noticed St. Mars's fever.

She wished she could make that point, and she was wondering how she could do so without appearing particular, when a lady whose daughter had been named maid of honour to the Princess of Wales asked Mrs. Mayfield, "What *did* you notice?"

For a moment Mrs. Mayfield was stumped. She had not had time to think of a credible lie.

"St. Mars didn't want me to dance with anyone else," Isabella offered unexpectedly.

This made the ladies glance around at one another. "Do you mean he was jealous, dear? Did he threaten you at all?"

Hester could not keep from snorting, though her snort went completely ignored.

Isabella seemed unsure. "No," she finally said on a drawn-out note. "I wouldn't say that he was threatening. He just seemed so serious, and I could tell that he wanted me all to himself."

Beneath the ladies' painted faces, Hester detected a cold, silent waft of suspicion. She sensed an uneasiness so deep, it threatened the very ground on which they stood. No one wanted to be the first to point an accusing finger at a peer, but the notion that violence in its most heinous form might have infected one of their rank had them examining their neighbours with barely-disguised fear. The security of their class rested firmly on the keeping of the King's peace. The aristocracy must always be above the sins of the rabble. This sort of violence must never be seen to spread.

If Hester had possessed the smallest degree of influence, she would have used it at once to quell their exaggerations. Dismayed, she found no opportunity to broach the subject until the next day when she was sitting with Mrs. Mayfield and Isabella in the back parlour. Then, she urged them both to demonstrate their faith in St. Mars.

Mrs. Mayfield took immediate exception to her suggestion. "I do not see that my Lord St. Mars's affairs are any business of yours, Hester. Your partiality for that gentleman is quite unbecoming. If I was you, and I did not wish to become a laughing-stock, I should keep my tongue inside my head."

Hester swallowed the cruelty of the taunt, as she had so many others—by ignoring it, although the teeth on this particular knife were sharp.

"You mistake me, Aunt. I merely think that Isabella could show more interest. Surely a note, consoling St. Mars on the loss of his father, would not be inappropriate? She was, after all, in his company when he received the tragic news. And if she is still entertaining his suit—for I am certain he means to propose when he is well—mightn't she write to inquire how he is healing?"

"I am not so certain that his suit will be welcome then, Miss Prig. We shall know more after dinner tomorrow. I have asked Sir Harrowby Fitzsimmons to join us. *He* will be able to tell us if these terrible rumours about St. Mars are to be believed."

"Surely *you* do not believe them! You, who have been so much in his company!" As Hester spoke, she could not keep the indignation from her voice.

Mrs. Mayfield gave a toss of her head. "I do not pretend to know everything the way you do, Hester. But I can tell you that I will never let Isabella throw her prospects away! Not when she could have the greatest gentleman in London."

"And who might that be, Aunt, if not my Lord St. Mars? I presume you to mean his Grace of Bournemouth. Has he spoken yet?"

Her aunt's smile was brittle. "Not yet, perhaps, but he will, when he sees that my little girl may be ready to accept someone else."

"Is she?"

"If you expect an answer to that, you must think me a greater simpleton than I am." Mrs. Mayfield tossed her head, as she rose from her chair by the fire, dropping her needlework to one side. "I must speak to Cook about the menu. I wonder if Sir Harrowby would prefer eels or salmon with his tongue? I had better check the colour of the gills on that salmon Cook bought this morning. Hester, you may finish the work I began on these sheets, but mind, keep your stitches as fine as mine."

Since Hester had never known Mrs. Mayfield to set more than five stitches in a row, she had no fear that her handiwork would throw a stain on her aunt's. Suppressing her frustration, she took the sheet from the mending basket, grateful at least to have this chance to speak to Isabella alone.

For all the reaction she had given to their conversation, Isabella might have been in a different room. Her thoughts seemed far away, as she slowly worked her needle.

Unwilling to wait for her aunt to reenter the room, Hester asked immediately, "Is it true, Bella? Have you decided on a suitor?"

Isabella gave a sigh. "I don't know. I think I should like to have Sir Harrowby, but if the Duke should offer for me, then Mama says I will have to jilt him."

"And if the Duke does not?"

"Then maybe I can have Sir Harrowby instead."

Hester felt a clutching at her heart. "Then your mama has given Sir Harrowby permission to pay his addresses to you?"

"No. But after tonight, she might. It all depends on what he says about St. Mars."

"You cannot believe that St. Mars killed his papa!"

"I don't know, Hester. Last night Mama told me that gentlemen can do terrible things in a passion. And everyone says that Lord St.

Mars fought with his papa."

"But you know him, Bella. You have danced and talked with him. Has none of your time together taught you that he would never do anything unjust?"

Isabella shook her head. "I told you that St. Mars looks at me as if he wants me. What if he wants me so badly, he decided to kill Lord Hawkhurst so he could be an earl?"

"I do not perfectly understand."

"Well, neither did I, at first. But Mama explained it to me. Lord St. Mars must have known that I would never marry him if the Duke offered. How could I, when he was not even an earl yet?"

A feeling of distaste made Hester grimace, but her thoughts turned in a whirl. "Does my aunt truly believe St. Mars would have killed his own father in order to improve his chances of winning you?"

Isabella gave an empty-headed shrug. "She says that he might, and Mama knows a great deal about gentlemen."

Hester closed her eyes to smother the retort that sprang to her lips—she would have liked to say something about *how* her aunt had gathered her knowledge of men. But she had no wish to hurt Bella. It was not Bella's fault that her mother was vulgar. Nor was she to blame for being too stupid to think for herself.

Opening her eyes, Hester drew her chair close to Isabella and took her by the hand. "Bella, listen to me. Whatever you do, you must never repeat your mother's notion to anyone else. Do you hear?"

Isabella's worried look did nothing to comfort her. "Mama says I will have to tell the justice what she thinks if he comes to question me."

A chill spread all the way to Hester's toes. Mrs. Mayfield, it seemed—either one way or the other—would have her daughter made a countess yet.

What puzzled her most was why her aunt seemed so determined to harm St. Mars when she had recently encouraged his suit. Had she altered her thinking in order to have her way and give Isabella hers, too?

Think not when Woman's transient breath is fled,
That all her vanities at once are dead;
Succeeding vanities she still regards,
And though she plays no more, o'erlooks the cards.
Her joy in gilded Chariots, when alive,
And love of Ombre, after death survive.
For when the Fair in all their pride expire,
To their first Elements their Souls retire . . .

Sol through white curtains shot a timorous ray,
And oped those eyes that must eclipse the day . . .

CHAPTER V

THAT afternoon, Hester's aunt outdid herself for their guest. Sir Harrowby was treated to a first course which included both the salmon Mrs. Mayfield had examined and turbot for fish, a Soupe de Santé, Westphalia ham and pigeons, Battalia pie, a dish of roasted tongues and udders, pea-soup, an almond pudding, olives of veal *à la mode*, and a dish of boiled mullets—all under the guise of a cozy family meal.

An extra lackey had been hired to serve, so that Colley, Mrs. Mayfield's butler, could devote himself exclusively to their guest. Sir Harrowby, who had arrived in a harried state, distracted by his family's troubles, received this courtesy with surprise. Then, as his hostess's profuse attentions worked their magic, he became expansive under the glow of her approval.

Throughout the meal, Mrs. Mayfield displayed a certain tact, expressing only her shock with regard to Lord Hawkhurst's death. But once the broiled pike, jellies and creamed tarts had been removed and the servants had retired, her questions grew more pointed.

It was clear that Sir Harrowby had been disconcerted by his uncle's death. "God'struth, but I never thought to see an end to the old man! Quite intimidating, my uncle could be, I assure you!

Naturally, I was fond of him and all that, but he wasn't the sort of fellow one ever imagines dead."

"And to be murdered!" Mrs. Mayfield exclaimed. "Do they have any notion who might have done such a terrible deed?"

Sir Harrowby threw her a flickering glance. "Oh, as to that . . . . Well, I am sure it is far too soon to say. Sir Joshua Tate, the JP, you know—a right Puritan if I ever saw one—has some questions he would like to ask my cousin Gideon. But poor ol' Gid is right out of his head."

"Has the doctor seen any improvement in his lordship's condition?" Hester asked, trying to keep the worry from her voice.

"Oh, he is taken very low, I'm afraid. This wound to his shoulder, don't you know. I had my own physician, Mead, pay a visit to him. But poor ol' Gid. It's Mead's opinion that things could go either way. He did have some mighty nice things to say about St. Mars's valet—says the fellow's better at tending wounds than half the doctors he knows. I must say, I have envied him that Philippe of his. What a fellow wouldn't pay to have a valet like that!"

Hester ignored the last part of this speech. The first had made her chest contract as if a corset had been laced around her heart.

"So my Lord St. Mars may not recover?" Mrs. Mayfield seemed to greet the news with eagerness.

"Wish I could say." To his credit, Sir Harrowby seemed truly to wish for his recovery. "Sick as a calf from all I've heard. Got the whole household working on plasters for his feet and drinks to relieve his fever. The whole place reeks of cinnamon and nutmeg—not that they are so intolerable, mind. That valet of his, Philippe, is a marvel with his potions and his linens and whatnot. Splendid servant! I just wonder if all his thingumabobs will work. They say that Gideon hasn't come 'round once since he collapsed on the steps of Hawkhurst House. If it were me, I'd have popped off in a sennight, but he's always been a robust sort of fellow, you know.

"Can't help wondering, though, why he would be such a dunderhead as to attend a ball with a cut like that on his arm. If it were me, I should have taken to my bed."

"Why, *indeed?*" Mrs. Mayfield remarked, with just the proper inflection to make Sir Harrowby give a start, his expression dim.

"Perhaps Lord St. Mars—" Hester began— "Lord Hawkhurst, I should call him—had a particular reason for not wishing to miss the ball." Hester directed a pointed look at her cousin.

Mrs. Mayfield issued a pleased, tinkling laugh. "For shame, Hester! You will turn my poor Isabella's head!"

After a moment of studious thought, Sir Harrowby's face lit up. "Why, by Jove, madam, I do believe Miss Kean could be right! How could anyone stay abed when Mrs. Isabella had promised him a dance?"

Isabella spread her fan and covered her uneven teeth as if to hide a blush. "Sir Harrowby, you do me too great an honour, sir."

Though practiced, her reply had been delivered with a charming air, enhanced by the fact that Isabella had inadvertently caused the tassel of her fan to sway between her breasts.

Attracted by its motion, Sir Harrowby's gaze came to rest on her bosom and he choked out, "Too much were impossible, Mrs. Isabella."

Even seated as he was, he managed to make a creditable bow. Hester had no doubt that if Isabella and he had been alone, he would have pressed her hand with a gallant kiss.

Mrs. Mayfield broke in, "I have always said that no one can make as pretty a speech as you, Sir Harrowby, not even Mr. Letchworth for all of his scribblings. The ladies always count you amongst their favourites, sir."

Astonished by this praise from a quarter in which he had always received otherwise, Sir Harrowby blushed more convincingly than Isabella ever had. Before he could respond, Mrs. Mayfield went on, "I daresay St. Mars did come to see my daughter, but she has other suitors besides him. And it would surprise me if they did not all try to steal a march on his lordship while he is down.

"If he truly wants my Isabella," she added sternly, "he had better heal quickly, or she will be spoken for."

This speech had the wished-for effect of planting an idea in Sir Harrowby's infertile brain. He glanced from Mrs. Mayfield to Isabella and his eyes grew round. "Steal a march, you say? Zounds, ma'am!

Poor ol' Gid!"

"Poor, indeed," Hester murmured to herself. Only Mrs. Mayfield gave a sign of noticing her remark, but her aunt's hearing was notoriously acute.

She glared spitefully at Hester, and her next words held a hardness no one could miss. "It seems that my Lord St. Mars may not recover in any event and, if that turns out to be the case, then you would be the new Lord Hawkhurst, Sir Harrowby."

Her target paled. His voice shook, whether from a secret wish or fearful dismay, Hester could not tell. "I had not thought of that, Mrs. Mayfield."

"Lud, Sir Harrowby!" With one of her swift reverses, Mrs. Mayfield gave a playful wave. "You will have me thinking you a slow-top, sir! Your modesty does you credit, but surely you must know that if his lordship was to die or *if*, for whatever reason, he was not to ascend to his father's honours, then you would be the next in line."

He laughed nervously, it seemed, although his flush had blossomed in colour as if fed by an inner burst of exhilaration. "Naturally one knows, but one does not—that is, I have always felt—so far from it—the succession I mean. St. Mars being so robust and all."

"Robust is as robust does." For all her absurdity, Mrs. Mayfield made a point. "I have told my Isabella that it is your hot-blooded young gentlemen who always get themselves in some trouble or other. Whether it be a wound, like St. Mars's, or something more serious—who's to tell?—they are not always there to be relied upon, are they? While more elegant gentlemen like you and his Grace of Bournemouth are just the sort that a girl like my Isabella should settle down with. Not that I can promise anything, mind. I would never try to tell my Isabella where to bestow her heart. But she's a good girl, and she does what her mama says."

Hester could not believe that the simplest of fools would fail to see through these ill-bred remarks, but Sir Harrowby appeared not to mind. If he failed to follow her aunt's twisted logic, it nevertheless seemed to increase his sense of pride to be placed on a level with the

Duke. He beamed, and his brightening smile could only now be attributed to hope.

Throughout this interchange Isabella had done her part by looking modest and lovely. Mrs. Mayfield had placed her directly across from their guest so he could feast his eyes upon her dashing toilette. Although his gaze had none of the depths of passion Hester had witnessed in Lord St. Mars's, it did show a connoisseur's gleam of approval as it dwelt on Isabella's dress.

For her own part, Hester would have preferred to see a bit more affection on a prospective lover's face, but she was beginning to think that she and Isabella would never think alike. In light of the more serious matter of St. Mars's recovery, she hurriedly dismissed this unworthy thought.

It was plain to see that Mrs. Mayfield had written St. Mars off entirely. She even wished for his death—a possibility that could only make Hester shudder. For a shining gentleman like St. Mars to be so easily dismissed was the greatest incomprehensibility of all. She despised her aunt more now than ever before.

Hester was burning with questions concerning the mystery of Lord Hawkhurst's death, but she could not very well ask them. Even if Sir Harrowby knew the answers, which he most likely did not, Mrs. Mayfield would quickly put a stop to any query she made. Her aunt had no interest in the truth. She regarded the death of Lord Hawkhurst, and St. Mars's life, only with respect to how they affected Isabella's prospects.

But Hester could not master her need to know. She was too recently acquainted with St. Mars to know anything of his father. If St. Mars had not killed him—and she was certain he had not— then who would have wished to do his lordship in? Why would any person take another one's life?

Murder was a stranger to Hester. Her only frame of reference to help her understand it was the Bible. And the Bible was often more eloquent on the matter of punishment than motive.

Why had Cain killed Abel? From jealousy, because Abel had found more favour in the eyes of the Lord?

But jealousy of a father? Envy, perhaps, because Lord Hawkhurst possessed an earldom. Would anyone kill for envy alone?

A man might kill if he stood to gain from the death of another. Her aunt had suggested as much. Mrs. Mayfield was prepared to believe that Lord St. Mars had killed his father in order to inherit his place, because as an earl, he would find more favour in Isabella's eyes.

The thought made Hester shiver, even as she refused to accept it. Surely there would be others who would suspect St. Mars of such a vile motive. But Hester could not believe that the prospect of a title he was sure to inherit would tempt a good man like St. Mars to murder.

Who else would stand to gain from Lord Hawkhurst's death?

A laugh from Sir Harrowby over one of Mrs. Mayfield's sallies brought Hester's gaze to his face, and a stunning realization took her breath away.

She had always thought Sir Harrowby Fitzsimmons a rather harmless gentleman—neither bright enough nor purposeful enough to be cruel.

But was he? Beneath that inoffensive exterior could lurk the heart of an envious man. So envious of his uncle's riches, and his cousin's handsome looks, that resentment had spread its ugly tentacles. Hester remembered her aunt's taunts on the night of the ball. Had she not on several occasions made her position clear? Surely before that night she had let it be known that Sir Harrowby could never win her daughter's hand as long as two men of superior rank were in the running.

How much did Harrowby want Isabella and the title of Hawkhurst? Enough to kill his uncle and cast the blame on his cousin? Hester stared at his ingenuous face. Could anyone truly be as fatuous as he appeared?

☙

Gideon awoke from a fog, to the odor of plaster and spice. For a long time, it seemed, his dreams had been filled with the stuff of nightmares. His tongue was swollen and his throat felt raw. He tried to speak many times before any sound emerged.

Instantly, Philippe seemed to appear from nowhere. "*Monsieur le comte! Dieu merci!* You are better, yes?"

Gideon weighed this strange form of address until he recalled. *Monsieur le comte. Yes.* A wave of dizziness threatened to render him sick. He was the earl now. His father was dead.

"I must be getting better," he said, through a rush of bleakness. He wished he had never emerged from his oblivion. "How long have I been in this state?"

"Close to a fortnight, *monsieur.* You have been very ill."

"And my father?"

"My regrets, *Monseigneur.*" An unaccustomed kindness softened Philippe's voice. "*Monsieur votre père* is to be buried in three days. I asked the messenger why they do not wait for the son of *monsieur le comte* to recover before he is interred, but this messenger he did not know."

Gideon felt stunned. "Who gave the order to have my father buried so quickly? Do you know?"

Philippe did not. But only one person would have had that authority—Lord Hawkhurst's executor, whoever that was. Gideon could not imagine why the funeral had not been postponed until he could attend. His father's body would have been embalmed to allow it to lie in state for as long as desired. Gideon did not know if he was well enough to endure the journey, but he must go home as quickly as possible. He must have a glimpse of his father before he was entombed forever. To have him die so suddenly—then to feel as if all trace of him had vanished— It would be intolerable.

Feeling weaker than a fop's limp wrist, he struggled to sit. "Please help me to rise," he said. "I must get to the Abbey."

"*Mais non, non, non!*"

At Gideon's look of shock, Philippe apologetically fell to one knee, his eyes respectfully lowered. "I am sorry, *Monseigneur.*" Tears filled his voice. "But you have been very ill, and I cannot bear it if *monsieur* were to go out of his head again. It would be *insupportable.*"

"Sorry to inconvenience you," Gideon's voice croaked out his irony. "I was under the impression that your wages had been set sufficiently to cover even this eventuality."

"*Monsieur*, Philippe does not speak of wages. He speaks of a much greater importance. It is only due to Philippe that *monsieur* is still alive. These men below the stairs—they are all *imbéciles!* They would insist that *monsieur* have speech when *monsieur* did not have the head to speak his own name."

"What men?" Exhausted, Gideon fell back against the pillows. "No, don't answer yet. Bring me some water first."

"*Oui, monsieur.*" Leaping to his feet, Philippe disappeared no more than a second before he returned with a goblet of spiced water. As he helped Gideon raise his head and held the vessel to his lips, he whispered, "Sir Joshua's men have been waiting below since the night *monsieur le comte* was killed."

"To see me? Have they caught the villain who murdered my father?"

To Gideon's immense confusion, Philippe assumed a guarded look. "Not yet, *monsieur*, and *moi*, I must ask myself if these English are not all fools."

Gideon was much too tired, and too full of grief, to attend to this speech. And he had to get up. He had to go to his father's funeral. Then he would find his father's murderer and make him pay.

A sip of the cool water soothed his dry throat, and he rested until his head felt clearer. Nothing could dim his revulsion of the moment the justice of the peace had stated his news. Gideon knew his only comfort would be in bringing his father's assassin to the gallows. He had to discover the details of the attack—no matter how painful—and take the purposeful steps to bring the killer to justice.

His regret for the fury he and his father had exchanged would take a longer time to heal.

"Help me to stand, Philippe."

"No, *monsieur*. You are very weak. You must remain abed."

"Confound you! I know how weak I am, but I must speak to Sir Joshua. Tell his men to send him word I wish to see him."

Gideon tried to lift himself, but as he struggled to sit, the room revolved.

"*Mais voilà*, what did Philippe tell you?"

In spite of his pain and dizziness, Gideon gave a frustrated laugh. "You impudent dog! I shall have your tail hacked off for that. If you will not help me to stand, I shall call Thomas Barnes. *He* will obey me."

If Gideon thought this lie would spur his valet, he was grossly mistaken. The suggestion that a stable servant would be preferable seemed to carry no offence.

"This Thomas will agree with Philippe when he sees *monsieur* be so stubborn, *n'est-ce pas?*"

As if their words had miraculously conjured him from the stable, Thomas suddenly appeared at his bedside, determined, it seemed, to press his master back down onto the bed. "That's right, my lord, just you let the Frenchy take care of you like he's done. There's no call to get riled."

Gideon was sufficiently astonished to find Tom in his chamber that he easily fell back.

As soon as he found his tongue again, he said, "Tom, I insist upon getting up! What the devil are you doing in here?"

"Waiting on you, my lord, seeing as how the Frenchy needed help whenever you was bandaged—which was more often than you'd think. Though I never expected to say it, he does have a way with that lint and those pots of his. Welcome back to the living, Master Gideon."

These last words were uttered in a voice so full of emotion that Gideon's eyes were drawn to his face. A beard of several days growth, dark circles under his eyes and rumpled clothes revealed that Tom had spent the better part of the fortnight at his side. He must have fallen asleep on the floor and only been awakened by the valet's plaintive tone.

A fresh look at Philippe discovered similar signs of wear, though his valet would never have allowed himself to appear in such a slovenly state. His hair was coifed with almost his usual care, and his face made up, but weary circles beneath his eyes betrayed his sleepless nights.

Gideon said, "It seems I have you both to thank. You should seek your beds now, however. Send a footman up to tend me."

A meaningful glance exchanged by the two sent him a new surprise. It hinted at a complicity entirely at odds with their former animosity.

"My lord—" Tom, as the servant of his childhood, had the courage to speak first— "those men downstairs, Sir Joshua's men— they mean your lordship harm."

"Nonsense. Why should they wish me harm? They have come to give their report, and I wish to hear it. If neither of you will help me, I shall have to find new servants. Which I would be sorry to do since you have served me so well."

"*Monsieur*—" Philippe began in an anguished voice.

With a look of resignation, mingled with a different emotion that might have been guilt, Tom put an end to the Frenchman's protest. "Better do as the master says. Likely, he knows what's best."

Gideon was thrown for a loss by this sudden docility in a man who had never scrupled to scold or instruct him. Upon reflection, he could ascribe it to only one of two possible things. Either Tom had the intention of according him more respect, now that he had succeeded to his father's honours, or else, he did not wish to let his lord's valet see how disrespectful he could be.

Whatever the cause, in spite of his still-considerable weakness, Gideon soon found himself fed with a restorative broth, washed and coifed, and wrapped in a striped silk banyan to receive the officers. He would have argued with Philippe about the choice of garment, but he hadn't the strength to overcome his wishes. And he would need all his strength to question the men.

Sitting up in bed, he ordered Tom and Philippe to take themselves off, to find a meal and get some rest. They went reluctantly.

Unexpectedly, Sir Joshua himself appeared in his door. He must have received Gideon's message and come immediately, though his eagerness had not led him to put on a welcoming face. With his short, square wig covering a large head and a frown on his fleshy features, he entered first, followed by a man Gideon did not know.

This second fellow, a burly man with coarse, dark curls tied back in a queue, seemed afraid to trespass in an earl's bedchamber. Gideon made an inviting gesture to put him at ease.

"I am sorry I have been indisposed. You have come to tell me about my father's murder. Have you found the killer?"

"As to that, my lord, there are questions to be answered before any charges can be made."

His unwontedly hostile tone raised Gideon's hackles. What could he mean by being so damned offensive? An uneasy memory, something that had been said the night of the ball, gave Gideon pause, but he answered tightly, "Surely, sir, the servants who attended my father at Rotherham Abbey could give you a better idea of what occurred than I can. Though painful to me, their account is something I fear I must hear."

Sir Joshua replied, "They say you quarreled."

Startled—and surprised—Gideon frowned. "What passed between my father and me is no one's affair."

"But you admitted as much at Lord Eppington's ball."

Startled again, Gideon took a moment to assess this news. He tried to remember what had happened after he had learned of his father's death, but that evening was a blur. He wondered why the justice of the peace had come to confront him rather than to inform him of what he wanted to know.

Alarm, from some danger he could sense but not see, threatened to weaken him, when outrage should have been his response. His father would never have allowed Tate to speak to him in this insolent manner, but Gideon was not strong enough at the moment to throw the Roundhead out of his house.

"I was not myself that night. The injury that has kept me abed had started to fester."

"So your servants have said, my lord. Perhaps you would be good enough to tell me how you came about that wound."

Gideon related the attack as best as he could recall.

"You could not identify the man you say attacked you?"

"No, he wore a mask. If you wish to know more, ask my groom, Thomas Barnes. He was there. He carried me in."

"We have spoken to your father's servants, my lord. There is some disagreement as to when you received your injury."

Gideon experienced a jolt. "There *could* be no argument. More than one servant saw me carried in. There was blood on my coat."

Sir Joshua's silence let Gideon know he had no intention of volunteering names. And nothing could force him to. The law did not require him to divulge his witnesses.

The constable—for that was what he was, Gideon realized with amazement—glanced nervously from Sir Joshua's righteous expression to Gideon's tense one, from the smug, stodgy figure of the justice of the peace to the lean aristocrat.

"I insist," Gideon said, losing all patience. "You must tell me the circumstances of my father's murder. Who did it? When did it occur? And why are you posing these unnecessary questions?"

At Sir Joshua's continued silence, the constable finally spoke. "Your father was attacked just after you left 'im, my lord, in a first floor closet they're callin' 'is liberry. There must 'a been some kind o' turn-to, 'cause your father 'ad blood on 'is sword."

It took no more than a second for Gideon to realize his meaning. "You think that is how I got my wound?"

Sir Joshua spoke. "Perhaps you have confused the two incidents, my lord."

Gideon exploded. "Are you saying that *I* killed my father? That I lied about the attack on me?"

"It is possible, my lord. The coincidence would seem to be remarkable."

Incredulous, Gideon tried to shake off the fury that had rendered him dizzy again. "That is impossible! Ask anyone." The very notion that he could injure his father pricked him more than anything Sir Joshua could say.

"There are some who think it probable."

"Who would accuse me of such a thing?" His anger spiraled out of control, bringing him off the pillows to raise his voice, before weakness made his head swim. "I'll kill the man who would say it!"

"Perhaps your lordship's famous temper is to blame. We have proof you left your father's house in high dudgeon."

Betrayed by his hasty anger, the first thing he had inherited from his father, Gideon fell back, spent. "That was different," he said, remembering with pain his last exchange with his father. "My father and I often had words. That did nothing to diminish the strong affection between us."

"But there are greater attachments than a son's for his father. Wouldn't you say so, my lord?"

Alerted to Sir Joshua's train of thought, Gideon clenched his teeth. "What the devil do you mean?"

Sir Joshua gave him a mean, satisfied look. "It will do you no good to curse, my lord. We have laws against swearing. I only refer to your quarrel on that particular day. We have witnesses who heard it."

Gideon felt the breath being drained from his body. He recalled his father's words with respect to Isabella, and knew that Sir Joshua had heard Lord Hawkhurst's dictate. What a mortification for Isabella if the public were to hear the details of their fight.

"I say again that such matters were between my father and me. They are not to be discussed."

"But they will be discussed when this matter comes to trial."

To trial? Weak and wan, Gideon could not believe his ears—not when this conversation was more twisted than a dream.

He could not combat his frustration now. Nor could he refute Sir Joshua's charges when he had barely enough strength to raise his head. "You must come back another time. I have talked long enough. Tell me one thing, at least. Was my father robbed?"

"No. Strange, is it not, my lord?"

"How do you know?"

"Your father's agent insists there is nothing gone missing. It seems that a different motive inspired this killer."

Gideon could not mistake his meaning. The murder had been committed for personal reasons. And if Gideon were the murderer, he would have no need to rob his father of things he would inherit himself.

Rage, pure and primal, infused Gideon with a coldness he had not known he possessed.

"Go!" Rising up from his bed, he stared furiously into Sir Joshua's malicious face. "If you wish to speak to me again, you can reach me at Rotherham Abbey." He forestalled the protest forming visibly on Sir Joshua's lips by adding, "I plan to attend my father's burial. If you have not come to charge me with a crime, you can do nothing to stop me from going."

This proved undeniable, which told Gideon that Sir Joshua could not be confident of his ability to accuse the new earl with impunity.

"Very well, my lord. My constables will attend you, however, and I would advise you not to leave the country until this matter has been resolved."

Gideon had no desire to leave England. He would travel to his home, uncover the facts that Sir Joshua refused to supply him, find out who had accused him, and bring his father's killer to justice himself.

It was absurd, he thought, as the two men bowed themselves out. Absurd to fear them. They could not possibly bring him to trial for a crime he had not committed. The government would not stand for a peer to be so mistreated. How dare they make these false accusations?

But as Gideon's rage played out, so did his strength. Impatient with himself, he leaned back against his cushions and waited for his pulse to resume a normal pace. *Damn*, but he was weak! How could he pursue his father's murderer when he could barely lift his head, much less a sword?

But he must. It was clear Sir Joshua had formed his suspicions and had no intention of looking further. Who could have put such an impossible notion into his head? Someone who hated Gideon, that was sure.

But it was also true that Sir Joshua's prejudice against his family would dispose him to use any tool in his power to bring an Earl of Hawkhurst down.

Gideon tried to recall when the animosity between the Tates and the Fitzsimmons had started. It was long before his own birth—something to do with the execution of Charles I and the Restoration. The Fitzsimmons had been Cavaliers, the Tates firmly on Cromwell's side.

Skirmishes over property and elections had been common during Lord Hawkhurst's and Sir Joshua's youth, resulting in suits and counter-suits between their parents. Gideon had been taught to despise his Whiggish neighbours. Though having no particular love for Sir Joshua or his Puritan family, he had still possessed too great a knowledge of his father's intolerance to be completely swayed. Sir Joshua, however, seemed determined to carry on with the hatred passed to him from his.

Was this hatred so deep as to lead him to commit murder?

The thought nearly brought Gideon to his feet. If Sir Joshua had been his father's assailant, he would have a powerful motive for throwing the blame on Lord Hawkhurst's own son. Gideon knew he had to ride to the Abbey as soon as possible. The question—who the killer was—had begun to eat at his aching heart.

By tomorrow, he insisted, he would be strong enough to travel. Meanwhile, he would see what he could do to discover what nonsense had led to Sir Joshua's accusing him.

A large handbell had been left beside his bed. He rang for a footman, but an anxious Tom answered the summons instead. He had done nothing more than change his clothes before returning to the corridor outside Gideon's room.

"I thought I told you to rest." Gideon frowned as Tom bent his knee.

"I did rest a bit, milord." His obeisance completed, Tom showed no expression as he moved to plump Gideon's pillows. He added, "Never could sleep in the middle of the day, milord."

"Well, I wish I could say I was sorry to see you, but the truth is I need your help. I want you to find out why Sir Joshua Tate is able to convince himself that I stabbed my own father."

As his bitterness escaped, Tom's hands grew very still. In a moment, they resumed their activity, but Gideon could feel Tom's anger vibrating beneath the calmness of his words. "I told the constable that your lordship was attacked here in the street. The Frenchy and Will did, too."

"It appears, nevertheless, that someone in this household disputes what patently occurred. See if you can find out who it is. Will you, Tom?"

But Tom had been thinking, a frown on his forehead. "Mayhap it's that new boy, milord. That Jim we just took on. He said your lordship was in a rare heat when you came back to town. Looked like he'd tooken your lordship in dislike, if you'll excuse the liberty. I had to speak to him sharp-like for abusing your lordship when he stabled your horse."

Gideon considered this, but the notion that a stable boy with a grudge could sway a justice of the peace when all the other servants supported his story seemed ludicrous. There had to be more behind Sir Joshua's accusations than this.

More angry than concerned—though a niggling fear warned him not to dismiss Sir Joshua's bias lightly—Gideon instructed Tom to find out if the new groom had been questioned by the law.

Later that night, Tom came back to say that Jim had indeed been questioned by a constable and later by Sir Joshua himself. Tom could ruefully add that none of the other servants' stories—his own included—had been accorded that much attention by the officers of the law.

'Twas He had summoned to her silent bed
The morning dream that hovered o'er her head;
A Youth more glittering than a Birth-night Beau,
(That even in slumber caused her cheek to glow) . . .

O say what stranger cause, yet unexplored,
Could make a gentle Belle reject a Lord?

CHAPTER VI

THE next morning, Hester was sitting at her aunt's writing table responding to the invitations Isabella was reading out, when Mrs. Mayfield bustled into the room and hurriedly shut the door.

"Quick, Hester!" she whispered in a panicked voice. "St. Mars is below. You must hurry down to speak to him."

Hester started to her feet. "Lord St. Mars? He has come to see *me?*"

"No, foolish girl! It is Isabella he wants to see. But I will not let her go to him."

Isabella erupted with, "Oh, no! I do not wish to see him, Mama!"

"There, there. Nobody will make you, pet, as I've said. I would not have you talking to murderers, would I? But you, Hester, tell him Isabella is too unwell to receive visitors today."

By now, Hester had composed herself, ashamed of her revealing outburst. She had worried so much over St. Mars, it had almost— ridiculously—seemed natural that he would come to her if he survived. She welcomed the news of his recovery with such a full heart that it took a moment for her aunt's words to sink in.

"You wish me to lie to him, ma'am? Why not say yourself that you forbid Isabella to see him? For if you turn him away today, I make no doubt he will call again tomorrow."

"I don't forbid it, insolent girl!" With a flush, Mrs. Mayfield took a few nervous turns about the room. "I have no wish to offend his lordship. I merely wait to see which way the wind will blow."

Hester knew how frantic her aunt had become over Isabella's prospects. As she herself had predicted, the Duke of Bournemouth's attentions had waned. He had not visited Isabella once since Lord Eppingham's ball. Neither had he sent her any more verses or gifts.

Even Mr. Letchworth had stopped his daily inquiries at the house, and the pace of his missives had slowed. With St. Mars ill, Bella's most determined suitor had disappeared, so her mother had thrown herself into the pursuit of his possible successor. Only Mrs. Mayfield's encouragement of Sir Harrowby had kept that gentleman coming, however, for with all the matters attendant upon Lord Hawkhurst's funeral, he had barely had a moment to call.

The result was that the house had seemed unsettlingly quiet, and Mrs. Mayfield had grown more anxious by the day. With the Duke apparently out of the running, her goal had naturally fixed upon the earldom of Hawkhurst. Yet, she could not be certain which gentleman would inherit.

Rumours continued to fly. Everyone had heard of the constables at Hawkhurst House. Sir Harrowby had grown less reticent by the day and had let some of the Crown's information out. With Mrs. Mayfield's encouragement, he had begun to suspect his cousin more openly. Hester had done what she could to counteract her aunt's influence, but since Sir Harrowby's personal interest coincided so completely with Mrs. Mayfield's, she had had no success.

Mrs. Mayfield shooed her out of the room before Hester could protest again. "Tell him that my daughter is unwell. But do not offend him, Hester. And for Isabella's sake, do not let on that she fears him. You will know what to say. You always do."

Nervous, and feeling unequal to the task, Hester took a moment to compose herself at the top of the stairs. Mrs. Mayfield had slammed the bedroom door behind her and would not notice if she tidied her hair. The hallway had no glass, and she could only hope that her clothes looked neat and her colour normal. She had not been dowered with a complexion to blush.

For once, grateful for this distinctly unromantic characteristic, she hurried down to the withdrawing room and opened the door.

Inside, she found three men—two burly ones who must be constables, standing near the door with their arms crossed, and his lordship, pacing the room.

Dressed in black from head to toe, St. Mars looked extremely pale, but nearly as eager and restless as ever as he glanced up to see who had entered. Hester felt a moment of intense relief to see him so much like his former self when she had feared his death. She prepared herself to witness his disappointment, but all she saw was surprise as his mind adjusted to the sight of her instead of her cousin.

As he came forward to greet her, Hester dropped into a deep curtsy. "My lord, I am glad to see you restored to health."

In his gallant way, he took her hand to help her up before bowing, equally low. "Thank you, Mrs. Kean. I seem to remember that I have you to thank for your solicitude the evening of the ball."

She *did* blush. She could feel it. But seldom had Hester been thrown so far off guard. "My lord, I am only sorry I could do nothing to spare you the pain of that gentleman's news. You have my deepest sympathy on the loss of your father."

Gideon felt the sincerity behind her words, and it made him falter. It was a moment before he could respond. "Thank you, Mrs. Kean. Perhaps because of the circumstances of my father's death, I have received fewer words of consolation than you might imagine. Everyone seems more earnestly intent on accusing me of the murder."

He ignored her cry of protest to add, "You will have to beg Mrs. Mayfield's forgiveness for my bringing these men into her drawing room. They insist on accompanying me wherever I go."

He had not meant to let his bitterness show, but it had slipped into his voice. Instead of condemnation, however, he read her understanding of his mortification in her eyes.

After only a moment's hesitation, she seemed to take some resolve. She retreated to the door and opened it. "No apology is required, my lord. Nevertheless, I see no need for these constables to stand while we conduct our visit. They may descend to the kitchen, where I am certain the cook will find them something to drink. A glass of sack, perhaps?"

The constables gave a eager jump, then glanced at each other as if for permission.

Gideon had been privy to all their many complaints about this unusual duty away from their homes. As unpaid officers of the Crown, these petty constables had been asked to come away from their real occupations and leave their families to go up to London to act guard in a hostile household. Under the circumstances, Gideon was sure that his servants had not been the most gracious hosts to these two men, the one a butcher from Flimwell, the other an innkeeper from Cranbrook. He understood that the constable in Hawkhurst, who knew him, had refused to come on the grounds that it was a fool's errand.

In spite of his embarrassment and the anguish he had wakened to the previous morning, he almost had to laugh at the play of emotions across their faces. Duty demanded that they watch him, but the mention of sack, when they had had nothing better than his meanest beer for the past several days, was more temptation than they could resist.

He decided to give them a push. "If you men agree that you should respect this lady's wishes in her own house, then I for one will swear an oath not to flee until you have taken up your duties again."

He was tempted by a light in Mrs. Kean's eyes, to add, in a serious tone, "And, if I were to attempt to leave, I am certain that a lady of Mrs. Kean's noble character would be prepared to sacrifice her life rather than to allow a heinous felon like me to escape.

"Is that not true, Mrs. Kean?" He directed the constables' gazes her way, then indulged his own desire to smile.

He could see that she would be forced to think of something dire to avoid breaking out in a laugh when both constables quickly urged her not to do anything foolish, but to call on them for help at the slightest provocation.

"I promise not to restrain his lordship myself," she conceded, "although I doubt it will be necessary. He has given you his word."

"Just you leave the door open, ma'am, and we'll be sure to hear."

Gideon was astonished to note that her rather pale cheeks bloomed with a sudden infusion of pink.

"It is not my practice to receive men—even such perfect gentlemen as my Lord St. Mars—in a closeted room. I shall call you, however, when he goes."

The warm colour became her. And it intrigued him to discover that a girl as level-headed as Mrs. Kean could be put out of countenance by something as harmless as these men's social ignorance. But then, he reminded himself, she *was* a parson's daughter.

She ushered the constables out and handed them over to a servant.

When she returned, her face—and her colour—were once again composed. She was careful to leave the door half-open, however.

"Now, my lord," she said. "Perhaps you would care to be seated?"

Gideon laughed and waited for her to take a chair before lowering himself onto a sofa. "That was well done, Mrs. Hester. I should beg you to act for me with Sir Joshua Tate. If once you could speak with him, I am certain I would be relieved of those men."

"They must be a dreadful nuisance, my lord." Though she kept her tone light, he could sense the sympathy underneath.

During her absence, Gideon had had the time to ponder why she had received him instead of Mrs. Mayfield or Isabella. As he studied her, he could see that she was trying to show him the same calm, friendly mien she always had, but that something was bothering her. In the silence that fell between them, she found it hard to meet his gaze.

"Are you not afraid to be alone in the room with a possible murderer, Mrs. Kean?"

She started, in embarrassment, not fear, before she frowned. "That is plainly nonsense, my lord."

"I am glad you seem to think so. May I ask if your cousin and your aunt both share your opinion?"

He could see her reluctance to hide the truth from him.

"You must be wondering why I received you," she said. "And I apologize for leaving you to wonder. I am afraid your companions diverted me from my errand. My aunt sent me down with her compliments, but instructed me to tell you that Isabella is too unwell to receive visitors today."

"She is ill?"

"Not so very ill, my lord." She reassured him with a gentle smile. "There is nothing to fear."

He hoped his stare would encourage her to say more, but she stayed silent, her hands folded nervously in her lap.

Gideon stood her silence for as long as he could. Then he jumped up and started to pace. A glance at Mrs. Kean revealed her chagrin.

He moved to stand in front of her. "Tell me, Mrs. Kean. Would your cousin's illness have anything to do with the fact that two constables dog my every step?"

She looked down. "I am certain that Isabella would be . . . very distressed to learn of your lordship's troubles, if she could see how unpleasant they have become."

"And Mrs. Mayfield? Is she too ill to receive me?"

She threw him an unhappy glance. "I am not fully aware of my aunt's state of health, my lord."

"Then, tell me this, Mrs. Kean. If I were to return tomorrow— or the day after, or the week after this—would Isabella be at home to me then?"

With a straightening of her spine, she looked him in the eye. "I fear not, my lord. Not until my aunt should approve your visit."

"Ah." He started pacing again.

He tried to master his anger, but his need to see Isabella was driving him to distraction. He had passed here before leaving on his journey to Hawkhurst because he knew he would not be able to come back until he had found his father's killer. Last night he had been tormented by the possibility that the Duke of Bournemouth had declared himself while he had been unconscious. Fortunately, Philippe had been reading *The Daily Courant* and had not seen any announcement of that kind. He had hoped to have received some sign of regret from Isabella for his loss, but no note had been sent. If he could not speak to her soon to reassure her of his innocence, he was terribly afraid she would become engaged to someone else.

Aware of Mrs. Kean's eyes upon him, he stopped again and tried to smile. "I suppose the only course for me, then, is to prove without a doubt that I did not kill my father, even though the notion is *ludicrous*. But Sir Joshua Tate, the magistrate—who hates my family—seems to have taken it into his head that I am the only suspect. I have no idea what he bases this theory upon, for he refuses to tell me what evidence he has, and he has the law behind him. I cannot force him to confront me with my accusers, and no one else has the courage to tell me to my face the information that has been laid."

Gideon picked up his tricorn hat from the chair where he had laid it and started to bow himself out.

Mrs. Kean reached out to stop him. "My lord, if I could be of assistance . . . Perhaps it would help you to hear what is being said?"

A rush of sparkling relief filled his lungs. "If you would do that, Mrs. Kean, you cannot imagine how grateful I would be."

Obeying her gesture, he threw his hat back down and drew a cane-backed chair to face hers. "Please, tell me, Mrs. Kean."

He leaned forward, the better to look into her eyes. All he found there was truth and kindness.

"I am afraid I have heard that two of your father's servants have been questioned repeatedly about the events of that day. One—a groom, I believe—told Sir Joshua that you returned from Rotherham Abbey in a disheveled state, and with a painful expression, as if you might have been injured."

Gideon grimaced, and she could feel his exasperation. "I have heard something to that effect. Sir Joshua seems to believe my father wounded *me* when I sneaked back into my own house to attack him, and that I managed to conceal my wound and my blood until my cut miraculously opened up on the ballroom floor. Besides the fact that I would have had to ride seventy miles thus injured, it sounds like the final denouement in a tragedy, don't you agree? I find it impossible to believe Sir Joshua would listen to one discontented servant when all the rest are ready to swear I was attacked in the street."

"Perhaps it *is* their very willingness that keeps Sir Joshua from wanting to believe those men, my lord."

He stared. "You mean that he finds a servant more credible who hates his master, even if he lies?"

She nodded unhappily. "If—as you say—the magistrate is biased, and more interested in finding your lordship guilty, he can use such an argument to justify his blindness."

"True. Go on. Who else among my father's staff hates me?"

She glanced at her tightened hands, less willing to discuss the next. "Your father's receiver-general—a Mr. Henry I believe—is said to have related the details of the argument you had with your father. It is rumoured that certain threats were exchanged."

Gideon shifted uncomfortably in his chair. "There was an argument. I said as much when they came to inform me. I was angry, but so was he. My father made some unfortunate remarks I could not overlook."

She met his next glance with an anxious stare. "I can easily believe that he did, my lord, but what was said has done nothing to help your case. It is believed to have given you a motive for wishing your father's death."

"Does your cousin know of this?" he asked, chagrined.

She nodded. "I am afraid that everyone knows it, my lord. As far as I can tell, there has been no attempt to guard your lordship's privacy."

"*Damnation!*" Gideon clenched his teeth. "Is Isabella to suffer for my infernal temper? How dare James Henry eavesdrop on a private conversation?"

Then, aware that he had let his temper provoke him to an offensive outburst, he begged Mrs. Kean's forgiveness.

"Not at all, my lord. It is quite understandable that you should wish to swear. I have sometimes felt the need myself and wished I had the freedom of a gentleman."

That made him laugh. "If we should ever find ourselves alone again then, Mrs. Kean, and you should feel the need to swear, I will engage not to be offended either." The smile on his face turned rueful. "Now I can understand why Mrs. Mayfield keeps Isabella from seeing me."

She hesitated. "There is more to it than that, my lord. In her partiality for Isabella, my aunt finds it easy to convince herself that a gentleman might be willing to do murder to have her. She goes so far as to spread that notion, I'm afraid.

"I am sure," she added dryly, "that I have heard her mention a hundred times the violent professions of love Isabella has received from any number of gentlemen."

Gideon felt a flash of pain. And he saw her regret for the words she had let slip. She must know that he had come today to try to secure Isabella's pledge.

The sound of the constables' returning, made him sit taller and reach for her hand. He pressed a kiss on its back.

"I must be going. But you have helped me enormously, Mrs. Kean."

"Have I, my lord?" Standing anxiously, she held on to his fingers, engaging his gaze. "Is there anything I have said that might help you overcome this misfortune?"

"I believe so. I must find out why my father's agent should wish to cause me trouble."

They exchanged a quick look, before she added, "I wish you success in answering all your questions, my lord."

The constables returned, accompanied by Mrs. Mayfield's butler, who regarded the room's occupants with an arrogant air. He bowed frostily to my Lord St. Mars.

"Miss Kean," he said, with no attempt at civility. "Mrs. Mayfield desires you will go to her at once. She has been waiting for your assistance these many minutes, she says, and I am afraid that our mistress is very displeased."

Gideon felt an instant anger. He could sense Mrs. Kean's annoyance at being summoned in such a rude manner.

She remained poised, but gave her chin a little lift. He admired her grace.

She started to rise, but he answered for her in a harsh tone he seldom used, "You may tell your mistress that *Mrs.* Kean will join her when we have made our good-byes."

The servant made an instant bow, much lower than the one he had made on entering the room.

With the butler silenced, Gideon turned back to Mrs. Kean. "Please give your aunt and Mrs. Isabella Mayfield my best regards, with my hope that their indispositions will not long prevent my pleasure in seeing them."

"I will, my lord."

As she stood from her curtsy, she seemed to hesitate as if she would add more.

But the constables were looking on, and the butler's resentment was clearly growing.

"My thanks for your unparalleled kindness, Mrs. Kean."

She gave him an apologetic smile, and his eyes were drawn to the curve of her lip. "If there is anything I can do to assist you, I hope you will let me know what that is, my lord."

∅

Late that night, Hester was alarmed by a visit to her aunt from Sir Joshua Tate. She had been conferring with the cook about the need to pare the extravagance of his menus due to the number of unpaid tradesmen, when the sound of a summons at the front door drew her into the hall. She arrived just in time to hear Sir Joshua ask to speak to Mrs. Mayfield alone on a matter of the strictest urgency. Colley showed him upstairs into the small withdrawing room and went to call his mistress, while Hester followed helplessly.

She passed her aunt on the landing. The eagerness in Mrs. Mayfield's expression did nothing to reassure her. It was clear that her aunt would do anything to secure Isabella's fortune no matter what the effect on another person's life. Hester wondered how Sir Joshua had learned of her aunt's wish to speak to him, and she determined to try to stop her if she could.

She climbed a few more stairs as if heading for her room. Then, as Colley descended again to his post, she waited and retraced her steps. There was a separate parlor, smaller and behind the withdrawing room. She slipped inside and tiptoed up to the door between them, hoping to hear the two talking. She could not open it without being detected, so she found herself with no choice but the eavesdropper's undignified pose of ear to keyhole.

As she had feared, little sound made it through the heavy oak door, but by leaning her cheek against the plate, she was able to pick up her aunt's tones. Words she knew so well, she might have invented them herself, began to reach her. "My Isabella . . . all the gentlemen . . . so hot for her"—were all she could hear—as well as her aunt's exaggerated outrage and annoyance, and all the vulgar coyness of which she was so capable.

None of Hester's usual resourcefulness came to her aid. Short of bursting in and urging Sir Joshua to ignore everything her aunt said, there was no possible way for her to interfere. And casting herself as a lunatic would only do her harm and be of no service to St. Mars.

She was immeasurably distressed to learn that Sir Joshua would listen to the testimony of a greedy woman. Surely, an honest man would have the gumption to see through her aunt's obvious machinations. Mrs. Mayfield's wishes were not proof.

Hester waited until Sir Joshua had gone and her aunt had climbed the stairs to her room, before seeking her own. It would be another sleepless night.

What Time would spare, from Steel receives its date,
And monuments, like men, submit to fate!
Steel could the labour of the Gods destroy
And strike to dust th'imperial towers of Troy;
Steel could the works of mortal pride confound,
And hew triumphal arches to the ground.

This to disclose is all thy guardian can:
Beware of all, but most beware of Man!

CHAPTER VII

GIDEON set out for Hawkhurst immediately after their conversation, accompanied by two postilions, four outriders, Sir Joshua's two constables, and his valet, riding in a separate coach with his baggage. Tom rode Gideon's favourite horse.

Having never, since achieving the age of eight, suffered himself to be driven in a coach between London and Hawkhurst, he was considerably mortified by the slowness of the journey. The roads in the Weald of Kent were notoriously poor, slick, and deep with clay when wet and pitted and rutted when dry. On a horse, he could cover the distance in one day, but he counted himself fortunate that they made it in two by coach. The stretch of road from Sevenoaks to Tunbridge Wells had recently been turnpiked, else it would have been impassable by carriage at this time of year. The narrow highways that brought him the rest of the way posed constant hazards to his vehicle. He would have given anything to ride, but he had not yet recouped the strength.

After two miserable days of being tossed about with each turn of the wheels, with a night at an inn on the way, he arrived to find Rotherham Abbey cloaked in a spring rain. A light but steady drizzle soaked the lawn. Carriages filled the drive, nearly obscuring Gideon's view of the main portal and indicating the presence of visitors. The nobility and gentry for miles around would have come to pay their respects.

As his coach advanced, he saw that the façade of the house had been shrouded in black. Yards of black baize had been draped from every window, and he could see nothing but black through the window of the upstairs room, where his father would lie in state.

Except for the hangings, the Abbey seemed much as usual. The present house had been built during the time of James I, on the site of a former Cistercian abbey that Gideon's ancestor had been granted at the Dissolution. All that remained of the original buildings was a tumbled set of ruins, the tallest portion of which held the remnants of the abbey church. A house of enormous proportions, with carved stone windows in prominent bays, had been built upon a neighbouring hill out of abbey stones. The house was a relic of ancient times when the Court of England had wandered from one nobleman's house to another, when all that could raise one man above the other was the favour of the king.

King James I had often visited Rotherham Abbey, though not so often as to bankrupt his loyal subject upon whom Court appointments and offices had been heaped. Those several honours had been lost in the Civil War. Then, at the Restoration, the chambers had once again been honoured by a visit from a king.

They had been empty now for many years, along with the queen's chambers in the opposite wing. Gideon's parents had used the king's audience chamber for their own.

In spite of its unfashionable character, Gideon loved the Abbey with all his heart. The recollection of what he had to face upstairs in the Great Chamber, however, robbed him of his pleasure in coming home.

His coachman drove up to the central doorway. An outrider had been sent ahead to alert the servants to his coming, and as many of them as could be assembled were awaiting him outside.

Although he had often chafed at his father's antiquated notions of ceremony, Gideon was grateful for them now, as he faced the scores of familiar servants who had gathered to pay their respects.

He paused to speak to each one and to receive his condolences, which, for the most part, were sincere. If one or two of the newer servants eyed him askance, he was at least reassured that the ones who knew him well had nothing but sympathy in their gazes.

Then, as he crossed the threshold into the Great Hall, the people inside—his father's tenants—parted for him, bowing and murmuring words of regret. There were even fewer nervous glances here. If his tenants had heard the rumours of Sir Joshua's suspicions, they seemed not to have been influenced by them at all.

Inching towards the stairs near the end of the hall, Gideon made his way past the standing suits of armour, and the weapons and beasts' heads mounted on its walls. He tried to speak to each of his visitors. The traces of their work lingered on them, from the pungent odor of human sweat to the sweeter smell of hay mixed with manure. Those scents reminded him of his childhood among these people, before he had left on his European tour. Their loyalty would be to him now, as would their dependence be on him.

Robert Shaw, his father's steward, came forward and, anxiously lowering his gaze, went down on one knee. "Welcome, my lord. Your message reached us yesterday evening. Mr. Bramwell is awaiting your lordship's pleasure, and Sir Harrowby is here. He has begun receiving your lordship's guests for tomorrow."

The death of an earl was a momentous event, to be marked with ceremony. The number of carriages in the drive signaled that quite a few of his father's friends had come. Gideon wanted to ask Robert Shaw whom his father had named as his executor and why that person had not waited for his recovery before scheduling the burial. But there was something he had to do first.

"Thank you, Robert. I should like to see my father now. You may tell Mr. Bramwell I am here and will speak to him later."

"As you will, my lord." Robert paused. "My lord—may I express my deep regret for your lordship's loss? His lordship—Lord Hawkhurst—"

Moved by Robert's tearful expression, Gideon filled in for him, fighting the catch in his own throat, "Yes. He was a grand old gentleman, was he not?"

"Indeed, my lord, he was."

Then Robert, noting his pallor perhaps, gestured to a footman stationed near the stairs. "Assist his lordship upstairs."

Gideon waved the man away. "No, thank you. I had rather go up alone."

He looked behind him for his two constables, but they had vanished somewhere between the carriage and the end of the hall. He had to assume their way had been blocked by his servants, and he could only be relieved.

On the stairs he passed the hired mutes, with their schooled expressions of sadness, stationed at intervals up the wide stone steps. The depressing sight made him forget the weakness in his legs, until he reached the top, when he was forced to remember, for they began to shake. Two long days in a closed carriage, on top of a fortnight in bed had sapped his vigour, just when he had need for twice as much.

He fought a wave of impatience. It was the unfortunate result of his countrymen's insistence on having no police force that the burden of bringing offenders to justice had to be borne by the victims of crime. It was the price they all paid for the extraordinary freedom England gave her citizens, but Gideon could not help feeling that more could have been done in the case of his father's murder than Sir Joshua had seen fit to do.

Upstairs he passed through an antechamber hung with more baize, then through another, the walls of which had been completely covered in black cloth. Beyond this second one lay the Great Chamber, which had been shrouded in heavy black velvet, his family coat of arms attached by nails on every wall.

Whoever had arranged the details, while he had been too ill to see to them himself, had ordered them as his father would have wished.

Raised on a dais, on a bed of state beneath a canopy, lay his father's shrouded body.

A sudden whine came from near the foot of the bed. Gideon stooped to pet the dog that came to greet him. The sleek, grey body of his father's favourite lurcher whipped about his legs in a frenzy of relief.

"Hello, Argos. How are you, boy?" He had to fight a tightening in his throat at the unfailing loyalty of his father's dog.

No one else was in the room. Undoubtedly it had been cleared to allow him to express his grief in private. He gave a look about him and took a deep, aching breath before approaching the bed.

The room had been kept very cold, which was easy to do at this time of year with the weather still chill. Gideon glanced once at the empty fireplace, which at Christmas had been blazing with logs. He suppressed a shiver and moved on.

His father's body had been preserved with sawdust and tar to give his mourners these few weeks to pay their respects. Its unnatural appearance was not to be wondered at, but Gideon could not help but be affected by the insult that had been done to it. He sought some sign of the man he had known inside this pale, cold shell. He stroked his father's face and felt the impartialness of death.

This corpse no longer housed his father. The vigorous, iron-willed man that had been Lord Hawkhurst had long since abandoned it to go to another place. No matter how many days his soul had been allowed to reanimate his body by this formal delay, it was gone for good. Seeing his effigy brought Gideon some minor comfort, but there was nothing here to which to cleave. He had missed the chance to say goodbye, to ask for forgiveness, and nothing would ever bring his lost chance back.

He had never felt so alone. With neither parent nor sibling living, he was without kin in the world. He would not count his cousin Harrowby or his more distant relatives, for there was something about close family, the people who had watched one grow from birth, that could never be approached by anyone else.

His painful musings turned to fury at the person who had taken his father from him, especially at the moment when they had suffered the worst falling out of their lives. Gideon stood over his father's body and swore an oath to bring the man to justice if it was the last thing he did.

Questions and worries that had been plaguing him since he'd recovered consciousness began to tumble through his mind. He wondered how his father had been wounded. If his sword had been near enough to grab—and apparently it had—how had his murderer managed to deal a mortal blow? In spite of Lord Hawkhurst's age, he had been a large and powerful man with a long reach, and gifted with a sword. He had kept up his practice, even here in Kent.

Gideon's curiosity led him to examine the body. His father's white shroud had been made of linen, in defiance of the statutes. Even in death, he would never have condescended to wear wool next his skin, but it was unlikely that Mr. Bramwell, whose duty it was to report the infraction, would ever think of questioning his father's right.

Before he quite knew what he was doing, Gideon had untied his father's cravat and the chin cloth to his cap to get at the slit in his shirt.

The shroud had been folded about his feet and tied at the end. The opening over his breastbone had not been stitched together, as by custom, no dress for a corpse was to be sewed with thread. Gideon parted the linen layer and gently pushed it back to reveal his father's injuries.

Starting at his heart and running to the middle of his abdomen, was a long, ugly rift with sharp, blue edges pulled badly together with stitches. The sight of it made Gideon pull back in horror, until he realized that this particular injury had been made by the embalmers themselves. Even knowing this, he needed a moment to marshal his will to carry on. He regretted his impulse to investigate, but now that his own disrespect had been added to the insults to his father's corpse, he did not want to have acted in vain.

He forced himself to ignore his feelings and scanned his father's thick chest for evidence of a mortal wound. His eyes soon found a small, surprisingly thin slit—no more than half an inch across—in the region of his heart. He could not imagine that his father would have allowed a swordsman an opening like that, no matter how gifted his assailant had been. And the wound was neat, as if he had been unable to deflect it at all.

The wound was too neat. There was no sign of scraping or bruising or tearing. It was as neat as if a piece of beef had been pierced by a fork.

With a sudden hunch, Gideon pushed the shroud completely off his father's left shoulder and turned him over on his right side. On his back he found another slit, only this slightly wider. The skin where the blade had entered had been scraped. And a small circular bruise around it showed where the edge of the hilt had hit.

His father had been stabbed hard, and from behind. A small-sword with a small, round hilt—a shape that Gideon had never seen before— had been thrust with so much force that it had run clear through him. It had been his murderer's intention to kill him from the outset. There had been no fight.

As he eased his father's corpse onto its back and began to redress it with gentle movements, his mind filled in the likely scene. Lord Hawkhurst had turned his back on someone he had known. Someone for whom he had apparently had no fear. He had turned to fetch something, for it would have been impolite otherwise to turn his back on a guest. And his killer had used that moment to murder him.

He had drawn a blade and thrust it into Lord Hawkhurst's back, and only then had Gideon's father been aware of the treachery. He would have fought—Gideon knew his father well enough to know that nothing could have brought him down immediately, not even a blade through his heart.

He would have reached for the sword that was never far from his side. He would have turned—perhaps with the other man's blade still inside him. His murderer would have been defenceless, in that case, for only a few seconds before the impact of his father's wound brought him down.

In that brief moment, however, at least his father would have had the satisfaction of getting in the last blow.

And then, while he lay bleeding to death, his murderer stayed to withdraw his blade. Because he might be identified by it? It was likely. Swords were crafted by hand. A fine blade—and this had been very fine, judging by its narrow size—might have been easy to trace to its maker and, through him, to its owner.

As Gideon finished dressing his father, pulling the shroud back in place, relacing his cravat, and tying the broad chin cloth to his cap, he realized how very tired he was. The emotion of this day would not be something he would ever want to live through again.

When his father's corpse was laid out as neatly as it had been before, he knelt on the floor beside the bed, took his father's left hand in his, put his forehead against the mattress, and prayed.

He fell asleep like that and no one disturbed him until later that night when the Reverend Mr. Bramwell sent a servant to see if his lordship would receive him. Gideon learned that his cousin Harrowby was entertaining his guests in one of the Abbey's large withdrawing rooms, information he welcomed because it absolved him of his hosting duties for one more day. Considering how widespread the news of his own illness had been, he believed he would be excused from receiving people tonight.

He revived himself with a visit to his own bedchamber and a bit of water splashed on his face, and ordered a supper to be brought up to his rooms. Then he met the Reverend Mr. Bramwell in the gallery with the intention of strolling up and down inside it, knowing that the sooner he exercised his strength, the sooner he would regain it.

Mr. Bramwell entered and made him a deep, ceremonial bow.

Seeing the distress on the priest's face, Gideon hastened to help him up and embrace him. Feeling the old man tremble beneath his palms, he gave up thoughts of walking for the moment, and instead led him to a wooden bench against the wall.

"I should not say it," Mr. Bramwell said, "I, who spoke the prayers over his body as he lay there dying—But I cannot accept that his lordship is gone. The Abbey always echoed with his voice, and now that voice has been stilled."

Gideon did his best to soothe him, though the silence the priest described had enhanced his own sense of loss. Eventually, Mr. Bramwell achieved a certain degree of calm.

After a few minutes' talk, Gideon perceived that no small part of Mr. Bramwell's sorrow was linked to his anxiety over the loss of his patron. A learned, nonjuring priest, he had long ago sought the protection of Lord Hawkhurst when all state positions had been barred to one of his tenets—not for his religion, which was conformist, but for his deep, unquestioning belief in the divine right of succession. When William of Orange had supplanted James II, Mr. Bramwell had refused to swear allegiance to the Crown, and he had refused to take the oath of loyalty to all subsequent monarchs, whom he regarded as usurpers of the legitimate line.

Gideon consoled the tutor of his boyhood years with a promise that he would always have a home at Rotherham Abbey. Then, he asked him why the funeral had been scheduled when it was doubtful he would be able to come.

"That was James Henry's doing. You know how your father trusted him with all of his business. He made him his executor, and as such Henry insisted that the funeral should not be delayed. I begged him to wait until you were recovered, but he said that since your own life was feared for, we had better finish with one funeral in time for the next."

Gideon wasn't sure that his motive had been quite that simple—not since he knew that James Henry was the servant who had relayed the facts of his argument with his father to Sir Joshua Tate. But at least some reason had been given. He would speak to James Henry himself, tomorrow after the service, and find out how deep his hostility was.

"I should have liked to know of my father's wishes before all the arrangements were made."

"As to that, I believe you will be satisfied. I had expected your father to wish to be interred in Westminster Abbey, where most of your forebears have been laid," Mr. Bramwell said, "but his will was very clear on the subject. He wished to be laid here in his own chapel. He did not want to be put to rest alongside so many traitors. Of late, he had become more hopeless about our cause, but his loyalty to our rightful king never wavered."

Gideon hid a small smile. It would be impossible to tell how much of these sentiments had come from his father and how much from the person who reported them. Without a family to care for, Mr. Bramwell had always been rather unguarded in his Jacobite speech, and age had done nothing to make him more discreet.

"But the details are as he asked?"

"Right down to the number of pairs of mourning gloves and the rings that should be ordered. You will receive yours tomorrow after the service."

"Mr. Bramwell, did my father express any fears to you before he was murdered? Was there anyone he especially feared?"

"You are asking me if I know who might have done this terrible thing. That toad-eating Whig, Sir Joshua Tate, tried to ask me the same thing, but I had to tell him I was not in his lordship's confidence."

He glanced over at Gideon. "You stare because you must have imagined that if anyone was in your father's confidence, it would have been I, his spiritual advisor. But I will tell you something I never would say to that scheming magistrate. Your father always kept things close to his chest. He knew the risk of entrusting too many people with a secret. That is why he was so trusted himself.

"He also knew that, as an old man, I could be of very little use in spite of my constant devotion. I am sure his tendency not to confide his private business to me was more to the purpose of keeping me out of harm's way than due to any lack of trust."

He paused, then added in a voice full of grief, "He always protected the people who depended upon him, as well as those he loved."

Gideon suddenly got the uneasy feeling that Mr. Bramwell had, if nothing else, believed that some great matter was afoot. He would not press him now, but after tomorrow's service he would see what more could be got out of him.

He asked Mr. Bramwell to walk with him up and down the gallery a few times before he went to eat his supper. They strolled at a more moderate pace than Gideon would have chosen, but even this slight movement helped to clear his mind.

As they passed a portrait of his great-great-grandfather, painted by Van Dyck, he asked, "Had my father had many visitors of late?"

"Very few, I am afraid. The Tories, you know, have been quite unsettled by this German prince, and I am afraid the most recent parliamentary elections have tended to drive them apart rather than bring them together. Your father was greatly distressed both by the elections and by the nature of the attacks the Whigs have made on our former party leaders. I am certain my Lord Bolingbroke sent a messenger here with notes describing their vicious nature, with a plea for his old comrades not to desert him.

"I am afraid that some of our old friends have not shown the courage of their convictions as they should. But —" he gave a sigh— "I suppose it is one's Christian duty to forgive them."

They had walked to his father's portrait painted by Michael Dahl, a Swede. Lord Hawkhurst had refused to let "that Whig" Sir Godfrey-Kneller have the job. Neither man could approach the talent of a Van Dyck, and Gideon had never much cared for this lifeless portrait. Now, pausing to stare at it, he was grateful that at least a shadow of his father remained.

The painter had done only minor justice to Lord Hawkhurst's fiery character. It was there, certainly, in the hook of his nose, in the craggy brow, and in the stern, disillusioned lips. But the artist had failed to capture his lightning-quick temper and his equally strong urgency to forgive. Gideon had understood his father's impulsive emotions, so very much like his own, as well as the reason and fairness that always triumphed over them. But had someone else taken offence?

Looking up at the picture, Mr. Bramwell said, "Various people have suggested that your father had a harsh face, but I always tell them that appearances can be deceiving."

Gideon gave him a smile. "Which one of his features was deceiving, do you think? The hawk-like beak, which all the male members of our family seem to be cursed with, or his threatening brows? I confess I can hardly remember him before they became so wild and thick."

"I cannot pretend to know what other men saw in him, but he was a good man who always put duty before his personal wishes. For a man like that, he lived in difficult times. He made few attachments, but those he had were deeply sincere, even if he did not express his feelings well."

Gideon knew that Mr. Bramwell's intention was to console him for the manner in which he had parted from his father, but all he could feel was guilt for the part he had played in provoking him. The words they had exchanged had been laden with hurtful emotions he would be condemned to remember all his life.

They had reached the end of the gallery, and Gideon would have turned to continue, but Mr. Bramwell asked to be excused in order to prepare for tomorrow's obsequies.

Recollecting that supper awaited him in his rooms, Gideon was about to bid him goodnight, when Mr. Bramwell said, "I believe I said that appearances can be very deceiving, my lord. But while that is so, I might also say that they can hold truth for those who choose to search for it.

"Goodnight, my lord," he said, turning to leave.

And Gideon was left to ask himself just what Mr. Bramwell had meant to suggest with such a curious remark.

℘

The funeral had been set in the day, instead of in the evening which would have been more customary, to allow the mourners to return at least part way to their homes. After breaking their fast in their respective bedrooms, they spent the better part of the morning dressing in their suits of black superfine, most of which had been last worn for Her late Majesty Queen Anne. The peers among them had added scarves and hatbands in black Alamode, while the servants had all received new black livery for the occasion.

As Gideon walked from his rooms in his parents' wing towards the Abbey chapel, the two constables he had managed to lose for one precious night appeared at the top of the stairs. He ignored them as they fell in behind him like sentries.

He came across his noble guests in the antechamber to what had once been the queen's suite. Here they had gathered, framed by the tapestries that hung on the walls. He saw that the mourning gloves had already been passed out among them.

The noise of the gentlemen's conversations dwindled to a close as one by one they marked his entry. In the midst of the crowd stood his cousin Harrowby, clad in a splendid mourning suit, with black lace trim, heavily embroidered with lilies. A new raven-coloured wig fell softly onto his shoulders.

Harrowby had the agreeable air of a host at a private party. He seemed on the verge of inviting his guests inside, when he started at the sight of Gideon.

"Zounds! Dear Cuz, how you do give one a fright! You look positively ghastly, you know."

The others watched the interaction between the two before their eyes were drawn in shock to Gideon's two constables. A few of the gentlemen stepped backwards as if to avoid an unpleasant odour. Others seemed not to know where to direct their eyes.

Among them, Gideon noted a score or more of his father's friends—Sir William Wyndam, the Duke of Ormond, and Lord Mar among them. He was on the point of making them a bow when he spied the Duke of Bournemouth, standing off to one side.

Taken aback, he resumed his welcome, then said to his cousin, "I must thank you, Harrowby, for taking care of my guests."

One of his father's plainest-speaking cronies, Lord Peterborough, his short, stout body encased in thick, black velvet, examined him grimly through a quizzing glass. "St. Mars. Didn't know you would come."

The suggestion of a challenge in the old man's voice made Gideon say, "I must suppose you to refer to my recent illness, my lord. For no other reason would I be absent from my father's funeral."

"Of course not!" As if ashamed of the suspicion that had appeared to tinge his greeting, the earl quickly stepped forward to take Gideon's arm. "Glad to see you up and about. Shocking business this, an't it? Your father would be incensed by all this foolish talk. For myself, I do not credit one word of what is said! You must not allow it to distress you, my boy."

On the contrary, it had come as a severe shock to learn that even one of his father's closest friends could harbour a shred of suspicion against him, if only for the briefest of moments. Gossip must be truly going against him if this was so, and Gideon had been too seriously ill to counteract it. In a society where everyone's letters were filled with false rumours of people's deaths and marriage speculations, no one could afford to be entirely silent on his own account.

If this had been a normal situation, he would have ignored the gossip and let it sort itself out. But today he decided he had better take advantage of this olive branch, or risk alienating the few friends he seemed to have. He gratefully accepted Lord Peterborough's arm and invited the others to enter the chapel so that the service could begin. They would watch it from the gallery, while his father's servants and tenants sat on the benches below.

After taking his seat centre front as the chief mourner, Gideon waited for the noise to subside, before giving a nod to Mr. Bramwell, who stood below in his clerical robes.

The chapel, with its two-story ceiling, was the Abbey's crowning glory. At the Restoration, with Charles II's blessing, Gideon's grandfather had had it redesigned after the fashion of Rome, with marble columns, leafy Corinthian orders, painted Italianate ceilings, and a fine gilt altar. A set of marble crypts had been built into the floor.

It was into one of these that Lord Hawkhurst would be lowered. At the sight of his father's casket, covered in a black velvet pall and decorated with the family coat of arms, Gideon felt a squeeze in his heart.

As the sacrament began, his mind moved in painful directions. Never would he forgive himself for the words he had spoken to his father. Cruel memory revealed their argument in stark relief, every hurtful phrase, every threat that had been made. Only now, drained of his selfish passions by grief and guilt, Gideon could hardly recall the vicious anger that had made their last conversation so bitter. He could hardly recall Isabella's face.

It would be so much easier to bear this day and the days to come if he could draw on her beauty and her affection to see him through. He should not be ready yet to forgive his father for the harsh words he had said about her, but Gideon could no longer feel justified by the emotion he had experienced on hearing them. For the moment he had too great a need to avenge his father's death.

Contrary to Philippe's dire prediction that he would make himself sick again and end up back in bed, Gideon felt his strength rapidly returning. The bit of exercise last night, a heartier meal and a decent night's sleep had put an end to the shaking in his limbs. He could feel his body growing stronger with every step he took. And with this strength, his longing for Isabella would surely return.

At first, the pain from his loss had made him want her more, but he could not help feeling torn by his father's opposition to their match. He should not think of her now when his father lay covered by a pall. The comfort he wanted and needed from her would come later, after he had brought Lord Hawkhurst's killer to justice.

A short break in the ritual caused him to raise his eyes to his father's servants and friends. Looking on their bowed heads, Gideon realized suddenly that one of these people was most likely his father's murderer. The sickening notion made him examine each one of them with a searching eye.

To all appearances they mourned sincerely, the commoners more loudly below. To his father's tenants and servants, Lord Hawkhurst had been both a father and a god, a powerful being who exacted their obedience just as surely as he bestowed his blessings. Had one of these people turned on his domineering master?

Up here, the nervousness of the listeners spoke of the suspicion under which Gideon laboured, as well as the uneasiness of their times. His father's friends would want to believe in his son's innocence, but they could not be certain that Sir Joshua's accusations were false.

As Gideon glanced about the chapel, one thing struck him enough to make his thoughts take another turn. The men who had gathered to mourn his father's passing—with the notable exception of his cousin and the Duke of Bournemouth—were all at outs with the new King. They were all known privately to espouse the cause of the Pretender. With George of Hanover now installed, they were all living in the shadow of suspicion themselves.

Later, after the mourners had been served with wine and food and had been given the mourning rings and gifts his father had willed them, Gideon stood upstairs in the Great Chamber to bid them farewell. As the last of them departed, his Grace of Bournemouth appeared unexpectedly at his elbow.

Seeing the Duke reminded Gideon of Isabella, and he tensed to think of the progress her other suitors might have made. He wondered why his Grace had come when, to his knowledge, he had never been one of his father's friends.

After expressing his condolences in a conventional way, the Duke cast a glance at Gideon's two shadows, the two constables—too far away to hear—and said, "I wonder—what disposition, if any, has been made of your father's papers, St. Mars?"

"I beg your pardon, your Grace?"

The Duke gave a tight, little smile, which might have been intended to express sympathy, but failed. "Forgive me. I have surprised you. You wonder why I raise such a mundane matter on this unfortunate occasion; however, your father was keeping certain papers of mine, and I naturally wish to have them restored."

"I have only just arrived. As you may imagine, there are matters more pressing to me than disposing of my father's papers. If you will describe them, I will ask my father's agent to search for them in due time."

"You mistake me," Bournemouth said coldly. "I will take them from you and from no one else. I expect them to be returned before they are examined by other men for whom the contents can be of little interest."

It was a moment before Gideon recognized his words as a threat.

He narrowed his eyes. "You say they hold no interest? Then I fail to see the cause of your Grace's concern. When, and *if* I find them, I will, of course, return them to you—provided I agree on their provenance."

The Duke gave a start. A flash of fear showed on his face before his eyes were filled by a rage he barely managed to check.

"You would be wise not to offend me in this, St. Mars. You have few friends at Court just now. Your father's cronies are too busy defending themselves in Parliament to come to your aid, should you find yourself in need." With a tighter smile, he let his gaze veer towards the constables and back. "Let us say that in your current predicament, it would be a grave mistake to offend those few friends you have."

His allusion to the intolerable accusation Sir Joshua had made caused Gideon to curl his fingers into a fist. He did not know if the Duke would go so far as to back the accusations, but he could only think of one motive why he might.

"I am aware of your Grace's designs on a certain lady of our acquaintance, but I will not be discouraged. I mean to marry her."

If he had expected to anger the Duke, he was soon undeceived.

Bournemouth merely laughed. "Have at her, my boy, and I wish you joy. I would advise you to make haste, however, before someone cuts you out. I believe her mother is eager to make a decision. But, now that you raise the point, one has heard—has one not?—that you will stop at nothing to have her.

"Have a care, St. Mars," he said, turning to depart. "Take care that that temper of yours does not bring you to an early grave."

He strolled to the top of the stairs, leaving Gideon to stare after him. The two constables moved up to flank him.

Before his Grace descended, he threw an amused glance back over his shoulder. "I will have the lady if I want her, St. Mars. Make no mistake about that. For the rest . . . you should consider all that I have said."

He left Gideon angrily torn between a desire to make him eat his words and a fear he could not wish to acknowledge.

He looked down at his hands, tightly balled into murderous fists. The weight of his solid gold mourning ring had been added to his fingers just minutes ago.

The Reverend Mr. Bramwell had assured him that his father had chosen the image that adorned it—a death's head, in the centre of his family's coat of arms.

Gideon managed to shake off his constables for another short while. He could hardly bear their presence in the face of the glances he had received today. The Duke's casual remarks about Isabella had raised a fear inside him that could only add to his burden.

He could not lose her, too, not when he had just lost his father. Life could not be so unfair.

He needed to get back to London to see her. But he could not—and would not—stir from home until he had unmasked his father's killer. He had not been able to question his guests, and no one had volunteered any theories on who might have committed the crime. It would be entirely up to him to uncover it, and now was the moment to get his questions answered.

He gave orders for his father's receiver-general, James Henry, to attend him in the library where his father had been attacked. This was the room where his father had been murdered. It was also the place where Gideon had last seen him alive.

James Henry, he recalled, had been outside the room when he had stormed past the servants after their argument. He should be able to tell Gideon something of the details of that day.

The library occupied one of the larger closets in the king's wing, in a twisting set of chambers that led to the former king's suite. One of these had been converted into a library by his father, who had enjoyed a rare collection of nearly three hundred volumes. A system of cabinets and presses had been designed to protect his books in folio behind doors, while a separate leaf had been hinged to fold out into a desk.

The room had been cleaned. Whatever books might have been left out had been placed behind their cabinet doors. The leaf that opened into a desk had been locked and all his father's papers tidied away. For an instant, Gideon wondered if the Duke's papers could be found inside that desk, before he was distracted by an unusual sight.

The Turkey carpet had been removed.

Normally, it covered the floor. It had undoubtedly been stained with his father's blood. As Gideon looked on the scene of the murder and their last, vicious argument, he was nearly overcome by pain.

James Henry chose that moment to appear. He paused in the doorway, a strong, square figure of medium height with harsh facial features, dressed in the sober brown clothing of a superior servant, his manner stiffly correct.

"You asked to see me, my lord?"

Unlike the other servants in the household, he had not come to offer his condolences. Nor did he now.

Gideon felt the strange discomfort he had always known in this man's presence. For some reason, his father's man of business had never taken to his open ways. His failure now to show any regard for Gideon's suffering made him angry. It had not escaped him that neither James Henry nor his father's friends had once honoured him with the title of Hawkhurst.

"I have some questions to ask you," Gideon said. "Will you please tell me where my father was found?"

James Henry hesitated, as if considering *whether* —not *how*— to respond.

"Over there," he finally said, "quite near to the far door. I came in to see if there was anything his lordship needed and discovered him, dragging himself across the carpet."

Gideon looked up swiftly. "Did he suffer much?"

For a brief instant, Henry's eyes revealed a flicker of emotion, before he shuttered them, and said, "My lord displayed his usual courage. He gave no indication of suffering, although his wound was deep enough to impede his breathing. He insisted on trying to speak instead of allowing me to fetch aid."

"What did he say?"

Henry's expression was guarded. "He did not name his assailant, if that is what you are asking. He only managed to get out that he had wounded the coward. He spoke of treachery, and his distress was obviously heightened by thoughts of betrayal."

His voice had taken on an edge. Gideon was shaken by the accusation he saw the man's eyes.

Hurt and anger kept him from responding to it now. "Sir Joshua Tate came to see me in London. I presume he questioned you and the rest of the household?"

A stiff nod was his only answer.

"How was the murderer able to enter and leave the house with no one's knowledge?"

"It is presumed—my lord—" and here Henry's insolent tone

made his opinion clear— "that he came up the small back stairs beyond this closet and vanished the same way. There were drops of blood on the stairs."

"How long after I left did you find him?"

"Not *very* long, my lord. No more than half an hour . . . Long enough, I suppose."

Gideon's mind reeled. No wonder it was thought he had killed his father. The back stairs would only be used by someone very familiar with the house. It was one of the improvements his father had made to facilitate the movement of servants through a building with more than two hundred and fifty rooms. Tightly wound and narrow, the staircase was never used by outsiders.

"A search was made?"

"We began immediately after my Lord Hawkhurst died. We don't know how much lead his killer had, but presumably not long. Again, it is presumed that he took the road for London. We found no sign of him then, and the search was cut off as soon as Sir Joshua was sent for."

"Had no one seen any horse or carriage waiting?"

"No."

"And all the servants were accounted for?"

In Henry's eyes, he saw a sneer forming. "There is little reason to suppose that this was the work of a servant, my lord."

"Why not? What reason and *whose* reason should be applied to this? I do not like the tone of your voice, Mr. Henry."

As James Henry's gaze followed the unconscious movement of his hand, Gideon relaxed it before it reached his sword.

Would every burst of his anger and every attempt to defend his honour be interpreted as the action of a murderer?

A footman entered the room, and Gideon was arrested by the signs of agitation on his face.

"My lord—there are gentlemen to see you."

Gideon felt that this was no polite visit.

"Have they sent up a name?"

"One of them is that magistrate, Sir Joshua Tate, my lord. He insisted on being taken to you immediately. Mr. Shaw tried to tell him that you was recovering from your father's burial, but he said his business cannot wait."

"Take me to him then," Gideon said, anger pressing at his jaw. "I find I am ready to say a great deal to Sir Joshua right now. Mr. Henry, you and I will continue this conversation soon. Please be waiting to come to me as soon as I call you."

As Gideon strode from the oppressive room, he could not help but notice James Henry's failure to bow.

Four Knaves in garbs succinct, a trusty band,
Caps on their heads, and halberts in their hand;
And particoloured troops, a shining train,
Draw forth to combat on the velvet plain.

Form a strong line about the silver bound,
And guard the wide circumference around.
Whatever spirit, careless of his charge,
His post neglects, or leaves the fair at large,
Shall feel sharp vengeance soon o'ertake his sins,
Be stopped in vials, or transfixed with pins;
Or plunged in lakes of bitter washes lie,
Or wedged whole ages in a bodkin's eye:
Gums and Pomatums shall his flight restrain,
While clogged he beats his silken wings in vain .

Think what an equipage thou hast in Air,
And view with scorn two Pages and a Chair.

CHAPTER VIII

SIR Joshua had refused to be shown into a room. He waited for
Gideon at the base of the great stone staircase, the two constables
by his side.

"Well, my lord." As Gideon descended, the magistrate addressed
him with barely concealed smugness. "You are come back into Kent
in time to save me a great deal of bother."

Gideon took the last few steps, taking offence at the man's glib
manner. "Am I to believe that you have caught my father's killer,
sir?"

The justice of the peace returned an unamused smile. "I have,
my lord, although I doubt it will bring you much joy—I have come
to arrest you, Gideon Charles Francis Fitzsimmons, for the murder
of your father, Charles Edmund Fitzsimmons, fifth Earl Hawkhurst."

Gideon's heart gave an angry leap. He heard a gasp from the
footman behind him, and revulsion filled him. "You cannot possibly
mean this!"

"Aye, but I do, my Lord St. Mars. Your family's tainted blood
has caught up with one of you at last. I make no doubt your father's
head should be hanging on London Bridge, but you have saved His
Majesty that bit of trouble.

"You will accompany me to my chambers where your deposition will be taken before you are remanded to the King's prison in Maidstone." To the constables, he quickly ordered, "Tie his hands."

Gideon made a reach for his sword, but the constables were much quicker than they looked. Jumping him from both sides, they each grabbed an arm. He struggled with all his might, but his weight was no match for two burly men. Accustomed to subduing unruly prisoners, they spared no blows.

His body was bruised and scraped before they managed to tie his wrists behind him. Then, breathless, and with fury burning a hole in his side, he had to give up his struggle.

By the time they had secured him, more servants had run into the hall, attracted by the sounds. He heard Robert's wails and Philippe's Gallic curses, but none of his servants took up the fight.

He could not expect them to. None of them was armed. But it galled him to be taken like a common thief in his own house.

He was pushed and pulled out of the hall, the servants trailing after him. The grooms and coachman had gathered in front. Tom, who must have heard of Sir Joshua's arrival and come to see what message he brought, instantly stepped into the constables' path to block their way.

"You let his lordship go," he said to the magistrate, "or there'll be hell to pay!"

"Hush, fool, or I will put you in chains alongside your master! And who do you think will help the two of you? Never fear, your lord will have his fair trial. The next assizes will sit in August."

"The assizes!" Gideon came to such a sudden halt that his captors nearly lost their grips. "I shall be tried in the Lords, according to my rights."

"No, you will not. You have never received a writ of summons, have you, St. Mars? You have never been received as a peer, and I believe their lordships will not insist on granting you those rights— not when you killed your father to get them."

"That's a lie!" Tom shouted.

"Stand aside, man," Sir Joshua said. "I've told you he will get his fair trial. Although I warn you, it is not at all likely that he will be cleared. The lot of you have tried to hide his guilt, but happily there are *some* men on this estate who have respect for the law."

"They're liars, too!" Tom clenched his fists, ready to do battle.

Gideon's mind had been whirling in shock at what his imprisonment would mean. Nearly five months until his indictment and trial. He would rot in a prison cell, unable to act. He could not allow himself to be gaoled when giving in would mean that his father's murderer would go free.

He saw that Tom had drawn back a fist and hastily spoke. "It is quite all right, Tom. They have no proof. This is nothing but a foolish misunderstanding. They cannot possibly convict me of something I did not do. Besides, you can serve me much better here than you can from inside a gaol."

He had tried to sound convincing, but deep down he knew that the cards were stacked against him. He would not be allowed to seek counsel or even to face his accusers, not unless Sir Joshua wished, and clearly he meant to establish Gideon's guilt and no one else's. Sir Joshua would likely sit upon the Grand Jury, which had been loaded with Whig justices of the peace since the recent elections. The Crown had no obligation to provide him with the least defence. Nor would it allow him to furnish his own, other than a plea. Even questions about the evidence against him could be ignored.

The Duke of Bournemouth's remark about his lack of friends at Court came to taunt him now like the ringing of his death knell.

Tom must have noted his doubts, for he started up again. "Master Gideon—let me come with you."

"No." Just that quickly, Gideon thought of a plan. He must, and he would escape.

It would not be easy. He would have no more than one chance.

If Tom could only be made to understand.

"You must do me a service, Tom. I want you to take Penny to the blacksmith at the crossroads—the one we've often used. Ask him why she keeps throwing her left hind shoe. Do not ride her since she is lame. Take a horse for yourself, and make sure to choose a good one. This is one errand I dare not trust to anyone else."

As he had feared, Tom's face took on a look of deep confusion.

There was no blacksmith, and Penny was far from lame. Gideon could not name the exact spot he had in mind either or Sir Joshua, who knew the neighbourhood well, would suspect what he planned.

Fortunately, before Tom could speak, a light dawned in his eyes. He hooded them and bowed his assent.

Before Sir Joshua could prevent more words between them, Gideon added, "And take my sword. I shall certainly have no need for it in prison, and I would hate to think that a family treasure could end up in this gentleman's possession."

The insult was intended to divert Sir Joshua's certain protest. Otherwise, he might have stopped Gideon from passing the sword to Tom. But, not wishing to appear to covet Gideon's belongings, he allowed Philippe and Tom to remove the belt from about his hip.

At a signal from Sir Joshua, the constables gave a jerk on the ropes binding Gideon's wrists. He was shoved into the carriage, the door was closed, and with a jostling lurch they started from his home.

He would not believe that this would be his last moment to see it. Penny was his copper-coloured mare, got by Mr. Darley's famous Arabian, and she could run like the very wind. He only hoped that Tom would think to take one of the faster horses for himself, instead of a groom's plug. Gideon knew he had been cryptic. But Tom knew horses and he would understand the need for speed.

For a long moment Tom stood with the other servants in silence. Their lord had been dragged away like a common footpad, and the shock of it had left their mouths agape.

After a few minutes, Robert Shaw recalled the dignity of the house and started to urge the others inside. He paused before Tom, staring down at the sword in his hand.

Shaw started to take it, but Tom pulled it out of his way. "Shouldn't you give that over?" Shaw asked. "It should be hung with the weapons in the hall until his lordship returns."

"No," Tom said. "He wants me to hold it for him."

"Philippe would be a more proper person to take care of the master's sword. He could clean it."

"Not now." Tom waited until Shaw had turned to go back into the house before giving the Frenchman a meaningful look. "Pack up some fresh shirts for my Lord St. Mars, and anything else he will need for a few nights' stop. And send it to the stables. I'll be leaving within the hour." With that, he turned and hurried to the stables at some length behind the house.

It had taken him a moment to catch his master's drift, but as soon as he had dismissed his first thought—that his lord had taken leave of his senses—Tom had understood the message his words held. There had never been anything wrong with Penny's shoes. She was spirited, young, and fast, and Tom kept her hooves in perfect trim. If any fault could be laid at her door it would be her flightiness, but from the first her nervous wildness had suited St. Mars to a tee.

Escape was what his young master meant. If he could overcome the guards, then he would need his fastest horse to flee. The crossroads he had spoken of must be the one between Sir Joshua's estate and the old Roman road that went north towards Maidstone. The constables would have to take him through places where the woods would be thick on both sides. The first crossroads would be a perfect spot for an ambush, as a few unlucky travellers had discovered to their dismay. It should be possible to hide Penny, then wait for the magistrate's coach on its way to the gaol.

But, if he failed, what gaol would that be? The nearest thing to a proper one in Maidstone was that ancient set of rooms called the Dungeons, the old prison, belonging to the Archbishop of Canterbury, built in the days when the Papists' yoke had lain heavy on the people of that town. Master Gideon never belonged in a place like that.

Anxiety nearly robbed Tom of his breath. He had never in his life done anything to thwart the rules of his world. He had never handled a small sword. What he really could use was a brace of pistols to shoot over the constables' heads. But guns were not permitted among the stable staff. Only the head gamekeeper had that privilege. Tom knew how to load a pistol, having worked briefly for the keeper as a lad, but he had never discharged one in his life.

Now he would have to save his master without the skill it would take to beat those men. He doubted his ability to do it. But he had already failed Master Gideon once. He must not fail him again.

He knew he was supposed to take one of Lord Hawkhurst's finest steeds. Tom assuaged his guilt with the knowledge that Lord Hawkhurst would no longer be needing them. The horses would have to be exercised in any case.

He had finished saddling one of his lordship's hunters—a large horse, but fast—when Philippe, himself, appeared in the stall door bearing a large portmanteau. Tom looked up in astonishment in time to see him tripping through the scattered straw and manure in a pair of soft, dark shoes.

"You've got his lordship's things, then?" he asked.

With a distasteful glance at the corner of the stable, where a pile of muck waited to be carted to the garden, Philippe wrinkled up his nose. "But of course I have brought the things of *monsieur le comte*, although I was forced to imagine what sort of garments *monsieur* would need."

Tom gave a snort as he lifted one of the horse's hooves to check for stones. "I doubt he'll be wanting any of your fancier togs."

"Nevertheless, I have packed *monsieur* another wig, the brushes for the teeth and the hair, a set of small clothes, some shirts, his *surtout*—and these." As he finished, Philippe pulled a medium leather case from the portmanteau.

Giving a careful glance about him, he opened it to reveal a pair of dueling pistols with silver filigree worked over the light burled wood.

Tom gave a cry of joy. "You thought of these?" Quickly he covered the three steps between himself and the Frenchman to take the leather case in his hands.

Philippe sniffed. "A *valet de chambre* with my talents always foresees his master's needs."

"Well—" as Tom stared down at the wished-for pistols, he struggled with his pride— "you did a fine job. Yes, you did." He took out one of the guns and examined it for cleanliness. "Don't suppose you happened to find some powder and shot?"

"But, of course. That was much more difficult, *entendu*, but nothing is too much for Philippe. I had only to look in my Lord Hawkhurst's bedchamber. He kept his powder horn there." Philippe gave an eloquent shrug. "It is, of course, regrettable that *monsieur le comte* did not have his pistol with him when he was killed. Otherwise, *Monseigneur* would have no need for them now."

Tom nodded, too elated to let this reminder of the tragedy damper his spirits. With two fast horses and a good set of pistols, he just might succeed.

He waited just north of the crossroads, where the lane was tightened into a narrow strip, where the undergrowth —in contravention of the statutes—had been allowed to encroach as a thicket. He sat in his saddle for what seemed like hours, till the sun dipped so low its light barely pierced the thick stand of leafless trees. Darkness was moving in, raising shadows of threatening shapes, and causing Tom to shiver in his skin. He could not be sure there were no brigands about, though his mind tended to dwell more on ghosts and goblins than on human threats. He had both of Lord Hawkhurst's pistols loaded and primed, but from time to time he had to transfer them from one hand to the other in order to breathe some warmth into his cold fingers.

The hour grew so late, he had almost decided that Sir Joshua would keep Gideon at his manor overnight—either that or that the whole experience had been a nightmare. He prayed he would wake up to find himself in his bed over the stables at Rotherham Abbey, with both Gideon and his father safely asleep in theirs.

The sound of carriage wheels awoke him from this dream. He suddenly smelled the pungent odor of leaf mold and realized he must have dozed off. But now a vehicle was slowly making its way towards the main road.

It would be the one. Few other souls would travel this close on night. The highroads were notoriously unsafe, although this one— since it did not go into London—was relatively free of predatory men. Sir Joshua would hate to risk moving St. Mars during the day when he could not be certain that the Abbey's tenants would not revolt. His arrest was sure to be unpopular.

As the carriage approached the crossroads, Tom pulled a scarf over his nose. Better for the coachman to believe he had a highwayman to contend with.

Tom urged his lordship's horse to the edge of the thicket. The dark made it almost impossible for him to see, but he was able to recognize Sir Joshua's low-slung vehicle lurching along by the light of its lantern, held aloft by a sleepy postilion. With a deep, bracing breath, Tom spurred his horse into a charge.

He crashed out of the bushes, feeling the scrape of twigs against his knees. The team of plugs that pulled Sir Joshua's coach veered at once. They shied and whinnied to see the figure suddenly rushing upon them. As the coachman struggled with the reins, a constable in front raised his blunderbuss to fire.

Tom pulled on one of his triggers, praying to God he would never injure a man. He had aimed above the constable's head. But with luck, his shot nicked the roof of the carriage, and a splinter ricocheted and hit the constable's ear. The shock made the man drop his gun.

The horses refused to be quieted. They neighed and plunged, tangling their legs in the straps. The motion unbalanced the two men riding on the coachman's seat. Both held on for dear life.

"Stand and deliver!" Tom shouted, pointing his pistols at the men.

Still struggling for balance, they raised their hands in surrender as a series of muffled shouts and thumps erupted inside the coach. The constable began to explain they had no wealth on them, only a dangerous prisoner to deliver into Maidstone gaol, when the door of the coach burst open and Gideon jumped out.

His hands were still tied behind him, and his wig gone. The tousling of his hair made Tom wonder if he hadn't used his noggin for a battering ram. Gideon spied Tom immediately and ran to his horse's side.

Leaning down, Tom breathed a sigh to find his master all in one piece. He had not wanted to shoot his way into the carriage, but he would have risked the gates of hell if Gideon had been trapped.

Hooking elbows with him, Tom pulled the lithe body up behind him.

"Can you hang on?" he asked, ready to run.

"You know I can," came the low voice. "It was you who taught me."

Gideon heard Tom's satisfied grunt, before he spurred Beau and dived into the woods.

Exhilarated, Gideon managed to hold on with his knees, while bracing himself with his numbed hands behind him. The ropes burned his wrists, and both arms ached. The one that had been so recently wounded felt as if the blade were still in it. He would not forgive Sir Joshua the humiliation of these bonds. But for the moment, he inhaled victory.

Tom put only a few hundred yards between them and his captors before pulling to a stop. "Penny is here, my lord."

Even as he spoke, Gideon heard her high-pitched greeting and caught a glimpse of her copper-coloured hide in the faint moonlight. He would have slid quickly off the back of Tom's horse, if Tom had not grabbed his arm again to ease his descent.

When both were on the ground, Gideon said, "Can you loose me from these accursed bindings, Tom?"

"Very willingly, my lord."

With the help of the blade of his sword, which Tom had left on Penny's saddle, Gideon's hands were soon freed. He took a moment to shake the numbness from his fingers before belting the sword to his hips and urging Tom to mount again. Quickly, Tom threw him up into the saddle before climbing into his own.

"Where to, my lord?"

Gideon had spun Penny in a tight circle to keep her from flying homeward. "Not that way, my girl." He softened his command with a pat upon her neck. "I wish I knew," he said to Tom. "But for now, we should put as much distance between us and Sir Joshua's men as we can."

"Will they follow us?"

"They will try, but it will take them a while to unhitch those horses, and with Sir Joshua's nags, they don't stand a chance of catching us. Well done, Tom."

With a glance at the moon for direction, Gideon pushed Penny through the woods until they came to another lane. Like most of Kent, this part was full of enclosures. They would have to use the roads. In the dark they could not set too fast a pace without risking a serious tumble. Gideon rode east towards the coast, then turned north at the next crossroads. After a while, he doubled backwards and urged the horses on faster. They had ridden for only a few minutes in this direction when Tom called out from behind him, "Pardon, my lord, but isn't this the way to Maidstone?"

"It is," Gideon replied. "But, if I am right, they will head for Deal, where my yacht is moored. They will expect me to flee to France. The last place they will think to find us is nearer the gaol."

Tom grunted. Gideon could not be sure that he approved, but he pushed on, until the excitement that had carried him this far no longer could. He had been tried very hard that day, had eaten little, and still felt weakened by his convalescence. He pressed on, though, hoping to find an inn he had seen once while hunting this far away from home.

In another moment, he spotted a sign post pointing towards another highway some three miles off. Gideon slowed. He began to search for a little-used path just past it, among the trees. After slowing to a walk, he eventually found it, cutting through a dense area of the forest. It was hardly more than a drovers' trail.

They turned onto it, and the darkness seemed to swallow them whole.

They had ridden for hours already. After they followed this narrow bridle path awhile, batting limbs out of their faces, Tom said, "I mislike the looks of this area, my lord. I think it best we turn back to the road."

"I would agree with you, Tom, but unfortunately, this is the sort of path that I must take for now."

Just as he finished speaking, they came upon a small clearing, a former swine pasture filled with a cluster of untidy dwellings. It could be nothing but a common-land settlement, consisting of squatters' cottages and hedge-alehouses in this lonely part of the Weald.

One larger structure with a second story dominated the small group. Its three broad bays seemed to huddle under a sagging thatched roof. Its yard was large enough to hold the stock of the drovers and carriers most likely to stop at such a house. Minor sounds came from inside, but only one small light in a window proclaimed that anyone was at home.

As they approached, Gideon found the swinging sign he had noticed before, bearing the undignified figures of a fox and a goose.

He pulled Penny to a halt and Tom moved alongside.

"You can't be planning to stop here, Master Gideon! Even if the sheets be free of lice—which they will not—the place is sure to be full of thieves!"

"I've no doubt you're right, but I'm afraid this will have to suffice for now. I cannot return to the Abbey, and I will ask no friend to shelter me." He could have added that now that his elation had worn off, he would be happy to accept the first pile of straw that came their way. He couldn't drag himself another mile. "Besides, if the keeper of this house is not too particular about his guests, he cannot object to a pair of suspicious-looking strangers. He will not want to call down the law upon his house."

"But, milord—"

"There must be no 'my lord' or 'your lordship' here, or I shall be discovered straight away."

"What *can* I call you then?"

With his face concealed by the dark, Gideon smiled at Tom's shocked tone. "You may call me 'sir.' And, for the time being, I must be plain Mr. Brown."

"As if that'll fool a set of cutthroats longer than it takes to pinch your purse! My lord, I beg you to ride on!"

"I am in no mood for argument, Tom." Gideon knew that fatigue had lent an angry edge to his voice, but he could no longer deny that his very bones were spent. He was not accustomed to feeling pain or tiredness, but the accumulation of his wound and the constables' blows had taken their toll. He could no longer ignore the desperate nature of his situation. He needed rest and time to think.

He had expected a low grumble from Tom, who must always capitulate, though he would usually let his displeasure show. So he was surprised to hear in a low, meek tone, "Yes, sir."

"There's a good man," Gideon said, when he had recovered from his surprise.

They turned their horses into the yard. When no ostler came forward to take them, Tom dismounted to raise the house. After a spate of increasingly vicious knocks, he finally managed to stir the innkeeper. As Gideon slowly eased his aching body out of the saddle, he heard the throw of a lock and the creak of a sagging door.

In a harsh voice, Tom demanded a room for his master, bedding for himself, and stabling for their horses.

"It's rooms you'll be wantin', is it?" In the dark, their host raised a lantern over his head until its faint beam encompassed them both.

He must have noted the quality of their horses and Gideon's clothes, for his manner underwent a rapid change.

"You here! Avis!" he called back into the inn. "Come take care of these gen'lemen's horses!" He rushed out to shoulder Gideon's portmanteau.

A curious haste was in his actions. Gideon was used to the bowing and scraping that generally greeted his rank. But this innkeeper wasted no time in bows. He bustled them inside his dimly lit house.

"You can sit here in the parlour—I've got a nice fire goin'—and let our Avis tend to your horses. He's handy with a nag." He called again to the sleepy boy who had stumbled in from the corridor beyond the kitchen, "Walk these two gents' horses, and put 'em in the stalls near the door to the cellar. Give 'em a good rubbin', too, before you bed 'em down."

The boy went to do as he was told, and their host turned his face back towards them, in it a mixture of wariness and curiosity. "It's a pleasure to greet you gents. The name's Lade, and this is my house. Look's as if you've been doin' some hard ridin' for this hour of the night. Did ye meet wif trouble on the road?"

"No trouble," Gideon answered, taking a look about.

The dingy room they were standing in appeared to be the inn's only parlour, and it only scantily furnished with a table, one bench, and a pair of chairs. A fire illuminated the far wall. The rest was lit by a sputtering tallow candle in a shallow earthenware dish.

He took a chair by the table, noting the stains of grease on the floor. "I want a mug of your best ale and a good meal."

"I can give you better than that. I can offer you gents a bottle of the finest French wine. You won't get another one like it this far from the coast."

Gideon was hardly taken aback to discover smuggled wine in this out-of-the-way place. Free-trading was rampant along the coast, and even the cellars at Rotherham Abbey had been stocked by carriers making nocturnal journeys from Rye. An occasional bottle even made its way as far as London.

He had already surmised that his host did some trafficking in illegal wares. Mr. Lade had mistaken him for a gentleman of the road, seeking shelter after a robbery, no doubt. Why else would a well-dressed horseman take a room in an inn of this class?

"A glass of your wine would be welcome, and a mug of ale for my servant. He can take his supper in here with me."

"My—!" With a startled protest, Tom caught himself just in time. "I should take a look at them horses, sir. Beau may have took a few scrapes."

"See to them first. Then join me in here."

Tom departed gratefully, but the innkeeper's gaze had already shifted. He had noticed Tom's slip and the deference in his manner and must have realized his guests were no ordinary pair of robbers. "I'll bring you that wine," was all he said. But this time, he bowed himself out.

Gideon watched him disappear down the dark corridor to the kitchen. The inn was laid out in the form of an ell with a small square in front, containing this dingy parlour, a drinking-room, and some rickety stairs, and a leg-like wing that bordered the yard. Presumably the chambers ran along the wing upstairs, with the innkeeper's rooms, stables, and storehouses below. On Gideon's way inside, he had noticed a separate brewhouse in a corner of the yard. A few husky voices came from the taproom next door. The sound of a woman's laugh told him that Lade had someone to help him with his chores.

The very femininity of that laugh made Gideon think of Isabella, but there was nothing to comfort him in the thought of her. In fleeing, he had removed himself from her just as certainly as his father had hoped he would. That he had done so out of necessity did not change the fact that he would be unable to see her until he had proved his innocence. He could only pray that she would sympathize with his refusal to be caught and wait for him before bestowing herself on someone else. And he hoped he could rely on Mrs. Kean to help her believe that he was not the murderer his peers accused him of being.

For the moment there was nothing else he could do. Isabella could be nothing to him right now but an inspiration, a symbol of the comfort he would receive when he had discovered the truth behind his father's murder. He would use his memory of her face as a talisman, if only he could, but he found that her features eluded his desperate attempt to recall them to mind. His body still yearned for her, but wanting her was a torment he could ill afford.

In frustration he turned his attention again to his poorly-lit surroundings. The parlour had nothing in the way of comfort in it, except for the dwindling fire. There should have been plenty of faggots available in these woods to feed a blaze, with the help of an occasional bit of coal, stolen from the iron smelters working in the Weald. The furniture was all of plain oak with not a single cushion amongst the chairs.

If what he had wanted was a hair shirt, here it was.

Lade returned just then with a bottle that glowed a rich, burgundy red, two earthenware mugs, and a murky finger-bowl.

He placed the bowl on the table before pouring Gideon his wine. As Gideon reached for the chipped mug, his host said, "How 'bout a toast to his Majesty before ye drink?"

Gideon stopped, the mug suspended halfway to his lips.

Lade was watching him closely. Gideon took a moment to study his angular features, the wary gaze, the crooked nose, and a puckered scar that marred one cheek.

The man was tall and lean, with long, clumsy bones. He seemed to be missing a few of his teeth. Gideon could almost feel Lade's bated breath as he waited for him to drink his wine. His tension infused the air with an acrid smell.

Lade had offered him a reason to explain his stop in such an unlikely place.

Slowly, with his eyes fixed on his host's , Gideon reached his free hand and pulled the finger-bowl near the edge of the table. Then he raised his mug.

"To his Majesty." He drank, making a show of holding his mug over the water.

A satisfied gleam lit a spark in Lade's eyes. "So, that's the way of it, is it? Well, you'll not be meetin' wif any troubles here. There be no troops about. Nor any prignappers, neither. And I'll never squeak beef on ye. You can bet on that. I know my business, and it's to make you coves as comfy as you like—so long as you tip me my earnest, that is."

A few of his colourful expressions passed Gideon by, though he had caught the gist. He had overheard similar speech in London, in the seamier parts of town, and he knew it for thieves' cant. The boys of his childhood acquaintance had often tried to imitate it when their elders weren't around. He had indeed landed himself and Tom in a den of thieves.

Tom had been forced to assume the role of highwayman to free him. Now, he had branded them both as Jacobites, too, in their host's eyes at least. That had been the meaning behind the finger-bowl. To drink to the king "over the water" was to drink to James Stuart in exile in Lorraine.

For the rest, he had not missed the meaning of Lade's final words. Money always spoke a language of its own.

He reached into his pocket and tossed the man a silver piece. "There will be another like this if you take good care of our horses and give us two good, stout beds with clean linen. I'll be wanting hot meals for us both."

Lade's face brightened again at the sight of the coin. He caught it nimbly, then tested it between his teeth.

"That'll be right, then. I always likes a bleedin' cull. I'll get you and your man that grub."

As he disappeared into the kitchens, Gideon considered their situation. And, for a moment, despair made him think he had made a mistake by fleeing the law.

But truly he had been left with no choice. Sir Joshua's examination in his chambers had been conducted with the same determined disbelief as his earlier questioning. The group of witnesses he had bothered to quote had been chosen for one reason only—to help him obtain a conviction. With Sir Joshua as the magistrate presenting the evidence to the assizes, he would have no hope of a defence.

And now Gideon had landed in this gruesome spot, mistaken for a Jacobite or a highwayman—or both. He could almost smile at the irony—that he, who had never been enthusiastic in his politics, should be taken for a traitor to King George.

Even his father had been more cool-headed than that. Lord Hawkhurst had never taken up arms in James's cause, no matter how loyal his sentiments had been. Perhaps he had reluctantly concluded that to bring the Stuarts back into England would plunge the country into another bloody civil war, when James insisted, as he surely would, on a Roman faith. Gideon believed that himself, while regretting the necessity of accepting a dull-witted, turnip-loving foreigner on the English throne. He was willing any time to drink to the Chevalier St. George—the only title the Pretender was ever likely to have. Gideon would even drink to him as king, if it would throw his landlord off the scent.

Nevertheless, he wondered if he had helped himself by convincing a stranger that he was not only a thief, but a traitor, too. Alone for the first time in many days, he sank his face into his hands.

No cheerful breeze this sullen region knows,
The dreaded East is all the wind that blows.

A Sylph too warned me of the threats of fate,
In mystic visions, now believed too late!

A constant Vapour o'er the palace flies;
Strange phantoms rising as the mists arise;
Dreadful, as hermit's dreams in haunted shades,
Or bright, as visions of expiring maids.
Now glaring fiends, and snakes on rolling spires,
Pale spectres, gaping tombs, and purple fires:
Now lakes of liquid gold, Elysian scenes,
And crystal domes, and Angels in machines.

Down to the central earth, his proper scene,
Repaired to search the gloomy Cave of Spleen.

CHAPTER IX

IT was in this position that Tom found him, just minutes after he had satisfied himself that Beau's scratches had been salved and both mounts had been well tended. The boy Avis had pleased him with his scrupulous handling of the horses, until he had artlessly informed Tom that a mysterious "Mr. Jack," who had kept a room at the inn until he had ended his days at "Paddington-Fair," had taught him to care for his own horse— "a rum prancer."

Disturbed by the boy's vocabulary, Tom had left him with the intention of warning his master that they had better leave this place before their throats were slashed. Finding Gideon in an attitude of obvious despair, however, undid his resolve. He decided to hold his tongue until St. Mars had refreshed himself.

Not knowing what to do to comfort him, Tom merely entered and set about making the parlour more comfortable. He had not been trained to indoor service, but certainly he knew how to stoke a fire. He knelt in front of the smallish fireplace and poked the dwindling coals with faggots until a blaze roared.

He cleared his throat.

"Them scratches is nothing much. Just a few licks from some thorns in the thicket. Beau'll be right as rain come morning."

Gideon raised his head and gave him a grateful smile. "That is good news. Thank you, Tom." He lowered his gaze once again and continued soberly, "I have much to thank you for, but it has occurred to me that you should return to Rotherham Abbey. You must get there as soon as possible to avoid the appearance of being in league with me. You were wise to cover your face when you stopped Sir Joshua's carriage. No one will ever be the wiser.

"I doubt you've been missed in all the confusion," he continued, "but it would be better for you to seek your bed, so you can leave before dawn. If anyone sees you returning with the horse, you can simply say that you rose early to exer—"

To Gideon's astonishment, Tom crossed the room towards him in one desperate stride and, as Gideon broke off, he fell to one knee.

"Please, Master Gideon, don't send me away! I know it was my fault as got your lordship in this fix, but I swear it'll never happen again. Please, my lord!"

Gideon was stunned. "Whatever do you mean? How can it possibly have been your fault?"

"When you were wounded there in the street. I should have gone after the devil—like you said—but I was worritin' about your shoulder and what Lord Hawkhurst would've wanted. I should have obeyed you, and none of this would ever have happened."

As the moment came back to Gideon, weariness made him shrug. Then, as he recalled two distinct instances in the past few days when Tom had obeyed him without his usual grumbling, he smiled instead. "So *that* is why you've been so docile. You've been blaming yourself for letting him get away?"

"It was due to me, my lord. If I had gone after him, Sir Joshua would never have been able to insult you like this."

At the mention of the justice of the peace, Gideon gave a wry grimace. "So, in order to atone for this sin, you would attach yourself to a fugitive like me? I can't let you do it, Tom."

Tom stiffened. With terrible dignity, he stood and glared stubbornly down into his master's face. "You can send me away, my lord, but I won't go back to the Abbey—not without you do. I'll sleep in the woods if I have to, but I *will* stay."

Despite a glimmer of amusement, Gideon was genuinely touched. Although he had been raised to expect it, he felt he had no right to exact such loyalty from a servant. The class that ought to have rallied behind him was his own, but it had not. It had scattered like a flock of geese seeking cover from a hunter's gun. The only true friend he could count on was this one man. Thomas Barnes.

A lump began to form in his throat. "That will not be necessary, Tom. You are more than welcome to remain, believe me. Call me selfish if you like, but after all that has occurred, I would hate to see you go."

He saw a hint of tears in the hazel eyes staring down at him, before Tom sealed their bargain with a bow as full of grace as any Gideon had ever seen.

Just then, Lade entered with a large wooden tray of meat and some plain loaves of bread, which he plunked on the table. He was helped by a fair, buxom lass—in her late twenties Gideon guessed— who gave Tom an interested look when she set his tankard down. He scowled at her, but his gaze seemed drawn against his will to her glowing cheek and the ample curves of her bosom. When, with what seemed like a Herculean effort, he removed his gaze, Gideon teased him with a lift of his brow, then grinned at his answering flush.

Taking up his knife, Gideon thanked the woman for pouring his wine. As she leaned forward to serve him, he flicked her carelessly under the chin. She smiled politely, but clearly it was Tom who had caught her fancy. She glanced at him repeatedly, but he had turned his shoulder to the fire.

After Lade and the girl departed, Gideon said, "A charming wench, that. She seemed to take a liking to you, too. You ought to see if she won't keep you company tonight."

"Master Gideon!"

Gideon laughed, and rankled as he was, Tom seemed moderately relieved by the sound.

"Have I offended you?" Gideon asked. "I thought I detected a glimmer of interest."

Tom moved closer to the table, but he kept his eyes fixed on the floor. "I keep no company with whores, sir. You ought to know that."

Gideon would have teased him, but a suggestion of something serious in Tom's face warned him not to. "Well, you're a better man than I," was all he said.

He started to slice a piece of beef just as his stomach gave a loud rumble. It was the first glimmer of life he had felt since Sir Joshua had arrested him. Now he felt like lighting into the meat, but the thought of eating alone from this meal forward threatened to rob him of his appetite.

"I don't suppose you would agree to sharing this meal with me?" he asked Tom.

The horror of the suggestion dyed Tom's face a ghastly colour. "I couldn't never do that, my lord!"

Gideon gave a sigh. "Well, I wish you would. I have no taste for eating alone. And I tell you again frankly, unless you wish to see me hanging from the gallows, you had better drop that mode of address. Lade's suspicions are already aroused. He thinks he's taken in a desperate pair of scoundrels, and he seems perfectly delighted by the notion."

"I think we should leave this place."

"We will do that, *if* we can find a better one. For the moment, however, I don't find either it or its staff so uncongenial as to make me wish to seek another retreat. I stopped in many a worse place during my three years on the Continent. The meat is good, and if the ale is decent, I propose to make this our headquarters until we find my father's killer."

Tom started up. "Is that what you mean to do? Find the man and clear yourself?"

"It is what I had intended to do before Sir Joshua paid his disagreeable visit. Are you with me?"

"Of course."

"Good. Then, let's eat."

In the end, Tom condescended to take a trencher of meat into a corner, where he gratefully wolfed it down, but he would not sit at the table with his master. Gideon did not mind so long as he wasn't alone.

When he had finished, Tom insisted on standing by Gideon's chair to serve as his footman. Then he went to rouse Lade and demanded to be shown the rooms. When he asked for clean sheets, Lade grumbled about the unnecessary work involved and would not comply, despite Tom's attempts to bully him, until Tom advised him that he had better deliver them if he wanted to keep his well-heeled guest. He said that his master was used to all the comforts—and to paying for them neatly—so Lade had better act fast.

As if by a miracle, then, two surprisingly clean sheets appeared. Tom's liberal pledges of Gideon's money had served far better than his threats. As the maid from downstairs—Katy her name was—said, as she leaned across the bed to make it up, Mr. Lade had lost a good piece of business when Mr. Jack had been taken up by the law. When Tom uttered a disapproving growl, she hastily assured him that no harm would come to his master at the Fox and Goose. Mr. Jack had been taken when a hue and cry had been set up after him on the "Lunnon road."

Tom listened in a fuming silence that would not be assuaged. The tempting sight of Katy's round bottom as she bent to her work exacerbated his temper. He did not want to be in a place where his very soul was threatened, and it hurt him to see his master in such a low house.

Later, as, feeling clumsy, he tried to arrange Gideon's effects in the room, he told his master that a highwayman had been its previous tenant. "And that bed isn't fit for nobody better. I make no doubt you'll pass a sleepless night on them lumps."

"I doubt it." Yawning, Gideon had already collapsed onto the bed with his boots still on. "It will take more than a few lumps to keep me awake tonight. If we remain for a while, I'll send you into Maidstone to buy a better one."

Tom pulled off his master's boots and set them aside to clean. Then he finished unpacking St. Mars's portmanteau.

"Master Gideon," he said, after a few minutes' thought, "how can you prove you're innocent?"

"We'll talk about it in the morning." St. Mars's voice was hardly a mumble. "But for now you'll have to wish me goodnight, Tom."

"Goodnight, my lord."

Tom waited in the chamber until St. Mars's breathing seemed even. Then he covered him with a sheet and a pair of coarse woolen blankets. He didn't have long to wait before Gideon was snoring as deeply as a man without a care in the world.

Tom settled himself on his bed, leaving his own door ajar. He would hear if anyone tried to enter St. Mars's room unawares. Nearly every night of his life since he'd become a groom, he had easily been awakened by sounds in the stables. Part of his job had been to see that no harm came to Lord Hawkhurst's horses during the night. He had no fear that he would lose that watchfulness now.

Not when he had so many things to worry about.

In the morning, Tom went down to check on the horses before rousing St. Mars. He was pleasantly surprised to find Avis already tossing them hay. Tom unbent so far as to ruffle the boy's blond hair and express his approval, before a near slip of his tongue sent him frowning back upstairs to find his master. He had almost been careless enough to suggest that the boy come to Rotherham Abbey if he ever wanted a position in one of the country's best stables. A mistake like that could have cost St. Mars his life.

He found Gideon dressed in a fresh lawn shirt and a pair of breeches, with his long, fair hair combed back into a queue and tied with a black ribbon. Someone, probably Katy, had delivered a bowl and pitcher to the room for his use. Tom breathed a sigh. He had feared Gideon might need him to act as his valet. Undoubtedly something would have to be done with his clothes, but Tom was grateful not to have to dress him.

Finding himself in the inn this morning must have caused St. Mars a rude awakening, for he wore a grim look on his face. At the sound of Tom's entry, he purposely squared his shoulders and wished him a good morning before leading him downstairs for his morning pint.

Lade brought in the food and drink, obviously in a garrulous humour.

As he set the tray down, he said, "Mornin', gents. Mind if I asks ye, what's the difference between an Orange and a Turnip?"

Tom would have chased him off, but Gideon shook his head. "I'll have to give up. I'm not much in the mood for riddles this morning," he said.

"Like is to like—as the devil said to the collier. Both are pernicious to England." With a hearty guffaw at his joke, he left Tom to serve the meal.

Gideon barely touched his meat or his beer. He remained lost in thought until Tom, uttering grumbles under his breath, threatened to clear his trencher away.

Gideon gave a quick grimace into his tankard. "I wonder if any chocolate is to be found in this village. It would be more conducive to thought of a morning than my host's fine ale. You must tell him to get me some from London."

"Yessir."

Tom was dismayed to see him sink into his musings again. Clearly, something had bothered him deeply.

After a few more minutes of this, Tom grew frustrated and said loudly, "Sir, you said you would tell me this morning what we needed to do."

"I am afraid I have done quite enough already, Tom."

His shameful speech startled Tom. "You cannot blame yourself, Master Gideon. You've done nothing wrong."

Gideon threw him a grateful glance, but the corners of his mouth turned down. "You are wrong—though nothing can be altered by regret. There is no doubt in my mind that the argument I had with my father gave his killer the chance to assault him and to cover his crime."

"How do you mean?"

Gideon pushed his chair back and, with characteristic impatience, started pacing the floor. "Whoever it was must have heard our row and decided to wait until I had left before using the fact of it to murder my father."

"Who could it have been?"

As Gideon came to a halt in front of him, the furrow on his

forehead deepened. "I don't know, but I have an idea. I have been wondering why James Henry would be so willing to set Sir Joshua on me. I have asked myself what he stood to gain by killing my father and doing his best to implicate me. And the only thing I can conjecture is that he might have feared being discovered in an irregularity with his accounts.

"He might have been stealing from the estate. My father trusted him implicitly. He was getting older. He might not have examined Henry's ledger for some time."

"Do you truly think so?" Tom had never had an uncivil word from Mr. Henry, but it was true that Lord Hawkhurst had placed an unusual degree of confidence in him. "How will you find out if it's true?"

"By having a look at his ledger myself."

Tom felt an uneasiness stealing over him. "Have you taken leave of your senses . . . sir? Sir Joshua'll have his men all over the Abbey. If you try to go back, he'll have you took up before you can say Jack Robinson."

Normally Tom would have been glad to hear St. Mars laugh, but not when his laughter came with that reckless gleam in his eye.

"You were very well named, most doubting Thomas. Endeavour, however, *not* to suspect me of being a complete fool. We will go after dark, and I know a safe way to get inside. If Sir Joshua has his men posted there, they will none of them be in my father's closet where the money chest is kept, or in the chamber upstairs where I shall make my entrance."

They went that night, long after sunset, and rode at a trot, weaving their way through the dark, hilly Weald on paths that drovers had made, cutting past fields of hops with their long wooden poles standing like soldiers with pikes, until the woods and the night enveloped them again in its ghostly air. Coming on Rotherham Abbey near midnight, they left their horses under the cover of a thick grove of trees and approached the ruins on foot.

Tom had lived on Lord Hawkhurst's estate for most of his life without learning that a secret entrance had been built into the house from the ruins of the original abbey. St. Mars led him through the familiar game park to the bottom of a hill below the main house, where a centuries-old bridge spanned a ditch that had once held a stream. The stream had long-since been diverted, but the arched set of stones that had carried the monks across it on their way to the neighbouring abbey, some twenty-five miles away, was still strong enough to bear any weight. They aimed for the southeastern corner of the old religious complex where a huddle of crumbled walls stood. If Tom had been asked earlier, he would have said that the monks lying buried there had slept undisturbed, but apparently in the last bloody century someone had ordered a passage to be carved into the hill.

Squeezing past a barrier of tangled vines and caved-in stones, Gideon pushed his way into the ruins surrounding the abbey church. In this section, he had explained to Tom on their long ride down, the chief monastic buildings had stood apart from the abbey infirmary, the novices' cloister, and the quarters for the aged monks. Most of the stones from those, the original chapter house, the refectory and storehouses had been taken and used to build the first Earl Hawkhurst's manor on the site of the abbot's house, but the rest had been left as an interesting bit of antiquity under its cover of trees and vines.

Tom peered down into almost total darkness. He could make out nothing but the queer silent shapes of tumbled stones.

The stables, kennels, and mews that supported the present house had fortunately been built on the far side of the house. Neither the horses nor dogs could hear them from here, so they needn't fear a ruckus.

Safely out of sight from any window, Gideon withdrew a book of Congreve matches from his pocket and struck them a light. They had brought torches with them, and the instant flames revealed a set of worn stone steps leading down to a vaulted area below ground. In the days when the abbey had been filled with monks, this had been an undercroft. Now it was empty and remarkably free of dirt or refuse. Its cold stone flooring was probably too inhospitable for any beast to make it his home.

In the silence behind him, Gideon could hear Tom's wary tread and his gasping breath when without any preamble, he made his way across the floor towards a blackened opening in the wall.

"You're never going in there, my lord!" Tom whispered.

The horror in his voice made Gideon turn to examine him with the help of his light. Square and dependable—but with his face shining with sweat even on this cold night—Tom appeared as white as the moon.

"I have to go in. There's a passage that leads underground and climbs a few hundred yards farther along to lead into the house. If you'll come, you'll see that it's not so bad."

In a strangled voice, Tom blurted, "I can't."

Gideon had never heard just that note of panic from him before. "It's not haunted, you know—though I haven't been inside it for years. The point was not to use it, you see, except in the case of direst necessity. I doubt, however, that it has been taken over either by bats or ghosts."

"You know I'm not afraid of any of them things, my lord."

"Do you think the roof will tumble down on you? You run a far greater danger of being arrested for consorting with me."

If possible, Tom's face had grown even paler at this suggestion, but he stood his ground. "I'm not afraid of anything I can see. I just—I just never have liked—being in dark, little places."

His horror was obviously real, even if it was one Gideon did not share.

"Very well. There's really no need for you to go in, but I wanted you to see where the passage is, in case you ever need it. It might be better if you were to stand guard anyway. If someone should stumble upon us, you can cover my back."

Gideon turned and prepared to walk stooping through the passageway. "Keep your torch lit, and stay out of sight of the windows."

"When will you come back?"

At the worry in his voice, Gideon smiled. "I can't say how long it will take me to read Henry's ledger. If you'd rather, you can wait outside."

Gideon stooped to pass through the low, dark passageway and felt his way forward on the irregular stone floors. Once inside, his torch cast a beam only a few steps in front of him into a dank, earth-smelling void that seemed to expand and contract with the movement of his light. The underground passage had been constructed over a walkway from the abbot's house to the base court of the abbey. The walkway had sunk over the years, since the abbey had been built some 600 years before. The grounds about it had been filled in, and gardens had been built over it, but whomever Gideon's great-grandfather had hired to construct the passageway had known just where to look for it. All Cistercian abbeys had been built along the same plan, with an east-west passage linking the abbot with his church. The architect had only needed to dig for it and to build a long, arched corridor along it for any priest—or family member—who had a reason to flee Cromwell's men.

As far as Gideon knew, the passage had never been used, but there had been many a time when Cromwell's Roundheads had struck terror into Kent on their way to sack Canterbury. He remembered the moment, on his eighth birthday, when his father had taken him up the stairs to show him the important secret, which he'd said must be preserved in case the Reverend Mr. Bramwell should ever find himself in danger from a resurgence of the religious violence.

Gideon recalled the immense feeling of responsibility he had felt for keeping the secret. In all these years, he had divulged it to no one save for Tom now, no matter how great the temptation had been. Many times he had wanted to use the tunnel as a play place, but each time he had thought of revealing it, he had remembered his father's stories of the Civil War, and he had contented himself with an occasional foray into it alone.

Now he had told Thomas Barnes, who was as trustworthy as any man alive. Whatever happened to him, the secret would not die.

He came to a place where the walls were coated with a sheen of moisture and knew that he was more than halfway along. The monks' original watercourse had intersected the walkway here, flowing under it before resuming its journey to the mills. The stream had been rerouted to supply pastures farther from the house, but nature had obviously decided to leave some water behind.

The air in the tunnel grew scarce as Gideon drew near the house, so he was relieved to see the wooden door at the end. Before extinguishing his torch, he tried the latch and managed to open it after only a few jerks to scrape off the rust. Then he smothered his flame and, in total blackness, opened the door.

He felt a slight but welcome flow of air from the staircase built inside the Abbey wall. Feeling with the toes of his boots, he scaled the tight spiral staircase, scraping his knees and hips on the stones with every step. Even with a thickness of a few feet, there was hardly room enough to squeeze himself up as he inched his way to the top. He had remembered the stairwell as bigger, but it was he who had been smaller the last time he had ventured here. Prudently he advanced with a hand held high to avoid locating the next step with his head.

His hand collided with a roof. For a moment, he listened for sounds, but nothing came from the other side of the panel. Hoping that the spring that moved it still worked, he pushed on the latch he located with his thumb.

The panel sprang open. A surprising amount of light greeted him from a window near the bed. His eyes had grown accustomed to total darkness, so the moon glowing on the bed curtains shone nearly as bright as a beacon, making his errand all the easier.

Gideon stepped out of the stairwell and closed the panel behind him, then quickly sat down on a chair to pull off his boots. Years ago, this tiny chamber had been furnished for a superior servant, but lately it had only been used when a visitor of rank required the space for a member of his retinue. It was seldom needed, and no one would be likely to come across his pair of boots while he padded about.

The small chamber—hardly more than a closet—stood upon the first floor near the chapel gallery and the queen's set of chambers. Gideon cracked open its only door, peered into the deserted rooms beyond and crept out.

The great chest, which held his father's money, had usually been

kept in the London house, but since his father's retirement from
public life, it had been brought back here. Gideon knew he would
have to cross the open gallery to the other side of the Abbey before
he could search through it for James Henry's ledger.

The house—*his* house, though he had been made to feel an
intruder in it—was as silent as his father's grave. An empty air seemed
to have settled over it. Gideon felt all the weight of his loss as he
moved in stockinged feet through the warren of rooms which had
been shrouded in ghostly holland sheets. Angrily he shook off the
pall that threatened to overcome him. Action would be the only
cure for his grief. He couldn't afford to wallow in emotions.

The gallery yawned before him, lit by a long row of leaded
windows that faced the collection of portraits. Gideon's ancestors,
their friends, and monarchs who had figured in the family affections
for generations watched as he passed. He needed no candle. Every
nook and corner of this place was as familiar to him as his own face.
He even knew which squeaking boards to skirt.

As he turned right into the wing that housed his father's
chambers, a sense of excitement built in him at the idea that he
might be on the point of discovering something important.

As they had many times that day, his thoughts drifted to his
conversation with Mrs. Kean, who had alerted him to James Henry's
role in his troubles.

He would never forget her kindness, when so many others had
turned away. If another young lady had done the same, he would
have wondered about her motives. But not with Hester Kean. It
had been clear from her manner that her intelligence and her true
sense of fairness had been offended by Sir Joshua's unprincipled
accusations.

Strange that he hadn't noticed before what an attractive smile
she had.

She had given him this first line of pursuit. He had to discover
why James Henry had so willingly thrown the blame his way. There
had been a new hostility in his tone when they had talked in his
father's library. Whether he believed that Gideon had killed his
father—or from some other cause—his animosity had never been

quite so apparent before. Gideon tried to recall the man's expression throughout their conversation, but his painful feelings in that room had made him less than perfectly observant.

Had James Henry regretted his indiscretion? Did he fear Gideon would hold him accountable for Sir Joshua's insults? Or had there been something else?

Gideon had often wondered at the amount of trust his father placed in his receiver-general. James Henry wielded all the authority of a superior servant, of the kind seldom employed any longer except in royal households, in which positions like his were still held by men of noble blood. Not so very long ago, every duke or earl would have employed an agent such as he, but as with everything else, customs were changing. Only a man to whom tradition was a major point of honour, like Gideon's father, would have clung to such a costly way of operating his estate. The difference was that James Henry had no pedigree to recommend him, but Gideon had been too preoccupied with his own education and later his three-year Grand Tour to question the running of Rotherham Abbey. And when he had returned, he had found James Henry more entrenched than ever.

Perhaps he should have asked these questions before.

Nestled among the suite of rooms that included Lord Hawkhurst's bedchamber, his library, his wardrobe, and his privy, was another with only one door. It had been locked with one of James Henry's keys, as would be the chest itself. Gideon had come prepared with a stout iron bar tucked firmly through his belt. He forced one end of it between the door and its frame, then pushed with all his weight. He heard the splintering of oak as the door broke free of the lock. The aged wood had held fast except where it had been weakened by a joint with the metal.

He listened for sounds of footsteps coming, but no noise would have carried through these thick stone walls unless someone had been near enough to see him. Satisfied that no one was coming, Gideon hastened to find a light. His servants knew their duties—an abundance of candles lay close to hand. He lit two and set them on

James Henry's desk.

He was much more reluctant to rip into his father's chest, the product of an Augsburg craftsman. It had been in the family for over one hundred years. The keys should have been handed to him the moment he had risen from his sickbed. He had to convince himself now that he risked losing all his fortune if he did not forfeit the chest.

His bar made short shrift of the finer wood, the carved wooden panels, and the flowers that had been painted with such skill. Gideon felt the injury to the chest as if he had torn into himself. Again, however, he pushed his feelings aside and, as soon as he had it opened, felt inside the chest for Henry's ledger. He found it alongside the neat stacks of notes on London goldsmiths, among the silver and gold coins.

Ignoring the money for the time being—though he would need to replenish his meagre funds—he took the ledger to the only chair in the room. With the light from the candle, he began reading through the household records, starting near the end.

Here were their lives, minutely recorded in James Henry's small, tight script, every penny accounted for, whether it be a pound and seven shillings for the wood and iron to make two umbrellas or one and six for a gargle for Mrs. Dixon. Gideon noted the payment of his own allowance, as he thumbed through the ledger, along with annual servants' wages, payments to the grocers and mercers, and the doctors called in on a regular basis to physic the staff. Other entries recorded the purchase of trees for the orchard, beeves for the table, and cloth for the servants' livery.

The mass of details made him impatient. He had never realized all the tiny bits of recordkeeping that went into maintaining a household of this size. He couldn't believe that somewhere in this minutiae, he wouldn't find what he sought.

Then a note caught his eye. A large payment made to James Henry at Michaelmas. A sum of one hundred pounds, when he had already seen another entry for Henry's salary at Lady Day. Gideon turned back to confirm that a payment had been made in March and found it. Then, with his senses on edge, he checked the other quarter days, and discovered that on each, James Henry had been paid—or had paid himself—another hundred pounds.

Four hundred pounds in one year. A fabulous sum, when most servants were paid only a few pounds per annum. When all their expenses for food, clothing, and shelter, physicking and education, and travel were covered by their master. Even a receiver-general should not expect a salary of more than fifty pounds. Gideon knew, because he had seen the entries, that James Henry's expenses had always been met when he traveled between Rotherham Abbey and London, or any of the other Hawkhurst manors.

He lived in his own house on the estate and had a separate lodging in London when he might easily have been assigned a room in Hawkhurst House. Yet, here was evidence that he had received enough money to live like a gentleman without any of those other rewards. He had received as much, in fact, as Gideon himself received every quarter from his father for allowance.

Sickened, Gideon checked as far back as he could in the ledger. These payments had been started only three years ago. No statement had been recorded as to their purpose—when normally not a shilling left the chest without its full purpose being inscribed. Even the guineas withdrawn for Lord Hawkhurst's personal use, or a gratuity of a few pennies for the bargeman or a beggar woman coming to the door had been faithfully noted and explained.

Gideon simmered as he wondered what sort of business James Henry had waged against his father. Something dangerous it was sure. Such a threat, he guessed, that his father had been forced into making these quarterly payments.

Had his father refused to pay more? Was that why he had been killed?

If Sir Joshua would have accepted this ledger as evidence Gideon would have carried it to him. But it would take more than a supposition to convince Sir Joshua of his innocence. And Gideon knew he needed to know more before he could be satisfied himself.

He started to replace the ledger inside the great trunk, before recalling his need for money. With a sense of irony, he counted out a quantity of coins, which would have amounted to his next quarter-day allowance, and slipped them into a sturdy bag used for carrying them to the goldsmiths in London. By next quarter day, Midsummer Day, he fully expected to be back in his country seat with the keys to the money chest in the trust of a better man than James Henry.

Gideon did not forget to record his own withdrawal from the chest. On James Henry's nearby desk lay quill and ink. He noted the day with his own hundred pounds for his personal use. Then, in a large flowing hand, much like his father's, he boldly inscribed the name that no one had yet called him, the name that was his right.

Hawkhurst.

Hear and believe! thy own importance know,
Nor bound thy narrow views to things below.
Some secret truths, from learned pride concealed,
To Maids alone and Children are revealed:

Know further yet; whoever fair and chaste
Rejects mankind, is by some Sylph embraced:
For Spirits, freed from mortal laws, with ease
Assume what sexes and what shapes they please.
What guards the purity of melting Maids,
In courtly balls, and midnight masquerades,
Safe from the treacherous friend, the daring spark,
The glance by day, the whisper in the dark,
When kind occasion prompts their warm desires,
When music softens, and when dancing fires?
'Tis but their Sylph, the wise Celestials know,
Though Honour is the word with Men below

CHAPTER X

AS Gideon made his way back through the house, a patter of
paws caught up with him at the entrance to the small
bedchamber. He drew his father's dog inside by its wide brass collar
and spent a few valuable minutes scratching its ears. He considered
taking Argos with him. His need for this one small contact with his
father and his home was strong, but he realized that even the comfort
of a dog could prove a serious distraction, when he had his father's
murder to solve. Resolutely, he put the dog back outside the room,
before returning to the hidden stairwell.

As he stepped behind the wall, his boot met something in the
dark. In a hurry now, he felt blindly about the floor until his fingers
came upon a roll of papers, left presumably by his father, for no one
else should have known of this passageway. Gideon couldn't see them
without his torch, and he had no wish to spend another second
more than necessary inside the dank space. But the papers must
have been important for his father to have hidden them in here. He
took them to examine in the light of day.

Tom was waiting for him—not inside the undercroft, but out
in the open air. He gave a start when Gideon parted the tangle of
vines.

"My lord!" The relief in his whisper was palpable. "You was gone that long—did you find what you was looking for?"

"I did. And it appears we have another errand tonight."

"We do?" The moonlight on Tom's face revealed his dismay.

"Yes." A resurgence of Gideon's anger stoked his impatience. "We have a visit to pay."

James Henry's house stood but a mile away. It had never been part of Rotherham Abbey, but had belonged instead to a prosperous Kentish yeoman, who had died without heirs. Gideon could recall when his father had bought the estate, which lay contiguous to his own. He had originally let it to a tenant, but for the past few years it had served as the receiver-general's residence.

The main house was a half-timbered building with a clay tile roof. As Gideon and Tom rode near it, they halted their horses beneath a grove of trees on a higher piece of ground.

"It's just as I said, my lord. There'll be no way to get in. Them windows and doors is certain to be latched."

Gideon ignored Tom's warning as he studied the house by the light of the moon and the stars. A dry breeze had cleared the air, and with the help of the sky and his eyes now accustomed to the dark, he could see almost as well as if by day.

"On a night like this, I would sleep with a window open to let the fire smoke out of the room."

"And likely die from the poisons in the air. I tell you, my lord, Mr. Henry is too smart to leave his windows open by so much as a hair."

"I hope you are wrong. However, if you are right, I shall have no choice but to go in by the front door."

Tom smothered his reaction. Gideon heard him grind his teeth with the effort to muffle his disagreement. He had told Tom of his findings on their way here. He'd had no need to explain his suspicions.

He guessed that it was now past one o'clock, time for all good farmers to be deeply asleep. In the past few years, since his mother had died, his father's household had kept country hours except when in London, where they could not seek their beds until well after midnight. Here, away from Court, Lord Hawkhurst had involved himself in county matters, and his clock had been dictated by the farming activities on his estate.

James Henry would have retired late, but not so late as to arrive at work after breakfast. Without a master to rule the house, he would be even more vigilant. He should be upstairs and fast asleep, unless affairs had taken him to London.

Gideon wanted to get inside the house. He could not rest until he had had this confrontation.

Abruptly, he turned his horse to circle the house. He drew close to a garden wall where the land sloped downward to the garden behind. He was grateful for the silence in the barn and the henhouse, for James Henry had no need to produce his own food. For years all his meals had been taken at the Abbey with Lord Hawkhurst, except when Gideon was at home, when he had eaten with the upper servants in their hall.

The fluttering of a drapery at a window caught his eye. And he saw it—his way in.

Motioning to Tom—for they were too close to the house to speak aloud—he handed him Penny's reins and made a sign for him to stay. Then he tickled Penny's ribs to make her sidle near the wall, raised his feet to crouch upon her saddle, and launched himself onto the top of the wall.

"Be careful, my lord," Tom whispered after him.

Gideon pulled himself up the rest of the way, then crept doubled along the foot-wide wall until he came to a place where the house was nearest. He studied the structure until he found what appeared to be a foothold—a place where two low gables met. He wished he had brought a length of rope, but he had not come prepared to break into a second house. Wryly, he promised himself that if housebreaking were to become a habit, he would have to learn to be more prepared.

Taking a breath, he leapt again and, grappling, caught hold of a corner that protruded from the roughcast walls. The weather-beaten wood had splintered and it drove sharp, little pieces into his arms.

His sword dangled interferingly at his hip, as he worked to swing his legs onto the beam. He hung from his elbows a few moments to rest. Then, calling on all his resources, he pulled himself up and onto the roof.

He rested there for a few minutes, his wounded shoulder aching and his chest heaving, until his breathing returned to normal.

James Henry had been right to feel safe with that window cracked, Gideon reflected later, after he had crossed over the top of the roof, slid down the other side, and hung precariously until he had found a toe-hold near the open window. No burglar would have been foolish enough to risk his life to reach it. But Gideon's need for justice had propelled him where another man would have quit.

Carefully, he perched on a small ledge, looked about for the window, and gingerly inched his way towards it. One hand inside the open casement was all the grip he needed to pull himself onto the sill. For another few seconds, he sat pressed against the glass, peering as deeply as he could into the shadow-filled room. For, once inside it, he would lose the moonlight that had illuminated his way.

The sound of steady breathing coming from the bed decided him. Without a sound he swung open the narrow casement and squeezed himself through it.

The person in bed could only be James Henry. The room was much too large to belong to anyone but the master of the house.

Gideon unsheathed his sword. Moving to a table beside the bed, he struck a match and brought a candle to life.

He grasped the bed curtain and ripped it open.

Wakened from a deep sleep, James Henry threw up one hand to shield his eyes. Fighting momentary blindness, he saw Gideon and started up violently. But Gideon had already brought the point of his sword to his throat.

Never a fool, James Henry leaned back against his bolster and fixed his eyes on the intruder's face. With a curling lip, he asked, "Have you come to kill me, too, St. Mars?"

Gideon reacted with all the fury he had suppressed, shoving the point of his blade under the other man's skin.

James Henry made a strangled noise, as a trickle of blood slid onto his nightclothes. Silenced, he glared at Gideon with more hatred than fear.

A sickening seized Gideon's stomach. His loss and the insults he had suffered were making him insane. But he refused to take more from a man who had cheated his father and possibly killed him.

With Henry pinned against his headboard, Gideon eased his hip onto the bed.

Facing his father's servant comfortably, he addressed him in an anger-filled voice, "You thought you could throw the blame on me, but I have been to the Abbey, Mr. Henry, and I have examined your books. You will find it hard to explain to a magistrate how you managed to extort such an exorbitant sum from my father.

"What happened?" he continued, as Henry's gaze widened in surprise. "Did my father threaten to expose you for the thief you are?"

Henry said nothing. But he betrayed none of the fear Gideon had expected him to feel. Instead, he scrutinized Gideon's face as if searching it for the answer to a long-held secret.

Gideon lost all patience. With gritted teeth, he tightened his grip on his sword. "You will tell me now why you murdered a man who placed so much faith in you."

"I didn't kill him. Nor did I extort any money from him."

"Then what were those payments for?"

To his surprise, James Henry gave a smile of disbelief. "You cannot pretend you do not know. You cannot think me such a fool as to believe that."

Gideon stared back, confused. A momentary doubt threatened to divert him from his purpose, but he shook it off. "Answer me now. Either I can kill you, or I can let you dress and we can go see Sir Joshua together."

"If you do that—" James Henry spoke with an astonishing calm— "you will force me to divulge a secret your father would rather have kept."

Here it was—the reason why his father had paid this man so

much money—the secret James Henry had used to extort hundreds of pounds from his master.

Gideon could not believe that his father had anything to be ashamed of. How, then, to account for this sudden sick feeling coming over him?

"That is a price we will have to pay." He reached with his left hand to take hold of Henry's collar to haul him to his feet, but the other man moved quickly, too. He grabbed Gideon by his neckcloth and pulled his face close.

"Look at me, St. Mars!" He bared his teeth in a vicious snarl. "Look at my features—and pretend you do not see."

A sudden motion in Gideon's mind—like the raising of a window—an awareness that those hawk-like features should have brought him years ago—made him recoil. His pulse began to race.

They were locked in a deadly grasp, two faces bared in the candlelight, Gideon's sword forgotten, although its point still threatened James Henry's throat.

Look at me, he had said, as if the answer was written in his face.

Gideon looked, and he saw his father's craggy eyebrows—thinner and tamer because they adorned a younger man. He saw his father's light brown eyes.

And there were other signs, too—in the determination he knew they both possessed, in the anger they both had failed to control, and in sheer physical strength. It did not matter that James Henry was square and Gideon slight, or that he lacked James Henry's restraint. He could no longer ignore the traits staring back at him. And he wondered how he had been so blind all of these years.

But James had never let on, and their father, who should have told him, had kept his older son a secret while bringing him steadily into the family.

Now Gideon knew the reason for those quarter-day payments. Lord Hawkhurst had seen fit to make an allowance to his bastard son, the eldest boy, who would never inherit his father's fortune.

And if the shock in James Henry's expression meant what Gideon thought it did, he had believed that Gideon had known all along. Had known—and had ignored him.

How he must have hated him, the brother who would not acknowledge him, who treated him like a servant, no matter how politely.

And mistrusted him, too. For Gideon realized that his jealousy must have shown. He had begun to resent his father's preference years ago, but he had never known why. Now that he did, he did not know what to make of his behaviour.

In the same instant, the two men released their holds. Gideon removed the point of his sword from James Henry's throat.

"I did not know," was all he could manage as he moved backwards off the bed.

James lifted his fingers to the wound on his neck. The cut had already clotted. Soberly, and with a pallid face, he raised himself to sit and felt for the wound again. "I find that hard to believe," he said.

"It is true, nonetheless. You have not answered me. Did you kill our father?"

His verbal acknowledgement took James aback even as he protested, "I would ask you the same! You had more reason to do it. Why should I?"

"I don't know." Confusion was making mincemeat of his brain. Now that one of his suspicions had proved false, he felt so tired. Besides the lateness of the hour and the strain of his climb, he felt as if the breath had been knocked out of him.

"Who was your mother?"

If James was surprised by his change of subject, he did not show it. "She was a refugee."

"A Huguenot?"

"Yes. From the merchant class. My grandfather lived near your estate of St. Mars. That was where our—our father met her. Later, at Versailles, he began to suspect that Louis would revoke the Edict of Nantes and attack the Huguenots. He persuaded my grandfather to bring his family to England. They opened an inn with the money they had taken out of France. It was when they came to England— when she was grateful—that our father seduced her."

Gideon winced, as much from the bald way in which it had

been stated as from the word itself. "Is she still alive?"

"No. She died in the last smallpox. I was not with her. My lord had already sent me to be instructed to become his receiver-general."

Hating to meet his half-brother's eyes, but determined to meet them, Gideon raised his gaze before asking the painful question. "Did you ever talk? You and my father? Did he explain why he did not marry your mother?"

James Henry shrugged in a gesture that betrayed his Gallic blood, his expression a careful blank. "I had already heard the explanation from my mother. We were not wealthy enough. My mother had no dowry to tempt an earl. There was also our religion." He gave a laugh.

"He gave me my name, though. He insisted I should be called after the Pretender."

Gideon understood the irony that had tinged his laugh. Their father had insisted on naming his son, but had not cared enough to marry his mother or to acknowledge him. Lord Hawkhurst's excuses were the ones that any noble would have used. Their code of honour extended to men, seldom to women. He wondered if James had been able to accept the reasons as easily as their father had.

"He never spoke to you of this?"

"Not until he lay dying. I tried to get him to name his assailant, but his mind was wandering. All he would say was that he had injured the man." His gaze shifted to Gideon's shoulder, then to his face, and his eyes grew hard.

"I did not kill him." Gideon fought a spurt of rage. After a moment, he went on, "What else did he say?"

"He told me that he had transferred this house into my name and that his will would insure me a living as receiver-general to his heir."

"Did he leave no words for me?"

"None."

His cold answer, delivered with a satisfaction he did not even attempt to hide, filled Gideon with an anguish he could hardly bear.

He gripped his sword. The impulse to slash at something became so fierce, he almost gave into it now. But a change in his brother's expression stopped him.

James was staring at him angrily, as if the emotion he read in Gideon's face had confirmed his worst suspicions.

Gideon's fury collapsed. He tried to speak, but frustration clogged his throat.

He stood immobile, until he finally managed to say, "I loved my father. I would never have harmed him. I know he was angry, but I would not let him keep me from marrying the woman I love. He understood there was nothing he could do to stop me. So, you see, I had no motive."

Reading nothing on his brother's face—neither belief nor condemnation—he did his best to conceal the emotions that were eating him alive. Slowly placing his sword in its sheath, he started backing towards the door.

"With your permission, I shall let myself out. I had rather not leave by the way I came in."

James's relief showed in the slight relaxation of his posture.

Gideon said, "I have taken some money from the chest at the Abbey. You will find my signature for it in your book. When I need more, I shall either apply to you, or find a way to take it."

His statement was a challenge, but his receiver-general—his brother—answered not a word.

Disappointed—for he had hoped for a small sign that his brother believed him—Gideon hardened his heart. With insolent grace, he swept James Henry a bow, grasped the door latch behind him, and fled from the room.

He took the stairs in leaps, afraid that James might take the opportunity to aim a pistol at his back.

And other demons were there, nipping at his heels and howling in his ears.

Once outside, he searched quickly for Tom, but Tom had heard his fumblings with the front door and had ridden around to meet him. Gideon spied him coming around the side of the house.

He snatched at Penny's reins.

"What happened in there, my lord? I was about to go in after you."

"I'm all right. But we should leave. And fast."

Tom held his tongue, and soon they were galloping north. Back to the Fox and Goose. As their pace slowed to a walk and they began the long, twisted journey through the Weald, Gideon's thoughts were as dark as a blacksmith's pit.

He should not care that his father had used his last few moments of breath to console his other son. He should not care that another son existed or that another woman had once tempted his father's heart.

He should not care that his father had left him ignorant. Or that his brother would accuse him of murder now.

But the expression in James Henry's eyes when he had seen the anger welling inside him would haunt Gideon all the way back to the inn and through his tortured sleep.

℘

On the following afternoon, Hester Kean found herself at the Theatre-Royal in Drury Lane, acting as Isabella's chaperone. Mrs. Mayfield, who normally would have reserved this pleasant duty for herself, had taken to her bed with a nervous cholic. Hester had dosed her with a potion of her own, a mixture of Dr. Stephen's water and powder of rhubarb, but Mrs. Mayfield had felt no relief. With a great sense of ill-use, she had pressed Hester to take her place so that Isabella would not be made to forego the delights of the theatre when she had suffered such a cruel blow. That very morning, the Duke of Bournemouth had announced his engagement to the daughter of a German prince.

The disappointment seemed not to have crushed Isabella, for she was enjoying a spirited flirtation with Lord Kirkland, their host. His footmen, dispatched in the forenoon to hold their places, had managed to secure this box on the stage. So they were looking down on the actors in comfort, while the majority of patrons elbowed each other in the pit. Like the fops in the neighbouring box, Lord Kirkland had spent a great deal of his time grooming his shoulder-length wig with an embellished ivory and tortoise shell comb, in order to attract the ladies' admiration. The lustrous female hair, which surely must have come from France, would have cost him all of three hundred pounds. He suitably lavished it with as much attention as he gave the flimsy piece of lace that failed to cover Isabella's breasts.

Hester had found the pair's conversation, which consisted chiefly of Lord Kirkland's lewd suggestions and Isabella's giggle, scarcely bearable. As a chaperone, she was a failure, for her presence had proved no deterrent to their vastly unbecoming behaviour. Since Hester was certain, though, that her aunt would not have her interfere with Isabella's fun unless their host's advances surpassed the conduct of his neighbours', she had said nothing as yet. She had derived her only pleasure in the evening from the play itself.

And she had enjoyed it, despite the *double entendres* and the lewd gestures which had provoked shouts and guffaws from the pit, for coming from a country village, she had never been treated to plays or spectacles. Improper conduct and rude notions were several times more amusing on stage than they were in real life, perhaps because the author devoted more wit to his lines. Unfortunately, most of the audience, including Lord Kirkland, failed to perceive the difference between the cleverness on stage and the foolishness in their chairs.

Was it too much to ask for a kindred soul who would also prefer such goings-on to be kept in private? Hester closed her eyes and her imagination took her away from the rowdy scene. She escaped to a place where ignorance and vanity had no place.

She became so engrossed in a vision of an elegant stone house and a husband who treated her with affection and conversed with sense, that she forgot her duty, until Lord Kirkland's low, insistent tone pulled her back.

"Just one, my angel. That's all I ask. Just one touch of your hair. Your cousin has drifted asleep. No one else will see."

"No, you mustn't. Oh—!"

Isabella's gasp, instead of the firm *"No!"* Hester would have preferred to hear, caused her to open her eyes. Lord Kirkland had possessed himself of a lock of Isabella's hair. And while he stroked it, the backs of his fingers stroked her breast.

Breathing in heavy gasps, like a footman near the end of a race, Isabella seemed frozen in place, her eyes wide as coachwheels. She did nothing to stop him.

Grinning at her enraptured expression, Lord Kirkland moved to work his hand inside her dress.

Hester sprang to her feet. "If you will excuse us, my lord, Isabella and I must go."

Lord Kirkland snatched his hand from beneath Isabella's lace, but where he had touched her, she glowed a pleasured red.

Hiding his annoyance, his lordship made Hester a mocking bow. "It shall be as you say, Mrs. Kean, but I regret the hour that takes Mrs. Mayfield away. I hope to be granted more of . . . the pleasures of her company very soon."

His look was full of meaning. Isabella's mother might encourage her to flirt, but she would be furious if she learned that Isabella had behaved so freely with Lord Kirkland. Though a peer, he had little to recommend him but a title. His debts were said to be as legendary as his estate was scant. Mrs. Mayfield would have to be desperate before she would allow Isabella to take him for a husband. Even Mr. Letchworth, who had recently resumed his attentions, would be a preferable catch in her eyes.

Creditors were now almost constantly at her door. With her excessive spending to enhance Isabella's charms, Mrs. Mayfield had come near to ruining herself. It had taken all Hester's tact and management to persuade the most importunate tradesmen to accept the small bits she could pry from her aunt's tight fist. The merchants in the Strand had refused to extend her any more credit, so Isabella had been reduced to retrimming her gowns.

Hester gave no hint of these thoughts as she draped her cousin's cloak over her shoulders, but she kept a sharp eye on the pair as they left the box.

As they made their way through the anteroom, a bustle in the corridor ahead drew their attention. Sir Harrowby, who had paid them a visit between acts, had just emerged from his box. A group of his friends had collected around him, as he read the note a messenger had brought.

As they passed him, an oath escaped his lips.

"What's towards, Harrowby?" one of his companions asked as they jostled each other, trying to hear.

Turning pale, he stammered out a tale that quickly spread. It reached Hester and her party before they reached the door.

Lord St. Mars had been arrested for his father's murder.

Isabella gave a shocked gasp. But Hester could not utter a sound. Her heart seemed to have stopped in her chest. She felt no air in her lungs, no blood in her veins. Nothing but a terrible stillness and an ache that stemmed from her heart.

Aware that she could not give in to distress here at the theatre, she forced herself to breathe. The stale scent of perfumed bodies nearly choked her, but she pulled herself outside, past Sir Harrowby's friends who were congratulating him on his certain inheritance of the Hawkhurst title and lands.

He seemed dazed, whether by good fortune or grief, she could not tell.

Outside the air was hardly better with the stench of refuse and coal smoke, but at least it was free of the heavy perfumes the ladies and gentlemen wore. Hester declined Lord Kirkland's improper invitation to show them his collection of curiosities and insisted that he call chairs to carry them home, pleading an indisposition of her own.

Leaving him to deal with the quarrelsome chairmen, she saw Isabella into one chair, before taking another. With her curtain closed, Hester could finally relinquish her pretense of calm. She buried her face in one hand and tried to weep, but her stunned mind denied her relief. The tears that might have soothed her remained painfully wedged in her throat.

They were still there when she and Isabella arrived at Mrs. Mayfield's house. As Hester descended, she saw that Lord Kirkland had used the unchaperoned minutes to his advantage. He had walked the whole way beside Isabella's chair. Whether or not he had kept his hands outside the curtains, which Hester doubted, he had somehow managed to provoke more breathless blushes from her cousin. Still feeling stunned, Hester could hardly muster the strength to be annoyed, not when she desperately wished for the privacy of her own room to reflect on what could be done to help St. Mars.

Mrs. Mayfield had been waiting to hear a report of their evening. She intercepted them at the top of the stairs.

"Well, my dearest," she said, palely anxious now that the Duke was out of play. "Did you enjoy yourself? Did you meet with any interesting gentlemen?"

"Oh, yes, Mama." Isabella concealed the excitement that had aroused her that evening. "Everyone was there. Sir Harrowby paid us a visit to Lord Kirkland's box, and he brought two very handsome gentlemen with him. Their clothes were as fine as anything I've ever seen.

"And Lord Kirkland was so good to us. You would have enjoyed yourself, Mama. I am certain I did."

Mrs. Mayfield missed the subtle hint. She ignored the reference to their host and fixed instead on her intended target.

"Sir Harrowby paid you a visit? Did he seem well? Had he any recent word from Rotherham Abbey?"

Hester had hoped to conceal the news from her aunt, at least until tomorrow. She did not think she could bear to hear her speculate on how this would affect Isabella's chances. But Isabella was quick to latch on to the change of subject.

"Oh, yes! He had a message from there just as we were leaving. A man must have ridden all the way from Hawkhurst to tell him. Lord St. Mars has been taken up for murder, Mama!"

Hester found she couldn't tear her gaze away from Mrs. Mayfield's face. Where there should have been shock, she only revealed a sense of deeply felt relief. Suddenly, all her pallor was gone, along with the pinched look she had worn of late. In her glowing eyes, hope triumphed again.

"Thank God," she said, not bothering to hide her greed. "First thing tomorrow, I shall write Sir Harrowby a note. We will invite him to call on us immediately. Isabella, you must wear your most becoming gown, the Pudsway silk with the silver lace. I will dress your hair myself. We must be ready to receive him at any hour."

Hester couldn't bear to hear her aunt's plans now. "If you will excuse me," she said, "I will leave you both. Good night, Isabella . . . Aunt."

"Come into my room," Mrs. Mayfield said to her daughter, ignoring Hester. She pulled Isabella through the door behind her. "I will tell you what you need to do."

They disappeared inside.

Hester knew she should stay to dissuade her aunt from whatever plot she was hatching, but she hadn't the heart for it now. Whatever plan Mrs. Mayfield had for Sir Harrowby, she was sure he deserved Isabella. He was not the one who merited her pity tonight.

How could Sir Joshua have been so stupid as to suspect St. Mars of killing his father? Had the world gone mad?

She seemed to be the only person who could see St. Mars for the gentle man he was. Friendless as he seemed, she could not reprove herself for these feelings, even though it had become fairly clear to her that she suffered more on his account than she would have for another man in his predicament. She could not fool herself any longer on that score.

Desperately she asked herself what she could do to help him. But there was nothing. There would be a trial. She did not know when the Kentish assizes were held, but she doubted she would be allowed to attend them, unless Mrs. Mayfield managed to secure Sir Harrowby for Isabella before the issue of St. Mars's innocence was resolved.

Which raised another question—how could her aunt be so certain that St. Mars would not win his release when the justices heard his case?

They would have to hear it. And the assize judges could not all be as foolish or as vengeful as Sir Joshua Tate.

Some nymphs there are, too conscious of their face,
For life predestined to the Gnomes' embrace.
These swell their prospects and exalt their pride,
When offers are disdained and love denied:
Then gay Ideas crowd the vacant brain,
While Peers, and Dukes, and all their sweeping train,
And Garters, Stars, and Coronets appear,
And in soft sounds, Your Grace salutes their ear.
'Tis these that early taint the female soul,
Instruct the eyes of young Coquettes to roll,
Teach Infant cheeks a bidden blush to know,
And little hearts to flutter at a Beau.
　　　Oft, when the world imagine women stray,
The Sylphs through mystic mazes guide their way,
Through all the giddy circle they pursue,
And old impertinence expel by new.
What tender maid but must a victim fall
To one man's treat, but for another's ball?

The Gnome rejoicing bears her gifts away,
Spreads his black wings, and slowly mounts to day.

Belinda burns with more than mortal ire,
And fierce Thalestris fans the rising fire.
"O wretched maid!" she spread her hands, and cried,
(While Hampton's echoes, "Wretched maid!" replied)
"Was it for this you took such constant care
The bodkin, comb, and essence to prepare?
For this your locks in paper durance bound,
For this with torturing irons wreathed around?
For this with fillets strained your tender head,
And bravely bore the double loads of lead?"

CHAPTER XI

IN the morning, Mrs. Mayfield sent a note to Harrowby, inviting him to call. Then she and Isabella sat down to wait. Hester tried to carry on with her duties, but heavy at heart, she worked through the morning's tasks at a burdened pace.

Harrowby sent word that he hoped to wait upon them later in the day, but that events had occurred which might rob him of that pleasure. Mrs. Mayfield nearly fretted herself into a panic at the thought that he might not come at all.

She was hardly relieved when a different caller appeared—Mr. Letchworth, his face covered over with a thick coating of white paint, punctuated with the bright red traces of Spanish paper.

At least his arrival provided a diversion from the tedious wait. Isabella's greeting revealed her relief, which made her seem warmer towards him than usual. She had never shown any particular liking for Mr. Letchworth, although her manners towards him, as to other men, were calculated to keep him hanging on the hook. His habitual references to his enormous wealth had the power to captivate her attention.

Unfortunately, no degree of fortune could make him attractive in anyone's eyes. His physique was good enough. He was tall and long-limbed, though his high, knobby shoulders gave him a clumsy appearance that belied the vigour in his stride. He had dressed with more care today, in a puce silk suit that sat better with his long black wig. His bamboo cane, which he carried in place of a sword, was very fashionable. But the paint he persisted in wearing, undoubtedly to cover up some bad scarring from the smallpox, had already begun to flake. His complexion resembled nothing so much as an unfinished bit of crockery left out in the sun to dry.

Previously, Mrs. Mayfield had discouraged his calls, using an ensemble of practiced excuses. Today, however, although the announcement of his name first annoyed her, she took comfort from the sign of his continued interest. Hester surmised that her aunt realized she could not afford to despise anyone with Mr. Letchworth's wealth, when Isabella's nobler suitors seemed to have vanished. She wondered how long it would be before her aunt came to understand that she had thrown the best one away.

Not today, it appeared, for no sooner had Mr. Letchworth taken a chair, his acquisitive stare appraising Isabella's beauty, than Mrs. Mayfield asked, "Sir, have you heard the shocking news about my Lord St. Mars? They say he has indeed murdered his papa!"

"I heard the gossip in the street. It would seem our fair young lord could not wait to inherit his father's estate."

"Well, as to that . . . " Mrs. Mayfield put on a coy look. "I am sure you have heard why he was become so desperate."

"Indeed I have." Mr. Letchworth had taken his eyes off Isabella when her mother had spoken, but he turned them back to her now. She blushed as if on cue, and a light as hard as diamonds lit his eyes.

Hester fancied she could see Isabella's reflection in the small, black dots that were his pupils.

Her aunt went on, "You will say I should be flattered that the heir to an earldom should be so deep in love with my Isabella, but I do not hold with murder, Mr. Letchworth, and I will not bestow my daughter on a gentleman who would attack his own papa."

This attempt at piety missed its mark. Their visitor, who never betrayed a hint of the slightest sense of humour, gave an unexpected twist to his lips. "You do not think that it is better to kill for a woman than to die for one?"

"Oh, how shocking you men are! If you must, I suppose you will have your silly duels and your quarrels! But we ladies do not wish to hear of them, I assure you. Our sensibilities are much too refined for that."

"You prefer us to hide our passions . . . . Very well."

He engaged Isabella in awkward small talk. Sitting in her quiet corner, Hester observed how he tried to draw her cousin out. Mr. Letchworth's conversation held little art. If indeed he possessed a sense of humour, it was once again invisible. He made no silly jests of the type favoured by Harrowby or double-entendres like Lord Kirkland's. Instead he preferred to tell her of his recent purchases, offering to take her for a ride in his new carriage, which he seemed to have bought with no better intention than to impress her. Isabella's eyes grew round at his talk of silk upholstery and wheels trimmed in gold.

She was far from immune to the excitement most girls felt for precious metals, jewels and silks. But this morning her responses were almost mechanical—nothing like the breathless passion she had revealed last night.

Hester worried that her cousin might have formed her first real attachment to an ineligible man. Up until now, Isabella had seemed willing to let her mother choose her husband. But what would happen if she decided she wanted Lord Kirkland, who had no fortune?

Mr. Letchworth's visit ran longer than any of them liked, and he gave no sign of remarking their fidgets. Anxious—undoubtedly that Harrowby would be offended by his presence, should he come— Mrs. Mayfield eventually stood and told their guest that they must wish him a good day.

He scowled at her interruption, but immediately said, "If I might have a few words with you in private, Mrs. Mayfield."

For once, Hester's aunt was nonplussed. She had nothing to say to discourage him, but a proposal from Mr. Letchworth just now would surely destroy her plans.

She could not afford to offend him, however, so she stiffly

acquiesced, asking him to accompany her to the smaller of the two parlours.

Before they departed, he bowed over Isabella's hand, and pressed it with a kiss. This was more than a polite brushing of his lips. Instinctively, Isabella tried to free her fingers, but he held fast to them, not relenting until she relinquished control. An edge in his smile revealed his displeasure at her reluctance, and two knots in his neck reddened and bulged above his neckcloth.

As he and Mrs. Mayfield disappeared behind the door, Isabella collapsed into a chair. For the first time in Hester's memory, she seemed distraught. And who would not be, with a greedy mother negotiating her future with a man as unappealing as Mr. Letchworth.

Up until now, Bella had seemed unaware that reality awaited her after the flurry of suppers and balls, but after all, hadn't these amusements been designed expressly to conceal the truth from their innocent guests? Yesterday, she might have entertained an offer from Mr. Letchworth with no more notion than a butterfly of the obligations marriage would entail, but last night, at Lord Kirkland's hands, she had received her first inkling.

Hester was moved by sympathy to say, "I would not worry, Bella. Your mother would rather see you wed to someone other than Mr. Letchworth. She will know what to say."

Isabella threw her the glance of a startled doe. "She said I must catch Sir Harrowby or we will lose everything. What if he doesn't come? What if he doesn't want me?"

Then, your mother will sell you to the highest bidder, were the words that ran through Hester's mind. But loath to frighten her cousin, she kept this thought to herself. "There are many other gentlemen who would give a fortune to marry you. You must not despair."

But clearly Isabella believed that her choices had narrowed to Harrowby or the unattractive man closeted with her mother.

An angry voice from behind the parlour door startled them both, but it was soon silenced. In another moment, they heard Mr. Letchworth's heavy steps in the hall, accompanied by the sound of his cane striking the floor. Isabella clung tightly to the arms of her chair, but his footsteps passed by the withdrawing room and proceeded to the stairs. Hester and she had barely taken a new breath when Mrs. Mayfield came back to join them.

"Well!" She entered on a triumphant note, though the lines on her face were strained. "I have something wonderful to tell you, my dearest. What will you say when I tell you that Mr. Letchworth has made me a very pretty application for your hand? I cannot tell you how much he has offered, for I have not yet accepted, and it remains to be seen if we cannot do better. But I will tell you that it is a very handsome offer indeed, and you should feel very proud."

"You will not accept it, Mama?" Isabella's anxiety was strong. "I thought you wanted me to get Sir Harrowby."

Her mother's features hardened. "I *do* want you to get him, and you *will* get him if he comes. But if he does not, I expect you to do as you're told. That is understood."

"But—"

"Do not argue with me, child!" Mrs. Mayfield's voice rose on a note of hysteria. "I will not abide disobedience. We have spoken often enough of your duty. And, God knows, I've done everything in my power to see you handsomely wed. But if, in spite of everything, you fail, you will have no one but yourself to blame. So do not anger me with your tears."

Isabella shrank back, stunned by a tone of voice that had never been directed at her before.

Even Hester was shocked. And if she could be shocked, knowing her aunt for her greedy self, what must Isabella's feelings be?

"Go upstairs now and lie down on your bed. That's a good girl," Mrs. Mayfield added weakly, as Isabella, with a fearful glance, nearly ran from the room. "I will call you when Sir Harrowby comes and you will do as I have taught you."

"If you do not need me, Aunt," Hester said, "I shall go up, too."

Mrs. Mayfield turned blindly towards her. She seemed to be talking to herself when she said, "He's demanded an answer when he returns from Bedford at the end of the week. He was furious when I would not give my consent immediately.

"But she almost captured a duke! I should have done something else to help her get his Grace. If Sir Harrowby fails to come, I shall have to give her to him."

Her reasoning made Hester feel sick. It would be useless to point out that Isabella could never come to love Mr. Letchworth, no matter how wealthy he was. "I should go up and make sure she gets the rest she needs."

"Yes," her aunt said, beside herself. "Do go up and make sure her eyes don't turn red. Tell her it won't matter—tell her she can have any man she wants—just not until after the wedding night."

As Hester climbed the stairs, she vowed that she would never repeat such cynical words, no matter who had said them. Undoubtedly, they had been true of Mrs. Mayfield. And they were also true of many an aristocrat Hester had met.

But they would not be true for Isabella, were she so unfortunate as to marry Mr. Letchworth.

They had almost despaired of Harrowby when, late that night, a knock sounded at the door, and a few moments later, he entered the drawing room with an unsteady gait and a happy, flushed face.

"I am sorry to appear at this inconvenient hour, and I will not stop. I should have come sooner, had I not been occupied all day with the most astounding business.

"My cousin—Gideon, you know —has escaped his constables and fled. It's assumed he's gone to the Continent, although they searched for him at Deal with no success. And the devil of it is that Bolingbroke is missing, too. He was to be called to account for his traitorous activities, but no one has been able to find him since he left the play a few nights ago. And now with poor ol' Gideon—St. Mars, don't you know—vanishing—well, they are saying that he must be embroiled with the Pretender, too, and likely the pair of them have gone to join him. There is a motion before Parliament to strip my cousin of his honours, and they say it has every likelihood of passing."

As Hester gave a distressed gasp, Mrs. Mayfield uttered a cry. "Oh, my dear Sir Harrowby!" Revived, she could hardly contain her elation. With an adoring gaze, she dropped into a profound curtsy. "Forgive me, I should say, 'Lord Hawkhurst', for such you will surely be. My most ardent prayers for you have just been answered."

She turned a beaming face to her daughter. "Isabella, is it not wonderful that our dearest friend in the world should have come by such wonderful fortune?"

Indeed, Isabella was so overcome that tears sprang into her eyes. "Oh, my dear Sir Harrowby."

"You must not call him that now, foolish girl. He must be 'my lord' now."

Harrowby beamed, with no trace of emotion that remotely approached either guilt or humility. He did not notice that Hester refrained from adding her congratulations to theirs. All she could think was that St. Mars would be unjustly deprived of his rights and possessions.

The travesty made her furious even as she accepted that his flight might have spared him a much worse fate. He would not have to languish behind bars, as she had pictured him half the night. He would not have to face execution, as fantastic as that possibility had seemed. The news that he was gone, however, was very painful. She could never hope to see him again. But at least he was free.

Harrowby—for Hester promised herself never to think of him as Lord Hawkhurst—accepted their praises, then made as if to go.

"No, no!" Mrs. Mayfield quickly stopped him. "You would not be so cruel as to leave us before we have drunk a toast to your good fortune. Let me call for a bottle of champagne. We *must* be allowed to celebrate."

Hester observed that he had probably drunk a bottle or two with his friends before coming, but she would not interfere with Mrs. Mayfield's plans. Whatever her aunt had in mind, it could not be as horrible as the thought of Isabella's marrying Mr. Letchworth.

Isabella had embraced the role her mother had designed for her. She urged Harrowby to take a chair, then sat on the floor to worship at his feet. She leaned against his knee while, with an engaging innocence, she clutched his hand to her cheek.

With Isabella smiling up at him and occasionally drawing his dangling fingers near her modesty piece, it was no wonder that colour began to infuse his cheeks.

Mrs. Mayfield pressed a glass into his free hand. She watched him drink, then made certain he was poured more and more. Mother and daughter kept up a lively chatter, wanting to hear about his plans for taking over Rotherham Abbey, wondering when he would move into Hawkhurst House, asking him what sort of entertainments he would give. And throughout the merry talk, both women gave him the impression that he was a hero to be adored.

Before long he forgot that he had intended to leave. He stared dazedly into Isabella's eyes with a happy, half-satiated smile. Isabella alternated between shy, downcast glances and eager gazes filled with rapt admiration and a soft, seductive charm. Taking an occasional sip of her own champagne for courage, she laughed unrestrainedly at Harrowby's addled jokes, no matter that they were becoming more suggestive with every passing minute.

Gazing on them with a look of indulgent approval, Mrs. Mayfield suddenly turned to Hester. "I would like you to fetch my fur tippet. It is all the excitement, I make no doubt, but I'm getting gooseflesh on my limbs. I left it upstairs in my wardrobe. You should have no trouble in finding it."

Aside from the unusual degree of courtesy in her aunt's request, there was nothing in it to take Hester by surprise. She was used to Mrs. Mayfield's demands. On this occasion, she was even glad for the opportunity to escape from the parlour, for she had never enjoyed the spectacle of intoxicated persons, and it appeared that Harrowby and Isabella were both headed that way.

She wished to be alone to grieve for St. Mars. She felt powerless in a way she never had before. Her one aim had been to help him win Isabella's love, since that was what he had wanted. Then she had hoped to help him clear his name. She was grateful to know that he was safe, but she could not be happy when she suspected her aunt had done her utmost to encourage Sir Joshua Tate in his suspicions. And since last night, she had known exactly why. Mrs. Mayfield had wanted to rob St. Mars of his fortune so that Harrowby Fitzsimmons could inherit it.

Hester wondered what Harrowby's part in this scheme had been, whether he had killed his uncle and cast the blame on St. Mars to win himself an earldom. Did a murderer sit in their drawing room now? With a sigh of despair, she asked herself how she could find the truth, and if it were not too late now to help St. Mars.

If only she could find some proof that someone else had killed his father.

But how would she—a waiting woman—ever come by such proof, even if it existed?

Far from eager to return to the drawing room, she took her time in searching for her aunt's wrap. It was not to be found in Mrs. Mayfield's wardrobe. After looking carefully through all her aunt's garments, Hester sighed again at the thought that her aunt might have left it anywhere in the house.

She looked in the bedchamber, her aunt's privy, and every other closet nearby before deciding she had better resume her search downstairs in the small parlour where Mrs. Mayfield sometimes sat. She walked back through the bedchamber and had almost left it when a flash of brown, peeking out from behind the bolster on the bed, caught her eye.

Hester turned, and there, folded and stuffed behind the high, plumped cushions, lay her aunt's fur tippet, wedged carefully as if hidden.

A sudden suspicion brought flutters to her stomach.

She could not imagine that an accident had led to the wrap's being placed there. It had been purposely tucked behind, where she would not find it without turning the room upside down.

With a sense of foreboding, she took it from behind the pillows and made her way down to the first floor.

Outside the withdrawing room door all was quiet. There was nothing strange. Undoubtedly, Mrs. Mayfield had meant to get Hester out of the room so that Harrowby might find it easier to declare himself.

To knock on the drawing room door in defiance of all convention would indicate that she suspected something improper. Her sense of tact would not allow her to embarrass Isabella by doing that. She could only be as self-effacing as she knew how to be.

Taking a deep breath, she squared her shoulders and passed quietly into the room.

She would have gasped at the sight in front of her, had her lungs not already been full of air. As a consequence, her entrance made insufficient noise to alert the two tightly wound in the chair. The hinges of the door were well-oiled—too silent to protect her from a scene she would rather not have witnessed.

Isabella was sprawled on Harrowby's lap. They must have been locked in their embrace for quite some time, judging by the fact that his hands were no longer visible. The little bit of lace that had protected Isabella's modesty from probing male glances was no longer in place. It had been tossed aside to provide greater access to the treasures underneath.

Isabella held his face to her breasts and arched her back in a passion that could only be real. Even as Harrowby—in his drunken fog—became aware of Hester's presence and tried to extricate himself from this compromising position, Isabella whimpered in protest.

Hester felt a jolt of shock, then a warmth beneath her skin. Chagrin at her untimely arrival would have overcome her feelings had it not been for the rapt expression on her cousin's face.

"Oh, my! Oh, my dear!" From close behind her came a loud, theatrical cry.

Hester whipped around to see that her aunt had entered the room behind her, making no noise. She must have descended the stairs close behind her niece.

But no, Hester realized as, stunned, she watched her aunt walk past. Only seconds had separated their entrances. Mrs. Mayfield must have been waiting for her to come down, lurking perhaps in the small room next door, to follow so closely on her heels. Had this been her plan?

Hester turned back to see Harrowby furiously smoothing Isabella's skirts which had risen well above her knees. With horror, he tried to move her off his lap, but Bella had latched onto his neck to bury her blushes in his disheveled cravat. As she bewailed her shame at being caught in such a compromising situation, he stared at Mrs. Mayfield with round, frightened eyes.

He must have expected her to scream and throw him from the house, but Bella's mother was far too cunning for that.

She moved to within two feet of the chair and stood looking down at him, her thick arms folded.

"I never should have left you two love-birds alone," she said, with a mixture of harshness and coyness. "I should have known not to turn my back on you for an instant, but I thought Hester would return soon enough and that I might escape to the privy for one minute without any harm. Thank heaven she did come in time, or my poor chick would be ruined for sure!

"But—" and here her voice turned on a positive note— "nothing's broke that can't be fixed.

"You should have applied to me, my lord." She gave Harrowby a saucy wag of her finger. "If you was desirous of wedding my Isabella, I would not have withheld my consent, not when I know how much her heart has been set on you from the first. Oh, but you're a shrewd one, an't you! You wanted to make good and sure of her before you applied to me, and I cannot blame you—not when half the beaus in London have been vying themselves to death for love of her.

"But you see now that she loves you more than anyone else, and I will do nothing to put myself in the way of my daughter's good fortune. It is a good thing for you that you are becoming an earl. But I can't have you sampling the goods before the marriage now, can I? You two love-birds will have to let each other go, so you and I can conduct our business, my lord."

Throughout this one-sided exchange, Harrowby looked stunned. His fuddled mind seemed unable to grasp how he had been trapped in this fix. He did not look in the least like a man who had been granted his heart's greatest desire.

He looked lost—in fact, so dazed—that Hester began to wonder if he had only then realized that an earl could aspire to a greater match than to Isabella Mayfield. He had been attracted to her silliness, her immense popularity, and her sense of fashion, and he had obviously enjoyed her attentions enough to allow himself to be seduced. But Hester doubted he was very much in love.

"Oh, Harrowby!" Isabella raised her face to look joyfully into his. "We shall be so happy. Think of the clothes we will have! We shall be the most admired couple in London!"

She could not have said anything surer to remove the horror from his eyes. Her delight was infectious, despite her spotty teeth. He was not immune to her happiness, but more powerful than either of these was the satisfying image she had drawn of the elegant figure the two of them would cut.

Especially when Bella gave a wriggle of delight in his lap, followed by a ripe giggle. He nearly forgot himself again, imagining all the fun they had in store.

"By gads!" he said, beaming. "We shall make a dashing couple, won't we? Zounds! I doubt but I'll be the envy of all the beaus. They'll be ready to tear me to shreds for snatching such a beauty away. Stap me, if they won't! It shall all be great good fun!"

Hester was nearly sickened by his shallow sentiments, but her cousin obviously shared his feelings. If Isabella could find happiness with such a fool, she would not say anything to spoil it. But Hester could not believe that a marriage founded on such feeble grounds would stand a chance of bringing anyone a lasting joy. At least, Isabella would be spared the worse fate of being married to Mr. Letchworth.

Some feeling of disillusionment must remain, however, when she thought of how easily Isabella's passion had moved from one gentleman to the next. For the unfeigned ecstasy she had surprised on her cousin's face had been every bit as intense as Isabella's expression with Lord Kirkland last night.

Her aunt made certain that Harrowby did not leave the house until he had agreed to her conditions. Though the shock of his impending nuptials sobered him to a degree, he would never be sharp enough to outfox his future mother-in-law. She took him into her parlour and extracted a promise of a generous settlement for her daughter with a thousand pounds in pin money per annum. Hester would not have been surprised to learn, either, that she had wangled a number of lavish benefits for herself.

Others on earth o'er human race preside,
Watch all their ways, and all their actions guide:
Of these the chief the care of Nations own,
And guard with Arms divine the British Throne.

Our humbler province is to tend the Fair,
Not a less pleasing, though a less glorious care;
To save the powder from too rude a gale,
Nor let th' imprisoned essences exhale;
To draw fresh colours from the vernal flowers;
To steal from rainbows e'er they drop in showers
A brighter wash; to curl their waving hairs,
Assist their blushes, and inspire their airs;
Nay oft, in dreams, invention we bestow,
To change a Flounce, or add a Furbelow.

CHAPTER XII

AFTER his encounter with James Henry, Gideon had spent the rest of the night struggling with the news that he had a brother. His emotions were so complex, he had been forced to try to sort them from his suspicions, a difficult task that had kept him awake until dawn. By noon the next day, when he awoke from a troubled sleep, he had still not decided once and for all if these revelations had cleared his brother from the murder.

If James spoke the truth, he would have had no reason to kill their father. But what if he had lied? What if the payments their father had made him had been extorted rather than given? Gideon did not question the essential facts of his birth. The evidence in his face was too strong. But there was no proof that the payments had been made out of affection. Gideon wished he had a stronger sense of intuition to help him through the fog in his mind.

Rubbing his face, he laughed ironically. His family motto had never been more inapt than it was now.

Invisibilia non decipiunt.

Things unseen do not deceive us.

How long had he believed that his family had greater powers of discernment than the rest of mankind simply because of that phrase?

He had deceived himself badly. James's heritage had been carved in flesh for all to see, and still he had not seen it. Gideon wondered how many people had guessed the truth and kept silent. He recalled the words the Reverend Mr. Bramwell had used the last time they had spoken and realized that the old man had been trying to tell him.

But he had been too obtuse. Now, he had to question his ability to discover his father's murderer. If he had failed to notice the obvious, wouldn't he be equally incapable of uncovering a darker secret?

A whimsical notion came into his mind. If Mrs. Kean had only heard James's story, she would have been able to give him her opinion of its truth. Gideon had the impression that she had a key to people that he lacked. But, of course, he would not have an opportunity to ask her. He had only his own cloudy wits, and no one else's on which to rely.

He would have to live up to the Fitzsimmons' motto. He would have to hone his wits. And he needed activity to make them sharp.

He shaved himself, using a basin Tom had brought, but when his clothes were presented and he saw how poorly washed and pressed they were, he realized that something would have to be done to make his life at the Fox and Goose more tolerable.

"I want you to engage a sufficient staff for this place," he told Tom later, as he carved his way through a breakfast of bread, meat and cheese. "I may be hunted like an animal, but I see no reason to live like one.

"Talk to Lade. Get him to hire the people he needs to make this place decent. But make sure you approve them first. We'll need servants we can trust. I want someone to look after my clothes, and perhaps a few more in the kitchen. And I want a bed with warm curtains, a dressing table and stool with a looking glass, a desk, and a chair. And I'll need pen and ink."

"You want me to ride into Maidstone?"

Gideon nodded. Then, as he tossed back the rest of his morning beer, he noted Tom's worry. "Think you can manage the lot?"

Tom's brow puckered. "I've never worked in the house. What if I buy something you don't like? Or what if somebody cheats me?"

Gideon sent him a smile full of trust. "I doubt anyone will. It's like buying a horse off a stranger. Go with your instincts. And if you want to know the kind of clothing I like, take a look at what I have. The mercers in Maidstone can help you find the artisans and tradesmen you need.

"But if you're truly worried, take Katy. If Philippe were here I would send him, but I doubt there's a man in this village who knows anything about furniture or cloth. The girl has a neat style. I noticed it last night. She must know something about fashion."

"That's no job for a girl," Tom said gruffly.

Gideon saw that he'd offended Tom. Although he had to wonder if something other than offended sensibilities could account for the crimson in his cheeks. "No, it's not. But in my experience, women have a better eye for what suits. Do as you wish," he said, coming to his feet, "just get started. I don't know if I can bear many more nights in that bed."

"What should I do with them papers you brought back last night?"

Gideon had forgotten all about the papers in his eagerness to confront James, and later in the aftermath of their talk. At the mention of them now, he felt a certain relief. He would need something to occupy him while Tom was gone, for he could not very well ride about in the day when he might be recognized.

"Bring them in here." The little parlour, with its solid oak table, would afford him a place to examine them thoroughly.

Tom left and returned in a few minutes with a thick roll of parchments. Gideon took them all together and tried spreading them open on the table. Rolled as they been, he had to weigh them down with his mug.

"Will you be needing me for anything else, sir?"

"No, Tom. You may go."

With the papers before him, Gideon was reminded of how long it had been since he'd had any news from London. His own escape would certainly have caused a stir. "Bring me whatever news-sheets you can find," he called over his shoulder to Tom.

Then he returned to the papers, which consisted of letters in a few different hands, enough to amount to a formal correspondence. Among them was a list of names. With a hasty perusal, he recognized most as being his father's friends. The letters had all been directed to Lord Hawkhurst.

Gideon tried to leaf through the sheets, but their ends had been curled irreparably by the damp in the passageway. He uncurled one corner, and a loose object fell out.

He picked it up and examined it. It was a bronze medal cast with the figure of a man in Roman armour. Gideon didn't need to read the words engraved on the other side to know who the person was, for he had visited this man himself on his trip to the Continent. His father would never have let him travel through France without paying his respects to the Pretender.

He turned the medal over and on its back read the slogan, "Cuius est." To anyone versed in Latin, the double meaning would be clear. It meant not only "Whose is it?", but also "He whose it is," referring, of course, to the Crown that should have been James Stuart's. The phrase had been taken from the Book of St. Mark, from the passage in which Jesus advised his followers to render unto Caesar the things that were his.

It was not what the medal said, for he had heard similar words before, but rather its existence that disturbed him now. The words were the same sort of sly reference seen in the Jacobite press. But the medal's presence among his father's papers suggested that the earl had been in correspondence either with the Pretender or with his agents—both of which were treasonable acts. Gideon had seen these medals at James's court. Along with portraits and miniatures, they were given to his adherents as rewards or bribes. Some would also be sent as talismen to persons afflicted with the King's Evil who could not come to his court in Lorraine. For James, like all the Stuarts before him, practiced the Royal Touch.

It was a ceremony that Gideon had never given much credence to, although it had been carried out by both French and English kings for centuries and was a sacrament in the Book of Common Prayer. The sovereign was believed by some to hold the divine gift of healing. William III, as a genuine Protestant, had said the ceremony smacked of Papacy and refused to use it. Queen Anne, a Stuart, had resumed the ancient practice.

Another use for the medals was to acquaint the Pretender's supporters in Britain with his image, for despite the genuineness of their loyalty, most had never seen him. If he were to try to return for his crown, it would be imperative for his followers to recognize him as soon as he landed, so they could rise instantly to his aid.

Gideon's father would have had neither of these last two needs. Except for a touch of gout, he had been healthy right up until his murder, and he had seen the young James. He also possessed one of his portraits.

That meant that the medal had been sent for services already rendered or promised by someone else.

Gideon had convinced himself that his father's devotion to the Stuarts was hardly more than a sentiment, that he would have been too astute to risk his life and all he possessed for a futile cause. He had so often bemoaned the lack of good leadership at James's court, and he had mistrusted Harley, Lord Oxford, and other members of the October club, a group of extreme Tories to which he had belonged. Now Gideon realized that his father had been more actively involved in the Stuart cause than he had ever imagined.

Gideon had found it disappointingly easy to resist the famous Stuart charm when he had seen the sort of toadies with whom James surrounded himself. He had felt sorry for the prince who had been wrongfully deprived of his throne, but nothing about the Pretender or his favourites had inspired Gideon to join them.

To think that his father had been willing to risk everything—his life and estates, and his son's inheritance—for such a hopeless cause rocked Gideon to his very core.

He pored over the papers, examining first their broken seals and scrawled signatures. A number of the friends who had come to his father's burial were represented here, as were others who had not appeared. In every case they had pledged their support for James Stuart if he should come.

Then he came upon a name that so startled him, an erratic pulse started beating in his throat.

Here was the Duke of Bournemouth's hand and seal on a letter promising full support should his Majesty King James III arrive in England with a company of French troops sufficiently large as to ensure his victory over the newly-crowned King George.

These, then, were the papers the Duke had been so eager to retrieve. And no wonder, for the mere inscription of the name James III would brand him as a Jacobite and traitor to King George. The letter implied that the Stuart King had made him promises of greater land and honours in exchange for his support, something his Grace of Bournemouth would not wish to be known now that he had assumed a valuable place at Court. This letter would be enough to hang him.

With his nerves on edge, Gideon read on to discover the extent of his father's treason against the Crown. It seemed that Lord Hawkhurst had taken on the duty of raising a group of supporters in the southeast of England, in case the Pretender managed to march as far as London. An invasion was planned for the west coast as soon as James could persuade Louis to commit French troops.

The men on this list had pledged their support in exchange for greater titles or the promise of an appointment at Court, either for themselves, their daughters, or their sons. Lord Hawkhurst, apparently, had done it as a matter of conscience. He had asked for nothing more than the honour of serving his true king.

Gideon held evidence in his hands that could condemn a number of men to the gallows. But only one of these had put money on both sides and ended up in a place of trust in the Hanover court.

What if the Duke had killed his father to still the one voice that had the means to expose him? Clearly, he had wanted these papers, enough to threaten Gideon. Perhaps, his threats had carried more danger than Gideon had believed.

He thought through the details. If the Duke had plotted with his father, he might have been told of the small staircase leading to his father's library. He would not have wanted to be seen entering the house of a known Tory, not when most Tories were suspect. But they might have met in secret. Gideon found it hard to believe that matters of such importance had been discussed entirely through letters. Yet, his father had seldom left home.

The Duke could have climbed the staircase, hidden while Gideon and his father were arguing, then used the cover of that fight to kill Lord Hawkhurst and throw the blame on his son.

But, in that case, the Duke would have received the cut. He had been at the ball when Gideon arrived and had not appeared to be hurt, but his cut might have been shallower than Gideon's. And even Gideon had managed to conceal his for over an hour that night. Perhaps the killer had, too.

Then who had attacked Gideon if the Duke was already at the ball?

One of his lackeys? If so, the Duke of Bournemouth would not be the first man to use his servants to attack his enemies.

But would he have sent someone else to murder another peer of the realm?

Gideon doubted he would. The risk of taking anyone so deeply into his confidence would have been too great. It would have put him at the mercy of a servant who could use his knowledge to demand money.

The more questions Gideon thought of, the more frustrated he became. How could he discover if the Duke had even had the time to kill his father? He would have to find out where Bournemouth had been before his arrival at the ball, and what time he had arrived, facts that were impossible for him to gather in his current situation.

If he could ask Mrs. Kean, she might be able to answer his second question at least, for she seemed to have an observant eye. But how was that to be accomplished when he dare not show his face at Isabella's house?

As Gideon realized what he would have to do to prove a duke guilty of murder, an overwhelming sense of defeat threatened to crush him. How would he ever get his freedom back?

How could he find the truth if he had to hide? How could he prove anything against a favourite of the king?

He had been able to force his way into James Henry's house, but he could not do that to his Grace of Bournemouth. The Duke's numerous estates would be gated and guarded. And waylaying him would be next to impossible, for he traveled with an army of servants and enough outriders to guard a royal treasure.

Gideon was too unused to having his will thwarted to take frustration calmly. He had been raised to be obeyed, to receive almost anything he desired at a mere request.

He was not stupid. He had been accounted a good student and had enjoyed his studies far more than many of his peers. But he had never had to employ the sort of shrewdness necessary for subterfuge. He'd had no need to be unscrupulous or even very smart. He had always preferred action to invention and openness to trickery.

But those were tools reserved for people who could walk in the light of day. He would have to use the opposite if he wanted to catch his father's murderer.

His sense of caution warned him that there were other men named in these papers, any one of whom might have had a motive for murder. He would have to go through them and make a list of possible suspects. Then he would have to make a plan. And he would learn to use whatever means were possible for a fugitive from the law.

※

Before Tom set out for the county town of Maidstone, he discussed his master's requirements with Mr. Lade, telling him that the woman who had done his washing would not suit. He told him to call in the best workers he could find and have them ready for his inspection when he returned. Lade grumbled about "gentry coves what don't have the wit to keep upon the sneak" and how all this commotion "would bring the harman down on his house," but in the end he seemed to understand that if he wanted to keep his flush customer, he would have to improve his service.

Tom would never have asked for Katy's help, but when Lade heard that he wanted to use the only wagon the inn possessed to drive into Maidstone, he insisted that Tom take her along. He had purchases he needed himself, and could not leave the house to go.

Tom offered to run Lade's errands. He would have offered his soul to avoid riding in a wagon with a harlot, especially one with a face to make him wish his virtue were not so strict.

He had avoided looking at her on every occasion, which had been hard in this tiny place, where it seemed she was always near to hand. It had been tough at first when she'd assumed he'd want her, for how many of Lade's other clients had not? A few harsh words and a turned head had cured her of flirting, but it had taken all his will to ignore her when he often passed her on the stairs. He could not move through the narrow stairwell without brushing her body with his.

The first time it had happened, he had smelled the ripe, womanly scent of her, which had shaken him so deeply that when she'd smiled up into his eyes and said good morning, he had almost answered back. Since then, he had made certain to hold his breath. Still, he could sense her sweetness in the air.

He would not be seduced by a trull who made her living keeping strange men's beds warm. He knew too much about the suffering that came from sin. His own father had taken the pox from whoring after Tom's mother had died. He'd gone full mad with the pain, and there had been nothing in the end Tom could do to help him but hand him the knife he'd begged for.

He had heard that Hell's worst torments were reserved for those who refused to keep themselves clean. Most men ignored that teaching, because they didn't want their pleasures curtailed, but Tom knew it for the truth. His father had not had to wait for Hell for those torments. He had suffered them on earth.

And here at the Fox and Goose, deep in the Wild of Kent, Tom would force himself to keep clean when every fiber of his being yearned for the pleasure this woman could bring.

He almost cursed when Katy emerged from the back of the inn and looked about for the wagon. She wore a plain woolen dress, but a brighter scarf had been tied around her shoulders. Its bright, cheery red made the yellow of her hair glow like the warmest sun.

She looked different this morning. Cleaner, and not as bold as she did in the taproom at night. She even seemed shy, as she pulled herself up on the box beside him and arranged her skirts so they would not touch him.

She understood that he wanted nothing to do with her, but to Tom's dismay, she was even more tempting when shy.

Angrily he turned his attention to Lade's mules, who were reluctant to leave the yard. They repeatedly refused the gate in spite of his lively cries, and a snap of the whip did nothing to persuade them. Tom was about to get down to lead them through it, when Katy bounded down from her seat.

"I can do it. I know what these beasts be wantin'," she said.

She dug into the pocket of her skirt and brought out a handful of small dried apples, which she placed in her palm before backing through the gate. The ears of the largest mule pricked up, and as Tom gave a slap to the reins, it hesitantly walked out behind her.

Once the team was through, Katy rewarded them. Then she climbed back up, as Tom scowled.

"I hope you've got a bushel of them apples so we can make it the rest of the way to Maidstone," he said as he cracked his whip by the big mule's ear. Immediately, the team put their heads down and pulled with a will.

"We won't be needin' any more. That's Lucifer. He can't abide that gate, but he won't give you any more trouble now that he's through it. He's a good mule."

"He likely puts up that fuss 'cause he knows you'll feed him. Better to let me handle him. Beasts shouldn't be spoiled." Tom had spoken harshly to end a conversation he wished he had not started, but Katy straightened her shoulders at his rebuke.

"He doesn't fuss because I spoil 'im. He's scared. And that's why I have to feed 'im. He was walkin' under that gate once when it collapsed and cut him bad on the neck. I just give him a little treat so he'll forget it. He's a good mule, and I don't like to see a creature get whipped if he don't deserve it."

Tom was startled. He did not often use the whip himself. Certainly not to force a frightened animal to overcome a fear.

But since he did not want to appear too friendly, he said, "Spare the whip, and you spoil the beast."

How many times had he frowned at those very words, yet he

was producing them to frighten away this pretty woman?

The tactic worked. Katy herumphed and folded her arms. She looked about at the passing scenery with her chin in the air. Tom did nothing to break the silence, though every time the wagon gave a lurch to the left, and Katy was flung against him, he had to grit his teeth. He couldn't hold his breath all the way into Maidstone, but her smell was like a warm summer breeze, urging him to lie down in a pasture.

They made the rest of the trip without a word passing between them, through the dense forest of the Wild, bumping over deep cart tracks. Then they moved on through great fields of hops on either side of a road, and finally orchards filled with cherry trees in full white bloom. Near noon, they rolled past the ancient College of Priests, All Saints Church, the old Archbishop's Palace with its dungeons and the stables across the road. A medieval bridge took them across the narrow river Len before the wagon climbed to the High Town. Tom paused his team before they reached the market cross.

Maidstone was a prosperous county town. It stood near the middle of Kent, at the junction of two major roads and two rivers. The Medway to his left was the stream that was used to bring London goods from Rochester down to Tonbridge and beyond. It also carried Kentish ragstone back to London for buildings, as well as paper, and hops to the brewers for beer.

The High Street, which sloped sharply down to the riverbank was full of bustling shops and imposing houses. A community of artisans in fine linen made only one of the towns many guilds. Its mayor was a justice of the peace. The courts for the County of Kent and the gaol were also here. Tom tried not to think of these last as he steered his wagon onto a quieter street and pulled it to a halt.

The shop fronts on the High Street and the sight of well dressed ladies and gentlemen entering their doors had raised a panic inside him. He gazed longingly towards the river, towards the sight of ships and the decks of wharves, where workers would be loading paper and cloth, bricks and tiles, and the stones that were quarried nearby. Today was a market day, and purchasers were herding sheep, cattle and horses back through town after haggling for them in the fields across the bridge. Their droppings muddied the streets.

He could have dealt with those things without even a blink, but to enter these shops—he was bound to make a total fool of himself.

Katy started to climb down, leaving a cold space where her body had warmed him. Tom reached for her blindly, unable to find the words to stop her.

She turned in surprise. Seeing his look of helpless terror, she sat back down.

"What is it, Mr. Barnes? Have you took sick?"

"No." He dropped her arm and worked hard to compose himself. "I just need you to tell me where to get the things my master needs."

Confusion wrinkled her perfect nose. "What have you come for?"

Stiffly, Tom related Gideon's requirements, trying not to react to the delight shining in her eyes.

"Clothes!" was all she said. And she seemed to find a reason for joy in the thought that a servant would be needed to tend them.

By the time he had finished enumerating St. Mars's list, it was too late to refuse her help. Katy told him that her father had been a draper in Tunbridge Wells. She had grown up working in his shop, and there was nothing she had loved better than handling the cloth demanded by their prosperous clients.

Tom wanted to know how she had come to her current profession, but he stopped himself before asking. It would do him no good to know more about her, not when keeping aloof already took most of his strength.

Katy insisted on accompanying him into the shops. At first she watched him negotiate for the fabrics he thought St. Mars would want, but once or twice, as he was dithering over the price a shopkeeper was pressing upon him, he felt her touch upon his sleeve. Turning, he saw her frown and give a tiny shake to her head. With her close, her fingers on his arm, he found he could not go on. He had to step back and let her finish the deal.

By the end of the day, Tom was following her around like a pack mule, loaded with bundles of cloth and fine linens, acquiescing to all her choices. He paid a stout-looking boy to guard their purchases after he loaded them into the wagon. Then, they pressed on to order furniture for his master, "Mr. Brown."

Even Tom knew that the quality of workmanship here was not up to the standards at Rotherham Abbey, but at least St. Mars's new mattress would have more feathers than the one he had spent the past few nights on. Katy was having so much fun, he had a hard time convincing her that they had bought enough for one day.

They were walking back to the wagon, when she volunteered the information he had refused to ask. He felt the brush of her fingers in his palm, and her touch sent a jolt deep into his flesh.

With a jerk, he turned.

"I wasn't always at Lade's," she said, indicating her meaning by a sadness in her voice. "My parents sent me to work in a shop at Tunbridge Wells, where all the fashionable people come to take the waters, so I could learn to help them in their shop. They wanted me to marry their apprentice.

"Then, at the Wells I met a man. He told me he was a merchant from London, but he was a thief and I got culled.

"He nimmed a cloak from my master's shop when he was supposed to take me out for a walk. They said I had stood his budge—helped him do it, you know. They called me his doxy and they nabbed me and clapped me in gaol. But I wasn't his doxy. I was just a stupid chub."

Before Tom could cut off these confidences, she went on, "Mr. Lade got out of the clink when I did. I couldn't get any work—no one would have a budge who had bobbed her master. He said he would give me a room and feed me, if I would help him serve and clean, and keep his customers happy.

"I haven't minded it too much," she said, her gaze on the ground. "It's better than being hungry or alone. But I would much rather take care of Mr. Brown's clothes, if you could see your way to helping me get the work. I promise I'll do it as well as a man would."

This was not what Tom had been expecting, and relief took him by surprise. He had expected her to offer herself to him. It was what he had feared all day. But, with this fear removed, he felt a confounding sense of shame, as if he were the one who was indecent in some way.

But taking care of St. Mars's clothes—he couldn't bring himself to believe that a woman could handle a job always reserved for a man. The very notion was disturbing. Of course, women had always done the wash, but only a man could be expected to keep finery in order. To press his linen and clean his boots.

With Katy's desperate eyes upon him, Tom tried to shake his head, but he found he could not—not without offering her the kind of comfort he mustn't give.

"I'll talk to Mr. Brown," he said. "I can't make you any promises, but I'll tell him how you helped me today and how you used to be in the trade. He has to have somebody he can trust."

The thought of her spilling St. Mars's secrets on another man's pillow caused him to accuse her with an angry look.

Her eyelids flickered with a moment of hurt, before she met his stare straight on. "I won't go snitching if that is what you mean. I kept Mr. Jack's secrets, and he didn't pay me to, that's for certain. If Mr. Brown will give me this work, I won't have to keep Mr. Lade's guests happy no more, and I can be just as quiet as you need."

The idea that simply giving her another job could keep her from other men's beds started a fire burning dangerously near his heart.

He turned abruptly away. "I haven't promised anything. Just that I'll speak to him, like I said."

They had reached the wagon, and taking his hint that their talk was over, Katy climbed upon the seat. Tom paid the boy who had watched their wagon, feeling as important as the steward at the Abbey with his new authority to buy things for his master's house. Then he remembered what sort of house it was, and he recalled he was supposed to get what news he could from London.

He told Katy to wait and went back into the High Street to try to find a chapman in the market place.

Since the imposition of a tax of a half-penny per sheet, cheap newspapers for the poor had almost vanished from the streets. Tom searched for a pedlar who might have a news-sheet disguised as a pamphlet to evade the tax, but there was none to be found. His only recourse would be a bookseller who might have received a high-priced gazette from London.

He made one last trip down the unpaved street to a bookseller's shop they had passed and purchased a copy of the only journal he could find, *The Political State of Great Britain*, by A. Boyer. Then, as he realized how far he would have to come each time St. Mars wanted the news, he tried to make arrangements for the London papers to be delivered by carrier to Mr. Brown in care of Mr. Lade. The bookseller told him, however, that he would do better to subscribe to the journals through the post.

Minutes later, as he and Katy were making their way back out of town by means of a street paved with ancient stones, Tom noticed a house, the corner post of which was covered with public notices. He paused long enough to read them and was aghast when he saw Gideon's name and description screaming back at him in bold letters from a sign that had just been posted.

Taking a quick look around, he ripped the notice from the post. Tucking it into his shirt, he grabbed up his reins and slapped the mules into a brisk walk.

"What was that for?" Katy asked, looking at him curiously as the wagon lurched onward.

"Just you mind your own business," Tom said, and he was so upset by what he had read that he managed to return to the Fox and Goose with hardly a thought of her at all.

"Boast not my fall" (he cried) "insulting foe!
Thou by some other shalt be laid as low.
Nor think, to die dejects my lofty mind:
All that I dread is leaving you behind!
Rather than so, ah let me still survive,
And burn in Cupid's flames—but burn alive."

The hungry Judges soon the sentence sign,
And wretches hang that jurymen may dine;

CHAPTER XIII

THE announcement of Isabella's and Harrowby's engagement was sent to all the Whig news-sheets and *The Daily Courant.* Harrowby reported that the members of the Kit Kat Club had toasted him on his good fortune. They had drunk to Isabella's beauty, and Hester would not have been surprised to learn than several ribald jests had been made with respect to Harrowby's luck.

Harrowby was not remiss in sending a man to measure Isabella's finger for a ring. She could hardly wait to receive it.

Mrs. Mayfield's tea dishes and table had never seen so much use, as the number of ladies who came to congratulate Isabella on her extreme good fortune swelled throughout the week. Hester knew it would be useless to remind her aunt how dear tea was when presumably all their financial worries had been solved. She was kept very busy running errands in the City to replenish their supplies, while Isabella and Harrowby paraded their affection in St. James's Park every evening.

The goldsmith sent word that Bella's ring would be ready to be picked up on Friday. Harrowby would have gone himself to make certain that it had been properly made, but he received word from the Palace of St. James that the King would be happy to receive him that afternoon. The Princess of Wales invited Mrs. Mayfield and Isabella to wait on her at the same hour. In the wake of such an honour, the ring was nearly forgotten.

What they all should wear was the uppermost concern in their minds, and no one remembered the ring until after Harrowby had come, splendidly attired, to escort his bride to her presentation. Naturally, it was Mrs. Mayfield who remembered it as they were leaving the house in a bustle.

"Oh, my ring!" Isabella cried, too. She had been so happy, she had gone through the week without once thinking of it, but now that she was reminded, her mind latched on and would not let go. "How shall we get it today? I do not think I can wait another minute for it."

"Sorry, my dear. No time to send word to one of my men," Harrowby said, nearly beside himself with nerves. This would be his first visit with his Majesty as an almost-earl. "Afraid you will have to wait. Can't be helped."

Colley handed him his hat, and Harrowby roundly chastised him for ruffling the beaver fur the wrong way.

"Oh, I do so want my ring," Isabella wailed. Even her oblivious nerves were not immune to the stress of the impending interview. "Cannot something be done? Could one of our servants go?"

"You don't want a menial fetching an important thing like a ring," Harrowby said. "Better move along now. Can't keep her Highness waiting. Or his Majesty. Wouldn't be wise."

Mrs. Mayfield had been as anxious for the ring as Isabella herself, perhaps more so, since it would be proof positive of her daughter's engagement.

"Hester could go," she said.

Waiting for them both in the open doorway, Harrowby grew so fretful that he agreed. "But you must read the posy, Mrs. Kean, and make certain that all the words are there. These goldsmiths, you know—always trying to cheat a fellow out of his money. There should be —" he counted on his fingers, reciting the words of the posy in a whisper to himself— "there should be six words. If there aren't, you may tell the fellow for me that he's a knave and the Earl of Hawkhurst will never give him his business again. I don't think he will cheat me this time—wouldn't be prudent in a business sort of way."

Hester got the name of the goldsmith and his direction in Lombard Street, as they hurried out the door.

The goldsmith's shop lay farther along Lombard Street than Hester had hoped. She had left the hackney carriage waiting for her at Wool Church Market, so she could walk its length, not knowing where she would find the shop. Even with a footman accompanying her, she felt a bit uncomfortable in this male part of the City, even though she had been to the Royal Exchange many times with her cousin and aunt.

It was somehow more pleasant to be strolling arm in arm with Isabella, when she was certain that all the gentlemen only had eyes for her cousin, than it was to be walking alone several paces in front of a footman, who would not exert himself for her comfort. She attracted more men's attention than she would ever have believed possible, and she found that she did not particularly enjoy the sensation. Some women might find it amusing to be ogled and to have every one of their features loudly discussed, but she did not. She even reflected that if beauty were not believed to be essential for attracting the one gentleman one liked, then she would give off wishing for it altogether.

She dodged the idle men of business clustered on the footpaths, who seemed reluctant to let her pass, and the frenzied stockjobbers who ran up and down, darting into the coffee-houses dotting both sides of the street. She walked past St. Mary Woolchurch and the entrance to Exchange Alley across the street, hoping soon to be greeted by the sign of the Seven Stars.

She had almost made it to the entrance of the George-yard and could see the coaches and horsemen passing in and out of it, when she spotted the sign. The shop was small and dark, with stout shutters to close it up at night.

She had no note from Harrowby to allow her to take the ring, but the goldsmith, Mr. Shales, was willing to let her take it, as long as she signed his receipt. She told him to present his bill at Hawkhurst House. Then, before he wrapped the ring up, she asked to examine it, and he showed it to her, proudly awaiting her approval.

As she had promised, she counted Harrowby's words worked into the gold. There were, indeed, six. Since the posy had presumably been written by Harrowby, she would not at all have been surprised to find that it read, "Two made one. Great good fun!" But, instead, the couplet was a standard, "Two made one. By God alone."

His words would have been unobjectionable if Hester had any reason to believe that God had had anything to do with the engagement. Mrs. Mayfield seemed to have had a larger hand in it than God.

Chastising herself for having thoughts that some might have considered blasphemous, she told Mr. Shales that the ring was lovely, glad that she did not have to read him Harrowby's lecture. She took the package he handed her and walked back into the street.

By this hour, the daylight had started to wane. Hester told the footman to follow her back to Wool Church Market, and she started off at an eager pace. If she got back to the house before the others, she could have a little time to herself.

She needed to think about her plans. She was not sure she wished to stay on with her aunt after all that had occurred. She knew she would feel guilty for benefiting from St. Mars's losses. She didn't see how she could continue to serve her aunt and Isabella and be polite to Harrowby who had so willingly seized his cousin's property. She did not have any ideas about whom else she might live with, but she felt painfully compelled to make the effort to find someone.

Lost in thought, she retraced the length of Lombard Street sooner than she realized. She looked up to see the market place just ahead. Glancing back over her shoulder to make certain the footman was still with her, she didn't watch when she stepped in front of the traffic coming from Sherbourne Lane.

A man bumped roughly into her, and she dropped her parcel. As she reached after it with a cry, afraid that a pickpocket might have jostled it from her grasp, she encountered the thick, knobby wrist of the man who had bent to retrieve it.

His wrist was quickly covered up by the fall of long lace at his cuff. Reassured by this evidence of a gentleman, she nevertheless glanced up to see whether he intended to return her property to her, and was surprised and relieved to see that the hand belonged to Mr. Letchworth.

"Oh, sir, I am most dreadfully sorry. I was not attending."

He did not immediately know her. He had never paid her much mind, not with Isabella in the room.

"I am Mrs. Mayfield's niece," she reminded him. "Hester Kean is my name. I thank you for picking up my parcel."

"Of course, Mrs. Kean. I remember you now. And how is your cousin?"

In the confusion of the moment, Hester had forgotten that he had planned to come back in one week to demand an answer from Mrs. Mayfield. He seemed to have taken Isabella's engagement very well, considering how ardent a suitor he had been.

"She and my aunt are both very well. I thank you, sir." She curtsied, then took Mr. Shales's parcel from his hand. She was glad it had been wrapped. It would have been awkward for Mr. Letchworth to know he had handled Harrowby's ring.

"You may tell your aunt that I shall be by tomorrow. We have an important matter to discuss. I told her I should be back after taking the air in Bedfordshire. She will be expecting me."

His tone as much as his words implied an ignorance of the true state of affairs. Although she could not like him, Hester felt she could not let him labour under a deception. She imagined the chagrin he would feel on speaking to her aunt on the morrow, although it was more likely that someone would break the news to him tonight. She thought she should try to soften the blow for him.

"I gather that you did not receive the London newspapers while you were gone, Mr. Letchworth, else you would have read the news concerning my cousin Isabella. She became engaged to Sir Harrowby Fitzsimmons, recently named Earl of Hawkhurst."

For a moment, she thought that he had decided to take her news in graceful part, but in the next, he grabbed her by the shoulders and gave her a desperate shake.

"That is a lie! Isabella Mayfield is mine!"

Hester tried to extricate herself from his grasp. "I assure you, sir, that I am speaking the truth. If you do not believe me, you may apply to my aunt. My only thought was to spare you the pain of a call."

Hester's footman, slow to notice anything was wrong, came up to them, and requested the gentleman to release Mrs. Kean.

Mr. Letchworth paid him no more attention than he would a pesky fly. "I will go and see her," he said. As before, when she had seen him annoyed, angry knots appeared on both sides of his neck. His face was so dry beneath his cosmetics, she wondered how he could have fooled himself that a beauty like Isabella would consider marrying him.

"Here, what is going on? Sir? Madame?" A plainly clothed man came up Sherbourne Lane behind Mr. Letchworth. "Mr. Letchworth, is that you?"

"Leave me alone, Vickers! Go back to your house and mind your own business!"

"I beg you to release me, sir," Hester said in a clear voice. The man Vickers seemed reluctant to interfere. He stopped a few paces short of them to look on uncertainly.

"You may tell *your aunt* —" Mr. Letchworth nearly spat the word— "that I will be around to see her very soon. And I shall know who to blame for this."

"Sir, won't you let the lady go?" Mr. Vickers ventured timidly.

Mr. Letchworth released her by nearly thrusting Hester from him not, she supposed, because he had been requested to, but because he had said all he intended to say. He stalked off, and only then did Mr. Vickers and Hester's footman show a proper degree of solicitude.

"Are you quite all right, madam?" Vickers asked. "Is there anything I can fetch you?"

He was staring inquisitively at her, as if wondering what she had done to provoke his acquaintance to such anger.

"I shall be all right when I have found our hackney coach and gone home."

"Why do you not send your man for it? I shall be happy to wait with you here until it comes."

Hester thanked him and asked the footman to bring the coach to her here.

"I would invite you into my house," Mr. Vickers said. "It is just here in the lane where Mr. Letchworth was so good as to seek my service. But I fear you would find yourself uneasy accepting an invitation from a stranger."

"You are very kind, sir. And quite right. I should much rather get home."

"And where might that be, Mrs. . . . ." He let his question trail expectantly.

"I am Mrs. Hester Kean, and I live in Westminster."

"Oh." His voice fell flat. "I take it you are not the young lady my friend hopes to make his wife?"

"No, she is my cousin. Although during Mr. Letchworth's absence this week, she became engaged to another. That is why he was so upset."

Mr. Vickers looked very grave. "Dear me," he said, biting his upper lip. "I am certain he must have been very disappointed."

A hackney carriage pulled up by the kerb, and Hester's footman jumped down.

"I hope you will not hold his temper against him," Mr. Vickers begged. "He has had a great deal to unsettle him of late. I would hate to see more added to his burden."

"I will try not to blame him overmuch, sir." Stifling her resentment, she disengaged herself and climbed into the carriage as hastily as she could. With her arms still hurting from Mr. Letchworth's grasp, she would not be willing to forgive him all that soon, although she still pitied him.

Apparently, he had loved Isabella far more than she had given him credit for.

℘

A hue and cry had been set up, and a reward of three hundred pounds had been posted for his capture.

When Tom delivered him the news, Gideon was constructing a plan to meet the Duke of Bournemouth. He had searched all day through the papers in Lade's parlour, and had come up with the repeated fact that the Duke of Bournemouth was the only conspirator on the list who had gone over to the Hanoverians. The other names were very familiar to Gideon, as they would be to anyone, for they included a number of the most prominent Tories in Britain.

The Duke of Ormonde, the Duke of Marlborough's great rival—an undoubted Jacobite—as well as others long suspected of leaning towards the Pretender—Bolingbroke, Strafford, Prior, and Attenbury, Bishop of Rochester. But none of these others had gone over to the Whigs. And none had threatened Gideon except the Duke of Bournemouth.

Even allowing for his own bias, Gideon could not deny that the Duke of Bournemouth was the only logical suspect on the list. The others were already under suspicion. They had retreated from Court. Murdering a fellow conspirator could only have exposed them to greater danger.

Only the Duke had much to lose.

Gideon had been thinking up a way to lure the Duke into a meeting when Tom arrived with the handbill, and the immediacy of his danger temporarily drove everything else from his mind.

His description had been spread all over the county. It could not possibly take long before someone, to whom the sum of three hundred pounds was an inconceivable fortune, would think of the stranger, Mr. Brown, who lodged at the Fox and Goose.

He became aware of Tom's anxiety and forced a grin. "Well, it's not nearly the hundred thousand placed on the Pretender's head. Still, it's not an unattractive sum. I suppose I should be flattered. Thank you for bringing me that information, Tom."

"Shall I have Lade bring you a bottle of his good French wine?"

"So I can drown my sorrows in a rousing spate of drunkenness? I will admit, the notion has appeal. But I think we had better put our heads together and figure out how much it will cost me to keep friend Lade's tongue quiet when he sees this handbill, which he undoubtedly will."

Gideon could see that Tom had not thought of the danger from Lade, which was greater than the chance that someone else would recognize the Viscount St. Mars in this out-of-the-way place.

"This notice describes the clothes I was wearing when I escaped, right down to my wig. Fortunately it was brown and was lost. I shall make do with my own hair from now on, but surely Lade will recognize the 'black mourning suit' I was wearing when I stumbled in here."

"I'm sure he's noticed the ring you're wearing. I've seen him eyeing it, as if he'd like to know how much it'd be worth if he pinched it. That's in the notice, too. You had better take it off."

Gideon looked down at the massive ring circling his finger, with its death's head wrought in finest gold. In a very short while, it had become more than an emblem of his mourning. He wore it in place of the signet that had belonged to his father, and which, by all rights, should be his. It reminded him of his father's murder and of the role he had played in it.

He toyed with the ring, turning it with his fingertips.

"No, Tom. I can't take this off. Not until I've found my father's killer."

He could see that Tom was about to launch into a protest, so he cut him off. "It will not matter at any rate. With my hair a different colour from that description and modest clothes, I will be able to deceive most people. And Lade won't need the ring to tip him off.

"Unfortunately we won't be able to prevent him from putting two and two together, though, which means we will have to buy his cooperation."

Tom herumphed. "And what's to keep him from taking your money and the reward money, too?"

The only solution that presented itself struck Gideon as distasteful, but he knew that he couldn't afford such qualms. Again, he realized how much his situation would force him to disguise his nature.

"I shall have to threaten him," he said. "I will lead him to believe that if he betrays me, my band of confederates will make certain he suffers."

"And what band of confederates would that be?"

At Tom's wry tone, Gideon laughed for the first time that day. "Why, Tom, I am sure you can fill the positions alone. Haven't you gone from being merely a groom to groom, valet, butler, and general man of business in just a pair of days? But, don't worry—I won't ask you to murder Lade. There's simply no need for him to know how friendless I am at this juncture. Let him think I've got an army of villains to support me."

A later thought came to worry him. "But what about the woman? Katy? Shall I have to frighten her, too?"

He was surprised by the look of shock on Tom's face, followed by signs of an invisible struggle.

"No, sir," Tom said, and the uneven tone of his voice suggested that the words were costing him aplenty. "I don't think she would snitch on your lordship. She'd like a job—tending your lordship's clothes. I told her it was no kind of work for a woman, but her father was a draper in Tunbridge Wells and she was used to dealing with fine folk, she said. I know it's not the usual thing, but I don't see how you would find a good man here in the Wild for the job."

"You're certain she wants it badly enough to resist that reward?"

Tom squirmed miserably. "I just don't think she's a squealer. But, yessir, she does want it very much."

"Good. Tell her she can have the post with my blessing, and ask her to make me some clothes. I'll want a couple of sober suits, of the kind a Quaker merchant might wear. And I should have some plain pairs of breeches and shirts like yours for riding out at night. I want clothes that will make me disappear."

"She'll be disappointed," Tom said, as if he drew some comfort from that. "She had her mind set on handling your lordship's silks and satins."

Gideon smiled. "Tell her I'll let her make some of those, too. I should be ready for anything. In fact—" he recalled the plans he had been working on when Tom had returned— "It looks like I'll be needing a good set of clothes very soon."

With a grimace, he returned to the unpleasant chore in front of him. He stood and began collecting the incriminating papers. "Let's have Lade in, then, and we'll see what can be done with him before we set up household here."

Gideon spent the next hour or two playing a mental game of chess with his landlord over a bottle of his fine French claret. He had alternately to woo and intimidate Lade without revealing the nature of his Achilles' heel. And in the process he learned something about his host that could come in useful should he ever step out of line.

Although Lade was a thorough scoundrel of the sort who would have no qualms in cheating his own grandmother, he seemed to have one sentiment which, though founded on nothing but superstition, would provide a basis for dealing with him in a consistent manner. He had a thorough hatred for the Hanoverian Succession, and he blamed it for most of his ills.

Like others with no sense of right and wrong, he had to have a scapegoat to blame for his faults and their resulting miseries. The Jacobite principle that, in deposing the genuine heir to the throne, the English had invited a punishment from God, had taken root in his brain, to fester in a stew of self-pity and resentment.

As soon as Gideon got wind of this, he turned it to his advantage. Lade already believed him to be an escaped Jacobite of some sort. He was willing to believe, too, that a fellow partisan of the Pretender would need to set up his base in friendly territory. And he was more than ready to accept the inducements Gideon offered.

For a stipulated sum, far in excess of its real value, Gideon engaged to rent all the private rooms of the Fox and Goose, leaving only the public taproom for Lade to run. A regular income to be paid in advance was never to be refused. And Gideon made a sufficient number of veiled references and toasts to their "love o'er the Main" to confirm Lade in his early suspicions.

He only hoped Lade's superstitions would serve when he read a copy of the handbill and realized that his fellow Jacobite Mr. Brown was none other than the Viscount St. Mars. But—should they not—Gideon had collected enough evidence from Lade to see him hanged.

The next morning, after a night of thought, Gideon handed Tom a folded sheet of paper and told him that he needed him to ride into London to put a notice in *The Daily Courant.* While there, he was to arrange for the news-sheets to be posted to him on a regular basis.

Seeing Tom's curiosity, he said, "That notice refers to a set of lost papers that have been found in the possession of a deceased gentleman in Kent. It directs their owner to inquire for a Mr. Mavors at the Catherine Wheel in Southwark in four days."

"Mavors? Who's he?"

"Mavors is a Latin form of Mars. If the Duke of Bournemouth knows his Latin—which we have to assume he does—he should come at the appointed time to meet me."

"You don't mean you're riding into London!"

"Only into Southwark. They've never seen me at the Catherine Wheel, which is why I've chosen it for the rendezvous. And don't worry, I will go disguised."

Gideon watched Tom struggle to suppress his protest and was relieved when he did. He would have to come to the same realization that they could not afford to play it safe, if they wanted to find his father's murderer and clear his name.

After Tom had left, Gideon had to fight off a sharp attack of loneliness. A hopeless voice inside him told him that what he should do was get drunk and take Lade's wench to bed. He would feel a bit better for feminine comfort, and he was unlikely to get it from the lady he'd wanted to make his wife. Try as he would, he could not keep an image of Isabella in his mind. The closest he could come was a hazy vison of a tiny waist and the ghostly sound of a teasing laugh, hardly the memories to console him when what he needed was support. Mrs. Kean's kind words, uttered in their brief encounter, had done more to calm him in his moments of desperation. He could summon *her* face, with its intelligent eyes and sympathetic smile, with no trouble at all. He wondered whether she still believed in his innocence.

Impatient with himself for letting his mind wander, he tried again to conjure Isabella's face. He had to keep her face before him. He had to hold on to his love for her, or that last argument with his father, the one that had led to his father's death, would have had no meaning. That was one possibility he could not contemplate.

He hoped by now that Mrs. Kean had convinced Isabella that the charges against him were false. If not, he must find his father's killer in time to convince her himself.

But, for the meantime, a generous dose of debauchery was the only comfort he would be allowed.

In the end, he did not call for Katy. Instead, when night came, he asked Avis to saddle his mare. He had another yearning—to see his home again. And he needed to discover if he had an ally in the Abbey.

Tom had informed him of Philippe's role in obtaining his father's pistols. Gideon wanted to thank him. He also knew that Philippe could be a valuable source of information. In his impudence, the valet had always known his master's most intimate business. It remained to see whether his loyalty could survive an even greater test, now that his master had been declared outside the law.

The night's ride home was faster than his last. He and Penny were now both familiar with the drovers' trails. As they covered them at a spanking pace, Gideon resolved to use his days to learn all the twists and turns of the roads and paths between his new home and London, too. That was what highwaymen were said to know. It was what made it easy for them to get away when other horsemen set up in pursuit. If he was to keep his gentleman-of-the-road cachet with the host of the Fox and Goose, he would do better to learn a highwayman's skills.

As he rode, Gideon welcomed the freedom of being on his own, outdoors, and away from Tom's ever-pressing worry. No matter how much he valued Tom's loyalty, Gideon both wanted and needed to feel that nothing could hold him back or weigh him down. If he was going to survive this forced concealment, he had to break loose from the *mores* that had governed his life—honesty, openness, and politeness, and all the other restrictive behaviours that had made him an acceptable inhabitant of the world that rejected him now. If he had lost one kind of freedom, he must have another to take its place.

It was this need that pushed him to spur Penny to a reckless run. He rejected Tom's caution and let her have her head. Together they whipped past trees, through narrow gaps where the bushes nearly met. He put her over dimly seen hedges and deep ditches, feeling the powerful thrust of her hind quarters and the jolts of her front hooves. With the lightest touch of his hands, and whispers of encouragement, he urged her to race to her heart's content, feeling her exuberance through his legs, and knowing the selfsame need to run. He felt the wind whipping past his face, smelled the trees and hops, and the occasional scent that said beast. Grateful to feel pain, he even welcomed the thorns that tore at his knees.

He did not rein Penny in until she stumbled. Then he soothed her into a cooling walk.

With his pulse beating a strong tattoo against her lathered neck, he heard her great bursts of air. They thundered with every beat of her gait and every gasp from his lungs.

Now he felt both exhausted and cleansed. In his wild, dangerous ride, he had felt himself transformed.

Oh thoughtless mortals! ever blind to fate,
Too soon dejected, and too soon elate.
Sudden, these honours shall be snatched away,
And cursed for ever this victorious day.

With his broad sabre next, a chief in years,
The hoary Majesty of Spades appears,
Puts forth one manly leg, to sight revealed,
The rest, his many-coloured robe concealed.

Then flashed the living lightning from her eyes,
And screams of horror rend th' affrighted skies.
Not louder shrieks to pitying heaven are cast,
When husbands, or when even lap dogs breathe their last;

Now meet that fate, incensed Belinda cried,
And drew a deadly bodkin from her side.

Sudden he viewed, in spite of all her art,
An earthly Lover lurking at her heart.
Amazed, confused, he found his power expired,
Resigned to fate, and with a sigh retired.

CHAPTER XIV

THE Abbey seemed grave, as if the house mourned the loss of
the people who had loved her. The underground passageway
felt evil and damp.

He had walked Penny until she was cool, then, hiding her inside
the crumbling ruins, he had used fistfuls of grass to rub every inch
of her hide. No need for recklessness or despair would make him
neglect her care—unless, in their wild midnight ride, they had both
found paradise.

Inside the house, he tiptoed to his suite of rooms, where he
hoped to find Philippe ensconced in the small valet's chamber near
his wardrobe. The silence of the Abbey was so complete, Gideon
wondered if the constables had given up their watch. Sir Joshua
could not expect them to forsake their trades forever to wait for his
possible return.

He reached his rooms with one of his pistols in hand. The need
to carry it was regrettable, but he could not risk being taken again.
And in any case, it was unloaded. For all Philippe's talents, telling a
loaded weapon from a harmless one was not one of them.

A ragged snoring emerged from the valet's closet. At another time, Gideon would have been amused. On rare occasions he had needed to waken Philippe from his deepest sleep, and he remembered the sound. For now, he was only grateful that his time would not be wasted.

A gentle shake, then a vigorous one, and Philippe opened his eyes.

His startled *"Mon Dieu!"* was quickly muffled by a hand pressed over his lips.

As the Frenchman froze, Gideon whispered a greeting and immediately sensed Philippe's relief.

"O Monseigneur!" As Gideon uncovered his mouth, Philippe sat up and gasped for breath. "You must not frighten Philippe so! I thought milord's killer had come to murder me, too."

"Then you believe I am innocent?"

He was glad to hear the sound of indignation in his servant's voice. "But, of course! Who should be certain of *monsieur's* innocence if it is not his valet?"

Gideon gripped Philippe on the shoulder before turning to light a candle.

Philippe leapt up to assist him, but Gideon made a motion for him to sit, so he returned to the bed and perched himself on the edge. If he was uncomfortable sitting in his master's presence, in typical Philippe fashion, he did not show it.

He asked, "How did *monsieur* get into the house without being seen?"

Unwilling to share the secret of the passageway with too many people, Gideon temporized, "I know a way. And no one saw me, so I assume we are safe to speak."

He asked Philippe, "Is James Henry staying in the house?"

"No, *Monsieur* Henry has traveled to London to see *monsieur's* bankers. He should be back . . . after the others come."

The tenor in his voice made Gideon react sharply. "What others?"

Philippe was visibly disturbed. "I thought *monsieur* might have seen it in the newspapers. I thought that was why you have come. . . . His voice failed. Then, in a mood of resignation, he said, "A messenger came tonight. We are to prepare the house for visitors.

Monsieur's cousin, Sir 'Arrowby, will arrive the day after tomorrow with a party—two ladies and their servant."

"Ladies? What can Harrowby be about?"

He felt a sudden dread at the regret in Philippe's eyes.

"It is said that he brings his fiancée. The note said that we are to expect Madame Mayfield and her daughter."

Gideon felt a kick in his chest. "No—the messenger was mistaken. Or he lied! Isabella would never marry Harrowby."

"*Monsieur*, there is more. It pains Philippe to tell you, but your *villain parlement*—the House of Lords—has taken *monsieur*'s inheritance away. The papers say that *monsieur* has been accused of treason, but without a trial, you cannot be attainted. Still, it has taken your father's rights and given them all to Sir Harrowby."

Throughout his valet's agonized speech, Gideon listened as if in a nightmare. The Lords could not have stripped him of his rights. He could not be so ruthlessly deprived of what was his.

He had always known Harrowby for his heir, but he had never believed that his cousin would succeed him. Certainly never that he would supplant him.

Harrowby was the older cousin. Gideon had planned to marry and father children who would come between Harrowby and the title.

Now, even this reasonable illusion had burst—and in the unthinkable scenario that Harrowby had inherited while he was still alive.

Unwilling to voice his pain, he could do nothing but go.

As he turned blindly, he felt Philippe's gentle grasp urging him down onto the bed. He sank his face in his hands and tried to rub away the shock.

The Duke of Bournemouth's warning resounded in ears. It was true—*he had few friends at Court*. He had only to wonder how much the Duke himself had had to do with these events. If he feared exposure of his own treason, how better to win his own security than to accuse the one man who might have the means to expose him.

"Did you read the accounts yourself? Did no one try to defend me?"

"*Monsieur*, it is said that none of your father's friends dare to have courage, for they are all under suspicion. They retire to their estates in the hope that they will not be accused themselves."

There would be no one. With none but Whigs in the government, he would have no one to appeal to. His only hope would be to prove beyond a doubt that someone else had killed his father.

Even then, if the motive had anything to do with the Jacobite conspiracy and his father's involvement was uncovered, he would still lose his estates. The laws of attainder punished the families of traitors, taking away all they possessed. Those penalties had been renewed under Queen Anne in view of the Pretender's threat.

How much better a solution had been devised by the Lords. By denying him his summons, they had removed a Tory peer and replaced him with a Whig. Harrowby had always preferred membership in the Kit Kat Club to conformity with his uncle's opinions. Since he had never stood for parliament or shown a talent for statesmanship, Gideon's father had dismissed him as a fool and had not been overly concerned with his politics. Like Gideon, Lord Hawkhurst had never imagined being replaced by the likes of Sir Harrowby Fitzsimmons.

Gideon was now forced to wonder if Harrowby had planned this all along. Could he and his father have been deceived by Harrowby's imbecilic air? They had both thought him harmless, but— What if *they* had been the fools?

Harrowby had made off with his fortune and, if Philippe were to be believed, was about to make off with Gideon's woman.

A surging rage brought him abruptly to his feet. Philippe, who had been hovering miserably, took a hasty step backwards and anxiously searched his face.

"When did you say they were coming?" Gideon asked.

"They should arrive the day after tomorrow. They will break their journey two times since they are traveling in Monseigneur's coach."

That would give him plenty of time to plan an interception.

Isabella would be made to understand what a terrible mistake she was about to make.

But how had she been persuaded to marry Harrowby?

Gideon had no trouble convincing himself that Mrs. Mayfield was behind her rapid decision. If the Duke had not proposed, she would be eager to secure an earl for Isabella, and Harrowby had always been there in the background, no threat to Gideon's happiness until he had come into possession of the title.

"*Monsieur* . . ." Philippe sounded unusually tentative, which made Gideon believe he was sincere. "Is there something Philippe can do to help?"

"Yes, I would like you to stay on, if possible. I expect that my cousin will wish you to serve him as valet. He has never been happy with the man he engaged. And I know how much he admires your talent.

"My only question, then, will be whether you can continue to serve me, when it will be my cousin who pays your wages?"

He was relieved to see the haughtiness return to his servant's features. "*Monsieur le comte*, my wages shall come from the money that is rightfully *Monseigneur's, n'est-ce pas?* And when *Monseigneur* is restored to the place he should occupy by right, then Philippe will be his valet once again."

"And not a moment too soon for me, I assure you." Gideon smiled, for once entirely willing to pander to the little man's vanity. "You can see that I am much in need of your valuable attention."

"I did not like to say it, but *monsieur* is correct, *évidemment*." This was offered with the most Gallic of shrugs, which almost made Gideon laugh, until the weight of his losses tamped his amusement.

"I will stay in touch. Though it may be some time before you hear from me again. If you have any messages for me, you may send them to Mr. Brown at the Fox and Goose in Pigden."

A measure of caution came over Philippe's face. "I do not suppose that *Monseigneur* will be requiring Philippe's services at a place that sounds like that?"

"No. Never fear. You can serve me better by keeping me informed of anything important that goes on inside this house. But I shall soon receive the news-sheets, so confine your messages to essential news only. I would not want Sir Joshua to notice a sudden burst of exchanges between the Abbey and my current lodgings. Is that understood?"

Philippe assured him that it was, and Gideon started to leave. Then he remembered that he had also come to obtain some of his clothes. They moved into his dressing chamber.

As Philippe made up a bundle of shirts and riding clothes, Gideon thought about his plan to waylay his father's carriage. "I shall need something to disguise myself—some garments unlikely to be recognized as mine."

Philippe halted his packing and turned to look through the smaller items in a drawer of Gideon's commode. He withdrew a black loo-mask. "If *monsieur* wishes not to be recognized, he should ride masked, and may I suggest his *tricorne*, pulled low in front, *comme ça?*" As Philippe talked, he moved Gideon in front of the mirror, fastened the mask, and placed the cocked hat at the angle he believed it should go.

Gideon saw that with his hair tied at the nape of his neck and these accoutrements, he presented a very different appearance from his normal look. "That will do," he said. "Now pack my greatcoat, and that will suffice."

Philippe shook his head. "*Non, monsieur.* Not the greatcoat. *Monsieur* is forgetting how many times Sir 'Arrowby has complimented him on the greatcoat. It must be something that he has never seen."

He turned, and Gideon waited for him to emerge from another pilgrimage to the wardrobe, but when he saw the item in Philippe's hands, he gave a restrained sigh.

"You will not be content until I have worn that damned blue cloak, will you, Philippe? I am of a mind to wear it once, just so you will stop pestering me about it."

"But *monsieur* will see—" he rushed to drape it across Gideon's shoulders— "even with those intolerable garments under it, how elegant an appearance it makes. And if *monsieur* has formed the intention of stealing Mademoiselle Mayfield from his cousin, he must think of how the lady will feel. He cannot lead her to think that she has been abducted by a common ruffian."

Gideon could no longer be astonished by anything Philippe said. Still, he had to be amazed at his servant's ability to fathom his most intimate thoughts.

He refused to be drawn into a discussion about them, however.

Exasperated, he turned back to the mirror, and was surprisingly pleased by what he saw. The blue satin reflected even the smallest amount of light from the candle he had lit. It glimmered with a midnight eeriness that seemed appropriate for his plans. With the mask and hat, he looked sinister enough to feel sure he would not be recognized.

"If this won't frighten the very stuffing out of Harrowby's escort, I do not know what will. You seem to have found the answer, Philippe."

"But, of course, I have, *Monseigneur*. Philippe is *un homme de talent*. That is understood."

ﬆ

Tom rode back from London at a breakneck pace, having learned the news of Gideon's dispossession from the papers.

Gideon told him of his plan. "I may not be able to save my inheritance, but I'll be damned if I'll let Harrowby take everything away from me without a fight."

"You mean to call him out?"

The question drew a wry smile. "No—for that would be murder for certain, and I cannot afford to have another charge like that laid at my door. What I mean to do is waylay him long enough for a chance to speak to Mrs. Isabella Mayfield."

Tom stayed silent, for no matter how risky this errand would be, he would not try to stop St. Mars from securing what he wanted.

ﬆ

Hester Kean was the only person in Harrowby's boisterous

carriage who seemed to be aware of the injustice that was taking them down to Rotherham Abbey.

The scheme had been decided within a day of her encounter with Mr. Letchworth. For, as he had promised, he had stormed into their house and in the most unpleasant language imaginable given Mrs. Mayfield to understand that he would not be trifled with in such an unscrupulous way. He had then gone directly to call on Harrowby, but fortunately, that gentleman had still been at the palace.

That evening, after hearing about Mr. Letchworth's call, Harrowby formed the fear that the man intended to force a duel upon him, and nothing Isabella could say would convince him otherwise.

It had not taken Mrs. Mayfield long to see an opportunity in her future son-in-law's terror, especially when she lived in fear herself that something might happen to snatch Isabella's prize away. She had learned enough of Harrowby to know that he lacked resolution. It was not inconceivable that, even after presenting Isabella to the Court as his fiancée, he would find a way to get out of the marriage if he wanted to. And if Mr. Letchworth, or anyone else, threatened him, he might find that sufficient reason to rethink a decision which had, in some respect, been forced upon him.

The timing of their engagement, when Harrowby was supposed to be in mourning for his uncle, had always been inconvenient. But now, the threat of violence had given her just what she needed to persuade him to a secret wedding. Clandestine ceremonies were very fashionable. Whether because a great many young people married against their family's wishes, which was often the case, or whether they simply hoped to avoid the traditional expenses of a public wedding, secret marriages were all the mode.

And nothing appealed to Harrowby so much as being *à la mode*.

It had not taken Hester's aunt long to persuade him that a quick trip to his country house would remove him from Mr. Letchworth's anger and provide him with a chance to surprise the Court. A few indelicate references had also been made to the pleasures attending him on his wedding night without the interruption of an endless stream of visitors, who would expect expensive ribands for favours, and the riotous bedding by the bride men and bride maids, to be repeated early the next morning, complete with the drums and fiddles whom he would have to pay.

Harrowby listened to all her arguments, and as Hester might have foreseen, gave in.

So, although he might rather have remained in London to be fêted and to enjoy the attention of the gossips at Court for at least another week, he resolved on a secret ceremony. The journey to Hawkhurst would be made in the interest of discretion and his personal safety. Mrs. Mayfield had always longed to see Lord Hawkhurst's country seat, and Isabella was as eager to visit her future home.

The next morning, before Mr. Letchworth could call again, Harrowby went to obtain a license. Word was circulated that the Mayfields had gone to visit relatives in the North. Sir Harrowby was to be imagined retiring quietly into the country in view of his mourning for his uncle. And only Hester seemed to care about the grand hypocrisy of that particular lie.

Their first night had been spent in Sevenoaks, after Mrs. Mayfield had worked on Harrowby all day. The initial plan had been for the wedding to take place as soon as they arrived at Rotherham Abbey. The Abbey had a chapel. The former Lord Hawkhurst's chaplain could read the vows.

But once inside the coach, Mrs. Mayfield had thought of objections to this plan. What if the King became displeased when he learned that a nonjuring priest had performed the new earl's wedding? Would he not expect one of his most faithful subjects to uphold the principles he had sworn to protect?

Another clergyman would certainly be wanted, and that being the case, wouldn't it make sense to look for one in Sevenoaks?

After a day of sitting next to Isabella in the carriage, with her body pressed intimately to his side, and her hands caressing him skillfully whenever the occasion offered, Harrowby had been no match for his mother-in-law's logic. The prospect of bedding Isabella even one day sooner had been enough to tip the scales.

So, they had been married in the parlour at the inn in Sevenoaks by a minister the innkeeper had fetched. Harrowby had tipped the curate a Guinea and his clerk a Crown, and within twenty minutes, they had all been drinking healths to the happy couple.

Isabella was now a countess. Her mother was ecstatic. And for two days, Hester had been subjected to the carryings-on of the lovers who, since the wedding last night, had made no effort to spare her blushes.

Harrowby had repeatedly allowed that it had been "great, good fun" to sleep with his wife, and Isabella had also been gratified by their activities, if her adoring looks and surreptitious movements were anything to go by. Hester was well prepared to believe that the marriage act was enjoyable. Every person she knew with any experience of it had said this was so, and during her short sojourn in London, she had been faced with enough examples of indiscretion to be convinced that coupling was practiced more often just for the pleasure of it than for its more religious purpose. But that did not mean that she wanted to watch Isabella and Harrowby pawing each other all day.

After two days on the road, she was looking forward to being anywhere other than in this carriage or with this company. And it was not only the lovers who tired her.

Mrs. Mayfield was never a stimulating companion, but in her house she might be avoided for hours on end. She was happy now, but already she had begun prodding poor Harrowby to get her way. Hester wondered how long it would be before she had complete control of him and all of St. Mars's fortune.

Two complete days and one entire night with this lot had stretched Hester's toleration to its limits.

Her aunt had insisted she come to wait on Isabella. She also wanted to hear her opinion on the economy of Lord Hawkhurst's household before taking it over. And she most certainly wished to give as forward an impression of her own menage to the Abbey servants as she could, which bringing a waiting woman would accomplish. For Mrs. Mayfield had made it clear that they would both make their home with the new couple.

Feeling her neck grow stiff from resting her head against the cushions, Hester sat up to look outside at the passing scenery. They had left Sevenoaks that morning, with the intention of reaching Cranbrook tonight. This second leg had been much rougher than the first, since they had left the turnpiked portion of the road at Woodgate where it turned off for Tunbridge Wells. From that point on, the surface of the highway had been so poor that they had lurched over ruts as deep as their wheels, and a rain earlier in the day had made the clay so slippery, that if not for the skills of Lord Hawkhurst's coachman and the excellence of his vehicle, they would surely have turned over in a ditch.

The rain had mercifully stopped near noon, but it had delayed them by an hour or more. Isabella, on whom the motion of the carriage had begun to wear, had begged her new husband to let them put up for the night in a village nearer than Cranbrook. She had cajoled him with the promise of their conjugal bed, seeming to look forward to a resumption of the previous night's activities even more than Harrowby did.

But on this he had shown a degree of firmness Hester had never witnessed in him before, since he was absolutely convinced that there was no inn between the Wells and the George in Cranbrook that could provide him with the level of comfort he required.

The length of the journey began to wear on them all. Even Isabella and Harrowby could not keep up a lewd banter forever, not when they had enjoyed so little sleep.

Quiet eventually fell. Isabella and her mother settled their heads to rest, and Harrowby dropped his jaw in a doze. Hester used this first peaceful silence to peer through the marvelous glass on Lord Hawkhurst's coach to gaze on the rolling hills and thickening woods of the Kentish countryside.

The woods had grown denser with every mile, and she understood herself now to be in the Weald, or the Wild of Kent. Having come from a county in which a tree was scarcely to be seen, she had been astonished by the number of ancient oaks, elms, and beeches and the wooded acres that seemed to cover leagues. The trees stood so tightly compressed in places that her eyes could not penetrate beyond the first few feet. Their branches, most still leafless from the winter, often met overhead. When this happened, daylight nearly vanished, due to the number and thickness of the limbs. Although by now Hester had accustomed herself to the eerie changes in light, she realized that its present dearth was due more to the lateness of the hour. Night was fast coming on. If Cranbrook lay more than a few miles farther, they would not reach the inn before dark.

The carriage gave a sudden plunge into a particularly deep rut, throwing them all off balance. It was all the four could do to keep from falling on top of one another. Before they could recapture their seats, a brisk shout, followed closely by a pistol shot, startled them from outside.

As they gripped their benches, hoping for the reassuring sound of their coachman's voice, they heard a blast from the blunderbuss. It rocked the carriage, before two more pistol pops assaulted their ears. Isabella shrieked and grabbed for Harrowby's hand. A deep voice ordered, "Hands up!" And something clattered as it hit the ground.

"Good lord!" Turning pale, Harrowby looked about the coach as if searching for a place to hide. "*Banditti*, by gad!"

The carriage had rolled to a stop. The silence from their servants was ominous. Then the door flew open, they gasped, and a polite man's voice said, "Ladies, may I beg you to step down?"

Something in the voice caused a tingle in Hester's spine—more than just her surprise at being addressed with such politeness by a highway robber.

But she could not see him because the door was hinged on her side. Isabella could, and something about him made her shrink back against the cushions, calling on Harrowby to protect her.

Hester had never been stopped by a highwayman before, though their numbers were alarming in the heaths and the woods about London. Each time a merchant or a person of consequence was held up, there was a flurry of debate. Demands for a real police force, a hue and cry, and indignant reports from the people who had been robbed died down only to be repeated at the next occurrence.

Hester felt a shove in the small of her back. "You go first!" Mrs. Mayfield hissed from beside her.

As the one nearest the door, Hester had no hesitation in going first. Her curiosity was nearly as great as her fear. So she gathered her skirts and stooped to pass through the door.

She felt a shock when a man gently took her arm to help her down. She glanced up and saw a masked face, the point of a dark cocked hat, and a pair of startling blue eyes. She could not be certain in the evening light, but they appeared to be friendly.

Her heart gave an unreasoning skip. She felt she had seen those eyes before.

As the man released her to help her aunt step down, she turned to examine him from the rear. He wore the most elegant cloak she had ever seen, with three huge shoulder capes, in a remarkable blue tint.

"Madame . . ." He handed her aunt away from the door, then reached in for Isabella.

"Better step back!" a gruff voice from the right shouted at Hester and her aunt.

With a start, they turned to see a second man mounted on a horse in front of their coach. The coachman, guard, and postilions had all climbed down to stand with their hands in the air. This man had them covered with one pistol. The other was trained their way.

"Scoundrels!" Mrs. Mayfield yelled like a fishwife. "You shall both be hanged for this!"

The more courteous of the two begged her not to be afraid. He spoke tensely, as if he waited for something important. "You will not be harmed, but you must do what we ask."

Harrowby had begun to descend, and, as his head emerged from the coach, he made a shaky attempt at joviality. "Never travel with money, y'know. I've heard stories about you chaps. You may take what little there is and be off. It won't do to frighten the ladies, y' know."

This diverted the highwayman. "In that case, you will not object if I check your pockets myself."

The man on the horse loudly cleared his throat. Hester was surprised to see a disapproving frown on his lips. She quickly returned her gaze in time to see the man in blue roughly turning out Harrowby's pockets.

"Hey, there! Impudent fellow! You will be called to account for this!"

"Undoubtedly, but the temptation is much too great. What have we here? A gold watch and a signet ring? These will do very nicely, along with your purse. And you must have forgotten these guineas in your waistcoat pocket, for I'm certain you wouldn't have lied to me, when if I were angered, I just might shoot you."

"No! That is—yes, yes! Take the guineas and begone! But you should leave me the signet ring—it was just bequeathed to me."

Their robber went still. In a moment he spoke, in a voice that chilled her. "But I have conceived quite a fancy for this ring. I am very certain you would not wish to refuse it to me. Would you?"

"No—take the blasted thing! And I hope they hang you for it! I had heard that you chaps comported yourselves in a gentleman-like manner, but I can see that it was all a hum! Just let me go!"

"Not so fast." With a bow full of irony, the highwayman took a few steps backwards. Then he purposefully turned towards Isabella, and his mocking smile softened until Hester could see both yearning and passion on his lips. She felt a powerful jolt as she recognized St. Mars.

She couldn't tell if Isabella knew him or not, but as he moved towards her, the girl let out a terrified shriek. "Harrowby, help!"

Her terror startled St. Mars. He halted, then started towards her again, with his arms outstretched. Hester heard him whisper, "Isabella, do not be afraid."

Hester doubted she heard him before shrieking louder and backing away. He halted again, stunned. Then, as his mouth turned fierce, he grabbed her by the shoulders, as if he would shake her to death.

Isabella fainted in his arms, and her mother screamed.

Hester started forward to help, but a shout from the other man stopped her. Bleeding inwardly at the grief on St. Mars's lips, she called gently to him, "Please, sir. It will be of no use. She has given— she has nothing left to give you."

Then she added, in a voice she hoped that only he could hear, "They are already married."

She hoped he realized that she knew him, and that he must no longer hope for Isabella's love. Isabella had made her choice, no matter how foolish it was. He would not be able to shake her into loving him.

Still holding onto her cousin, he gazed quickly up at Hester. The moon had risen, breaking over the trees to cast a soft glow of light. He must have seen the plea on her face, for he gave a sudden hard nod—a gesture that hovered half way between fury and heartache—before scooping Isabella up and in two quick strides, replacing her in the carriage.

Mrs. Mayfield, who had been too shocked for speech, uttered a hysterical cry.

Harrowby had started an ineffectual protest the moment the robber had touched his wife. Now he said on a gasp of relief, "Oh, I say!"

Abruptly turning his back on those two, St. Mars strode by Hester without even a glance her way. She felt the punishment of having been the one to tell him. The weight of his disappointment pressed a dull pain inside her breast.

They watched him climb quickly into the saddle of a waiting horse and signal to his friend. The other man turned in their direction, his pistols lowered. Hester ached, fearing she would never see St. Mars again.

Then, before anyone could budge, St. Mars spurred his horse in her direction, swooped down, and grabbed her by the waist. She felt the air being knocked out of her lungs, her feet leaving the ground, a turn in mid-air, and the connection with his pommel as she was swept up and into his arms . In a wink she had flown to the back of a horse and was galloping away.

Love in these labyrinths his slaves detains,
And mighty hearts are held in slender chains.

Say why are Beauties praised and honoured most,
The wise man's passion, and the vain man's toast?
Why decked with all that land and sea afford,
Why Angels called, and Angel-like adored?
Why round our coaches crowd the white-gloved Beaux,
Why bows the side-box from its inmost rows;
How vain are all these glories, all our pains,
Unless good sense preserve what beauty gains:
That men may say, when we the front-box grace,
'Behold the first in virtue as in face!'

CHAPTER XV

IT had all happened so fast that Hester had barely had time to register the shock on her companions' faces.

With the breath knocked out of her, she gasped for air and felt St. Mars's strength holding her on his horse, as the trees flew past them and the wind whipped her hair into her face.

They had not gone far before he slowed to a more rocking gait, and she could begin to feel the thrill of resting within his arms. He had one crossed in front of her breast. His other moved against her back as he directed the reins. To keep from falling, she had to lean into his chest. Not daring to peer up, she remembered the look he had given as he had ridden towards her.

For one instant—and one instant only—she feared what his grim determination might mean.

Before too long—in fact, in much too short a time to suit Hester—they emerged into a clearing, where St. Mars paused. He spun his horse around once, as if to check the area, before bringing it to a halt. Then he jumped to the ground and reached up to swing her down.

"Sir?"

Hester had forgotten the other rider until she heard his horse crackling through the brush behind her.

"Take Penny and walk her. I would like to speak to Mrs. Kean."

He *had* understood. Her shoulders, which had grown taut, relaxed.

"Is this a good idea, sir?" The servant lingered.

"Whether it is or not doesn't concern me right now. Please leave us alone."

"Yessir."

The man, who was clearly his servant, took St. Mars's reins and led both horses away. As their hoofbeats faded behind some trees, St. Mars ripped off his mask and hat, tossed them down, and started to pace. She could just make out his features, lit by a three-quarter moon.

The shadowy clearing was small. He could only take a few steps before being forced to retrace them. He paced them again and again, never looking up or uttering a word.

Even the open air seemed too confined for him. Like Mrs. Mayfield's parlour, it was simply too constricted to contain his energy. But at least the walls of this room were trees, its ceiling the sky, and its plaster branches of leaves. He belonged out of doors in a way he had never seemed to inside.

Through the dark, Hester made out the black ribbon that confined his hair at the nape of his neck. Having never seen him without a brown wig, she was struck by how handsome he was with his own fair hair worn in such a casual fashion. He seemed unaware of his magnificent cloak as it swirled about his limbs at every turn.

"She did not know me," he said in a tormented voice. "She should at least have known me."

He did not speak again for what seemed like a long while. Then suddenly he glanced up and around, as if searching for something he had forgotten.

"I'm very sorry," he said. He averted his gaze, as if only now regretting his impulsive behaviour. "I have no chair to offer you but that fallen tree over there."

Hester looked in the direction he indicated and spied a large trunk on the ground. She thanked him and walked the few steps to settle herself on it. In truth, the past thirty minutes had been so exciting, she was relieved not to have to stand.

Her calm reaction to his invitation seemed to soothe him. But she had no sooner sat than St. Mars resumed his pacing.

After a few more minutes of silence, Hester offered, "You have my sympathy, my lord. I can only imagine the disappointments and shock you have suffered in the past several days."

He gave a mirthless laugh as he glanced up in the dark. "Disappointments and shock—you put that quite accurately, Mrs. Kean. Tell me—how long has *your* cousin preferred *mine* for a husband? Did her love for him begin the instant he gained my fortune, or am I to believe that his manners were always more engaging than mine?"

Hester had prepared herself for the question, but his bitterness still had the power to make her wince. "As strange as it may seem, my lord, Isabella has always evidenced a certain preference for Sir Harrowby."

He halted as if she had slapped him. Then, after a moment's pause, he spoke in a humbler tone. "I hope you will pardon me, Mrs. Kean. I seem to have expressed myself in an abominably conceited way. I did not mean to suggest that anyone should prefer me to my cousin."

"Please believe me, sir, when I say that I meant no rebuke. It is impossible for me to comprehend how she *can* have formed a preference for a man as silly and witless as your cousin, but she has."

She was relieved to hear his chuckle. "Thank you, Mrs. Kean, for that balm to my vanity. I am glad to find that your innate good taste is as sound as ever." As he stood before her, his smile faded and his gaze sought the ground.

She tried to help. "Knowing how much you—loved Isabella, it has pained me to see her affections directed elsewhere. But she does care for Sir Harrowby, my lord. I cannot say that she might not have come to love someone else, but my aunt gave her no time or opportunity to choose."

His tone grew hard. "This is her doing, then?"

Hester nodded, no longer caring if her aunt's character were exposed to him in all its ugliness. "She has been determined to make Isabella a splendid match. When the Duke of Bournemouth became engaged to another, and you disappeared, she threatened to marry Isabella to Mr. Letchworth if she did not catch your cousin. And the only thing that made Sir Harrowby acceptable in my aunt's eyes—for, as you know, she had always discouraged him before— was his increase in fortune."

"The Duke of Bournemouth did not offer for her?" he asked sharply.

"No, an announcement was made that the king has arranged a marriage for him—to the daughter of a German prince."

Hester did not understand why this news seemed to excite him. She started to ask him, when he said, "And she would have married her to Letchworth. Ye gods, it doesn't bear thinking about!"

"She was encouraging him to feel hope until your cousin proposed. I am afraid he took the news very badly, which is one of the reasons they were married secretly last night in Sevenoaks."

"Poor man." He spoke absentmindedly. After a few moments, he glanced over at her and said, "I beg your pardon, Mrs. Kean. My mind was wondering."

"You must not think of it," she said, painfully aware that it was the thought of Isabella that had distracted him. "What is it that bothers you about his Grace, my lord?"

He shook his head dismissively. Then, seeming to think better of her interest, he stood for a moment, irresolute, before abruptly sitting beside her on the fallen tree.

With his elbows on his knees, he wearily raked his head. "I have been trying to discover who killed my father. And I have reason to believe that his Grace of Bournemouth might have done it."

Hester's stomach gave an uncomfortable leap. "What reason would that be, my lord?"

His hesitation reminded her that she had no right to ask. She was about to withdraw her question, when he answered, "This is something I have told to no one. Not even to Tom, my servant, even though he has sacrificed his security for me."

He turned towards her and in an earnest voice said, "It is not a comfortable secret, Mrs. Kean. You may wish I had not told it to you, yet I'll admit that I have more than once wished for your advice."

He leaned closer. "Will you hear it, and will you promise never to repeat a word? I know this is much to ask, but you have been my friend before, and I have never been more in need of one than now."

Hester was stunned that he had thought of her at all. A warmth spread from the bottom of her heart to the tips of her limbs. She answered without the slightest hesitation, "I would be honoured to assist you, my lord."

Even in the dark, she could sense his relief, which was all the reward she asked. Then she listened in fascination, as he told her of the peculiar request the Duke had made at his father's funeral, of the papers he had found implicating him and others in a Jacobite plot, and of his certainty that the Duke was the only man on his father's list who had changed his allegiance to King George.

"Oh, dear." She felt a flutter of fear in her veins. "I can see why you suspect him, my lord. What may I do to help you prove it or disprove it?"

His startled laugh took her by surprise. "My dear Mrs. Kean, I believed—no, I *knew* you would not disappoint me, but your willingness to help is a greater blessing than I would have dared to hope for."

Warmth suffused her from the pleasure in his voice.

He continued, "I have wanted to ask you if you remember what time the Duke arrived at Lord Eppington's ball."

She pondered. She could certainly remember when her aunt had noted his arrival. Mrs. Mayfield had always made sure of the presence of Isabella's suitors.

"He came later than we did, and we arrived at ten o'clock because Isabella had promised a dance to someone at that hour." Hester instantly regretted reminding him of Isabella. She was grateful for the darkness that concealed his reaction, though his body did seem to shift. "I cannot say for certain, but he must have come near eleven o'clock."

He turned away as if to think. "That was before I was attacked in the street. And the attack was designed to throw the blame on me. Whoever killed my father overheard our quarrel and waited until I was gone before entering the library to murder him. The argument must have given him the idea of making me his scapegoat, but he had to make it look as if I was the person who had been wounded by my father's sword."

He mused a few moments. "If his Grace did it, he would have had to ride to London in time to dress for the ball. But he could have sent a footman or another servant to attack me."

"When would he have left the Abbey?" Hester asked.

"Half an hour or so after I did. My father kept country hours, and I spoke to him before breakfast. I came to town after dark, but I would have arrived at the ball much earlier if Philippe, my valet, had worked faster or if I had not been attacked."

"Is his Grace capable at his age of making that ride in one day?"

She could tell that her question was one he had asked himself.

"He could have when younger, certainly. He fought in the war with Marlborough, which would have meant long days in the saddle. And he must have a dozen horses, at least, that could handle a journey at top speed. He never misses a meet at Newmarket."

"But, what about now? Would he be able to ride that distance and still appear at a ball in the evening?"

"I don't know. I suspect he could, but whether he could conceal his fatigue and a wound to his arm—that is what I cannot decide. How did he seem to you that night?"

Hester began apologetically, "I was not looking at him with that sort of question in mind, so I cannot be sure, but I do not think there was anything extraordinary in his appearance or his manner. The only thing I noticed was that he only stood up for one dance with Isabella, which, at the time, made me believe he had lost interest in her."

"It might have been because he was fatigued."

She agreed reluctantly, then added, "I know my aunt feared it was due to a loss of interest because she began to grow desperate at that point."

She wanted to be as honest with him as he had been with her. "Her eagerness to see Isabella well married had as much to do with her troubles, you see, as it did with ambition. She has large gambling debts that must be paid."

St. Mars gave her a sideways glance, before shaking his head ruefully. With a touch of wry humor, he said, "I thought there was nothing more you could tell me to depress me, Mrs. Kean. But now it appears that not only has Harrowby made off with my title, but I must also watch my fortune be wasted on Mrs. Mayfield's gambling debts. At least that is one aspect of the business I will not have to envy him."

Hester admired his ability to laugh even in these disheartening circumstances. She wished she could reach out and stroke his hair.

Unwilling to let this feeling run away with her, she referred to something else that had been on her mind. "Has it never occurred to you, my lord, that Sir Harrowby has benefited more than anyone else from your misfortune?"

"You are asking if he could be the murderer?"

"Yes, that is what I must wonder, although I know it sounds preposterous."

A sudden shaft of moonlight illuminated his face and she saw a quick grin, soon tinged with grief. She wondered if he had thought of his father . . . or Isabella.

"I admit, I have a hard time envisioning Harrowby as a villain. He has never been a good horseman, and you've seen how long it takes a carriage to make the journey here."

"If his ambition were as large as the stakes, would he never be able to ride a horse?"

Her suggestion sobered him. "You are right. I should think of it that way." He pondered again, then said, "I know how you can discover it for me if you will, Mrs. Kean. My valet, Philippe, is still loyal to me, and if I know anything about Harrowby, I know that he has coveted my valet. Not enough to do murder to get him, perhaps, but he will quickly overcome any scruples he has in employing my servants for himself. He will most assuredly employ Philippe."

"You wish me to ask him if Sir Harrowby has a wound on his shoulder?"

"Yes—on his left side—although Philippe will remember. He was the one who tended me throughout my illness."

"Could your cousin have employed someone else?"

He gave his head a shake. "It is more inconceivable to think of Harrowby's dealing with a cutthroat, than it is to imagine him as an assassin. He would not have the courage.

"No," he continued with a sigh, "the only reason I can even entertain the notion of Harrowby as my father's murderer is the cowardly way in which it was done."

He told her how his father had been stabbed, describing the bruise from the oddly-shaped hilt on Lord Hawkhurst's back.

"I still cannot understand how my father turned his back on a man carrying a sword. It *must* have been someone he trusted."

She could feel every hurt and every bitter thought that stoked his grief.

"Is there no one from the Abbey who might have done it?"

In his long hesitation, she read another source of pain. She could do nothing but wait.

In the end he told her of his discovery that James Henry, his father's most trusted servant, was a half-brother he had never known he had. He described their midnight confrontation and James Henry's suspicions of him.

Hester knew that it pained him to talk of this brother who hated him, but she felt she must ask, "Are you certain that he told you the truth, my lord? If I understand you, you have no one's word that he is your father's son but his."

"When you see him, you will wonder that his face didn't tell me long ago. But I was gone for three years, you see, and it was during my absence that he gained such an important position in my father's household. When I came back, I was so eager to assume my own place that I had very little time to think of anyone else. My father had tried to arrange for my election to Parliament, but in those three years, Kent had gone entirely to the Whigs. His bitter disappointment when I lost—and my own wish for society, I confess—kept me in London most of the time. I was dimly aware of James Henry's dislike for me, but I seldom saw him."

"Do you have any suspicion that he might have killed your father? I thought he was the one who reported your quarrel to Sir Joshua."

"Yes, he was. Although *if*, as he said, he had an affection for our father, I can see how he might have believed me guilty, particularly with his hatred for me.

"He might have done it," St. Mars went on, "but I find it hard to see what he would have gained. My father was making him an attractive allowance, which he has now lost. If he did commit murder, it was for a reason other than money."

"When you confronted him, did you see if he had been wounded?"

"No. I'm afraid that the shock of discovering a brother, on top of everything else, drove every useful thought from my mind."

Hester could imagine the swarm of emotions he must have felt on making this discovery. Chagrin would have been the very least of them. Not knowing what to say, she tried to think of a way to help him determine James Henry's innocence or guilt, but before she could, he asked her, "I would be very grateful if you would tell me your impressions of James Henry after you have met him. He will certainly wait upon my cousin, and you might find an occasion to engage him in conversation. I—I had a feeling about him. But with such animosity between us, I cannot trust my own feelings. Your opinion may be helpful in settling my own."

"I will do my best, my lord. But where can I reach you?"

"Send a message to Mr. Brown at the Fox and Goose in Pigden. And be sure to include whatever Philippe has to say about Harrowby."

"Will there be a difficulty in posting it?"

"It would be better if no one saw the address. If you go into Hawkhurst, you can give it to the postmaster yourself. If not, tell one of our pages, Clem, to take it in for you. He is a bright boy, but he cannot read. As long as no one else sees your letter, he will not question it.

"But no," he said, suddenly changing his mind. "I had rather get your answers sooner than that. And you might find it hard to send a servant on an errand when you are new to the household."

He turned towards her. "Would you be willing to meet me? In a week's time?"

"Yes, but how—and where?" She felt her heart speeding up just at the thought.

"When you get to the Abbey, you will notice the ruins just below the house. No one goes there. The servants believe they are haunted."

"Dear me!"

He grinned. "I hope you do not believe in ghosts, Mrs. Kean?"

"No, I don't, however, I daresay there is something vastly unpleasant about them if no one visits them at all."

"I'm rather fond of them myself. Will you meet me there or not?"

"Of course I will meet you, my lord. You have only to say when and tell me how to go about escaping from the house of an evening, for I assume you do not mean to meet me in a haunted place during the day. I would be bound to miss the ghost, and you could be caught."

"I shall be there among the ruins one week from tonight. That should give you time to get an answer to one of my questions at least. Do not concern yourself with the hour. I will arrive near dark and can hide until you come, whenever that might be."

"I may be able to leave the others when they are at cards. Since I have no money to wager, I am often excluded from their games. I doubt that anyone will miss me."

"There's a good girl." He told her which door would be closest to the ruins and from which her departure would less likely be noticed by the servants. "Although if anyone asks you, you can say you have always had a romantic turn of mind and adore a ruin."

"I *have* always had a romantic turn of mind, and I *do* adore a ruin," she said. "Thank you for reminding me of it, my lord. Now, if only your servants will believe that when they see me hard at my stitches and my household chores."

She had made a joke of it, because she did not want him to know how near the truth he had been. How could she think of meeting him in an ancient ruin in the dark without thinking of fantastic things that would never be?

He laughed, fortunately. As they had been speaking, Hester had got the feeling that his spirits had partially recovered, so she was not surprised when, on hearing Tom's return with their horses, he sprang up with all his former vigour.

"I shall leave that for you to contrive, Mrs. Kean, for I must get you back to Harrowby. I won't ask if you can think of a plausible story to explain your abduction, for I'm certain you will. But the less time you have to explain away, the better."

Hester fought a feeling of nervousness. She could think of some very uncomfortable questions which might be asked. "I will come up with something, my lord."

"Good girl."

A polite gesture invited her to accompany him to his horse. Along the way, he stooped to recover his mask and hat.

"I hope you will be more comfortable riding postilion this time, Mrs. Kean. Tom, will you help us up?"

His servant, a square, broad-chested man, came over to give him a leg up. He waited for St. Mars's lively horse to settle down before turning to Hester.

"Give me your right hand and rest your left on Tom's shoulder," St. Mars ordered.

She obeyed, as Tom said, "Pardon me, madam," and bent in front of her with his hands clasped. In a second he had tossed her up on the rump of St. Mars's horse.

"Put your arms about my waist," he quickly warned her, as he soothed his sidling mare. "Penny isn't used to carrying two, I'm afraid."

Hester overcame her timidity at the horse's first buck. She grabbed hold of St. Mars's waist for dear life. "Is that her name? She is very pretty, my lord."

"You see, Penny," he said, bending over slightly to pat his horse's neck. "I told you Mrs. Kean was a lady of uncommon good taste."

Hester felt an irrepressible bubble escaping in her laugh, which had very little to do with his remark, and everything to do with riding behind him on a cold spring night. She clasped her arms about his body and felt the strength of his back and the smoothness of his satin cloak against her cheek. The chill in the wind made her huddle close, and remarkably, she felt no shame or uneasiness. No reluctance—just a glorious thrill.

She did not ask him where he was taking her. For the time being she could pretend he was taking her away from her aunt's house and the dreariness of her future, as the trees sped past them and the moon lit their way.

At this, the blood the virgin's cheek forsook,
A livid paleness spreads o'er all her look;
She sees, and trembles at th' approaching ill,
Just in the jaws of ruin, and Codille.

(Sir Plume of amber snuffbox justly vain,
And the nice conduct of a clouded cane)
With earnest eyes, and round unthinking face,
He first the snuffbox opened, then the case,
And thus broke out—"My Lord, why, what the devil?
Z-ds! damn the lock! 'fore Gad, you must be civil!
Plague on 't! 'tis past a jest—nay prithee, pox!
Give her the hair"—he spoke, and rapped his box.

Now move to war her sable Matadores,
In show like leaders of the swarthy Moors.
Spadillio first, unconquerable Lord!
Led off two captive trumps, and swept the board.
As many more Manillio forced to yield,
And marched a victor from the verdant field.
Him Basto followed, but his fate more hard
Gained but one trump and one Plebeian card.

CHAPTER XVI

HE carried her all the way into Cranbrook, approaching it by a drovers' trail through the woods, then skirting the main road to cut in behind the church. They dismounted in the shadow of the building, leaving Tom with the horses. St. Mars had doffed his cloak, but Hester could not help fearing his capture as he walked her through the cemetery to the gatehouse, which stood within sight of the George Inn.

From the shelter of its walls, they peered out at an extraordinary bustle at the door to the inn. Men had crowded around it, and they all seemed to be discussing something disturbing. After a moment, a boy was seen to push his way through the crowd to run up the street.

The Hawkhurst coach was nowhere in sight, but it could already be in the yard.

"From the look of things, I would say that my cousin has called for a hue and cry after the rogues who robbed him. I'm afraid I will have to part with you here."

"Oh yes, please, do go! I shall be quite all right."

"And you will meet me?"

"Yes, of course. Please, hurry!"

But St. Mars would not leave until he had thanked her, and he insisted on watching her walk safely into the George. He took her hand and raised it to his lips. Then he held on to it, as he expressed his gratitude in a flow of humble words.

She was unable to find the right thing to say at such a moment. Fearing for his safety, but also afraid to give away more of her own emotions than would be prudent, she merely returned the pressure of his hand, before moving out into the street.

The George stood on a corner, with entrances in both streets. Since the men had grouped themselves around the door to the taproom, Hester made her way around the building to the other side. They were so engaged in their business that not one of them noticed a lady walking across from the church.

No matter how thrilling her ride had been, she still had found the discipline to make up a lie about her abduction. She was only nervous that her capacity to act might fail her when she needed it.

As she stepped into the corridor, she heard voices grumbling about a "blue devil" and a "blue Satan," and her heart skipped a beat when she recognized Sir Harrowby's plaintive tone amongst them.

"I insist on speaking to a magistrate. I tell you, a lady in my party has been taken. We must raise a posse to hunt down the scoundrel who took my guineas and my ring!"

If Hester had not been so flustered at the prospect of her own theatricals, she would have had a hard time not to laugh. Fortunately, her trembling was such as to lend her voice credence when she stumbled towards the inside taproom door, crying, "Help! Oh, help!"

A roomful of faces turned to stare at her in open-mouthed astonishment. She paused just outside the room and leaned dramatically against the door jamb.

"Oh, Sir Harrowby!" she said, doing her best to convey great relief.

"Gadzooks! Mrs. Kean!" For a moment, she couldn't be certain whether he was happy to see her or not. Then she recollected that the posse he'd wished for would unlikely be called out just for a few guineas and a ring.

Mrs. Mayfield chimed in, "Hester! How did you come here? And who was that man?"

Feeling suddenly queasy, Hester saw questions forming in their eyes, and with more presence of mind than she knew she possessed, she fainted right in front of them.

It had not precisely been a genuine faint, so she was uncomfortably aware of the bruises she caught on her way to the floor. The men of Cranbrook were not in the habit of catching fainting ladies, she discovered, but at least her apparent unconsciousness bought her sympathy and some time.

She prolonged her swoon as long as she could, hoping St. Mars would have more time to get away. But she "came to" when the people who had called for hartshorn and brandy began discussing the possibility of a chase.

Harrowby had taken it upon himself to administer the hartshorn to her. She shouldn't have been surprised that he carried a bottle of it in his valise, but she was unhappily made aware of it when he waved it under her nose.

It would have been impossible to hold out any longer, so she sat up woozily after giving her first jerk to evade the fumes.

"My dear Mrs. Kean!" Harrowby shouted in her face as if she were deaf. "What can you tell us about the rogue? The one in that marvelous blue cloak?"

She frowned, shaking her head as if to clear it. "I can tell you nothing about him, sir. He dropped me somewhere on the road, and after ascertaining that I carried no money on me, he left me to make my way here."

"Do you mean you have walked these last three miles?"

"No, a farmer—or a shepherd—I'm not sure which—picked me up in his cart and set me down near the church. I should have asked his name so that you could thank him, but I was so frightened—I forgot to."

Sir Harrowby dismissed this omission with an impatient frown. "But what about my watch and my ring?"

Hester looked affronted, and was rewarded by the indignation she saw on other faces. "I was hardly in a position to demand them back, sir," she reminded him.

As he became aware of their listeners' sympathetic grumbles, he testily said, "Well, of course, dear lady. I did not mean that you was to get them back, but I would give a pretty pair of guineas to have that ring.

"I don't know why my coachman refused to chase the scoundrels, but he shall answer for it, and so I assured him."

Hester had wondered if anyone had tried to pursue them. Now, with a start, she wondered if Lord Hawkhurst's coachman had recognized St. Mars.

"Did the villain hurt you, ma'am?" A polite man she took for the innkeeper inquired. "If he did, then it is your duty to report it."

"No." She did not have to fake a rush of colour at his pointed question. "He did nothing except to take me from my friends and leave me to make my way alone."

"That is all very well," Harrowby inserted in an injured voice, "but he must be had up immediately for highway robbery. I cannot believe that a magistrate will not consider this assault on a peer on his Majesty's highway a very grave offence."

The citizens of Cranbrook could not disagree. As Hester looked around, she saw many prosperous tradesmen among them. They would be just as worried about a new highwayman in their area as an aristocrat would—perhaps more, since they would not have the escort a travelling nobleman would have.

As they discussed what was to be done, and Sir Harrowby was assured by the innkeeper that a boy had been sent to fetch "Sir Harold," Hester excused herself and begged the aid of a maid to help her upstairs. The dishevelment of her hair—and the relative neatness of her clothes, she hoped—had convinced her audience that her story was true. She must not act so overturned that they began to suspect a ravishment as well as an abduction.

She was uncomfortably aware of Mrs. Mayfield who climbed the stairs behind her and followed her into a room where Isabella lay in bed, her hair already covered with a cap. She must have been tucked in as soon as they had reached the inn.

"Hester!" she exclaimed, starting up. "I was so afraid!"

And with that she began to cry with such a violent sobbing that Hester took her in her arms and mumbled soothing words, until Mrs. Mayfield lost all patience with her daughter. "Now that will be quite enough, Isabella. You can see that nothing has happened to any of us, and aside from a few guineas and a ring that Lord Hawkhurst can very well spare, now that he has come into his inheritance, no harm was done."

"Your mother is right, Bella. There is nothing to cry about. I am perfectly well, you see?"

Isabella pushed away from her to blow her nose. "But did you see how that man came after me? Almost as if he knew me?"

Hester felt a sudden uneasiness, which increased when Mrs. Mayfield asked, "Why should you think he knew you? Did you recognize him?" She gazed sharply at her daughter.

Isabella shook her head. She must have been too focused on her own shrieks to have heard St. Mars use her name. If not, she should have known—not that it was St. Mars, perhaps, but that their highwayman was an acquaintance.

"Did *you* know who he was, Hester?" Her aunt gave her a fearful glance, as if she suspected St. Mars.

"No." Hester shook her head and tried to look surprised. "How should we know a highwayman?"

Her open stare made Mrs. Mayfield look away. She would not want to encourage anyone to think that St. Mars was still around. Better for him to have fled to France as the government believed.

"There are have been stories that some of them come from noble families—younger sons, who would rather rob innocent people than take up an honest trade."

Hester shook her head again seriously. "I cannot think of anyone we know like that."

Isabella seemed comforted by her assurances, and Mrs. Mayfield evidently preferred to believe her, too, for she stopped posing questions. She told Isabella to get some sleep so that she could look beautiful on the morrow. Recalling what delights awaited them then, she put the robbery behind her. With a great deal of cheer, she bustled about Isabella, tucking her in again, and calling her "my lady" and "countess" until Isabella went to sleep with a smile on her face.

Hester took advantage of the moment to go unobtrusively to bed. She had not been offered any supper, but she reckoned that a small price to pay for returning from a false abduction with so few questions to address. Conscious of the friendship that had been forged between herself and St. Mars tonight, she, too, fell asleep with a smile.

ß

Rotherham Abbey was a sight to strike awe even into Mrs. Mayfield, whose raptures on seeing it were restrained by pure amazement.

It was a noble place, a proud place, and not even the wear of a hundred years could rob it of its impressive facade. Although it might not conform to the current taste for pediments and columns, its size alone was enough to satisfy even Mrs. Mayfield's wish for grandeur.

They were ushered in past an army of servants, most in the Hawkhurst livery of bronze and gold. Hester caught the names of a few of the upper staff, as they made their bows to their new lord and his lady. James Henry was not among them, but she overheard the steward informing Harrowby that Mr. Henry would be happy to wait upon him at his convenience as soon as he returned from his lordship's business in London.

Lord Hawkhurst's private chaplain, the Reverend Mr. Bramwell, greeted them inside. He congratulated Harrowby and Isabella on their marriage and assured them of his eagerness to serve them in all things spiritual. Harrowby dismissed him as soon as he could, and the old man retreated to his private sanctuary.

The first order of business after receiving the good wishes of the staff was the selection of rooms. Since Isabella came as a bride, Robert Shaw, the steward, had wondered if the new Lord Hawkhurst and his lady might not prefer to see the house before choosing their suites. He assured them, however, that all the likely rooms had been made ready for their comfort so that they might choose any chamber they liked.

Mrs. Mayfield and the lovers were delighted at the prospect of viewing their new domain. Hester followed them as Robert showed them over the first floor. Harrowby seemed averse to taking the chamber that had been occupied so recently by his uncle's corpse, but he had no qualms at all in choosing the king's chamber with its adjoining withdrawing room and inner chamber for his wardrobe. For in this day and age, as he pointed out, it could not be presumed that his Majesty would visit any country house but his own.

As soon as he determined on that one, Isabella was keen to see the queen's suite. She was, at first, deterred by its distance from her husband's rooms. They decided to share a bedchamber this week, but in the future, they should each have a suite of their own.

Keeping separate bedrooms was very fashionable. It was the French style, so naturally not to be debated. Hester wondered that a couple who seemed so besotted with each other would give up a perfectly good English notion of conjugal happiness on the strength of a fashion. Their decision would have made sense if they had married purely for property, as so many did, but they had seemed in love.

Isabella settled on the queen's bedchamber, and she and Harrowby immediately began discussing how their rooms should be changed. That left the queen's great chamber for Mrs. Mayfield, and Hester could see how her aunt relished the thought of having a room that had been used by a queen.

On their way back to the great stone staircase, Mrs. Mayfield peered behind every door until she finally stopped at a very small chamber, which had nevertheless been fitted with a bed.

"This will do very well for you, Hester. It has everything you can possibly want, and the advantage of lying between mine and Isabella's so you can be of easy use to us both. And it is not so large or so pleasant that we shall wish to use it for guests."

Hester, who never ceased to be amazed by the thoughtlessness of her aunt, thanked her with no demur. She had grown to be amused by the tactless remarks and, in fact, regarded them as one of the minor compensations for the dreariness of her life.

Taking a moment to examine the room, while the others moved on, she found that it did indeed meet all her requirements. She was grateful to have been placed on the first floor and not up under the roof where the servants lived. The room had a window which looked out over the ruins with their crumbling walls and high pointed arches. She had spotted them eagerly from the drive, thinking of her rendezvous with St. Mars. Seen through the large, clear panes, they offered a good place to hide from anyone gazing from the house, since the earth had made an effort to reclaim them, stretching arms about them in the form of trees, uneven ground, and clinging vines.

It would be a good place to meet someone secretly.

Fighting off a foolish romantic thrill, Hester turned to examine the other features of her room. It was not without character, for in spite of its small size, a great deal of trouble had been taken in the execution of the carving that adorned the panels on the wall across from the bed. The wood had been worked into representations of fruited vines. A skilled artisan had been employed in the work—surprising for such an insignificant space.

Hester caught up with the others as they climbed the stairs to the second floor and then went out onto the leads. Isabella was charmed by the roof's summer houses and she projected the supper parties they would give up there.

As the tour moved on, Mrs. Mayfield overcame her uncharacteristic delicacy to suggest several improvements they could make to the house. Hester was glad that her own room was so modest that she would not have to feel even more ashamed for profiting from St. Mars's plight.

Her aunt began referring to everything she saw as old or outdated. The amazing thing was how quickly Harrowby agreed with her, and how eagerly he entered into the notion of changing the furniture in favour of something more in style. Hester wondered that he could so easily shrug off any sense of guilt for usurping his cousin's place, and she became more determined than ever to discover whether he was the murderer.

She could not speak immediately to St. Mars's valet. The house was so enormous that she was unlikely ever to run across him. But, with the advantage of being little more than a superior servant herself, she did not doubt her ability to come up with a solution.

§

Two days later, after her aunt and cousin had settled into their country routine, Hester roused herself for an early breakfast, in the hope of having a few moments alone with Robert Shaw. She found him with the butler and two footmen setting up the table in the downstairs parlour where breakfast had been served on the previous mornings.

Having adjusted himself to the later hours kept by his new master and mistress, he was distressed not to be ready to serve her yet. Hester took advantage of his chagrin to explain to him the nature of her position in her aunt's household. She had been prepared to meet with a diminution in his courtesy, accustomed to such treatment from Colley, but she was pleased when Robert still accorded her the respect due a lady.

She told him that her aunt had asked her to inquire about the details of the Abbey management, since it would fall to her to act as messenger between the senior staff and their mistress on many occasions. She explained that her cousin, being young, had not yet learned to assume the responsibility of a large house.

She found that Robert was a man who took most things at face value. She doubted if he had ever formed an opinion for himself. Certainly he gave no sign of questioning either Harrowby's right to assume his uncle's place or the qualifications of his bride.

His only aim seemed to be helpful to his master, no matter who that might be. It was a pleasant quality in a servant, but Hester cautioned herself that St. Mars was unlikely to discover an ally here.

Deftly, she inquired about the number of servants, their names and each of their roles. When Robert mentioned his late master's valet, who had retired on a pension granted in Lord Hawkhurst's will, she knew she was getting close.

"If he has retired, who will assist my lord with his clothes?"

"His lordship has already made use of Lord St. Mars's valet, and he says the man will suit. He is a Frenchy," Robert pointed out with distaste, "but they are said to be handy with fashion and whatnot. Lord Hawkhurst did not bring his own man down, because he turned him off, expecting to keep Philippe. Philippe's the Frenchy," he added unnecessarily.

"Yes, well—" Hester grew instantly brisk. She did not want to hear about the other servants now that she had the information she had come to get— "if I might have a simple breakfast, I would like to start interviewing a few of the servants to get a better notion of their duties."

She gave him a list with a few of the names he had supplied her with, starting with the cook and finishing with Philippe. If Robert thought there was anything peculiar in her asking to speak to his lordship's valet, he gave no sign. Truly the time to make these inquiries was while the household staff was having to accustom itself to the new master's ways.

Breezing as quickly as she could through the other servants, Hester found that Rotherham Abbey was as well run as she could imagine a house of this size to be. References to Robert Shaw and James Henry told her that most of this efficiency could be attributed to them. She found also that not everyone was as sanguine about the change of ownership as Robert was. Although, as a member of the invading party, she was not to be trusted with their confidences, she found that more than half she talked to expressed a veiled bitterness or grief. Her heart went out to them, and she wished she could tell them that her present activity was nothing more than a ruse to help their real master regain his place.

It was not to be expected that Philippe would have a moment to speak to her when Harrowby required his services to dress. When Harrowby descended, however, after two blissful hours over his toilette, Robert arranged for Philippe to see her in one of the back parlours.

She had not figured out how to conduct this interview when she did not know how readily Philippe would accept her as an ally. But she found a quick way into his heart when she instantly switched their conversation into French.

Hester had learned French from a Huguenot who had married into a Yorkshire family. Without the money for formal instruction, she had known that without at least a spattering of French, she would always be regarded as inferior. So she had traded English lessons for French, and much to her surprise and her teacher's delight, had turned out to have an aptitude for the language.

As the only French servant on a staff of more than forty, Philippe was willing to overlook her few errors for the chance to speak a civilized tongue. He politely denied that she made any mistakes, but corrected them nonetheless.

"I have not spoken my language since my master went away," he sighed.

"You were attached to my Lord St. Mars?"

A reserve settled over him. She was afraid she had cost herself the progress she had made.

"I was 'appy to serve 'im, *bien sûr*," Philippe said, with a shrug, "but I shall be just as 'appy to serve my Lord 'Arrowby."

Hester stifled a smile, wishing that she could plead an ignorance of the proper forms of address and refer to the new earl as "my Lord 'Arrowby." While the name might elevate him in birth, at least it would not usurp St. Mars's right to his title.

"Well, he is certainly pleased with you," she said. "He praised your talent at the dinner table yesterday."

She was surprised to receive another shrug. She had thought that a conceited man like Philippe would be flattered to hear such a report.

But all he said was, "It is to be expected, *mademoiselle*," putting her in her place, and proving that it was confidence and not conceit that she had discerned.

"Still . . . . "She let the word linger in the air before saying, "One has to wonder if Sir Harrowby *can* fill a position that was destined for a gentleman like my Lord St. Mars."

"You knew my master?" Philippe seemed more alert.

"Yes, I did . . . and I know someone very much like him now. A Mr. Brown, who lives retired." She did not know where she had got the inspiration to use St. Mars's alias, but it proved to be the magic key.

"Ah," he said, regarding her eagerly. "Myself, I know this Mr. Brown. You have spoken with him recently?"

"Quite recently. We encountered him on the road, although my companions did not know him. He was wearing a marvelous blue cloak."

At this piece of news, Philippe sat up with delight and clapped his hands together. "So! *Monsieur* has finally worn his magnificent new cloak! Did it not enhance the blueness of his eyes?"

"Yes, it did, most magnificently." Hester could hardly restrain her smile.

He shook his head sadly, though, as he leaned to speak in a whisper. "I tried to convince him that he should wear it to milord Eppington's ball. Then, perhaps Madame Isabelle would 'ave married 'im instead of Lord 'Arrowby. But he would not listen to Philippe, and now the cloak will be wasted."

"Oh, no," Hester assured him. She could not share his regret about that, but she could say, "You must not think that. You should have seen how beautifully the satin shone in the moonlight. Sir Harrowby was so struck by it that he cannot stop referring to it."

This appeased him slightly, so she made haste to move on. Cautioning him never to mention the cloak to anyone else, she told him of the information his master sought. "When you were assisting Sir Harrowby this morning, did you notice whether he had sustained an injury recently?"

"*Non*. But *mademoiselle* must realize that Lord 'Arrowby does not have the physique that draws the eye. I put all my attention this morning into arranging his lordship's clothes, but I will examine his arm tonight and tell *mademoiselle* what Philippe finds."

Hester thanked him and assured him that she would get the message to his master. They named a rendezvous for that evening before the others retired to their rooms.

ø

That night found Gideon sitting at a table in a dark corner

of the taproom at the Catherine Wheel in Southwark. Seated on a wing-backed bench near the chimney-piece, with his back to the wall, he could easily make out the features of anyone stepping through the door.

At ten o'clock, most of the tables were filled in the low, smoky room. The men who conducted their business in the taproom during the day had given way to others who came to meet their friends and carouse. The general hum, broken occasionally by the raucous roar of male laughter would be excellent cover for his confrontation with the Duke. The busy motion of the drawers as they filled and delivered mug after mug, and of the wenches who flirted with the customers, would provide enough distraction to keep the Duke from spotting Gideon, if he decided not to be seen.

The innkeeper, sitting on a stool behind the counter, arguing with an acquaintance, had been told at a signal to direct the man who asked for a Mr. Mavors to his bench. Tom was stationed outside to see how many men the Duke brought with him. It would be his job to warn Gideon if the Duke's servants moved to enter the inn. He could be reasonably certain that his Grace would not call in the law as long as Gideon had his father's compromising papers, but he might choose to overpower him with a few of his men.

Neither one was likely to be recognized here, unless the Duke drew attention with his dress. Gideon had clothed himself like the tradesmen who frequented the place, and he had instructed Tom to cover his face. It was unlikely that the Duke or his men would know Tom, but in the event of trouble, it would be best if they could not describe him.

Having arrived much earlier in the evening, Gideon was growing impatient for the Duke's arrival. He hated to think that his Grace might not have recognized the significance of his notice. If this plan failed, he did not see how he could speak to the Duke without placing himself in too much jeopardy.

He was working on an alternate plan, when he heard the hoofbeats of a group of horses outside. Then a minor bustle at the entryway alerted him that someone was about to come in.

Gideon shielded his face, while keeping a sharp eye on the door,

and was soon rewarded by the appearance of the Duke of
Bournemouth. He had disguised himself in a suit of unfashionable
clothes.

The innkeeper would not be entirely fooled by an outdated suit,
which could only be a legacy to a trusted servant. Not when its
wearer was accompanied by a large retinue, as this one had been.
But he was unlikely to discover the exact identity of either of his
two distinguished visitors.

As the Duke approached this worthy, Gideon gave the man a
nod, so he pointed to the corner where Mr. Mavors was to be found.
Gideon kept the brim of his hat pulled low to hide his profile until
his Grace moved directly in front of him.

He raised his eyes and met with an astonishment he had not
expected to see, before it was quickly concealed behind a satirical
mask.

"Mr. Mavors," his Grace said, declining to bow. "I believed you
to be sojourning in France. I had expected an emissary, perhaps. I
had not thought you so foolish as to come."

"In what way foolish, your Grace?"

As Gideon had expected, his use of the Duke's title raised a
scowl on his face. He glanced quickly round to make sure that no
one had heard it, then fixed his eyes on Gideon again.

"Why, quite simply—" with an effort at insouciance he tried to
regain the upper hand— "that a rather large price has been placed
upon your head. Just one word from me, and the rabble in this
room would start fighting over the right to take you in."

"But if they did, I should have to tell them about your signature
on a very interesting piece of paper."

Bournemouth flushed in fury. "If you tried it, one of my men
would shoot you before you could open your mouth."

"And one of mine would see to it that a very damaging letter
came into the hands of the Lord Chancellor."

"You wouldn't dare! Your own property would be forfeit!"

Gideon raised a brow. "But would I not be dead? I was under
the impression that your servant had already dispatched me with a
bullet. And, in that case, I have to tell you that Harrowby's

inheritance is unlikely to be my concern."

His amused answer had a strange effect upon the Duke. He first seemed enraged. Then, as if a small sense of humbled arrogance seemed to infuse him, he collected himself and gave Gideon a measuring look.

Gideon decided that it was time to stop playing games. "Will you not be seated? It seems we have some matters to discuss."

The Duke still hesitated. He checked behind him again, before taking a seat on the bench across from Gideon.

"How much do you want for those papers?" he asked, as if the deal were understood.

"They are not for sale and never will be."

Bournemouth tightened his jaw. "Then why did you bring me here?"

For the first time since the Duke had entered the room, Gideon leaned forward. "I brought you here to get answers to my questions."

The Duke was not stupid enough to ask what Gideon would do if he refused to answer. The stakes had already been named on both sides.

"Did you kill my father?"

As the Duke started violently from his bench, his right hand reaching for his sword, Gideon said through gritted teeth, "Not so hasty, your Grace! I have a cocked pistol pointed directly at your stomach. You would never survive the wound."

Half-way to his feet, the Duke froze, then dropped back onto his bench, his face crimson with rage.

"How dare you try to pin your crime on me!" he said.

Gideon stared at his enraged expression and felt his first doubt. How he wished with all his soul that the truth could be read in a man's features!

"I did not kill my father," he said, "nor have I ever committed a treasonable act. I read *your* hand in the charges brought against me."

The Duke's eyelids flickered, and Gideon knew that he had, indeed, had something to do with them.

But the charges against him were unimportant. "You have not

answered me. Did you murder my father?"

The Duke's impatient scoff surprised him. "What possible reason could I have had?"

"He knew that you had flirted with the Pretender's cause. You are the only man on his list who turned coat and profited by doing so."

A defensive twitch appeared in the corner of the Duke's mouth. "I am not ashamed of being the only one sensible enough to embrace the realities."

"Especially when that reality conveys such advantage to yourself. Did I not hear recently that King George has arranged a splendid match for you?"

Unruffled, the Duke inclined his head.

"That match would never have been possible if my father had taken his knowledge of your treachery to the King."

Now it was his Grace's turn to lean forward, and he spoke with conviction. "He never would have given the King that information because he could not have done it without implicating himself and his friends."

He let the words settle in, before continuing in a dogged voice, "I did not kill Hawkhurst, because as long as he was alive, I did not have to fear that those papers would fall into the wrong hands. It was only after his death that I began to fear that someone—you perhaps—would use them against me. Your father was a true believer in the Stuart succession. He never would have jeopardized the Pretender's cause or his supporters."

He went on, "You say that you did not kill him. And I have to suppose you speak the truth, or you would never have arranged this meeting.

"But neither did I kill him. I had no motive. In fact, it was in my interest for your father to stay alive."

Gideon had intently watched his face throughout this monologue, and he had seen no signs of prevarication. No blinks. No averted gazes. And, in the end, it was he who first lowered his eyes.

"Please pass me your sword," he said.

Surprised, but betraying no uneasiness, the Duke removed his sword from its sheath and offered it to him sideways on his upturned palms.

Gideon reached for the hilt and examined it. It had an ornate basket design with the Duke's arms wrought into the steel and covered in silver. A peculiar curl in the metal tip satisfied him that this was not the sword that had been used to murder his father.

He handed it back without a word.

After the Duke had replaced it, and a few moments of silence had passed, he asked, "What is your intention with respect to those papers?"

"I shall keep them for a while. Eventually they must be burned."

"Why keep them at all?" Clearly, he had been astonished by Gideon's honesty.

"I have to keep them, until I find the man who killed my father. Until then, I cannot be certain that they have no significance."

In a more thoughtful tone than he would have expected, the Duke said, "The same reasoning is likely to apply to those other names as to me. Even more so, since his Majesty already suspects them. You will find nothing among them to help you, St. Mars."

Gideon shook his head. "I shall have to keep them. Once I have found my father's murderer, I promise to destroy them. I do not wish for my father to be labeled a traitor."

He could feel the Duke's lack of satisfaction with his decision, but also his acceptance that he could do nothing to change his mind. His Grace made ready to go, but before he stood, he said, "I should be grateful—and mind, my gratitude may count for something in future—if you will notify me when those papers are destroyed. It would greatly add to the peace of my sleep."

Gideon gave a nod, upon which his Grace rose to go. "I would offer to send you word if any information comes to me that could assist you; however, I do not know where to forward it."

"I will be receiving *The Daily Courant*. An advertisement would reach me."

The Duke inclined his head, and Gideon stood to repeat the courtesy. His visitor had turned to go, when he bethought himself of something else and turned back.

"You have undoubtedly by now seen the announcement of your cousin's engagement to Mrs. Isabella Mayfield. If it is of any consolation, I will tell you of my certainty that she will take a lover before the first six months of her marriage are out."

Gideon felt a tightening in his stomach. He made no response, however, only watched the Duke's retreating back as he made his way through the brawling, sprawling drunks and out into the night.

Tom joined him as soon as the Duke and his men had ridden off on their horses. He found him staring cheerlessly into his mug.

"You let him go?"

St. Mars gave a curt nod. "I don't believe he did it. He had no good reason. We shall have to start over, Tom."

Looking up, then around, he ordered, "Sit down and join me, or you will draw too much attention."

Tom obeyed uneasily, saying in a whisper, "Shouldn't we ride out of here in case his Grace sends for the law?"

"He won't. He has too much to lose if he does. Never mind why. Just know that we are safe from him.

"It is pleasant to be back in London, is it not?" St. Mars said, changing the subject. He drained the rest of his mug. "I suppose we shall have to establish a house to live in here, before long."

"You're never giving up!"

"No, Tom." St. Mars gave him a sad smile. "I am not giving up. I just wonder how long it will take us to discover the truth."

Some thought it mounted to the Lunar sphere,
Since all things lost on earth are treasured there.
There Heroes' wits are kept in ponderous vases,
And beaux' in snuffboxes and tweezer cases.
There broken vows and deathbed alms are found,
And lovers' hearts with ends of riband bound,
The courtier's promises, and sick man's prayers,
The smiles of harlots, and the tears of heirs . . .

CHAPTER XVII

THEY rode back all that night and half the next day. Without the ability to change horses at the posting houses where he was known, they could not make the time they were used to making. Penny had been bred to race, not to plod along at this pedestrian speed, but she performed like a royal trooper.

Gideon regretted the hours he'd been given to think, especially in the dark. He had tried not to think about Isabella's defection, but the Duke's parting words had forced him to consider her in a different light. His feelings on hearing her shrieks, when she had shrunk from him, had run from shock to dismay and revulsion. It was the revulsion that had bothered him ever since.

He had been repulsed by her fear, because of what it had meant. She had not known who he was. If she had loved him, if she had had any thought of him in the past few weeks, she would have looked for him in every face she saw. But she had forgotten him entirely—presumably even before his father had been murdered. He could no longer think of her smiles the way he had thought of them before. They had little to do with goodness, and everything to do with a childish happiness. There was nothing wrong with childishness, but that had not been the foundation for his love.

His father had been right, according to the Duke. And he had fought with his father—had made it easy for his assassin to kill him—all for a mistaken love for a lady who did not deserve his loyalty.

She had repulsed him at the moment in which he had realized his terrible mistake. But that revulsion was nothing compared to the self-loathing he felt for being such a fool.

$$\wp$$

The next afternoon gave Hester her first opportunity to speak with James Henry, St. Mars's illegitimate brother.

Her eagerness to see him had increased since her rendezvous with Philippe the night before. They had met on the first floor, outside the privy chamber nearest to Hester's own room, where she had headed after excusing herself from cards. She had chosen that place, since anyone seeing them would assume she had simply come to use the close-stool.

But she had returned to the withdrawing room not one step closer to solving the mystery of Lord Hawkhurst's death. Philippe had reported that, much to his regret, Harrowby bore no trace of a scar.

While Hester could not be surprised, since his lack of an injury merely confirmed what both she and St. Mars had always known about him, she had still been disappointed. She reconciled herself to his innocence, however, for she reasoned that they would never discover the real murderer until they had first eliminated other suspects.

This morning, Harrowby had finally taken the time to speak with the man who knew more about the Hawkhurst estate than any other. While a more intelligent heir would have asked to see his receiver-general immediately, Harrowby inevitably put business after pleasure. When showing Isabella and his mother-in-law about the Abbey and its grounds had begun to pall, he had sought James Henry out as a means of varying his day.

Since his days habitually started very late by country standards, the two were still closeted together when the dinner hour sounded.

Harrowby gave instructions for an additional place to be laid for Mr. Henry to join them.

Hester's first impression of St. Mars's brother was of a younger and humbler version of the portrait she had seen of Lord Hawkhurst in the gallery. To be certain, there were clear similarities between father and son, and she could only imagine that St. Mars's failure to see them must have been due to some overwhelming difference in the two men's characters.

As the introductions were made, Mr. Henry included her in his sober bow. Although his manners were considerate, he appeared to lack the openness and warmth that seemed so much a part of St. Mars. He apologized for not being here to greet them, but their marriage on the way down had not been foreseen.

The dining chamber was on the first floor in Harrowby's suite of rooms. The food invariably arrived there cold, but the hall and large parlour on the ground floor had traditionally been used for the servants' meals.

Hester found herself next to Mr. Henry, with her aunt and Mr. Bramwell across from them, and her cousin and Harrowby seated at either end. Mr. Bramwell said grace.

As Harrowby and Mr. Henry resumed their conversation about the estate, she was surprised to detect no trace of resentment on the latter man's part. He seemed to accept his new employer, when surely, as Lord Hawkhurst's son, he should feel that Harrowby had an inferior claim. After listening to him speak, however, she began to understand that his contentment sprang from his stewardship of the estate. *He* would be the one to oversee it and to preserve it for future members of the Fitzsimmons family, which was, after all, the task of the heir. He had no heirs of his own to be concerned for. And, while he performed his duties, he lived much more comfortably than most would ever live.

She understood from things that had been said that he possessed an independence—surely not too harsh a fate for an unacknowledged bastard.

She had hoped to dislike him enormously for St. Mars's sake, and more than half expected to decide he was the murderer. But he had just enough Fitzsimmons in him—some of the very same qualities that St. Mars had—that she could not help but find him attractive.

Mrs. Mayfield did not know what to make of a servant with his status. Coming from a humbler house, herself, she had never encountered his kind before. And since Harrowby's manner towards him varied wildly from a condescending *bonhomie* to plain uneasiness, tinged with ignorance, it was hard for her to gauge which precise sort of attitude she should take.

Never one to give an inch, however, when she might take a league, she tried in various little ways to assert her superiority over Henry. Hester could almost hear her aunt's reasoning. She was the mother of the new countess, which made her family. On the other hand, he was independent and a man, which, strictly speaking, gave him a leg up. Since she did not have the faintest notion about his breeding, she had to assume he was the son of a gentleman. A younger son, perhaps, but equal in birth to her, as most men in his post would be.

Her dilemma was exacerbated by the reality that James Henry controlled the purse strings at the Abbey, and plainly Harrowby had no intention of assuming them himself. Hester could imagine the worry this information had caused her aunt. To have to apply to Mr. Henry for every penny that came out of the estate, and to have to justify her expenses . . . .

His presence at the table today, though, gave her an opportunity to satisfy her curiosity on certain points, and as soon as a break fell in the men's talk, she asked him more particulars about the size of the staff and the assignment of duties to each.

They learned that the household staff, including the cook, was predominantly male. No more than a few women served as maids, although more from the surrounding farms and villages were often engaged for temporary tasks. The female housekeeper reported directly to Robert Shaw, who reported to James Henry.

"We lost our clerk of the kitchen in the last smallpox," Mr. Henry said, "and his lordship did not see fit to engage another, considering his retirement from Court and the small demands of his family. If you, sir," he said, "intend to host larger numbers, it would be wise to engage a new man."

Harrowby gave him a startled look, which revealed how little prepared he was to make decisions. He looked to Isabella for help. "A clerk?"

"Yes. His duty is to supply the kitchen with meat, game, fruit, vegetables, and dairy goods. Robert Shaw has taken over these duties for the time-being, but since he is primarily responsible for supplying all your lordship's houses with wine, groceries and coal, he has found these additional duties somewhat onerous."

"Complained about it, has he?" said Harrowby peevishly. "I cannot abide a servant who complains. You can tell Robert Shaw that!"

Hester thought she detected a cooling from Mr. Henry. "You will find no more dedicated servant than Robert Shaw," he said gently. "It shall be as your lordship wishes, of course, but I do not believe that one man can fill both positions if the household is to be larger. Taking on a new clerk will ensure that your comfort will never be disrupted."

Mrs. Mayfield spoke up. "Hester could fill that duty. She's done all my marketing this year."

Mr. Henry gave Hester a quick glance that, while assessing her in a new capacity, was not lacking in sympathy. "I hate to differ with you, madam, but the job I speak of would not be proper for a woman. It entails a great deal of travel—much more so than in previous years. With more than forty servants to provide for on a daily basis in this house alone, the clerk must see to moving cattle from his lordship's estates in other counties."

Isabella gave a good-natured laugh. "I cannot imagine Hester doing that!"

"No, my lady," Mr. Henry agreed with an indulgent smile.

It was his first of the day, and Hester found it surprisingly pleasant, though she reflected wryly that Isabella had managed to charm another Fitzsimmons.

"Oh . . . well, in that case," Harrowby said, obviously bored with the subject, "just do whatever you think best."

Mr. Bramwell, who had remained silent since giving his prayer, interposed, "You cannot go wrong by leaving everything to Mr. Henry, my lord. Your uncle placed all his confidence in him, and he was never disappointed."

Mr. Henry had acknowledged Harrowby's agreement with a nod. Hester admired how quickly he had learned to manage his new employer. She did not believe that Harrowby would ever take any direct role in managing his estate or his fortune.

"There is one more vacant post, which you may choose not to fill," he added. "That of gentleman of the horse."

Harrowby frowned, as if someone were trying to rob him of a treat. "How can I present a proper appearance without a gentleman of the horse?"

"I believe you will find that many of the great houses are dispensing with that position these days. And unless you mean to enlarge the kennels or to breed horses for Newcastle, I am certain your lordship's coachmen and grooms can attend to all you need."

"I *would* like to enter a horse at Newcastle." Harrowby's face lit up like a child's. "What do you say to that, Isabella? Think I could win a King's plate?"

She giggled, which was all the answer he required.

"And I do want a new chariot for town. I saw old Letchworth's the other day, and I can't have that scaly old villain making a grander show than an earl. I'd like a set of six matching bays to pull it, too, and you can't convince me that my coachman can be counted on to find *them*, not when he didn't have the sense to chase a highwayman down. No, a gentleman of the horse is absolutely necessary for my dignity."

"A highwayman, my lord?" Mr. Henry asked sharply.

"Yes. Now, don't tell me that none of the servants has seen fit to inform you of it. We were stopped on the road just before Cranbrook. There were two of them, and they took my watch and my uncle's signet ring."

"And don't forget, they took Hester, too," Isabella said ingenuously.

"Dear me!" Mr. Bramwell put down his spoon. "Did they hurt

you, ma'am?"

James Henry darted a concerned look at Hester.

She attempted to look properly distressed. "No, they let me go as soon as they found I had no money. The only horrible thing was that they left me to make my way to Cranbrook alone, but a farmer took me up and restored me to my aunt."

Mrs. Mayfield broke in, "Of course, he wanted my Isabella instead. And the only thing that saved her was that she fainted. I have never been so frightened in all my life. He was the meanest, lowest creature imaginable—quite enormous. I can only thank God for my daughter's extreme sensibility, for he could not very well take her—could he—when she was out cold. If Hester had had the good sense to faint then instead of later, she might have been spared the inconvenience. But she has never been as delicate as my Isabella."

Hester was grateful for her aunt's vulgar interruption which made Mr. Henry turn away. He had opened his mouth, as if to pose more questions, but her aunt's remarkable lack of tact diverted him at just the right moment. He quickly seemed to grasp the futility of addressing Hester when her aunt was around, for aside from another penetrating glance at her, he made no further effort to speak to her then.

It was with apparent reluctance that he turned back to ask Harrowby, "The signet ring is gone, my lord?"

"Yes, the scoundrel made off with it and with my purse! And after I had expressly asked him to leave it with me! He ought to be hanged!"

"I shall put a notice in the news sheets in case anyone tries to sell the ring. Did you describe him to the authorities?"

"I couldn't. The devil wore a half-mask and a hat—and the most splendid blue cloak you've ever seen! *Three yards* of the most extraordinary blue satin, or my name isn't Fitzsimmons! I could scarcely take my eyes off of it, I tell you. If they *do* catch him, I shall want to get the name of the fellow who made it."

James Henry had stiffened in his chair. "Blue satin, my lord?"

"Yes, the most dazzling sapphire blue!" Harrowby grew quite animated in describing it. "I told the constable in Cranbrook that a devil in blue had robbed us, ye know, but he had the insolence to make a joke of the whole thing. Said *I* must be blue-deviled after losing so much money, he bet! So, I changed the word to Satan. It has a better ring to it, don't ye think—Blue Satan—goes with the blue satin, don't ye know."

"That doesn't sound like the sort of thing a highwayman would wear, my lord."

"No," Harrowby agreed morosely. "I'll warrant he stole it from a gentleman. Poor chap! Must be ready to blow his brains out at a loss like that. Mind you, this Satan-fellow had polish. Wouldn't be surprised at all if he wasn't a gentleman himself—a demmed Jacobite or some such."

"You did not recognize him?"

Harrowby paled, then blustered, "How the deuce should I recognize a Jacobite? Or a thief, for that matter? I don't chum around with rogues like that, I assure you."

"No, of course not, my lord. I meant no offence. I simply wondered if—since you considered the man polished—if he might not have been the son of . . . someone important. Someone from this county, perhaps."

"Oh . . . well. . . ." Harrowby settled his ruffled feathers. "I don't think he was. Not among my acquaintance, anyway."

Hester had begun to worry that Mr. Henry had a particular person in mind, who could very well be St. Mars, so she was glad when his cousin failed to make the connection. She saw gratefully that his shoulders seemed to relax, as if his suspicions had been laid to rest.

He then asked if anyone could describe the man's horse.

Hester remained nervously silent while Harrowby retailed his argument with the coachman, who had insisted that the horse *he* had described as a copper colour, had in fact been a bronze sort of a bay with two white fetlocks. Mrs. Mayfield did not remember seeing the two white boots, but she had been so terrified for her daughter, she claimed, that the last thing on her mind had been the colour of the villain's horse. Isabella, who had long since lost interest in the conversation, had never seen it, since she had fainted soon after emerging from the vehicle.

Mr. Henry turned his stare on Hester and leaned towards her with a tenseness she understood.

The horse's description could clearly reveal St. Mars's identity. The beautiful mare he had ridden must have been a prize in the Hawkhurst stables. Anyone with a knowledge of horses would have noticed it and remembered it, and most men, and even most women, possessed that sort of knowledge.

She had begun to suspect that the coachman had recognized his master's horse and, out of loyalty to him, had deliberately misled the authorities. There could be no other explanation, and she could have kissed the old man for it. Now, having been given the time to think about what she should say, she could always describe the robber's horse as he had.

Then a slightly better plan came to her, and she answered, with as false and uneasy an air as she could muster, "If my lord believes the horse was a copper colour, then . . . why, of course, I must agree."

As she had hoped, Mr. Henry gave an impatient frown. He leaned closer to her. "You agree that the horse had that appearance? Did you notice any marks?"

Hester ventured a glance at Harrowby. Then, with a guilty suppressed look, she gave a quick, shy shake of her head.

He frowned even more deeply. "You are certain you noticed nothing different, Mrs. Kean? A slightly bronzer tinge, perhaps? The two white boots old Peter noticed?"

She strove to appear as uncomfortable as she could, smiling nervously in Harrowby's direction, lowering her gaze to her lap, and giving a fluttery laugh. "I cannot presume to have noticed something his lordship might have missed, Mr. Henry."

"I see." As he pushed back in his chair, James Henry tried to hide his disgust with a sigh.

"I shall need to have a new signet ring made," Harrowby said, changing the subject again.

Hester smiled inwardly. Her tactics had worked. Mr. Henry clearly believed that Harrowby—fool that he was—had made a mistake in his description of the horse, and that she, as his dependent, had been afraid to contradict him.

St. Mars would have to more careful in future, or his beautiful horse could get him hanged. The thought of the danger he was in made the muscles in her back ache.

She had a need to meet him now, and she would—eagerly— and with a warning.

But she would also have to tell him that she was no nearer to solving his father's murder.

Before she could meet him in the abbey ruins, she talked with James Henry again. He came across her the next morning in the housekeeper's room near the kitchen as she was speaking to the woman about a receipt for some pills to purge the head. Mrs. Mayfield had complained of a nervous headache, which had been bothering her for days. The country air had not agreed with her. Her nose had been a constant source of discomfort.

Hester would have waited to give her orders to Mrs. Suggs—an excellent woman—until Mr. Henry had finished with his business, but he insisted that she should finish hers first. It was not until he dismissed Mrs. Suggs with a courteous remark that she realized he had come in search of her.

"If you have a moment, Mrs. Kean," he said, detaining her with a light touch on the elbow, "I wonder if I might ask you a few questions about the men who held you up? Their description must be forwarded to the magistrates, but I could not get clear on the details last night."

She signaled her willingness to be helpful, but felt a flutter inside. Mr. Henry was not the sort of person to be easily fooled.

"I was a bit confused yesterday," he said, "by the conflicting opinions expressed by those who were there. But, now that my lord— and *yours*—is no longer within hearing, would you say that the younger highwayman's horse was a copper or not?"

This was said with such a dry understanding—though she could not be certain that his intention had been humorous—that Hester could not suppress a flush and a guilty smile.

Fortunately, these were signs which could be interpreted to her advantage.

"I do not like to contradict—Lord Hawkhurst," she said, nearly choking on his title. She fished around for a statement that would not be a total lie, but when nothing came to her, she took the plunge. "However, the horse the younger man rode—and upon which he carried me what seemed to be a terrible distance through those dark woods—*did* have some lighter markings. I should have called its colour bronze, rather than copper, too. I hate to say it, but I'm afraid I must agree with your coachman, Mr. Henry."

For a moment, she was certain that her answer had affected him more profoundly than it would if his question had not been prompted by a suspicion of the highwayman's being St. Mars. A shadow passed over his features. He quickly recovered, though, giving her a tight, formal smile.

"I have never known Old Peter to be mistaken in the matter of a horse. Still, I had wondered if he . . . ."

He broke off in mid-sentence, as if only then aware that he had spoken this last bit aloud. She could see that he was troubled, and trying to hide the fact.

"Is there something about the robbers that disturbs you—aside from the obvious?" she asked. Given his evident confusion, it was a logical question, and she felt safer asking it than not.

He tried to shrug his interest off. "Oh, no. It was just the satin cape that engaged my curiosity. You will agree that a robber's having such an expensive garment is out of the usual. And, *if* he stole it," he said, slipping back into a pensive mood, "which is entirely possible, I wonder why he would not sell it. If the reason for stealing in the first place is to get money, then surely a robber would sell everything he stole."

"I suppose that highwaymen have their vanities just like the rest of us," was all Hester could think to say. She had to admire him for his reasoning. She only wished his intelligence could be turned to helping his brother solve the mystery of their father's death instead of being used to unmask this fiction of a highwayman known as Blue Satan. She had heard the housemaids whispering about him only this morning, which told her that either the coachman or one of the footmen who had served them at dinner yesterday had regaled the other servants with the story.

She could not imagine that their exaggerations would do St. Mars any harm, but neither would she underestimate the cleverness of his brother. Something told her that it would be far better to have Mr. Henry on her side than to be opposed by him.

Her last remark had been intended to relax his preoccupation with the highwayman, and she was glad to see that it had had an ameliorating effect.

It had even struck a spark of humour in him. The sober lines of his face seemed to bend, and he and she turned, as if by consent, to walk towards the centre of the house.

"A vain highwayman," he mused. "I will admit, that is a notion I had not considered. But it is possible. I believe they regard themselves as a better class of criminal than footpads. A certain obligation of manners seems conferred on them for the simple reason that they are mounted."

"Is that why the populace so often gives them the title, 'gentleman'?"

"That's certainly one of the reasons. Being raised on tales of Robin Hood could well be another. Was your highwayman a 'gentleman' in that sense? Was he as 'polished' as my lord said?"

His reference to St. Mars as *her* highwayman unearthed a secret feeling she hadn't even known she had. She had been thinking of him as her highwayman.

She had to fight a serious discomfort when she said, "I would say there was an effort on his part to *play* the gentleman, but he could not maintain the role indefinitely. The truth, I imagine, would be somewhere between my lord's interpretation and my aunt's. He was neither so polished nor so rough as they said."

They had reached the Great Hall, and Hester used the opportunity to change the focus of their conversation. Looking up at the Fitzsimmons' coat of arms and the aged weapons and suits of armor displayed against the walls, she said, "This room is magnificent. I have never seen a better collection of arms. It must give you great pride to be associated with such a noble family."

She turned to witness his reaction, but James Henry had taught himself not to react to such comments. He must have heard similar ones all of his life.

"Yes, it does."

"Has your time here been happy? Was the late Lord Hawkhurst a kind master?"

She watched him close up before her eyes.

"He was . . . ."

The proper words seemed to fail him. She thought she detected grief in his pause, but it could have been a different emotion. Guilt, perhaps, or even dismay at being asked.

"He was a good master, and a fair one, I suppose, in his own way. He placed a great deal of faith in me, for which I shall always be grateful."

"It must have been a shock for you all to find he had been murdered."

He regarded her coldly. "More than you can imagine," he spoke, as if warning her off.

She flushed with shame this time. "I am sorry. I have trespassed on your feelings. But I was present at the ball when the magistrate carried the news to my Lord St. Mars, and I have naturally been curious. Is it so very certain that St. Mars murdered his father?"

She had hoped to be able to gauge his feelings about his brother, but his face revealed nothing, except that he had no wish to discuss Lord Hawkhurst's death with her. Or, perhaps, with anyone.

"I would not like to venture an opinion," he said. "If you are *curious*—" his emphasis on that word made her wince— "perhaps you should speak to Sir Joshua Tate. He is the magistrate who brought the charges."

Hester could not help reaching out to touch his sleeve. "Forgive me. I can see that you were very attached to his lordship."

Her sympathy disconcerted him. It did not seem to be unwelcome either, though he turned quite red. "I shall miss my lord very much." He stepped away from her suddenly and bowed. "I will bid you a good afternoon, Mrs. Kean."

As she watched him stride from the hall, she was reminded of St. Mars's reaction when she had expressed her sympathy to him.

Neither of Lord Hawkhurst's sons had, it appeared, been remembered in the scramble for their father's estate.

Here in a grotto, sheltered close from air,
And screened in shades from day's detested glare . . .

Just then, Clarissa drew with tempting grace
A two-edged weapon from her shining case:
So Ladies in Romance assist their Knight,
Present the spear, and arm him for the fight.
He takes the gift with reverence, and extends
The little engine on his fingers' ends;

CHAPTER XVIII

O N the night St. Mars had appointed, Hester excused herself from the withdrawing room just as the footmen were being called to light the candles.

Earlier in the day she had made references to a mild headache in the hopes that her absence, if prolonged, would be ascribed to her ailment. She had also taken opportunities to mention how glad she would be to take a walk down to see the ruins, in case she was caught coming back from her meeting with St. Mars.

She let herself out by a small side door, which led into the gardens, taking no torch to light her way. She did not want to run the risk of its being seen by anyone who might cast a glance out of a window. The illumination indoors had been dimmer than that outside, so it was still easy to make her way through the side gardens and across the lawn, past the lower remnants of the ancient abbey to the grander part of the ruins.

In the gathering dusk, she could understand why the servants said they were haunted. The uneven walls with their tall arched windows, and trees that had sprouted between the stones, some of them a hundred years old at least, cast indistinct shadows in the failing light. The sun had gone down nearly a half-hour before, and only a faint memory of it was left.

Lord St. Mars had not told her in which part of the old abbey he would wait, which made sense to her now, for she was unable to distinguish any of its buildings. When she was almost certain that a wall had been part of the sanctuary, she would find another behind it that seemed just as likely. She had visited the abbeys of Westminster and the city of York with their side aisles, and she tried to make sense of this one based on them. It was surprising, though, how easily one could be turned around.

Noting the rapidly approaching darkness, she hoped that St. Mars would show himself before she tripped over a stone and ended up lying in a sunken crypt like the one she had just passed. If he had not seen her coming, she feared she would never find him.

A strange, broken doorway, in the corner where two tall walls met, made itself visible to her in the dark. She stepped through it and nearly bumped her face on a curving wall of stone just inside it. As she gasped in surprise, a flutter came from her left. Starting at the sound, she saw the silhouette of her highwayman outlined by the faint light from an arched doorway on her right.

"I startled you," he said, in a low voice. "I did not mean to, but it is hard to catch up with someone in these rooms."

He had worn his tricorn and his cloak. As he moved nearer, she saw that part of his face was covered by a mask.

"I saw this doorway. It seemed a perfect place to wait." Nervousness made her fiddle with her hands. They were so very alone in this small, dark space.

"It is—or was—the night stairwell to the monks' dorter. You are in the old South transept. The monks tried to make it easier on themselves to perform their nightly rituals. Hence, this staircase directly into the church."

She wondered how he could possibly know. "You studied the history of these ruins?"

"As much as I was able. They have always fascinated me. Visiting abbeys that are still intact on the Continent was a big help."

"How I envy you that travel—but," she reminded herself aloud, "you did not come here to hear about my frustrated wishes, my lord."

"No . . . but I will be happy to wish them for you. So tell me," he said, with abruptness in his tone, "what have you discovered, my very dear friend."

She knew . . . perfectly well . . . that his expression was a reflection of the importance of anyone's friendship in a crisis like this, but she warmed just the same. "Unfortunately, your cousin Harrowby has no mark where your father might have wounded his assailant. Philippe is very certain. I am sorry, my lord."

Gideon was glad she hadn't beaten about the bush. He had been frustrated by the lack of news from every quarter.

The news-sheets from London had told him nothing. It was as if they all conspired to keep him in the dark. Little news from London or Westminster was reported, nothing about the political situation, although news from the Continent was copious. Only one item had caught his eye this week. Lord Peterborough had been forbidden the Court, which meant that the King's hostility to the Tories continued unabated. As long as that situation held true, he had no prayer of regaining his own, unless he proved the identity of his father's murderer.

"So," he said, with a sigh—surprisingly one of relief. "Harrowby is innocent."

"It would seem so, my lord. Are you not disappointed?"

"Actually, no. It is something of a relief to discover that my judgement in men is not more flawed than I had begun to believe it. I cannot blame Harrowby for what he has done. I don't know of two people who would have refused what the Crown and Parliament offered him."

He continued with more than a touch of chagrin, "Nor can I blame him for marrying your cousin. Not when she and her mother were both determined to have him."

"He might have had a little more consideration for your feelings," Mrs. Kean protested, and he was grateful for her bitter note on his behalf.

"Harrowby? No, Mrs. Kean. My poor cousin Harrowby has always been ignorant and shallow. Nothing can be expected of him, and nothing will ever be got."

She did not refer to Isabella's defection. No doubt she was trying to spare him the pain of recalling it. And he must not forget that Isabella was her cousin, and therefore, a person with a claim on her affections much greater than his own. It would be completely unfair to let her know how dramatically his opinion of her cousin had changed, but he was surprised by how strong his desire to tell her was.

He changed the subject. "Did you get a chance to meet James Henry, Mrs. Kean?"

Although she had, she could not tell him conclusively whether she suspected James Henry or not. Something in her attitude, however, gave him the impression that she had found his brother more likeable than she had expected to.

As he listened to her soft, reasonable voice, coming towards him through the dark, an unpleasant feeling—a feeling that couldn't be, yet it seemed amazingly akin to jealousy—made him frown at her description of his brother's evidently sterling character.

He tried to reason his resentment away. Mrs. Kean had been his only supporter in the society he had left. He quite naturally would not want to share her friendship any more than he had wanted to share his father's love. It was silly to care if she liked James, but the feeling still rankled as she continued.

"I must tell you, my lord, that I believe your coachman recognized your horse."

"Did he?" *Damn!* "I should have thought of that myself. He could recognize Penny as well as I could."

"You may be surprised to know that he described her as a bronze-coloured gelding with a pair of white boots."

It took a moment before her words sank in, but when they did he laughed, and some of the despair that had weighed him down since his meeting with the Duke seemed to lift. "Then, bless Old Peter!" he said. "I hope you agreed with him, Mrs. Kean, although Penny may never forgive you for it. She is a vain little creature."

"I made it as clear as I could that I could never contradict your cousin, who is my employer, and given that circumstance, I should have to contradict his coachman."

Gideon, who was coming to know the intricacies of her mind, immediately understood what she had done. "Did ye now?" he said, grinning in the dark. "Then I shall tell Penny that the truth was forced from you against your will." He wished he could see the sparkle he suspected would be in her eye.

Her mood sobered, though. "I do think I managed to convince Mr. Henry that the highwayman was not you, my lord, but I believe he was very suspicious of the possibility. The blue satin cloak intrigued him very much. Could he have known it was yours?"

Gideon grunted. "He might have, although the money for that garment came from my own income, not from my father's money. He approves every expenditure in this house, but does not approve all of mine. He wouldn't know about it unless Philippe raved about what a *formidable* garment he had commissioned for me. And knowing Philippe, that is very possible.

"Did James inform Harrowby of his suspicions?"

"No, my lord. Not that I know of."

"I wonder if he will?" He left that uneasy question for another day, and said, "If you would, Mrs. Kean, can you tell Philippe to say the cloak was sold or given away if he is ever asked about it? Chances are, he will not be."

"I have already warned him, my lord. He said he will say that you instructed him to give it to a beggar and he did."

Gideon was struck almost speechless by her foresight. She had done so much—*thought* of so much. "Thank you," was all he could say.

"And have you discovered anything to help you, my lord?"

He told her about his meeting with the Duke and his reluctant conclusion that his Grace had not had a logical reason to kill his father.

When she had heard the Duke's arguments, she agreed. "What now, then, my lord?"

"I do not know."

His bleak response was interrupted by a bird, which flew out of its nest behind her, fluttering its wings about her head.

"Oh!" She started forward, falling, and he caught her shoulders with his hands.

She smelled very sweet, like fresh spring grass. He remembered sitting with her in Mrs. Mayfield's parlour and thinking that she smelled very good.

When she pulled backwards, apologizing for her clumsiness, he helped her back onto her feet. "This isn't the perfect place to talk," he said, to cover her shyness. His voice came out a bit hoarse, and he hoped she wouldn't know why.

He did not want to frighten her. She had been very brave to meet him alone at night, and it was wrong of him to think of the pleasures he was thinking of now.

"Let's move outside. There's a low wall in the lavatorium you can sit on."

When they moved out into the night air, the stars and moon were shining. Gideon took her elbow to help her step through the maze of stones. He knew his way unerringly, having spent his boyhood amongst these buildings, but they could trip someone new to their groupings.

"Have you nothing else to go on, my lord?" Mrs. Kean asked, after he had settled her on the wall.

"I've been reading over the letters I told you about. And there is just one possibility."

"What is that?"

"Two of them refer to the Pretender's need for money to pay for troops. They both hint at the existence of a man who might be persuaded to pay for the cause if a certain inducement can be given. Neither the man's name nor the nature of the inducement is mentioned."

"Didn't the conspirators have money of their own?"

"Yes, but mounting an invasion takes more wealth than even these men could have raised. They were afraid to commit their own funds until they knew the Pretender could raise an army in France, in which case they would need their own money to pay for their troops here. They were looking for someone willing to send funds to the Chevalier before he landed—in exchange for something he wanted."

"What could that have been?"

Gideon found her naivety amusing. "An earldom or a dukedom is generally thought to be pleasing."

"But only the King can grant those."

"Precisely. But they may be *promised* to as many people as the Pretender can convince, and he loses nothing in making such promises. You would be surprised to know how many men are willing to risk their lives and their families in the hope of riches they may never see."

"I believe I *would* be surprised. It seems quite foolish to me."

He couldn't help laughing, but the truth of what he had explained to her sobered him quickly enough. "I want to find out just who this financier was. What if he only pretended to join their cause? He might have been a spy for the Crown. Or he might have considered joining them and changed his mind. He could have panicked and killed my father when he tried to back out. His name does not appear, either on a list or in a signature. If he did commit murder, none of the papers I found would implicate him in their plot."

"But how will you go about finding this out?"

"The Duke of Bournemouth may know. I shall write to ask him."

"Will he tell you?"

"I don't know."

"Is there nothing more?"

Gideon sighed. "Just one more thing . . . and I don't see how it fits, but it might."

She waited for him to go on, and tired of standing, he sat down beside her.

"There was a Jacobite medal, rolled up inside my father's papers." He described it for her, explaining its symbolism and telling her the reasons why it was sometimes bestowed.

"I do not believe it was intended for my father, for he was not a superstitious man, and he had seen the Pretender too many times not to know him."

"Could it have been for the man they hoped would supply them with money?"

"Possibly. But it might just as easily have been for someone else. For someone who needed the reassurance that James Stuart does exist."

Mrs. Kean sighed. "I'm afraid I see nothing in all this that I can help you with, my lord."

"No," he agreed. He became aware that he had prolonged their conversation longer than he ought. But he had always enjoyed being with her and, right now, he craved the companionship she gave. "I do not think there is anything else you can do for me, but I thank you for all you have done."

He could just make out the lines of her slender body in the dark. She sat very straight with her hands folded on her lap as if they sat in a drawing room instead of beneath the stars.

He tried to ignore a temptation to thank her in a way that would be more satisfying to him. Mrs. Kean was not that sort of a woman, and he would not insult her by treating her like one. She had not given him a reason to make him think she would welcome that kind of attention, and he mustn't abuse her friendship. She had started by trying to help him understand her cousin. Now Isabella was gone, and she was simply his friend.

He stood and held out a hand to help her rise. "I must permit you to go. You won't want to be discovered coming in so late."

"Yes . . . Oh!" Her voice was light. "I meant to tell you that you have become a figure of terror in these parts—not as yourself, of course, but as a highwayman, known as Blue Satan. Your cousin has a very romantic turn of mind. He named you himself."

"Ye gods! And what am I supposed to be capable of? Raping the dairymaids and making off with the butter?"

"At the very least, I should think. And he cannot forgive you for owning that cloak. Since we met you on the road, I believe he has mentioned it with regret some twenty times a day."

"Poor Harrowby! But I am happy to hear there is still something he envies me. I shall have to make certain that Blue Satan is seen again, so I can wallow in his envy."

She grabbed quickly for his sleeve, then dropped her hand, flustered. "I hope you will not take any unnecessary chances, my lord."

He had heard a tiny catch in her breath. Mrs. Kean should be warned that there was something very arousing in the sound of a woman's gasp in the dark.

He drew closer to her. "I will endeavour to be very prudent in my rides, if only to please you, dear lady."

She did not flirt back at him, but said, "Well, *if* you undertake to rob any more coaches, I hope you will take measures to disguise your beautiful horse. *Or* to hide her, although I do believe a disguise would be more serviceable. I know of a very good shoe-blacking that can be obtained in London. If you would like to try making her into a brindle mare, I should be happy to send a tin of it to the address you gave me."

She said it in the same tone of voice with which a physician might prescribe a poultice for his chest, as if she found nothing injudicious in recommending highway robbery to her friends.

He chuckled, and had to smother a deeper laugh. "Never a brindle, Mrs. Kean! You cannot imagine how insulted Penny would be. She has the blood of princes in her veins."

"So do you, my lord, if the Fitz in your name is anything to go by. Yet *you* wear a disguise."

"An interesting comparison. I will be certain to bring it up with Penny. Fortunately, should I ever take to the King's highway again, the job of altering her looks will fall to Tom and not to me."

He had led her to a sheltered spot beneath some trees within sight of the house. Low light from one of the rooms where a fire had been lit would provide her with a beacon as she crossed the lawn. "I hope your absence has not been noticed. I have kept you rather long."

He turned to her to say goodbye, but she forestalled him. "Please do not concern yourself with my return. I am getting very good at telling fibs. You had best be on your way, yourself. Good night to you, my lord."

She made him a curtsy, and he was too surprised by her sudden leave-taking to think. But before she got too far away, he called out in a loud whisper.

"Mrs. Kean, which room have they given you?"

She turned. "It is a smallish chamber on the first floor near the queen's suite. Why do you ask, my lord?"

"Does it face this direction, and does it have paneling that is elaborately carved?"

"Yes."

He smiled to himself. "That is a very handy room. I hope you find that it suits you."

"It is far more comfortable than I deserve, my lord."

He frowned. "Why do you say that?"

"Because none of us has a right to be here." The tremor in her voice told him of all the shame and anger she felt for her family, and for his cousin Harrowby.

Her sensibility moved him. He doubted that any of the others had experienced similar qualms.

He called softly to her over the grass, "My dear Mrs. Kean, it gives me pleasure to know that you are staying in my house, if being here brings you even the slightest bit more comfort than you had before."

"It does that, my lord. I cannot deny it."

"That is enough, then. Good night."

He watched her cross towards the house and disappear through a garden gate. The pleasure of her company left with her, and he was left to gaze alone on his house, which he could not enter except at night through a hole in the ground.

This evening with Mrs. Kean had helped to raise his spirits, bringing him contact with the world he had lost. But still he was not one step closer to finding his father's killer. She had helped him thus far, but he had no excuse for asking for her help again. And as her sweet, honest essence vanished in the cool night air, he felt bereft.

He had pored over his father's papers again, stopping to examine every name and consider its implications. But the same lack of motive held true for all the Jacobites as had held for the Duke. The murder of his father could only have put them at greater risk, for it might have led to the discovery of their intrigues by a Hanoverian supporter. Since his father had not seen fit to draw him into his treasonable activities, none of the conspirators could have been certain of his discretion.

Before learning of his Grace's engagement, he might have suspected him of killing Lord Hawkhurst and throwing the blame his way to make a clearer path to Isabella. But the Duke had never intended to offer for her, and if he had, he would have been certain of being accepted.

No, there had to be some other person. Someone he had not yet found. Either a wealthy man who had flirted with the notion of supporting the Pretender or a superstitious one who had wanted a talisman of his prince. Or both.

He tried to think of the kind of men the Chevalier pulled to his side. He attracted the discontented of every stripe and managed to give them enough of what they needed to keep them loyal. To the Catholic Irish, he promised religious freedom and put them into his private army. An allowance, paid by the French, kept them in food and lodgings along the French coast.

To the ambitious he granted titles and the promise of land. Both of these motives would stand him in good stead if he ever invaded England, for every man who fought for James Stuart would also be fighting for his own benefit.

The priests who supported him—and there were many—needed no glue to bind them. They secretly published treatises on the divine nature of authority and suffered the consequences of being barred from their posts. Whether rightly or not, it was these men who served the Pretender with the greatest purity of heart. And Gideon's father had been one to share in their beliefs. If he had been different from the nonjuring priests, it was in the fact that he would gladly have taken up arms in the struggle for which they only wrote and intrigued.

Gideon knew, however, that his father had always acted with his eyes and his ears wide open. A true Fitzsimmons, he was seldom deceived by things unseen.

Invisibilia non decipient.

His father had not been deceived by Isabella or her mother. Yet he had turned his back on a treacherous murderer. How? And why?

Had he known the financier or the superstitious man so well that he trusted him?

In this current dangerous climate, a person with a great deal of wealth would have to have a powerful motive to want to overthrow a king. Especially in the cause of one who might never make it to England's shores. A wealthy man had too much to lose, unless he had a reason that was more powerful than the temptation to keep his riches.

Something told him that his father had courted a terrible risk in attempting to raise money for the Chevalier. Again he wondered if the Duke of Bournemouth knew whom his father had approached.

Gideon went to find his horse, concealed in the woods beyond the ruins. Then, mounted, he made his way down the old monks' path through the woods and over the abandoned stone bridge towards the inn that was his current home.

He thought of James, sleeping in comfort in the house their father had bought him. Mrs. Kean did not believe that James was a murderer. She had not said so specifically, but he had read it in her tone. No matter. He had realized—stupidly—that it was unlikely that James could have done it.

If he, himself, had not been attacked in London, he might have wondered if his father had not drawn his bastard son into the Pretender's cause. James might have looked to treason as the only way to establish himself with a peerage of his own. In the tense emotional atmosphere of their confrontation, Gideon had failed to check his brother's arm for the sign of a wound.

But whoever had killed their father had either followed Gideon to London to attack him or sent a confederate to do the job. On that day, James had found their father dying, had sent for the magistrate, and presumably had remained at the Abbey to care for his father's body. He had not sent anyone after Gideon to give him the news until Sir Joshua had found him at Lord Eppington's ball.

Gideon knew that he could not be certain of James's movements after he had alerted the household. That was one more thing he might have asked Mrs. Kean to investigate for him. But there was something deep inside him that revolted at the notion of hounding his own flesh and blood.

Sir Joshua had made the long ride to London in one day, travelling a good portion of it after dark. The murderer would have followed much closer on Gideon's heels, but he had not overtaken him on the road. If he had, he might have tried to strike him before reaching London and left him for dead, in the hopes that it would seem he had died from his father's cut. Since he had not overtaken him, he had been forced to wait in the darkness of Piccadilly for Gideon to emerge, when he could not have been certain he would go out.

This last thought snaked around in Gideon's mind. The murderer could not have been absolutely certain that he would go out that evening. But he might have been reasonably sure. If he knew the gossip, he would have been aware of Gideon's intentions with respect to Isabella Mayfield, and many people had known she was to attend Lord Eppington's ball. Wherever she had gone, he had foolishly followed.

Perhaps the murderer *had* been certain that he would ride out that evening.

The long journey from the Abbey might possibly have been made by one horse, but it was far more likely that his attacker had stopped to change his horse along the way.

And if he had ridden up to London, then he had also ridden down—in which case an ostler at a posting house just might remember him.

But anxious cares the pensive nymph oppressed,
And secret passions laboured in her breast.
Not youthful kings in battle seized alive,
Not scornful virgins who their charms survive,
Not ardent lovers robbed of all their bliss,
Not ancient ladies when refused a kiss,
Not tyrants fierce that unrepenting die,
Not Cynthia when her manteau's pinned awry,
E'er felt such rage, resentment, and despair,
As thou, sad Virgin!

In the clear Mirror of thy ruling Star
I saw, alas! some dread event impend,
Ere to the main this morning sun descend,
But heaven reveals not what, or how, or where:
Warned by the Sylph, oh pious maid, beware!

'Twas then, Belinda, if report say true,
Thy eyes first opened on a Billet-doux;
Wounds, Charm, and Ardors were no sooner read,
But all the Vision vanished from thy head.

CHAPTER XIX

WHEN Tom came in from the stables the next morning, Gideon told him he had a job for him to perform.

"It will not be easy," he said, watching Tom's square face light with the prospect of action.

It had not been easy, either, for Tom to wait for him to have an inspiration, especially penned up in a small inn with Katy, who was trying very desperately not to make eyes at him. Gideon had watched them with a mixture of amusement and pity, and exasperation with Tom for being so hardheaded, when it was easy to see what he wanted.

Tom was hoping they would leave the Fox and Goose before temptation grew too strong for him, but Gideon was determined to stay. Lade had cooperated. He had not tried to sell Gideon to the law. They were close to home, yet hidden. With its out-of-the-way location and its dilapidated appearance, the Fox and Goose did not attract many new faces, and certainly no one who knew them.

His new furniture had arrived, and his rooms were nearly comfortable. Katy had worked wonders with his clothes. Avis was a reliable stable hand. The cellar was full of smuggled French wine.

The only two drawbacks were that they were *not* at home—and that Tom needed a diversion to take him away from a pair of cheerful brown eyes.

"I would do this if I could—" Gideon fretted at his own inactivity— "but having travelled the London road so many times, I would surely be recognized. I want you to visit every posting house between Cranbrook and Bromley and see if you can discover anyone who remembers seeing a man riding fast and alone, either on the day before or on the day of my father's death. If someone does, get the traveller's name or, failing that, his description."

"Some of those ostlers and post boys are sure to know me, too, my lord."

"Yes, but I doubt if they know you've left the Abbey with me. Be very careful, of course. But until I see your name on a posted notice, too, I think you can say you are travelling on Abbey business, and none will be the wiser."

"Is there someone in particular you're looking for?"

"No. But I hope the Duke can point me in the proper direction. Here—" he handed Tom a letter addressed to the Duke, with money for his expenses— "you can post that once you get closer to London. I've asked for a reply to be delivered to the postmaster in Smarden. I am not known in that village, so I can call for a letter there myself. I do not trust his Grace enough to have his reply directed here."

"You think he knows who killed my lord?"

"I think he may know *of* him, but does not suspect what he did. I hope he can give me a name. But it is only a guess."

He could tell that Tom had lost most, if not all of the hope he had had. But he would never let on. As long as Gideon could think of clues, he would pursue them.

"Yessir," Tom said, making his bow. Before he moved to the door, he said anxiously, "You won't get yourself tooken up by the law while I'm gone now, will you, sir? This calling at every posting house could take a long time."

"I promise not to get myself into trouble if I can help it. Be off with you, now, and keep your face hidden and your nose to the ground."

Gideon allowed three days before riding into Smarden to see if any messages had been delivered for a Mr. Mavors.

But there was none.

He tried to convince himself that the Duke had not yet received his letter and had time to respond, but he was very well aware that there were other reasons why his Grace might have chosen not to. Gideon's own letter might have been intercepted by the Crown. He had tried to phrase his message in a way as to lead anyone reading it to believe that he was inquiring about the provenance of a horse. If it was read by a government agent, he believed it would still go through, but if no answer ever came, he would never be certain it had.

There were other possibilities, too—ones that he did not care to face. The Duke might not know the name of the man the conspirators had approached. Or, he might know it and see no reason to help him. He might fear that in naming the man, he stood a chance of risking his own exposure. Gideon's gratitude could be counted on, but what was to keep the other man from betraying him?

If the Duke failed to answer him for any of these reasons, he would be left with no leads.

But worse than all of these was the lingering possibility that the Duke of Bournemouth was the murderer. In which case, Gideon had made the same mistake in trusting him that his father had made.

⟡

As the days wore on, Hester felt alternately helpless and hopeful. Helpless, because there was no longer anything she could do to help St. Mars. And hopeful, because it looked as though they might return to London soon, and she desperately needed something to take her mind off her uselessness.

Harrowby needed to return to take his seat in the House of Lords. The King had granted him leave to examine his affairs, but at a time when Jacobites and Tories were retreating to their country estates, no Whig could appear to be gone from Court too long.

When Mr. Hare, who was secretary to Lord Bolingbroke ceased to appear, it was rumoured that he had fled to France as well, when according to this morning's copy of *The Daily Courant*, he had only retired to his house at Skiffington.

There were other reasons to go back, too. Appointments were being made, and honours were being handed out. Although Harrowby could not expect, nor would he desire, to be appointed to some posts, there were always lucrative and influential positions for which few talents were required.

Every afternoon after dinner, as they sat in the withdrawing room, Hester read *The Daily Courant* aloud to the others. Harrowby had begun this task, but they had soon found that his reading was more laborious than Hester's, so they had begged him to give the task to her in order to "spare his eyes."

From these readings, they learned that the Honour of Knighthood had been conferred on Mr. Richard Steele, Mr. Robert Thornhill, and Mr. Samuel Letchworth, as well as other titbits that whetted their appetites to return to Court before the King departed for the summer.

A pension of two thousand pounds had been granted to the Earl of Pembroke and Montgomery from the Civil List. The daily news of others being rewarded made Harrowby very anxious not to be forgotten in the King's largess.

The Marquess of Wharton had died rather suddenly at the age of seventy-six. As a fellow member of the Kit Kat Club, Harrowby felt he should attend his funeral. Letters from friends had teased them with a scandal brewing over the death, and both Harrowby and Isabella hated being far from the gossip. Lord Wharton's illness, it seemed, had followed hard upon the heels of his son's elopement, and now Philip was blaming his bride for his father's death, even though he had disobeyed his parent in eloping with the girl when she refused to be seduced.

On all three of Hester's companions, for whom the peace of the country had begun to seem tedious, such goings-on were bound to provide strong inducement to pack their bags. Mrs. Mayfield had found that, after all her machinations, she did not particularly care for country life. After acquainting themselves with the house and the grounds, the only occupation that had amused her was planning the decoration of Isabella's bedchamber. But after the architect had come down from London, and the upholsterers and joiners had been to show their wares, she had found it best to remove herself from the scene of the actual work.

Mrs. Mayfield had not thought it prudent to suggest a return to London yet, hoping for a sign that Mr. Letchworth had recovered from his sense of injury. He had got wind of where Isabella had gone, and had written her a letter in his former vein, apparently unaware that she was already married. Mrs. Mayfield had read the letter herself, declared it to be nonsense, and advised Isabella not to think of it at all. It had been tossed into the pile of letters which had been forwarded from home. But they had judged it prudent to insert a notice in all the news-sheets announcing that the nuptials had taken place. It was now hoped that Mr. Letchworth's elevation to a knighthood would solace his pride and that they might soon receive his note of congratulations in the post.

"Here is your notice, Isabella," Hester said as they sat in the parlour on a Thursday afternoon. She had found it in the day's packet which had been posted to them on Tuesday. It says, 'Yesterday was Sevennight, a marriage took place between the Earl of Hawkhurst and Mrs. Isabella Mayfield, daughter of the late Honourable Geffrye Mayfield, at Rotherham Abbey, Lord Hawkhurst's country seat.'"

"But that is wrong! We were married in Sevenoaks."

"Yes, my dear," Mrs. Mayfield said, "but it sounds better to say that you were married at your husband's house, and so you *will* say to anyone who asks. They have put it very nicely, although I never have understood why they do not say more about the people who attended the ceremony. They should have said that your mama was there.

"What else does the newspaper say, Hester?"

Hester's eye had been caught by an advertisement on the third page, but since it was unlikely to interest her aunt, she reverted to the gossip. "There is more here on Lord Wharton's business. 'We hear the Marchioness of Wharton has taken out a Process in Doctors

Commons, to prove her Marriage with the Marquess, who is said to be going to travel.'"

"Poor Martha!"

Mrs. Mayfield's sympathetic remark could not fool Hester since, as she recalled, her aunt had not been so fond of the girl when the marquess had fallen in love with her. Lord Winchendon, as he had been then, had figured as one of Mrs. Mayfield's favourite prospects for Isabella, and she had been irate when he'd fallen in love with a general's daughter.

Mrs. Mayfield continued in a commiserating tone, "Only fifteen years of age, and already abandoned by her husband! Why, just think, my dear," she said to Isabella, "how that might have been you. But you was not so easily taken in by that rake, no matter how he courted you. And only see how fortunate you are to have married our own dear Lord Hawkhurst. I always said that Philip Wharton was a scoundrel."

Not always, Hester might have reminded her. Only after he'd rejected Isabella. Still, she felt sorry for the poor marchioness. Her husband was said to be an even bigger rake than his papa had been.

"I suppose we ought to return to town," Mrs. Mayfield said, in a carefully disinterested tone, "to see if anything can be done for her ladyship. I would not want her to think that all her friends have abandoned her. What do you say to our returning, my lord? I would not wish to inconvenience you."

Harrowby still bloomed beneath his mother-in-law's flattery, and obviously her suggestion was welcome. "I say we go back. What do you say, my dear?"

"Yes, let's do! I cannot wait to show Martha and all the others at Court my ring."

"Then that is settled. Not but what it has been very pleasant to be here, just the four of us. But we mustn't be remiss in remaining away from Court too long, and you will want to find a house for the summer."

They started discussing where they had best stop, whether nearer to Hampton Court or Kensington, but since this was to be King George's first summer in England, it remained to be seen how much time he would spend at either palace. They did decide, however, that Monday would be the soonest they should start out for London, since otherwise they would have to spend all of Sunday at an inn.

While they were talking, Hester listened with half an ear while she perused the portions of the paper that had interested her. The advertisement that had caught her eye was for a recently published pamphlet called *The Black Day, or, A Prospect of Domesday*. It purported to be about a great and terrible eclipse, due to happen on Friday, April 22, 1715—tomorrow—and it claimed that the like whereof had not been visible in the Kingdom of England for over 500 years. Hester might not have believed it, except that, according to the advertisement, the prediction had been based on calculations by Mr. Halley, Professor of Geometry in the University of Oxford, a noted astronomer and secretary to the Royal Society. Even as unschooled as she was, it would have been hard to miss hearing of this gentleman. She would enjoy seeing if the prediction was right. At least the eclipse would give her something to think about besides Lord St. Mars.

Her meeting with him had ended her part in his trials. He had no more use for her, that had been clear. It had been all she could do to hurry through their good-byes, knowing that the most compelling role in her life was to be taken from her. She had not wanted to reveal to him how absolutely vital it had become.

She was supposed to enjoy the luxury of his home and ignore his rights to it. Forget his losses, and pretend they had never touched her heart. Benefit from his riches while he was consigned to ruin.

She could not, although her daily life had never contained so many comforts as it did at the Abbey. How could she enjoy herself, when her mind refused to let go of his misfortunes?

If she were a man, she might have found a way to assist him that was more helpful. She could confront suspects and question them. But the only role open to her had been as an observer of the things he could not see, the little happenings in her limited circle that might have pointed him to his father's murderer.

And had not.

It was unlike her to mope. The very least she could do for him would be to discourage her aunt and the others from wasting his inheritance before he could resume his position. She obviously would not be able to keep them from spending a great deal, but she vowed to restrain them in every possible way.

With so many servants available for the menial tasks, her aunt was finding different employment for her. Instead of sending her on errands, she had begun to use Hester for her eyes and ears in this household, which had been run by men. Spying was not an unusual job for a waiting woman, but Hester planned to use her position to manage her aunt as well.

ʂ

Gideon got up early Friday morning, eager to ride to Smarden again. He had given the Duke another few days, but he felt impatient. He could not wait any longer.

Tom had not returned, so Avis saddled Penny for him as he went back in for his breakfast of beef and beer.

"Yer up early this mornin'," Lade complained as he plopped Gideon's brimming mug down on the table. "Yer not gettin' ready to pike, are ye, afore ye tip me my earnest?"

Gideon looked down his nose. He was not in any mood to cater to Lade's impertinence. "I am going out on business—*not* that it is any business of yours. I thought I had made it clear that I intend to reside here for some time. If I did not, I would hardly have spent the money I have on improving this fleas' nest of yours. Rest assured that I shall inform you if my wishes should change."

He dug into his beef, trying to ignore the slow grin that spread over Lade's features. "Ay, but ye're a rum cove, an't ye. Always soundin' so pretty-like. But you can stowe it around me. Thinks I don't know that yer a knight of the road? But that's Bob with me, so long as ye tip me my gelt."

His boldness prompted Gideon to try to put a damper on him. "A knight of the road? I presume you to mean a highwayman. Whatever gave you that idea, my good fool?"

Rather than being insulted, Lade appeared even more delighted than he had before. "Ay, you like to stick that gig of yours up in the air, don't ye? And them oglers of yers could fool the nubbing-cove that you was a gentry-cove. But 'tis all boman. I knows that yer a sneakin' budge. You and that other rum padder of yers, ye like to go it alone. But I don't mean to get in your way. I'm an honest bluffer."

"Any statement including you and the word honest in the same breath is patently false. I assume you to mean something by it, however, so you might as well out with it so I can finish my breakfast in peace."

His demand provoked Lade to lean closer and whisper, even though there was no one else in the house. "I heard that there's a new pair o' rummer pads workin' the highway near Cranbrook. I also heard that one of 'em must a' nimmed a togeman, on account a' it's silk, which no rummer pad has had in this neighbourhood before."

"Which I'm sure you would know. But what does this silk cloak have to do with me?"

Lade shrugged, and there was a world of knowledge in his gesture. "Well, I don't say nothin' about his togeman or his shappo, but I can say a thing or two about his horse, and it seems that he's got a fine little prancer."

"Oh, he does, does he? And is he the only person in Kent to have a fine horse?"

"No, but as sure as I'm an honest bluffer, I'm a sharp bluffer, too. And I say that a gentry sort o' cove turned up on my doorstep just about the same time that this Blue Satan bites a loge off a cully not too far from here. That's two and two in my book, that is."

Gideon smiled sweetly, and saw that his expression unsettled his host. "I suppose I am to be obliged to you for this useless piece of information?"

Lade straightened himself with a frown. "Ye might tip me a borde for it, seein' as how yer so well equipt."

Hiding his impatience beneath an indifferent look, Gideon reached in his pocket and pulled out a crown. "There," he said, slapping it into Lade's outstretched palm. "There's a crown for you, or a bull's-eye as you call it. You may have it, if you let me finish my breakfast in peace. But if you hear any more news of this highwayman, I hope you *will* bring it to me. I should hate to be his next victim. And, as you have remarked, I spend a great deal of time on the road."

Lade took the crown gratefully, but Gideon could see that his reaction had puzzled the man. If he heard any more of Blue Satan, he would certainly be back, and Gideon doubted that all of Lade's suspicions had been put to rest.

But he could not worry about Lade this morning. He was already annoyed by the delay.

As before, he wore a modest brown coat and a soft felt hat pulled low to conceal his face when he rode into Smarden. Before approaching the post office, he circled through the tiny village, making sure that no King's Messengers were lurking about.

Satisfied that the Duke had not turned his letter over to the Crown, he finally rode up to the tiny inn, tethered Penny to a post, and walked inside to ask for his letters.

The postmaster remembered him and eagerly brought forth an elegantly sealed letter, evidently much impressed to be speaking to a gentleman who had received a message embossed by a ducal coronet. Gideon thanked him and tipped him extra for holding it for him, mindful that he might need the man's services in future. Then he walked back outside, restraining his impatience to open the message until he was safely out of the village and had turned off the main road onto a path through the Weald.

In the deep, protective shade of the towering oaks and beeches, coming into leaf, he tore open the seal, fighting a quiver in his hands.

His Grace of Bournemouth did know the name of the financier that Gideon's father had approached.

In the same way that Gideon had concealed his query in a request for information about a horse, the Duke had framed his reply as if giving the name of the owner.

But Gideon hardly noticed the Duke's verbal subterfuge. His eyes traveled instantly to the name on the page.

And with a sudden grip in his stomach, he knew he was gazing on the name of the man who had killed his father.

⌘

That afternoon, as Hester was reading *The Daily Courant* to her companions, she skimmed down to the notices to see if anything more had been written about the eclipse.

The mapsellers and printsellers of London and Westminster had been selling an instrument that would show the course of the event in every instant of its duration. But aside from the eclipsometer, as it was called, there seemed nothing of interest.

Mrs. Mayfield interrupted her perusings, demanding to be read again the story of the two houses near St. James's market that had fallen, killing six people. While she, Harrowby and Isabella argued over which two houses they were likely to be, Hester resumed her place further down on the page.

The usual articles informing the public of the ships that had sailed or come in was preceded by news from abroad. The advertisements were mostly about the publication of religious treatises, which held little interest for her. Having grown up as the daughter of a clergyman, even a very poor one, she had read enough of such things. The papers were always full of them. Either of them or of miraculous cures performed by medical men.

She was beginning to smile at a combination of the two when the name of the clergyman in question leapt out at her. With a growing sense of excitement, she read,

"Mr. Vickers, the Clergyman, who hath cured several People of the King's Evil, livith in Sherbourne Lane near Lombard-Street."

The name Vickers and Lombard Street brought back her encounter with Mr. Letchworth in the City. Now that she remembered it, she had been trying to cross Sherbourne Lane on her way to the hackney coach that was waiting for her in Wool Church Market. The gentleman who had interfered and who had known Mr. Letchworth had certainly been a Mr. Vickers. He had given her his name. She had not taken him for a clergyman, but he had said that Mr. Letchworth had been to see him.

And he had spoken of Mr. Letchworth's burden.

Now she understood why he always wore such thick paint upon his face. She had noticed the greyish tint to his skin and the bumps on his neck that bulged whenever he was angry.

The thick paint was not to hide his scarring from the smallpox, but the gradual corrosion of his skin.

Mr. Letchworth had been to see Mr. Vickers for a cure for the King's Evil.

As the others' conversation took a louder turn, Hester sat back in her chair, her mind in a roil. It was a shock to discover that Isabella's suitor had been dying and selfish enough not to have been truthful about it. Mr. Letchworth had tried to conceal his illness, while demanding to have his addresses received by a young girl.

His enormous wealth might have persuaded Isabella to take him, if Harrowby had not usurped St. Mars's title. A shudder escaped Hester when she thought that her cousin might have been forced into such a marriage, if not for St. Mars's misfortune.

Then, a light flickered inside her head. She recalled the medal that St. Mars had found among his father's belongings. The token which might have been intended for a financier. A financier who must need a strong inducement to commit himself to treason. And the fact that the Stuarts practiced the King's Touch.

There could be no greater boon than the promise of a cure from death, especially when a man wanted to marry a woman. As much as Mr. Letchworth had wanted to marry Isabella.

She broke abruptly across the others' conversation. "Isabella, do you still have Mr. Letchworth's letter? May I see it?"

Three faces turned to stare at her.

"I think I have it, but why do you want it?" Isabella said. "Mama said that it is nothing but nonsense."

"And so it is, I am sure. But if you still have it, there is a point I would like to examine in it."

"What can you be thinking of, Hester?" Mrs. Mayfield said sharply. "I won't have Isabella upset just to soothe your curiosity."

"It's all right, Mama." Isabella stood and said, "Come with me, Hester, and I'll see if I can find it."

Hester followed her eagerly, but Mrs. Mayfield said, "If Hester wants that foolish letter, she can find it for herself. You do not need to be running errands for her. How will that look?"

"I am going up to use my close-stool, Mama. It's either that or call for a chamber pot in here."

"Oh," Mrs. Mayfield subsided, but she mumbled, "I should have burned that foolish letter the moment she received it—it's the most impertinent piece of rubbish I have ever seen. But you gentlemen," Hester heard her say to poor Harrowby, as they left the room, "you are all mad as dogs when it comes to my Isabella."

If anything could have strengthened Hester's urgency to see the letter, her aunt's words did. She followed Isabella up to her room where a basket overflowing with papers littered her dressing table. Isabella waved at it, and turned to disappear into her closet. "I believe you will find it in there."

With a sense of great anticipation, Hester flipped through the pile of bills, letters from friends, and invitations for the new Countess of Hawkhurst. Not far from the top she spied one with Isabella's name sketched in a man's crude scrawl.

She opened it, and her heart stood still as she read the threats he had made to Harrowby.

I shall marry you. No one will stop me. I will kill any man who gets in my way.

So this, according to her aunt, was the violent language of a man in love. To Hester it was proof of Mr. Letchworth's madness and St. Mars's innocence.

"Did you find the letter?" Isabella asked, stepping back into the room as she smoothed her skirts back into place. "Why, Hester," she said, gazing at her cousin with concern, "you have gone all white. Is something wrong?"

"No, there is nothing wrong. And something is about to become very right. Bella, did you never suspect that Mr. Letchworth might have killed Lord Hawkhurst?"

Isabella looked astonished. "But St. Mars is the one who killed him."

"No, he didn't. But listen to this letter. Mr. Letchworth says right here that he will kill anyone who tries to come between you."

Isabella laughed. "Don't be silly, Hester. Mama says that all men talk such nonsense when they are in love."

"No, they don't. Harrowby did not. And neither did St. Mars, and he loved you very much. Words like this only come from a person with too much violence in him, Bella. Mr. Letchworth threatened Harrowby, remember? I believe that he murdered Lord Hawkhurst in order to cast blame on St. Mars in order to remove him from your list of suitors."

And St. Mars must be told—as soon as possible, Hester thought, as Isabella puzzled over what she had said. She could not tell her cousin her other reasons for believing Mr. Letchworth guilty, of the Jacobite conspirators who had promised him a cure for his affliction in exchange for money to pay for troops, of Mr. Vickers who had promised him the same without the risk of treason, and of St. Mars's quarrel with his father, which had given Mr. Letchworth a reason to kill.

He was the one who had been wounded by Lord Hawkhurst. That was why he had not danced with Isabella at the ball.

Hester remembered thinking that his colour was even greyer than usual that night. He had obviously come in order to give the appearance that all was well, then retired immediately to nurse his wound. And he had not called on her cousin for several days afterwards.

"But I did not truly want to marry St. Mars," Isabella protested, still unconvinced.

"No, dear. But Mr. Letchworth could not know that. How could he, when even I did not understand your preferences until later. To the rest of us St. Mars seemed the man you would most likely choose if the Duke failed to offer for you, and your mother would have chosen St. Mars for you if he had not been arrested.

"I must go," she said, feeling even more pressed. She must take a letter for St. Mars into Hawkhurst in time to catch the evening post. She turned to leave the room, then thought of the precious evidence in her hand and how she must not lose it. Unwilling to waste the time to go to her own room, she said, "I will leave this in the top drawer of your dressing table, Bella, but it must be kept. It can prove St. Mars is innocent."

"If he is, will he want to come back here?"

Her anxious question brought Hester up short. She spun around in time to see worry forming on her cousin's brow.

She really had no time to reconcile Isabella to the loss of her new position. Mr. Letchworth must be found and stopped before he could kill anyone else.

Hester thought of the announcement of Isabella's wedding in *The Daily Courant*. If Mr. Letchworth had seen it—and certainly he had—he might be planning a way to kill Harrowby. She did not want to alarm Isabella, but surely she would choose to protect her husband over keeping a position to which she had never had a right in the first place.

"You mustn't worry about Lord St. Mars, Bella. He is a very generous man. I'm quite sure that he will provide for you and Harrowby both, once his rights are restored.

"But I must go quickly. Someone must be notified of what we have found."

She left Isabella with the impression, she hoped, that she meant to fetch Sir Joshua, and walked quickly to the small withdrawing room where she kept a pen and paper to write letters for her aunt. Without bothering to sharpen the quill, she scratched out a note and addressed it to Mr. Brown at the inn St. Mars had named. She sealed it with a wafer, then tucked it deeply into the pocket of her gown before running downstairs and out by a side door.

She wanted to avoid being seen by her aunt, who would demand to know where she was going. Hester walked as fast she could across the open ground not worrying about the light coat of dampness soaking into her shoes. A strange dull light seemed to still all movement around her as she broke into a run.

He saw, he wished, and to the prize aspired.
Resolved to win, he meditates the way,
By force to ravish, or by fraud betray;
For when success a Lover's toil attends,
Few ask, if fraud or force attained his ends.

He springs to vengeance with an eager pace,
And falls like thunder on the prostrate Ace.

CHAPTER XX

THE village of Hawkhurst lay no more than two miles to the south of the Abbey by way of the road. By taking a shortcut through the woods, she could be there in less than half an hour. As soon as she came to the trees, she turned onto a wide footpath.

She had gone no more than a few yards along it before she heard the soft thunder of horses galloping towards her with a speed that made her step quickly aside to avoid being trampled. As the two approaching riders burst out of the shadows into her vision, she gasped to recognize St. Mars.

He had donned his blue satin cloak and mask, she guessed, to keep from being known this close to home. She had no sooner seen him than he must have spied her, for he halted his horse sharply and started to turn it deeper into the woods.

"My lord!" She cried out to stop him, even as he seemed to recognize her. She gasped with relief as he walked Penny towards her, his servant Tom bringing up the rear.

"Mrs. Kean!" he called, before they reached her. "What is the matter? Has something occurred?"

The tenseness in his voice surprised her. But he must have suspected danger, or he would not be abroad in the light.

"Not yet." She waited for Penny to come to a perspiring halt. The state his horse was in told her that they had ridden fast, and she wondered what had brought them.

She continued breathlessly, "I was going into the village to send you a note. It was Mr. Letchworth, my lord. He has the King's Evil."

As St. Mars dismounted, she tried to make out his face, but in the failing light, his mask and hat hid his reaction. "Mr. Letchworth is your murderer, my lord."

He clasped both of her hands in his. Even now, his face was in shadow. "I know. Bournemouth supplied me with his name, but I did not know why he had considered risking so much.

"We must hurry," he said, leading her back to his horse. "We believe that Letchworth is on his way to the Abbey. Tom was told by an ostler on the road from London that he was headed this way. He must mean harm."

Hester froze. "Harrowby. He means to kill your cousin, my lord. Mr. Letchworth is in love with Isabella. He wrote her a letter, vowing to kill anyone who tries to take her from him. And the announcement of their wedding appeared in the newspaper a few days ago."

She felt an increased pressure from his hand. "I know where he'll be then. Come on."

Faster than she would have believed possible, he picked her up and tossed her in front of his saddle. Not waiting for Tom's help, he mounted swiftly behind her and spurred Penny back in the direction she had come.

They burst out of the trees, but the light Hester had expected in the open was not there. A dreadful stillness seemed to have fallen upon the world.

No birds were singing. Aside from the sounds their horses made, there were not even any rustles in the trees or the grass. They passed a lone oak tree, and Hester looked down at the strange shadow it made. Unbelievably, every single one of its leaves had cast a separate shadow of its own.

Some primitive instinct made her feel as if the world was sliding towards its end. No wind was in the trees. Nature had abandoned itself. And the earth seemed poised for a giant calamity.

Then the light grew dimmer, the shadows all merged into one, and they were plunged into a terrible darkness.

Behind her, she could hear Tom's dreadful curse. St. Mars tightened his arm around her, and then she remembered.

She covered his hand, turning her face up to his. "It is the eclipse," she said, hoping he heard her.

Gideon did hear. And the comfort of her touch made him relax his unconscious grip. He moved his fingers beneath hers until they clung.

The darkness was eerie. It was neither the absolute blackness of night nor the uneven light of a storm, but the tenebrosity of an Italian masterpiece. If God had appeared in the sky, Gideon would not have been amazed.

Holding on to Hester with a sense of impending fate, he reined Penny towards a corner of the house. The thick brick wall loomed above them. The stillness of the eclipse seemed to have frightened the inhabitants of the Abbey. No one was in sight as they rounded it from the east.

As they did, he saw a man approaching the house on foot, no more than twenty yards away. It was Letchworth, aiming for the small door tucked between two wings under an eave, the door that the murderer had entered to kill his father.

A white haze clouded Gideon's vision. He forgot the eclipse and the stillness. All he saw was the coward who had stabbed his father in the back.

Letchworth saw them coming and halted.

"There he is, my lord!" Hester's cry reminded him of the need for her safety. He pulled Penny up, and with a squeeze of Hester's waist, he said, "Stay here," and slid her to the ground alongside a hedge leading into the formal gardens. She moved behind it, out of his way, and he and Tom pushed their horses to surround their man.

Letchworth had frozen. Transfixed by the darkness or by the sight of a masked man riding out of it towards him, he stared at Gideon like one who beheld the gates of Hell. He had no weapon, just his cane, which he thrust up over his head to ward off the attack. Gideon urged Penny closer to him. A swing of Letchworth's stick made her shy and step sideways, but she was too weary to flee.

When no blows rained down upon his head, Letchworth lowered his cane. Hastily putting a hand inside his pocket, he shouted, "All the money I have is in this purse. Here, take it—" he reached up with it— "and leave me to my task. If you ride quickly, no one else will see you."

Gideon's mind filled with loathing. Letchworth was so intent upon Harrowby's murder, he would make his robber an accomplice.

"I do not want your money," he said, remembering all too well how he had helped this man frame him for his father's death. A chill of hatred welled up from deep inside him.

He wanted to use his sword. He wanted to run Letchworth through and make him suffer the way his father had. But the only thing that could restore him to his life was this man's confession.

"I am taking you to a magistrate, so you can confess to the murder of my father."

Letchworth staggered back. Even in the dark, Gideon could see the horror on his face—a fear of the vengeance that had ridden out of the night to take him to the gallows—a figure, cloaked and covered as he had been the night he had attacked St. Mars.

"St. Mars?" His voice trembled. His legs seemed no longer to function as he stumbled backwards, finally falling to the ground. He clutched his worthless cane to his chest.

Had his illness become so severe that he could no longer resist it? A hard ride on horseback would have weakened him. Letchworth had made that same trip and back a bare six weeks ago, yet how much more ill those weeks would have made him, as his disease rotted him from inside, stiffening his joints and mangling his bones.

Gideon dismounted and went to help him up. Tom took his reins.

Letchworth cringed, and still he made no move to pull a weapon. No sword hung at his side. Gideon wondered what injury he had planned for Harrowby. Did he carry a pistol or a dagger? Carefully, he bent over to take the man by the arm.

A sudden lightening of the sky as the moon moved away from the sun illuminated the look on Letchworth's face. It bore a look of cunning, not defeat.

How had this creature outwitted his father? *Things unseen do not deceive us.* Gideon's family motto flashed into his mind, and with it, a revelation.

Jerking back, and reaching for his sword, he just missed Letchworth's lunge as the man pulled a sword from his cane. Surging to his feet just a moment too late, he missed his mark, hitting Gideon with his shoulder instead of the point of his blade. Gideon was knocked sideways, but he recovered, leaping backwards to put more space between them.

"Careful, my lord!" Tom cried. He had not seen the attack coming, and remorse was in his voice.

"Put the sword down," Gideon said, struggling with his breath. The attack had caught him by surprise, disrupting his intake of air. So this was how the coward killed. "You cannot win. If I fail to stop you, my servant won't."

He saw Tom out of the corner of his eye. Tom had pulled a pistol from his saddle and was pointing it straight at Letchworth's chest.

"Don't shoot him! I need his testimony."

Letchworth laughed as he circled widely, the swordstick raised in his hand. He seemed unconcerned about Tom. "You will never kill me. I am the only one who can exonerate you, St. Mars—not that I will. I was too quick for your father—and I'm too quick for you. I'll outsmart you and get what I want."

"You weren't that smart. You were nothing but a coward. The only way you managed to kill my father was by stabbing him in the back." Gideon watched for an opening.

"He thought he could buy me with a medal from the Pretender, but I don't need the Stuart touch. Vickers will cure me, and even if he doesn't, I have another King now. His Majesty laid his hands upon me when he made me a knight."

Hester had followed close upon the horses' heels and had come to a stop within hearing distance of the two men. As long as the moon had blocked the sun, she had struggled to see their expressions, but ever since Mr. Letchworth had pulled his sword, the sky had been brightening. The flat, odd light had returned. St. Mars and Mr. Letchworth circled each other, casting unnatural shadows on the ground.

She couldn't understand why the murderer wouldn't yield. Two armed men could surely stop his flight. St. Mars would not kill him, which would be for the best. She had the letter with Mr. Letchworth's threats. But better no blood should be on St. Mars's hands.

Still with his weapon *en garde*, Mr. Letchworth pulled back near the horses, which stood where Tom had left them. Just as he reached for Penny's reins, St. Mars lunged.

Their swords clashed in a cross in front of their chests. St. Mars pushed Mr. Letchworth back with the strength of an angry man, but surprisingly Mr. Letchworth countered with an almost equal strength. His source was madness. It could not be anything else, for he responded with a terrifying frenzy.

Hester had never seen a sword fight. It was nothing like the brawls one saw in the streets of London or in the Yorkshire village where her father had been a clergyman. Those fights had been mere tussles compared to this, no matter how brutal they had been. She had not liked them. They had caused bruises and cuts, which had seemed like enough misery to satisfy the men who earned them. But this—this duel, in which St. Mars's life depended both on defeating his opponent and keeping him alive, frightened her more than anything she had ever seen.

At first, St. Mars did nothing but parry Mr. Letchworth's thrusts. Though wild, they still bore the mark of schooling. He was no novice to the skill of fencing. He must have trained with a master. A lack of ethics had led him to cowardice, not a lack of skill.

Skill that Hester was afraid St. Mars might lack, as she watched him evade lunge after lunge. He parried neatly, but Mr. Letchworth appeared to have the strength of seven men. How long St. Mars could continue to hold out under the force of the other man's attacks, she did not know, but she worried that his recent injury had robbed him of his strength.

A grim look settled beneath his mask. He stared into his adversary's eyes with the piercing gaze of a hawk, determined on a kill. His breaths came evenly, though beads of sweat collected on his forehead.

Slowly Hester became aware of the enormous skill he had held in check. His defensive posture had been intended merely to tire his opponent. Now she saw that his every movement was working towards Letchworth's disarmament, not injury. His smooth, rapid footwork, and well-timed thrusts began to drive Letchworth backwards towards the Abbey wall, where he would be helpless to retreat.

Letchworth kept backing, unaware of the wall behind him and the small door just off to his left. His skin turned a sickly grey as he sweated off his thick layer of paint. Beneath it, they could see the ravages of the King's Evil, the crusty eating-away of his flesh, then the knobby growths on his bones that he had striven so hard to hide. Hester would have shrunk from the pitiable sight if her fears for St. Mars had not kept her eyes glued on the movements of the two men engaged in mortal battle.

A piece of cracking paint slid into Mr. Letchworth's eyes. He gave it a swipe with his sleeve, leaving a streak of white and rouge from his forehead across his cheek. St. Mars hesitated. A look half of disgust, half of something like pity crossed his face. In that moment it seemed as if he would have pled again with this murderer to surrender to him. But Mr. Letchworth saw his pity, and he roared.

He rushed at St. Mars, just as his weapon was paused to parry a thrust. But Mr. Letchworth had not raised his sword. With the fury of a mad dog, lunging to bite, he threw himself bodily at its source.

St. Mars's sword caught him just beneath his heart. The weight of his body drove it home. Even with the pain of the strike, he could not recoil, but plummeted forward into St. Mars's arms, the blade burying itself to the hilt.

St. Mars caught him, and all the colour drained out of face. "No!"

Hester heard the desperate syllable even where she stood. Tom rushed to help, and she ran, coming to a halt at St. Mars's side.

Mr. Letchworth's eyes were still open. They had fixed in an expression of surprise, as if he had never believed in his own mortality.

With an anxious face, Tom pulled the body out of his master's arms and lowered it to the ground. They heard a gurgling sound deep in Mr. Letchworth's throat. Hester watched St. Mars's expression change to despair, as Tom loosened the man's neckcloth and felt for a pulse. Then Tom put his ear to Mr. Letchworth's chest.

"Is he dead?" St. Mars's asked, in a curt tone, even though Hester could see the anguish in his eyes.

"Aye, my lord, I'm afraid he is—not that the cur didn't deserve it."

"Yes, he did. But I have truly fixed things now. Sir Joshua will never believe the evidence of a corpse." He turned away from them both to run a hand over his face.

Hester stood helplessly by. She wanted to tell him about Mr. Letchworth's letter, but she was afraid to raise his hopes. It would take a great deal of convincing to persuade Sir Joshua or another magistrate that Mr. Letchworth had been responsible for Lord Hawkhurst's killing.

"But I was here, my lord," she started to say. "I can be a witness to what transpired here. I can tell Sir Joshua that you tried to deliver Mr. Letchworth to him."

St. Mars shook his head as he turned towards her, his hat shading his mask. "No, you must not say anything. How can you explain what he was doing at Rotherham Abbey when he heard my quarrel with my father? You cannot—not without exposing my father as a traitor and a Jacobite. I could not live with that, not when I am so much to blame."

"But, my lord—"

They heard a shout. St. Mars shoved her behind him as he whirled to meet it. Someone from the far end of the garden had seen them, but whoever it was, was too far away to be recognized.

He turned back to face Hester. Gripping her by the arm, he quickly walked her to the small door in the Abbey wall, shielding her with the spread of his cloak.

"Here—take these stairs," he said rapidly. "Say nothing. You did not see Letchworth. You must be as shocked as everyone else by his death."

"But—" Before she could protest, he opened the door and pushed her gently through it. The last thing she saw of him was a swirl of blue satin as he closed the door.

Hester took a stunned minute to recover, before turning and making her way up the spiral stairs to Lord Hawkhurst's library. Shuddering to think that the murderer had come this way, she nearly ran out of the library to Isabella's dressing room where she had left her with the letter.

Outside it, she paused to smooth her hair and gown, wiping the worry off her face, before she knocked on the door.

"Come in."

The sound of Mrs. Mayfield's voice caused her heart to give a queer leap. She entered the room where she found both her aunt and Isabella waiting.

They seemed to be waiting for her. Both sat erect in their cane-backed chairs, pulled up to the fire. No work was in their hands. Nor did they seem to have been chatting. The look in Mrs. Mayfield's eyes when they fell on Hester held more viciousness than Hester had ever seen.

"Where have you been?" She started in on her directly. "I understand you left this house without my permission."

Hester's glance flew to her cousin's face. Isabella looked afraid, but there was also a hint of guilt in her countenance. Hester knew at once that she had told her mother about Mr. Letchworth's letter.

She could do no worse than try to brazen it out. She answered casually as she crossed the room to Isabella's dressing table, "I had intended to send a message, but the sky grew so dark before I could reach the village, I had to turn back. It was an eclipse. You ought to have come outdoors to see it. It was quite remarkable."

"Send a message to who?" Her aunt ignored her other statements.

Hester had reached the table. With a trembling hand, she pulled open the drawer.

No letter was there. The drawer contained nothing but Isabella's brushes and combs.

Turning rapidly, she saw the triumph in Mrs. Mayfield's face, and the tearful shame on Isabella's.

"I put a letter in here. An important paper, Aunt. I would like to be told what has become of it." Indignation and fury burned like torches inside her.

"If you mean Mr. Letchworth's letter to Isabella, then you might as well forget it. It is no longer here."

"I need that letter. We must show it to Sir Joshua Tate. It proves that Mr. Letchworth was the man who killed my Lord Hawkhurst. He did it to cast blame on Lord St. Mars in order to remove him from your list of suitors, Bella." She cast her cousin a pleading look.

"That is nonsense!" Mrs. Mayfield bit out. "And so I shall tell Sir Joshua if you dare to mention anything of the sort to him. What are you trying to do, Hester, ruin us? Your cousin has made a splendid match. She is a countess now—a very rich lady. And you and I shall live much the better for it. I expect you to keep your mouth closed!"

"We cannot take Lord St. Mars's money. That is stealing. He was falsely accused, and we have the proof."

She drew herself up. "Where have you put that letter, Aunt?"

"Somewhere where you will never find it. As far as you are concerned, I might have thrown it in the fire."

Hester darted her gaze at the coals. They burned a clean, vivid red. If her aunt had thrown the letter into the fire, it would be nothing but ashes now.

Fighting a sick feeling, she spoke as calmly as she could. "But we all saw it. We can still tell Sir Joshua that Mr. Letchworth threatened to kill anyone who came between him and Isabella. We can tell him that he threatened Sir Harrowby."

She could not let them know that he had been killed—here—right outside, on his way to fulfill that threat. She hoped to use their ignorance against them. "Mr. Letchworth must be stopped before he tries to murder Isabella's husband. You wouldn't want that, Bella, would you?"

"Mama?" Isabella turned big, anxious eyes on her mother. "I know you said we mustn't make the letter public, but—"

"Hush! I've already told you that his ravings are nothing more than the words of a man who's violently in love. I am certain I received many a letter with exactly that sort of language both before and after I married your papa, yet nobody murdered anybody for all I know. If they wanted to fight a duel over me, there was nothing I could do to stop them, was there? And if Mr. Letchworth challenges your husband . . . well, then, Harrowby will just have to beat him, won't he? A lady is helpless to stop these passions gentlemen have. They just love a fight. So don't you worry about it, my precious. Just let your husband take care of himself."

"But you," she said to Hester, rising out of her chair to turn a withering look upon her niece, "you have gone too far. I cannot be expected to house a traitor to the family. You may have two weeks to find yourself another post, and do not expect me to do it for you. I have done enough to help you already, and if you have no other relations to beg from, then that is not my fault."

Hester couldn't speak for the fear that struck her. She had never wanted to live with her aunt, but with no other home to claim, she had no choice.

Pride kept her from begging to stay. She would find something—anything rather than that. A position as a housekeeper, perhaps.

But no sooner had these thoughts sped through her mind than Isabella cried out, "No! You cannot throw Hester out, Mama. She didn't mean any harm. She doesn't want us to be penniless. She just made a mistake. Didn't you, Hester?"

Hester was touched by her cousin's defence, even though Bella was the one who was mistaken. She had a generous heart when it did not interfere with her mother's will, her own limited grasp, or the wishes she had for herself. Still, Hester could not lie to her, if it meant betraying St. Mars.

She moved to take Isabella's hands in hers. "Thank you, Bella. I hope you know that I love you, and I would never do anything willingly to harm you. But, unfortunately, in this case, I have to tell the truth.

"I know that Mr. Letchworth killed Lord Hawkhurst. If I do not tell Sir Joshua, then I will be letting us take the things that rightfully belong to St. Mars."

Tears filled her cousin's eyes. "But Harrowby is the earl now, and he wants to be an earl. And I want to be a countess. How can you be so certain, Hester? You cannot possibly know."

Hester hesitated. St. Mars had instructed her to pretend no knowledge of Mr. Letchworth's death, or of his attempt to enter the Abbey. Without that information, how could she say that she was sure?

A sudden commotion came to them through the door, muffled shouts, running feet. A door slammed.

"What on earth is that?" Mrs. Mayfield turned to open the door and vanished through it. In a second, Hester heard her voice calling down the stairs.

Curious, Isabella dropped her cousin's hands to follow her mother out of the room.

Left all alone, Hester surmised that someone had found Mr. Letchworth's body. She prayed that they had not captured St. Mars, and she was comforted by the recollection that his horse had stood nearby. She remembered how swift Penny was.

Afraid, for him—and for herself, for it appeared she was to be thrown on the mercy of strangers—still she searched the dressing chamber thoroughly for any sign of the letter. She did not think her aunt would have destroyed it. She knew how little use it was as evidence, but she also knew its value. There might come a day when a person more sympathetic to St. Mars's cause would be in a position to restore him to his rights.

The letter was nowhere to be found. Still, she believed her aunt had kept it. If nothing else, the threat of making it public could give Mrs. Mayfield control over Harrowby. And Hester knew her aunt too well to imagine that she would not have thought of that possibility. She would never burn her advantage over another human being.

Defeated, Hester left the room and all of its secrets behind her to descend the stairs and play the role St. Mars had asked her to play.

Oh! if to dance all night, and dress all day,
Charmed the smallpox, or chased old age away;
Who would not scorn what housewife's cares produce,
Or who would learn one earthly thing of use?
To patch, nay ogle, might become a Saint,
Nor could it sure be such a sin to paint.
But since, alas! frail beauty must decay,
Curled or uncurled, since Locks will turn to grey;

Since painted, or not painted, all shall fade,
And she who scorns a man, must die a maid;
What then remains but well our power to use,
And keep good humour still whate'er we lose?
And trust me, dear! good humour can prevail,
When airs, and flights, and screams, and scolding fail.
Beauties in vain their pretty eyes may roll;
Charms strike the sight, but merit wins the soul."

CHAPTER XXI

LATE, on the following night, near midnight, when Hester returned to her room to sleep, she took a moment to pet the greyhound dog that had taken up his abode outside her door. Then she entered, and throwing off her air of composure, she turned to lean her forehead against the solid oak, hardly aware of the candle in her hand.

It had taken nearly all her strength to pretend ignorance. Unable to say what she knew, she had struggled under the burden of lies, forbidden to divulge Mr. Letchworth's motive for the murder to help St. Mars.

A gardener had spied the two masked men with their horses, looming over the body. He had not recognized them, nor had he been aware of the lady concealed by one of the men's bodies. Hester supposed she should be grateful he missed her, but he had spread the word that a villain in a long, blue cloak had murdered a gentleman just outside the Abbey.

A hue and cry had been raised for the highwayman, Blue Satan, whose description Harrowby had recognized instantly. In the shock and bustle of dealing with Mr. Letchworth's corpse, sending for Sir Joshua, and answering his questions, no one had bothered to ask *why* Mr. Letchworth had been found outside the door that Lord Hawkhurst's murderer had used to gain entrance to the Abbey.

Hester had glimpsed an occasional flicker of speculation in the gentlemen's eyes—Harrowby's, Sir Joshua's, and more particularly James Henry's. Still, no one had voiced his suspicions. Hester's aunt had made certain that she was given no chance to speak, and since it was presumed she had been inside and seen nothing, no one had asked her for her version of the events.

Hours later, when Sir Joshua had gone, Mrs. Mayfield threatened her again. Mr. Letchworth's appearance at the Abbey had convinced her of his guilt, Hester believed, but his death had released her from any worry she might have felt for Harrowby. She only wanted to be rid of the one person who might try to convince the magistrate of the truth and all would be perfect in her eyes.

But to all their amazements, Isabella had firmly put her foot down.

"No, Mama," she had said again, in a defiant tone. "I don't want you to send Hester away. And you cannot, for I won't let you. *I* am the countess and this is *my* house now, so I can say who stays, not you. Hester can be my waiting woman instead of yours. I want her to be with me, and she will be with me, so that's that."

Then, hugging her, Isabella had pleaded with Hester to stay, sensing the struggle she had with her conscience, even if she could not understand her reasons.

Hester had found herself embracing her cousin in tears, the only salve to her conscience being that in remaining, she could continue to search for the letter and provide St. Mars with another ally in his house.

If she ever saw him again, which was not very likely, she told herself, as she pushed her head away from the door. She walked to the small commode that served as her nightstand and set her candle down. She turned to look at herself in the mirror, noting the droop of her shoulders and her down-turned mouth. The only news she had to comfort her was that, so far, Blue Satan had not been found.

She looked down to locate the hooks to her bodice. She had unhooked two, when a deep voice sounded behind her.

"I shouldn't finish that, if I were you."

She turned and gasped, "St. Mars!"

He appeared from behind the heavy curtains to her bed, stepping around from the other side to stand just a few feet away from her. He paused at the foot of the bed, his black tricorn in his hand, his fair hair tied back with a black ribbon. He wore the blue satin cloak over a billowing white shirt.

On his face was a mixture of amusement and apology.

"I hope you will pardon the intrusion, Mrs. Kean. I did not mean to startle you."

"No! I mean, of course, my lord, you are excused. I am very pleased to see you. But how did you come in here?"

"I have a way, which I will show you. But first, I should like to know what caused you to rest your head against the door? I would have spoken sooner, but I was afraid to disturb you when it seemed you needed a moment to yourself. In any event, I should have said something before you started to undress."

His gaze dropped to the opening at her breast.

Hester felt herself roasting from her chin down to her toes. She covered the small opening hastily with one hand. With fluttering eyelids and a queer beat in her heart, she said, "It is of no importance, my lord. You spoke in time."

She ventured to peek at him from beneath her lashes. He seemed unnaturally still as he watched her silently from across the room. They stood that way for a matter of seconds, not speaking, with the bed between them.

St. Mars cleared his throat. "Yes . . . I did." He retreated to the window seat. Hester watched him walk towards it, his cloak swirling about his knees, when with a natural grace he turned and swept it behind him. "I hope you don't mind if I sit a while. I shall not stay long, but the ride before me is."

"You must sit, of course." When he did, propping one boot up on the wooden bench and draping an elbow across his knee, she asked, "Are you going away?" She hoped that her tone did not betray her dismay.

"Not tonight. But I may go to France. I should see to the business of my estate. No," he continued, "tonight, I have only to return to my lodgings at the Fox and Goose. But having ridden half the night already, I find I am a little tired."

"Why have you ridden half the night, my lord?" She spoke with unconscious sympathy.

He smiled wistfully back at her. "Perhaps for the same reason you rested your head against the door?"

She sighed and moved to hold on to one of the bed posts. Leaning against it, she said, "That is very likely."

"Then there is nothing more to say. We did our best. If Letchworth had given himself up—" He did not finish, but looked down at his hands. "I cannot be sorry for having killed him. My father would have done the same for me . . . though perhaps sooner."

"I quite understand you, my lord, and you must not blame yourself for what has occurred. Either on that day *or* on the day your father was murdered."

He gave an unamused laugh. "My dear Mrs. Kean, it is only the knowledge of my blame that makes my current situation tolerable. How else can I justify all I have lost?"

Her heart ached painfully for him. She wished he could spare himself these regrets. She only hoped that time would help him to see more clearly. He must forgive himself or he would never make another push to recover his position.

"Your friendship is the one blessing I have to be thankful for. If you ever have need of my help, no matter what it might be, at any time, or in any place, you have only to send for me. Will you promise to do that, Mrs. Kean?"

Her agreement would help to salve his conscience, but she would not give it without one condition. "Only if you promise to do the same, my lord."

His silence told her that she had surprised him. He laughed. "Very well, dear lady. Or, should I say, dear friend?"

"I believe that both are accurate, my lord." She felt herself burning. His laughter, which seemed to stem from delight, had the same effect on her as before, as if a slow-burning candle that heated but did not singe had been lit inside her.

"I know they are. And now, my very dear friend, Mrs. Kean," he said, springing to his feet, as if he had never claimed to be tired, "I shall show you the secret to my miraculous entry.

"Remember," he said, as she followed him to the wall across from the foot of her bed, "that I once told you that this room is a very handy chamber?"

Hester nodded.

"Well, it truly is. See this piece of carving that resembles the top of a pineapple?"

"I do see it, my lord"

"If you ever want to escape from this house, you have only to turn it so, and . . ."

Hester was amazed to see the shape of a door appearing in the paneling. It swung away from her, as if on a spring, making only a slight squeak. A small, dark closet stood revealed beyond, and a cool burst of earth-scented air floated upwards out of the blackness inside.

"It's a staircase!" she exclaimed in a whisper. "I had no idea that this doorway was here."

"This is the closet where I found the documents my father hid. I came in this way one night after I escaped from Sir Joshua's men."

He stepped into the tiny space and lit a torch. It roared into life, illuminating the narrow staircase with its damp stone walls. She peered down the stairs, as he held the torch out to help her see. But its beam only reached a short way into the dark. The steps appeared to descend into a black, bottomless well.

"At the base of these stairs is a tunnel that goes to an undercroft in the ruins, near where we met." St. Mars explained why it had been built, and he asked her to show it to Mr. Bramwell, if the King should ever change his current position and decide to persecute the nonjuring priests.

She promised him she would.

"No one else knows of this, except you and Tom. I know you will keep the secret to yourself. I wanted you to be aware of it in case you should ever have need of it." He showed her how the latch in the closet could be opened, should she ever enter her room from the ruins.

As St. Mars extinguished his torch and stepped back into her bedchamber, Hester assured him of her discretion and thanked him for honouring her with the secret.

"I thought it only fair to tell you about it—" he grinned— "considering that this is the passage I will have to use to enter my house. I will not use it often, but I should hate to frighten you when I do."

The idea that he might pass through her room at who-knew-what hour flustered Hester. "Not at all, my lord. Of course, you must use it as often as you wish."

Then fearing that he might take her words for an invitation he would not welcome, she added, "I do not suppose that you could give a little knock?"

His eyes danced with laughter. "I shall most certainly knock, and I shall take care not to disturb you at any more awkward moments, Mrs. Kean."

She could not help laughing back. "You are goodness itself, my lord."

They stood smiling. Then something sad occurred to him, for his look turned wistful. With a wry twist to his lips, he said, "I should be going now. But I meant what I said. If you should ever be in any need, I am your servant."

"You *are* kind, my lord."

"Not at all. It would give me great pleasure to serve you. More than I can ever express."

Hester curtsied, her eyes lowered so that he would not see how much she wished him to stay. But he raised her up, and taking both her hands in his, kissed them with more earnestness than was courtly, before ducking behind the wall.

Not bothering to light his torch, he called back up to her as he vanished. "Good night, Mrs. Kean."

"Good night, my lord."

Hester waited until no more sounds came from below— no footsteps, no falling pieces of earth, no brushes of air that might have been caused by a swirl of his cloak—before closing the secret door and laying her hands on the carving that could open it up again. She made very certain that she remembered which one it was, before turning to seek her bed.

She hugged a feather pillow to herself.

She *would* see St. Mars again.

THE END

For, after all the murders of your eye,
When, after millions slain, yourself shall die;
When those fair suns shall set, as set they must,
And all those tresses shall be laid in dust;
This lock, the Muse shall consecrate to fame,
And 'midst the stars inscribe Belinda's name.

AUTHOR'S NOTE

Some of my readers will accuse me of having Tory sympathies. I can assure them that I am neither pro nor con. My novel simply starts in a year when the Whigs had come into power. The tactics they used had been employed to only a slighter degree by the Tory party, which had invented them. It was the beginning of a Whig century, for they stayed in power for almost one hundred years. I think it fair to assume that in England, as in other places, history was written by the victors, so I have tried to be fair to the Tories and the Jacobites.

Up until the accession of George I, the social life of the aristocracy revolved around the Court. Then, since George had little taste for either pageantry or society and, speaking no English, never exerted himself to see that his British subjects were entertained, the social whirl began to revolve in the private sphere. The assemblies and balls that previous monarchs had hosted were gradually given more by the aristocrats themselves.

The eighteenth century has been called the Age of Aristocracy. During those years aristocratic prerogative reached its peak, with the resulting contrast of extraordinary beauty and brutal poverty.

As far as I can tell, very few novels have been set during the first few years of George I's reign. At first glance this seems strange because so many factors were present in that age that would seem the perfect material for fiction: a contested throne, spying and intrigue, and the ever-romantic (in legend, at least) highwaymen. These are the elements that attracted me to the period.

Then when one begins to research, one comes up against a strange phenomenon—a terrible dearth of memoirs, letters, and diaries. Several of the old news-sheets are available on microfilm, the *Daily Courant,* the *British Weekly Mercury,* the *Postboy,* the *Flying Post,* the *Post Man,* etc., but these are good only for certain facts and advertisements. There are no journals of the caliber of those written during Queen Anne's reign only a few years before, the wonderful *Tatler* and *Spectator* of Joseph Addison and Richard Steele, no opposition newspapers like Jonathan Swift's *Examiner,* or the independent *Review* from Daniel Defoe, just the unrelentingly pro-Hanoverian rant, the *Political State of Great Britain*, by A. Boyer.

The reasons for this were many. The Whigs had successfully co-opted the talents of Addison and Steele by giving them government appointments, in the same way that the Tory ministry had employed Swift. Swift, himself, had been banished to the deanery of Dublin. A process of libel had temporarily silenced Defoe. For other writers who might have criticized the Court and its party, there were two impediments, both of which had been raised by the government to suppress this increasingly troubling group. A heavy tax had been placed on newspapers, the effect of which was both devastating and immediate. As Swift wrote in his Journal to Stella, "Did you know that Grub Street is dead and gone last week? No more ghosts or murders now for love or money." The imposition of the tax saw the disappearance of all the good papers from the streets. Some that were bad still flourished—the first instance, perhaps, of the triumph of the lowest common denominator.

The second impediment was even more serious. Within two months of his coronation, King George instructed his justices of the peace to fully execute the laws at their command against printers and publishers. In all fairness, one must note that prosecutions against newspapers had already multiplied under Queen Anne.

Although the English press would recover from these setbacks, the years 1713-1716, or so, were among its hardest hit.

Newspapers are wonderful resources in their way, but they cannot supply the details of daily life, the gossip, and the attitudes that a historical novelist can find by reading memoirs, letters, and diaries. I am sure my readers will appreciate my disappointment at finding very few of these for the year 1715, in which this series begins. Again this seems strange when one understands the magnitude of the events taking place that year. It was George's first full year upon his throne. One can imagine the gossip and speculation that must have gone on in every family even remotely connected to the Court, the jostling for power, the wangling of influence. Then a major Jacobite rebellion took place near the end of the year. Why, then, is there so little evidence of the conversations and events that must have taken place?

In more than one diary or collection of letters, I would find an abundance of entries up until the first year of George's reign. Then there would appear an abrupt hiatus with nothing for a year or two, before the author of the diary or letters would gradually resume his or her writing. I had begun to suspect foul play, when I came across the following comment on the part of Elizabeth Lady Bristol, in a letter to her husband, dated April 7, 1713.

> "Pray send me word if you find my letters are open'd, for they tell me they do it to all."

and later, on October 25, 1716:

> "I will keep my letter open till he comes home in hopes of some news, though they make such a practice of opening letters that one dare not say anything but what is in the prints."

Lady Mary Wortley Montagu, who was nothing if not eloquent in her encouragement to her husband to get himself an appointment at Court, complained repeatedly about his failure to write her when she was stuck in Yorkshire with a baby.

> "I cannot forbear takeing it something unkindly that you do not write to me when you may be assur'd I am in a great Fright, and know not certainly what to expect upon this sudden change. (August 6, 1714)"

Later, he must have given her his reason for she reproved him for not telling her sooner that all letters were being opened.

One of the best memoirs of the period comes from Emily Lady Cowper. Her niece, who saw that the memoirs were published, writes in her foreword that her aunt and uncle had to burn many of their papers when Lord Cowper was accused of disloyalty by some of his enemies within the Whig party.

Lady Bristol and Lady Cowper were both ladies in waiting to the Princess of Wales, both approved by King George, and Lady Mary Wortley Montagu was a personal favorite of the king. If these ladies were made nervous by the government's practice of opening private letters and seizing ministers' papers, (this last first done when George took the throne), one can imagine how careful the Tories and Jacobites had to be to leave no trace of theirs.

The result for a novelist was that many times I had to rely on memoirs written later, from the safety of less hysterical years, and to extrapolate customs from the copious writings of just a few years before. If I've made errors in these, I hope my audience will forgive me.

A few more notes about some of the facts used in this book.

The King's Evil, which was essential to my plot, was the popular name given to scrofula, a form of tuberculosis that affects the bones. The name came from the belief that the sovereign's touch could cure it, a superstition, which dated back to the time of Edward the Confessor. The *Encyclopædia Britannica*, Eleventh Edition, notes that Samuel Johnson received the touch from Queen Anne in 1712.

There was indeed a Mr. Vickers, a clergyman who lived in Sherbourne Lane, who claimed to be able to cure it. I have no idea what method he pretended to use, but I assume it was something religious. He advertised in the *Daily Courant*.

Similarly, the news-sheets in that month advertised the prediction of a major eclipse on April 22, 1715, based upon Halley's calculations, even though the prediction was not his. I checked my *Britannica* and found that the eclipse did not occur then. Most interestingly, it had already occurred, just over two weeks before, on April 7. According to the *Britannica,* it is notable "for the careful observations made in England, and published by Halley in the *Philosophical Transactions.*" It is listed in a table of dates on which the shadow of the moon passed over some part of the British Islands.

I cannot account for the discrepancy, but I suspect an error in the *Britannica*. This is the sort of change that often occurs in transcriptions over time.

The last thing I should mention is my use of "Mrs." as a title for unmarried women. This was the notation used in plays and newspapers of the time. As far as I can discover, the abbreviation would have been pronounced "mistress," which had been the title used for women of influence since the Middle Ages. Our current pronunciation, "missis," dates from the nineteenth century. At the time in which this novel is set, the word "miss" was a recent invention, dating only as far back as the mid-seventeenth century, and its connotation was not good. This was a time of transition for women. By the middle of the eighteenth century, the custom of referring to unmarried ladies as "Mrs." was considered quaint.